Praise for Reon Laudat

What a Girl Wants

"Delightful!" —*Romantic Times*

"Ms. Laudat has found an interesting balance of comedy and drama that works well and is sure to please all of her fans." —*Romance in Color*

"Breezy . . . smart . . . sizzling . . . fast-paced." —*The Oakland Press*

"Bright . . . sassy." —*Detroit Free Press*

"Feisty! Highly recommended." —Wordweaving.com

"Fun . . . bouncy . . . charming." —MrsGiggles.com *Romance Novel Central*

"By turns tender, funny, and very sexy." —*Romance Junkies*

"Moving . . . Thoroughly enjoyable." —*A Romance Reader at Heart*

ALSO BY REON LAUDAT

What a Girl Wants
Wanna Get to Know Ya

ANTHOLOGY
The Sistahood of Shopaholics

If You Just Say Yes

REON LAUDAT

ST. MARTIN'S GRIFFIN
NEW YORK

Published in the United States by St. Martin's Griffin, an imprint of St. Martin's Publishing Group

www.stmartins.com

The Library of Congress Cataloging-in-Publication Data is available upon request.

ISBN 978-0-312-93363-0 (mass market paperback)
ISBN 978-1-250-80465-5 (trade paperback)
ISBN 978-1-4668-2935-0 (ebook)

Our books may be purchased in bulk for promotional, educational, or business use. Please contact your local bookseller or the Macmillan Corporate and Premium Sales Department at 1-800-221-7945, extension 5442, or by email at MacmillanSpecialMarkets@ macmillan.com.

First St. Martin's Griffin Edition: 2021

10   9   8   7   6   5   4   3   2   1

To Peter,
with all my love

Acknowledgments

As always I'd like to thank:

My wonderful parents, James and Yvonne
My cool granny, Sara
My super-sharp editor, Monique Patterson

Special shout-outs this time to:

Attorney Daryl Wood for our enlightening Q&A and brainstorming sessions. (Any mistakes in this book regarding legal terms and/or issues are my own.)

Extra special reader-friends Sharon McCalop, Nitesha Ford, and Nichelle Baviera, whose appreciation, support, and genuine interest have blown me away.

Other readers, who have taken the time to reach out to me with the nicest e-mails. It's uncanny how the encouraging messages *always* arrive just when I need them most.

Author-friends/critique partners Natalie Dunbar and Karen White-Owens for making our regular meetings so darn valuable and just plain fun!

Author-friends Tamara Sneed, Lynn Emery, Debra Phillips, and Cindi Louis, who make this challenging business we're in feel a little less crazy and lonely.

If You
Just Say
Yes

One

New York, New York

Michelle's morning played like something straight out of her favorite soap opera, *If Tomorrow Never Comes.* Minus the cheesy sets, musical crescendo, and obligatory fade-out to a fabric softener commercial.

"Do you make a habit of screwing every man you interview?" the irate female voice seared through the phone line like a lit fuse on a stick of dynamite.

Michelle rolled her chair closer to her neat desktop and computer. She didn't need this nonsense first thing on a tight-deadline Monday. After that bomb of a date last night with Ken Gerard, a crank call was about as welcome as the run zipping up the left leg of her panty hose and the painful zit rising on the tip of her nose like Mount Kanchenjunga. With the receiver tucked between an ear and a shoulder, her steady gaze remained glued to the monitor. Her fingertips fluttered over a kidney-shaped ergonomically correct keyboard. Early-morning newsroom activity bustled in the background.

Michelle responded with a half-distracted, "Huh?"

"You heard me," the voice replied.

Interview eventually registered; then Michelle got a clue. "Excuse me?" Poised over the keyboard, her fingers went still.

"I *said* do you make a habit of screwing every man you interview or is that personal touch only reserved for multi-millionaire CEOs going through a postmidlife crisis?"

Michelle swiveled her chair, her nervous gaze darting around the newsroom. Self-consciously she pressed the phone closer to her ear, as if her colleagues could overhear the caller's rant. The two reporters who usually occupied the cubicles flanking hers had yet to arrive.

"Who is this?" Michelle demanded in a stage whisper.

"How do you plan to maintain your journalistic objectivity and professionalism when it's obvious you're sleeping with my husband?"

Then Michelle recognized the voice. The impact felt like a dropkick in the solar plexus.

"Mrs. Chapelle?" Michelle pretended to humor an old friend. She cleared her throat. Both hands choked the receiver. "Mrs. Chapelle?"

"Did you call me *Mrs.* Chapelle?"

Michelle added a cocktail party chuckle. "Yes. This is Michelle Michaels. I think you have the wrong number." Another lighthearted chuckle with a sigh.

"Funny you used *Mrs.*" The woman broke into a scornful laugh. "I thought you'd conveniently forgotten that Stanford Chapelle is a *married* man. And I have the right number."

"Mrs. Chapelle, seems there's been a misunderstanding," Michelle replied with a low, measured calm despite the cocktail of anger and confusion now churning inside her belly. A massive tension headache arrived full force. "I-I don't know where you got your information, but—"

"Don't try to play innocent with me, young lady. And the *lady* part I do use loosely, of course. I'm no fool and I'm sure your editors at the *Business Journal* will be more than a little interested in what I have to say on this matter. When I'm done giving your supervisors an earful on your unprofessional behavior I'll make sure the rest of the media know just what a sneaky, opportunistic little slut you are."

That's it! Something inside Michelle unhinged. "Ms. Chapelle, for your information—"

"Instead of wasting time with a weak denial, I suggest you freshen your résumé," Mrs. Chapelle interrupted. "You'll need it when I'm done with you."

Michelle blinked at the abrupt click followed by the rude hum of a dial tone.

What the hell was going on? She gaped at the receiver. Her next impulse: Pitch it. Pitch something. Anything. Like Bliss Worthington would surely do. Bliss Worthington was resident daytime diva of *If Tomorrow Never Comes,* and the ballsiest concoction since the dang bubble gum machine. Bliss Worthington was Foxy Brown, Lois Lane, and Erica Kane all rolled into one.

But instead of unleashing a Bliss move, Michelle opted to fake cool instead. She was at work after all. And Thomas, the nerdy nosy news aid whose station was just a few feet away, gawked in Michelle's direction with his radar hitched high. She didn't need him poking around in her beeswax, nor did she need to add to the newsroom scuttlebutt. Michelle's alleged exploits read like Anna Nicole Smith's tabloid rap sheet.

Michelle acknowledged Thomas with a nod and pasted-on smile in hopes of convincing him that everything was just peachy in her world. He nodded, gave her a jaunty thumbs-up, then went back to his mail sorting. Pivoting in the chair until her back was to the news aid's station, she wrung her hands, then slumped forward, staring at the glowing green print on her computer screen.

"Think, Michelle," she muttered to compose herself. Her fingers stole to her temples, where the dull ache progressed to an unrelenting rhythmic throb.

She'd just finished putting the finishing touches on a major career-boosting profile on Stanford Chapelle, CEO of Luxor Enterprises, for her employer, the *Manhattan Business Journal,* a top national business publication.

Over two decades, Chapelle, known as one of the most

brilliant business minds in the country, had taken a half-dozen failing companies with flagging stock and made them Wall Street darlings again. An expert on business leadership and organization, Chapelle had been a hot commodity as far as interviews went. He didn't agree to many in-depth profiles, but Michelle had gone after him anyway. She hadn't been the first reporter to pursue Chapelle, but she'd been the one to succeed. And as much as she'd like to credit her intellect and ingenuity, there was more to Chapelle's caving in to her interview request. Utilizing choice connections, she'd crashed a tournament at his private racquet club, marched over, and introduced herself to him between tennis sets. For lack of a better word, she'd immediately realized there was a type of chemistry between them. But *not* sexual chemistry, for crying out loud. *Ewwww!* Michelle crinkled her nose and mentally shuddered at the thought. At sixty-six, Stanford Chapelle was old enough to be her grandfather, *and* the man was married.

Katherine Chapelle was paranoid, plain and simple, and completely off-base, accusing Michelle of sleeping with the man. The most ridiculous thing she'd ever heard!

She sighed, running her fingers through freshly relaxed auburn tresses as an unwelcome thought surfaced in bits and pieces. She couldn't lie to herself. She supposed that . . . maybe . . . if pressed . . . she could concede that she and Stanford Chapelle had made a connection beyond the norm between interviewer and interviewee.

There was something about him. Charming. Smart. Funny. Warm. She'd spent weeks picking his brain and trailing him for a five-part groundbreaking series on the man and his business machinations. In hindsight, Michelle would also admit that it probably hadn't been the smartest move to accept every "off-campus" invitation he'd extended away from Luxor Enterprises. That impromptu trip to Maui on one of the Luxor company jets while Chapelle did a personal check on one of Luxor's many business subsidiaries had no doubt come back to haunt her.

She could not deny that though she was working, she'd thoroughly enjoyed spending time with the man. And was more than flattered that he seemed to enjoy spending time with her, too. Any hesitation that surfaced Michelle had simply rationalized away. Most journalists had to do the tagalong thing at some point in their careers. Accepting Chapelle's invitations had been *necessary*—for the sake of thorough journalism—to get a handle on the real man beyond the tasteful Brioni suits and expansive cherrywood executive desk on high at Luxor headquarters in Midtown. Readers had come to expect certain things from a Michelle Michaels in-depth profile.

Michelle shrugged out of her black suit jacket as nervous perspiration dampened her palms and armpits and the back of her neck. What did this mean? What if her editors believed Mrs. Chapelle's wild accusations? Was a pink slip forthcoming? Michelle oscillated between panic and anger. She willed her rapid-fire breathing to stabilize. It was all just a big ugly misunderstanding that would clear up soon enough, she told herself to ease the tension tightly coiling the muscles in her neck. She'd simply talk to Larry about what just happened. Between the two of them they'd straighten out this mess.

Dizzily, Michelle watched her editor, Larry Morgan, squeeze the hell out of the rubber stress ball in his meaty grip and pace his corner office.

Settled in the leather chair positioned in front of Larry's cluttered desk, Michelle had just relayed the details of that heated call from Katherine Chapelle.

Larry stopped moving long enough to perch his beefy rump along the edge of his desk. The front of his rumpled khaki slacks strained across thick thighs. His nose and rounded cheeks burned a deep crimson from rosacea and anger.

"And you swear there's no truth to these allegations?" he grilled her in his thick Brooklyn accent.

"Larry!" Offended by his accusing look, Michelle gripped the armrests so firmly she felt her knuckles crack. "How could you even suggest that—"

"That you'd stoop to having an affair with a dashing mul-timillionaire CEO—"

"Who just happens to be married and old enough to be my grandfather," Michelle huffed, reeling from his insinua-tion. "How could you of all people even think that I—"

"Look, I'm sorry, all right?" Larry plunked the ball on top of his desk, then ran his fingers through his spidery brown comb-over. "Just need to make sure I've got all the facts straight. And besides, it's not as if something like this hasn't come up before."

Michelle rolled her eyes. "Is this about Maxwell Cole-man?"

Maxwell Coleman, founder and CEO of Coleman Elec-tronics. Michelle had profiled him for the *Business Journal* eight months ago. The paper wanted an in-depth feature, and that's what she'd given them. Michelle had turned on the charm and done the whole tag-along-journalist thing as usual. Michelle had found Coleman, like Chapelle, utterly fascinating. And Coleman had been so pleased with the job Michelle had done on his story, he'd sent a representative from Tiffany's to the *Business Journal*'s newsroom with a selection of pearls from which Michelle could choose as a token of his appreciation.

Michelle had been at once flattered and taken aback by his well-meaning but highly inappropriate way of expressing his gratitude for a job well done. She did not accept—or even consider accepting—such a grand personal gift. Not just because company policy prohibited reporters and editors from accepting "gifts or tokens of appreciation" valued at fifty dollars or more, but also because she simply knew it wasn't right. Despite the ugly rumors, she was *not* swayed by high-priced graft. Her personal and professional integrity was *not* for sale.

When it came to scoops, no one could deny that she kicked ass, though. To take her down a notch, some of her *Business Journal* colleagues gossiped about her "questionable" methods of gathering information. The disgusting newsroom rumors had been rampant: *Michelle Michaels was not beyond putting the moves—in every sense of those words—on top players in the business world to get them to open up to her.* But she refused to be broken by petty jealousy. She'd simply done her thing to the best of her ability. She wouldn't lose this job. She couldn't lose this job!

"Yeah, I was thinking of Maxwell Coleman." Larry nailed Michelle with his gray unwavering gaze. "*And* Desmond Bloomingthal of NitroTec last year."

Michelle's cheeks stung. She couldn't believe all this was coming from Larry, a man she thought of not only as her supervisor but also as her most loyal *Business Journal* supporter. "Don't tell me you've bought into the maliciousness spread by a bunch of insecure hacks, who've shown all the decency and sense of fair play of crabs in a barrel," she bit out.

"This isn't just about newsroom gossip, Michelle." Larry searched for the right words. "It's about . . . well . . . I suppose we should've had this discussion long before now."

"Discussion about what?"

Larry averted his eyes, then paused thoughtfully as the next few minutes of silence dragged like Michelle's beleaguered spirit. Dread settled in and her breath caught. Her stomach plunged like a bear stock market.

He was going to fire her.

"You see . . . ," Larry started slowly.

Here it comes. Michelle winced.

"I should have said something sooner, but hell . . ." He pushed out a sharp breath. "You were doing such a bang-up job on these showy profiles and grabby series. Who the hell was I to question your story-gathering techniques? Hey, you know, if it ain't broke . . . But I've had senior editors coming to me, expressing concern over how . . . what's the word . . . *close* you seem to get to some of your subjects, particularly the male CEO types."

"I have done nothing unethical or immoral," Michelle insisted, slapping the armrest for emphasis. "What female reporter hasn't used the charm-and/or-a-bit-of-flirting thing every now and then?"

"And beyond that?" He still seemed skeptical.

"I know where to draw the line. I am *not*—I repeat—I am *not* a mogul- and millionaire-fucker, Larry, if that's what you're getting at!"

Whoooops!

Eyelids twitching, Michelle wanted to snatch those words back the second she said them. Her butt was most definitely burnt toast, her professional reputation fried, and *she* wielded the blowtorch.

"I'm sorry. Th-th-that kind of language is uncalled for." Michelle downshifted to frantic backpedaling. "It's just that . . . I-I mean . . . This is all too much. These accusations hurled at me. I do not trade sex for scoops."

"Okay. All right." Larry lifted his hands in supplication and Michelle heard contrition in his tone.

He continued, "*But* there's a fine line between engaging subjects and presenting yourself in such a way that the subject is confused or misled to believe you're opening yourself up for a personal relationship."

"I haven't purposely misled anyone." Exhausted from having to defend herself, first to Mrs. Chapelle and then to someone she thought would always have her back at the *Business Journal,* Michelle released her grip on the chair.

"Maybe not on purpose. Look, I know it's tough, setting and maintaining boundaries and all. Even I've been tempted, but I've never once played where I worked, meaning no office romances, either. *And* I had even more rigid rules for when I was reporting, to make sure I didn't cross the line. For one, I never socialized with sources, because I believed keeping that distance was crucial to maintaining my independence."

"But it's different where beats are concerned—"

"Of course," he cut her off. "For beat reporting you do want to keep those relationships oiled and symbiotic, but at the same time it's vital to be well aware of the subtext and the agendas that abound. *Do* you understand?"

Michelle nodded, feeling like a third grader in the principal's office getting reprimanded for launching a spitball attack.

Upside: she still had her job.

So far.

Larry continued, "I've worked at major papers in Chicago, Washington, and Los Angeles. I got the hot leads and insider info without once partying with a subject or source, nor was I ever on a first-name basis with any of them. And for the record, I do know about that business analyst at Cooper-Braxton that you've become particularly chummy with."

Larry's reference to man-poaching Courtney Banks was like a jab from a rusty nail. Michelle's friendship with Courtney was no longer an issue because it was k-a-p-u-t. Courtney killed it after that stunt she'd pulled the night before when she crashed Michelle's date with Ken Gerard, then proceeded to steal the man away. Michelle had been relegated to riding out third-wheel syndrome as she guzzled lukewarm Kendall-Jackson and her insides heaved in gastrointestinal revolt. She began, "About Courtney—"

"Wait. Let me continue before you have a conniption

again. Maybe you don't even realize what's happening. But I recall how downright giddy you always were after you returned from one of your many meetings with Stanford Chapelle. You'd practically float into the newsroom like Tinker Bell on speed, then start chattering away about what a great meeting you two had."

"I was just excited about the story, my work, Larry. Is something so wrong with that? I thought you of all people would understand." Michelle slumped in her chair. "You've read that whole series. You worked with me on it, helping me shape it and polish it. You know how proud I am of it."

"Yes, and you did some damn fine reporting and writing, as usual. But can you honestly look me in the eye and tell me that you and Stanford Chapelle did not develop some sort of personal relationship?"

Michelle looked away from him to the wall where tattered construction paper and crayon art drawn by Larry's two grade-school-age grandchildren clung to a corkboard.

"Michelle, can you tell me that you and Chapelle did not develop a personal relationship while you were working on his story?"

Michelle bit her lip, looked down at her hands, then up at Larry again, breaking down faster than a perpetrator on an old *Perry Mason* rerun. "Okay. I guess you could say there was."

Dragging a hand down his face, Larry came to his feet. "Hooooh, boy," he said with a mix of resignation and weariness.

"But it's not what you or everyone else is thinking," Michelle added quickly as the corners of her lips lifted for a sad smile that pleaded for understanding. "We just became friends. But I swear to you, there was *nothing* romantic or sexual about it."

"Whether the relationship was about sex or romance is beside the point right now, and you know that." Larry twisted his lips with distaste. "Damn it, Michelle, you're not some wet-behind-the-ears intern. There was a personal relationship, a friendship, for crying out loud. If Mrs. Chapelle follows through with her threat and goes running off at the mouth about your relationship with her husband, it won't be good. She's even threatening to go to the *Media Monitor*."

Michelle wore a slack-jawed gape. The last thing she needed was her face splashed all over that supersnarky media watchdog rag. Her journalism career might never rebound.

Larry went on, "Even the exaggerated, erroneous blathering of a jealous wife could mean trouble for the *Business Journal*'s credibility. Don't you get it? We might have to pull the goddamn thing."

"Pull my series!" Michelle screeched. Yanking her series was the second-worst thing that could happen, running a pretty close second to getting a pink slip.

"Yeah, kill it." He jerked a flat hand across his Adam's apple. "Pull the damn plug on it because of, you know, perceived ethical breaches. I don't want to, but this paper has a reputation to uphold. We can't have anyone questioning our objectivity with this story or any other."

"But, Larry, this is the best work I've done yet." Michelle's voice quavered.

"I know, but we're talking damage control at this point. Sorry."

Michelle inched to the edge of her seat as desperation sank in. "Maybe if I talk to Katherine Chapelle—"

"Didn't you just hear what I said? No!" Larry scowled and leveled a warning finger at her. "You stay away from the Chapelles—Katherine *and* Stanford."

"But—"

"You just sit tight. I'll handle this." Larry's voice shifted from annoyed to sympathetic; then he glanced at the clock on the wall.

When Michelle came to her feet, he latched on to her by

the elbow to lead her to the door. "I'll discuss this matter with the senior editors at the ten o'clock planning meeting. As soon as I know what our strategy will be, I'll let you know."

Michelle had to summon every ounce of resolve not to break down in tears. Bawling on top of everything else would not only mean career suicide but also confirm that she was weak and in desperate need of psychological counseling. Hell, maybe she did need to put in her time on some therapist's couch. Look how she'd mucked up things here.

"I know I probably overreacted before, but there's got to be a way around this. Don't worry too much," he said jovially. "You look as if you could use a break. Forget that hot liquid crapola brewing in the coffee machine in the break room."

Michelle half-expected a condescending pat on her head to follow but contained her irritation. After all, she had brought all this on herself. How could she have been so stupid?

"Now, you mosey on over to that Starbucks down the street and get yourself that nice big coffee drink you like so much. What's it called?"

"Huh?" Michelle blinked out of her daze.

"Your favorite coffee drink?"

"Espresso?"

"Oh, it's more than that at those fancy-schmancy designer coffee places."

"The *venti caramel macchiato* with mint or Valencia orange," she replied as if still disoriented by the bum's rush he was giving her.

Larry chuckled, causing the belly lapped over his belt to jiggle. "And I remember when it was just about milk, Sweet 'n Low, or maybe a dash of Coffee-Mate."

Michelle managed a feeble smile, more like a glimpse of her front teeth.

"The coffee's on me." Larry reached inside his pocket,

where loose change jingled. He removed his wallet, then pressed wadded bills in her hand. Take your time." His chubby fingers stole to her upper back, where he patted her twice. "Just leave everything to me."

Two

Detroit, Michigan—one week later

Wesley Abbott zipped inside the *Detroit Herald* parking garage in the black sinuous form of his beloved Ferrari 612 Scaglietti. Late as hell and still pissed off at himself for crawling all up inside Brynn Devereaux last night like some loser-chump with his nose pried wide open. He should've turned in earlier when he had a long workday ahead of him—instead he'd spent half the night sandwiched between Brynn's well-toned thighs.

Damn. Brynn might as well have slipped a ring through his nose, then snapped on a leash.

Sit, boy.

Roll over.

Do me.

Heel.

Wes felt like a heel all right, because he should've told Brynn he was ready to end their "relationship" *before* that last romp for the road. He'd been satisfied gettin' it on with her for the past three months, and she had taken all he had to offer with gusto, barely giving him a break to gear up for subsequent rounds. He hadn't wanted romance, and that no-strings situation had not been easy to find. For women fresh out of college and those in their mid twenties—like Brynn—who were all wrapped up in their careers, Wes's inability to commit at age thirty-seven had not been an issue.

When Wes reached the top of the garage ramp and a level

surface again he manipulated the gearshift, with his love life, or rather the lack of love in his social life, still on his mind.

Brynn had been perfect. Her only demands on him had been sexual. Yet after three months he *still* wanted out. That morning she had taken the news well enough. They should cool it for a while. Wes suspected that, in Brynn's mind, he would be either (A) easy to replace or (B) poised to make yet another booty call sooner than he thought. She probably assumed a combination of both. Brynn could believe what she wanted. She'd realize Wes meant business when the weeks turned into months and Wes wasn't ringing her bell—literally and figuratively—anymore.

He lifted a Styrofoam cup filled with crappy gas station coffee from its holder, then cursed when he rolled over a speed bump too quickly, causing hot liquid to splash. He'd reached for the Kleenex in his glove compartment to clean the coffee spilled on his hands, the steering wheel, and the gearshift when his cell phone rang.

His mother with a quick reminder: "Wesley, honey, don't forget. It's your weekend to visit Patrick." Though she tried to mask the weakness evident in her voice, it rang in Wes's ears as clearly as a siren.

"I won't forget, Mom," Wes replied. "Are you and Dad all right?"

Both of his parents had been suffering from a nasty bug that had practically chained them to their Palmer Woods home for the past few days.

"We're doing better. The doctor told us the usual: get lots of rest and drink plenty of fluids. We're riding this thing out, but I think the worst is over."

"So how has it been with you two trapped with each other for days without an escape?"

"Not so bad. The house is big, ya know."

"But is it big enough for you two?" Wes wondered out loud as thoughts of the strain his older brother, Patrick, had put on their parents' marriage over the years surfaced. Patrick's latest brush with the law had torn the scabs off old, deep wounds. It wasn't long before his parents' blame hurling resumed.

Gloria Abbott had always been the stricter one of Wes and Patrick's parents. Their father, Winston, had a cool-breeze parenting style. He hadn't believed in tough love when his sons were growing up. He fell back on the "boys will be boys" reasoning when a teenage Patrick strolled in way past his curfew or borrowed the family cars without permission.

When Patrick stooped to petty crime it was Gloria who launched a diatribe against Winston for being way too soft on Patrick when a harsher, disciplinarian approach might have made a real difference and possibly scared Patrick straight. Then Winston, pushed on the defensive, would shout back, "A lot of good your screaming and overcontrolling antics did the damn boy! It's no wonder he chafed against all of your uncompromising rules and standards of perfection."

Many a night young Wesley went to sleep with a stress-related stomachache brought on by all the tension in the Abbott house. His way of coping? He took on the role of the family Golden Boy and peacemaker. That meant striving to be twice as good at everything to distract his parents from Patrick's many shortcomings. Wes had earned the best grades in school, had perfect attendance, excelled at his parents' favorite hobbies, such as tennis, you name it, then had made them proud by winning just about every prestigious journalism award out there but the Pulitzer. That had been next on his list until he realized that all the hustling to be the best at everything had brought him more mental exhaustion than personal pride or satisfaction.

"I'll come by after work to check on you two again, anyway." Wes still felt compelled to see for himself how they were coping.

"Oh, no you won't. You keep messing around here with

us and you're bound to come down with this bug, too. You stay away, you hear?"

Just before he ended the call, Wes made her a promise he had no intention of keeping. Instead, he would drop by their home later loaded down with a big carton of chicken soup from a little restaurant called Zoup!, their favorite reading material, fresh fruit, and an assortment of juices. His parents deserved all the extra TLC they could get after what they'd been through the past few months.

Patrick had been gone for four months, but his mother's prompt for Wes to visit him still brought on a wave of uneasiness in Wes's gut. A four-hour trek to a correctional facility in Michigan's Upper Peninsula was anything but his idea of a pleasure trip. Dread smothered him every time he had to see his older brother in his prison-issued blues. For weeks now Wes had been reflecting on Patrick's latest fuckup, one of a long string. This one, however, would cost him three years of freedom. *Served him right,* Wes tried convincing himself, but his fear still clung to him. He couldn't help fretting about the things that could happen to his brother in prison—even in a minimum-security facility like Davenport.

Wesley tried not to linger on the effect Patrick's troubles would have on Kelly, the five-year-old daughter he'd left behind.

Lonette Warren, Kelly's mother, who'd always had full custody, had done a fine job with the child for four years before Patrick had stepped up to the plate to take any parental responsibility. Kelly would be just fine without Patrick, Wes told himself. He would make sure of that, trying to take up the slack where he could. He needed to shift his focus from Patrick to Kelly. And it was about time, too.

Patrick, Patrick, Patrick. The first person Wesley thought of when he awoke most mornings and the last person he thought about before he went to bed at night. And it was Patrick Wes dreamed about when jolted from sleep at 3:00

a.m. Instead of facing his preoccupation regarding Patrick
head-on, Wes had attempted to distract himself by focusing
on his work and pushing his sex life into overdrive. Most of
the time neither worked, but Wes realized he had to stop ob-
sessing. Patrick was a grown-ass man. He'd made his
choices and now he had to suffer the consequences. Wes
wasn't his brother's keeper. The sooner he believed that, the
better.

Wes checked his watch. Had twenty minutes before a
scheduled phone interview. The engine hummed as he
smoothly scaled another spiraling ramp. Two more to go to
get to his assigned parking space. Did the math in his head.
One minute to park. Two to make it to the elevator. He'd
missed most of the early-morning building traffic, so he
shouldn't have to wait too long or endure too many stops to
get to the twenty-fifth floor, which housed the *Herald*'s vast
editorial department. He'd need about ten minutes to scan
his notes and refresh his thoughts on the subject at hand before he called his first interviewee.

Not long after he'd reclaimed his mellow vibe, he looked
up just in time to see a burgundy Taurus pull into his parking
space. His car came to an idling pause at the Taurus's rear
bumper. Wes lightly tapped his horn.

From the offending vehicle one bronze leg emerged, followed by its perfect curvy match. His gaze roamed from the
black pumps to the edge of the black skirt hem, which hovered just a couple of discreet inches above her knees.
Though the skirt wasn't snug, Wes could tell it covered a
very nice, round rear. The jacket, slightly fitted at the waist,
had big shiny buttons and softly angled shoulders. The hair,
fashioned in a shiny light auburn bob, flowed from her scalp
at a centered part, then softly curved inward at her jawline.
She turned and leaned back inside the vehicle to retrieve
something. Had she heard him?

When Wes tapped the horn again, she popped out with a

briefcase and a shoulder bag. He pressed a button and his driver's side window descended. He poked his head out. "Hey, lady, that's my space."

She looked as if she didn't believe him.

Wes pointed to a parking sign she'd obviously overlooked, then reached for the parking permit that he'd been instructed to hang from his rearview mirror but kept in the glove compartment instead.

With a smirk, he dangled the permit, emblazoned with a big green 58, out the window and waved it at her. She turned and looked at the brick wall in front of her vehicle, where the number 58 was painted in green.

From where he sat, he could make out that she'd twisted her features in annoyance. She turned and climbed back inside her car, then started its engine. Wes felt bad about making her move. He glanced down the row of parked cars and thought he saw an empty space about five slots down.

"Hey, stay put," he called out and gestured to her as he eased down the lane, only to discover the slot wasn't empty but occupied by a blue Mini Cooper. Vehicles filled every slot on this level, but he couldn't very well go back and demand that Hot Legs evacuate slot 58. He checked his watch again and discovered he was now four minutes off-schedule. He proceeded to the next level and found the same parking situation, then drove to the next and the one after that. No luck. He would need to drive out of the garage and seek a parking space on the street. Much to his chagrin, he only found a two-hour metered space about six blocks from the *Herald* building.

Just leave everything to me. Larry's last words from seven days ago echoed in Michelle's ears as she cut the engine of her rented Taurus and tipped her head back against the headrest in irritation. Little did she know that "leaving everything" to Larry would mean a trip right back to Detroit.

She'd circled the ramps of the *Detroit Herald* garage for the past half hour looking for an open parking space; then when she'd finally found one Speed Racer had almost ousted her. She'd already lost spaces to two other cars. She sighed, relieved when the black Ferrari kept moving.

The upside of her latest predicament: the opportunity to spend quality time with her family. That topped her list. She would divide her time in Detroit between her mother's Ferndale house and her cousin Fatima's Farmington Hills condo.

Not only did Michelle need to get to the bottom of her mother's odd behavior as of late, but also the two were long overdue for a serious heart-to-heart about Michelle's father.

Michelle's work at the *Business Journal* had kept her so busy the past year she hardly had time to travel to her hometown as often as she would've liked. Now she just felt ashamed for trying to fill that void in all the wrong ways.

Fortunately, she would not have to sit out the twelve-week leave the *Business Journal* senior editors had firmly suggested she take until the Stanford Chapelle debacle blew over. While the powers that be called it a vacation, Michelle knew it would be more like a suspension with pay while they pondered whether she still had a future at the *Manhattan Business Journal.* From what she'd heard through the company grapevine, Larry had fought like hell on her behalf and had opposed those who were in favor of simply firing her butt on the spot. The paper had managed to prevent Katherine Chapelle from going public with her allegations about Michelle and Stanford Chapelle's "affair" by paying Katherine off—under the table, of course. They would never publicly admit to bowing to that blackmailing harpy. But they'd promised Katherine they'd "deal" with Michelle, which at the time probably could have been interpreted as meaning that an immediate termination was on tap. But good ol' Larry had stayed true to his word and had come through for Michelle after all. He'd convinced *Business Journal* bigwigs to reconsider issuing Michelle a pink slip, or he had slowed down the process, for now.

While awaiting their final verdict, Michelle took up the editors on their offer to allow her to work elsewhere while on "leave" from the *Business Journal.* Keeping busy was the key to hanging on to her sanity while each day dragged like a week.

Roswell, Inc., owner of the *Manhattan Business Journal* and dozens of other newspapers and specialty magazines, boasted several options as part of its interstaff loaner or exchange program. Their newspaper in Detroit had a veteran reporter out on maternity leave, which created a temporary slot for Michelle.

She hated the idea of leaving the chain's most prestigious, flagship national publication for a smaller, midwestern one, but complaining had been the furthest thing from her mind under the circumstances. Technically, she was still on the *Business Journal*'s staff roster. Though Katherine had not made good on her threats to spew venom to the *Media Monitor,* an unidentified source at the *Business Journal,* aka resentful competitors on-staff, had still leaked the gossip about Michelle's penchant for collecting so-called CEO "admirers," complete with incriminating anecdotes. The one about the Tiffany's representative who had paid her a newsroom visit made for quite juicy column fodder. Michelle gritted her teeth and tried to push it all to the back of her mind. Just before she stepped out of the car, the cell phone inside her bag chirped twice.

Stanford Chapelle.

Michelle felt awful about leaving town without calling with some sort of explanation, but she knew Larry and the senior editors meant business when they decreed no further contact between Michelle and Chapelle. Despite the ruckus their friendship had caused, she was glad to hear his voice and risked engaging in a brief chat.

"I hear you're in Detroit to work for a while," Stanford said.

"Yeah, at the *Herald*. I'm not crazy about getting forced out of the *Business Journal* for now, but I hope to return soon if the editors don't decide to drop the ax instead." She already missed her old job and apartment and New York's charged atmosphere.

"You'll be back," Chapelle said. "Sorry about all the trouble."

"I'm not totally blameless here. I . . . um . . . we did cross the line if truth be told," Michelle admitted. It helped to verbally acknowledge her boneheaded blunder and take some responsibility for her predicament.

"It's a pity that people have a tendency to turn something that was nice and innocent, our friendship, into something else." Anger tightened his voice.

"Katherine's accusations about me to my bosses certainly didn't help," Michelle added drily.

"Katherine knows I wasn't having an affair with you. She had just enough facts to twist for her own devious purposes. It was all a setup to milk as much money out of me as she could to pave the way for her imminent departure from our marriage."

"She's divorcing you because of all of this?"

" 'All of this' came about because she's been planning to divorce me all along. She'd been scheming to find a way around a prenuptial agreement, which included an infidelity clause. Cheating would render the prenup null and void."

"Infidelity clause?"

"Yeah, can't believe I shot myself in the foot by allowing my lawyer to include one." He chuckled mirthlessly. "But hey, at the time it was the only way I could get Katherine to agree to some other things."

"So *that's* why she was so eager to cast me as the other woman!" Rage bubbled inside of Michelle.

"Believe it or not, during that time you spent interviewing me she had us tailed and got some photos. That's what she was using against me."

"But I'm innocent! We're innocent!" Michelle's voice cracked as she slapped the steering wheel. "They must be computer-manipulated fakes. What could she possibly have had photos of?"

"Remember when we were having lunch at that little restaurant in Maui and I tried to help you when you got something in your eye? And the time I was giving you a tour of the stables at our Hamptons estate and you got chilly? I removed my jacket and draped it around your shoulders. There were lots of little incidents like that when we made the slightest, fleeting physical contact. Then there were all the smiles, laughs, and such because we always had such a good time. You and I both know it was completely innocuous. But those things can look pretty damning in freeze-frame when you're predisposed to believe the rumors."

Feeling outdone, Michelle let her head roll against the headrest and moaned, "Oh, my God."

"I was going to fight but then reconsidered. It's just not worth it—the possibility of having those allegations *and* the photos out there for public consumption. I know she'd made some sort of deal with the *Business Journal* to keep quiet, but out of spite she could've still leaked those photos, then feigned ignorance. I don't need *that* kind of publicity. She can still screw me, but I had to agree to play by her rules."

"So she's won, then." Such vicious manipulation had been rewarded—not only by the *Business Journal* but by Stanford Chapelle, too. That left a bad taste in Michelle's mouth.

"Let's not call it that; winning, I mean. Let's say I decided to negotiate with that shark of a divorce attorney of hers to cut my losses. Besides, she's done enough damage already—what with you getting shipped out of town and all."

"But she's getting paid for her lies!"

"Well, um . . ."

"What?"

"Well, if truth be told, I might have pushed her into taking such drastic measures," he added sheepishly.

"Pushed her? But there was *no* affair!"

"Well . . ." Long pause. "No affair with you."

"What are you saying?" Michelle couldn't believe what she was hearing.

"Let's just say I've come to realize there's plenty of temptation out there for a man in my position. But Katherine has had one hell of a time gathering proof, and the prenuptial agreement she signed was far from fair. I have my own shark of an attorney who really worked Katherine's naïveté and the love she felt for me at one time."

"Sounds as if she wasn't as naïve as you thought if she managed to get you and your so-called shark of an attorney to agree to include an infidelity clause in what was supposed to be a bulletproof prenup."

"Don't remind me." He sounded annoyed. "She really has me by the short ones now."

This was Stanford Chapelle, the man of rock-solid integrity? Trying to take advantage of his bride all those years ago to safeguard his precious fortune, then cheating to boot? Michelle rolled her eyes at her own gullibility; then a sickening wave of disappointment threatened to overtake her. She couldn't believe this. It was official. Her world had disintegrated into a soap opera. A really bad one. Maybe it was as Larry suggested, Chapelle *had* gone out of his way to befriend Michelle to ensure that her stories about him had the most complimentary spin.

"Look, I'm sorry you got dragged into this ugliness and I'm sorry that after all that hard work you've done, the *Business Journal* decided to pull the series."

She'd just bet he was sorry. Now that she'd had a chance

to reflect objectively, those stories would have been valentines to Chapelle in newsprint. As much as she wanted to chew him out right then, she wouldn't. She was still way more disgusted with herself. "I'll survive that. What about you? Are you up for what we used to call a do-over when I was a kid? I hear they're sending a tag team, Janet Gordon *and* Carl Hooks, to reinterview you to remove the appearance of a potential conflict of interest, or partiality."

"Yeah, I've already heard from Hooks. He wants to schedule our first meeting in three days. What can you tell me about them?"

Aha! The *real* reason for this call. "They're good, fair reporters."

"And? What can you tell me about them as people? You know, is she married? Is he? Can they travel at the drop of a hat?"

"As in, would they be dazzled by an impromptu trip to Maui on the Luxor company jet? Better not get too friendly with them, lest someone accuse them of being in your pocket, too," Michelle bit out.

"You do know I wasn't using you," he said as if reading her mind.

"Sure you weren't," she scoffed.

"You going to be all right?"

"What's it to you, Chapelle?"

"Hey, listen, Chelle."

"It's Michelle." Her cool response was meant as a rebuke.

He continued. "For what it's worth, just let me say for the record I truly regret how things turned out, but this ol' fart doesn't regret meeting you and calling you a friend, young lady," Chapelle said with smooth obsequiousness she just recognized for what it was. What a phony!

She was now convinced that his motives for befriending her were not sincere. Who didn't love a sucker? And that's exactly what she'd been. With that realization her eyeballs stung and her throat felt as if it would close up on her. But she'd ride out this transfer—and demotion—sans the tears.

"I have to go now, *Mister* Chapelle, and I'd appreciate if you didn't call me again. It's not . . . *appropriate.* Goodbye," she said, her tone all business, as it should have been from the beginning. Not waiting for his farewell, she ended the call. She sucked in a calming breath, and her determination rallied as she clutched her briefcase and purse. She'd screwed up and misjudged someone *again,* but she still had a job to do. She would make serious waves at the *Herald* with her kick-ass reporting and *only* with her kick-ass reporting. She would refuse to be the source of fresh newsroom gossip. When her *Herald* colleagues spoke of her, it would only be in reference to her hard-hitting page-one, above-the-fold, groundbreaking, newswire-worthy pieces for the next three months. The *Herald* wouldn't know what hit 'em.

"I'm going to get my stuff in gear and in the process put this sleepy little paper on the map," she muttered as a fierce determination to redeem herself set in. "Then the *Business Journal* will beg me to come back!"

Wesley grabbed his briefcase, fed the parking meter, and slung his gray pinstripe suit jacket over one shoulder. Once inside the *Herald* lobby, he had a smile for the female security guard stationed at the front sign-in desk.

"Good morning, Crystal," he chimed cheerily, despite the hike to the building in early-morning heat that had plastered his Egyptian cotton shirt to his back.

"Hey, Wes." The fifty-something southern belle smiled back, at once tidying her uniform and patting her long acrylic-tipped fingers over red hair, teased up airily like cotton candy. "Did you remember to bring that Miles Davis CD?" she drawled.

Wes snapped his fingers "I knew I forgot something. Sorry about that. As soon as I get upstairs I'll plug a re-

minder of it in my Palm. You'll have it tomorrow. Promise."
He winked. "Chat with you later. Gotta run. I'm late," he
said, quickening his long stride to board an open half-full elevator. The air-conditioning cooled him as he adjusted his
collar and silk necktie.

The doors opened on 15 to reveal the woman who'd taken
his parking space. That's right; floor 15 led to the parking
garage. What had taken her so long to make her way here?
And where was she headed? The *Herald* newsroom? God,
he hoped so, he thought as a sly grin settled on his face.

He had not been able to thoroughly check her out from a
distance under that murky parking garage lighting, but
damn, up close—even under the elevator's unforgiving
fluorescents—the verdict was in.

Baby is fine!

Satinlike golden skin with a hint of a natural blush coloring her cheeks. Thickly lashed hazel eyes tilted up at the
outer corners. Flecks of gold and green made them look
ethereal, yet sexy. She'd slicked a nude hue on her lips that
gave them a natural, highly kissable sheen.

She boarded the elevator, then turned her back to Wes. He
eased behind her, close enough to inhale her perfume. A
unique blend of exotic hibiscus with a hint of peach. That
was it! She reminded him of a ripe, juicy peach. And his
mouth watered for a bite. Already an inch or two from in-
vading her personal space, Wes eased closer still, but she
didn't move. Just stood there, spine all stiff, chin held high.
The picture of detachment and cool efficiency. Man,
wouldn't he just love to melt the starch right out of that
crisply pressed blouse of hers. He checked out the breasts.
Perfect and generous. His gaze dropped to where her jacket
curved in at a slender waist, then flared out again to an ex-
traordinary booty.

He liked what he saw.

A lot.

He gave himself a mental shake. *Down, boy!* The elevator reached the twenty-fifth floor. Wes and the fine lady stepped out. She was probably there to have her picture taken in the photo department or to see one of his reporter colleagues. It would only take a minute to introduce himself, get her name, maybe even her phone number, then point her in the right direction for her appointment.

Time to make his move. "Miss, everything okay with the space?"

"Excuse me?" She stopped moving, faced him, wearing a pinched expression, as if she'd gotten up on the wrong side of the bed or something.

"The parking space. Number Fifty-eight. I was in the black car that pulled up to you this morning. Fifty-eight is my assigned space."

"I didn't realize 'Ferrari Man' was emblazoned on the space."

Just the opening he needed. "Make that Wesley Abbott." With the broadest smile he extended his hand.

She looked at it for a long moment before leveling her impatient gaze at him again.

Undeterred, Wes dropped his hand and cleared his throat. "I pay one hundred and thirty-five dollars every month for the privilege of parking there, you know."

Out came a loud put-upon sigh. Not quite what Wes was expecting for his gallantry. In a swift, efficient manner she reached inside her leather bag, removed a matching wallet, pulled out a bill, then slapped it in his right hand. "There. That should cover my squatter's rights for today." Then she turned away to march down the hall leading to the newsroom.

Amused by her cool chutzpah, Wes called after her, "Hey, I didn't catch your name!"

She glanced over her shoulder. "I didn't throw it."

Three

Michelle kept stepping.

She'd taken one good look at tall, dark, dimpled, and delicious Ferrari Man with his gleaming white teeth and smug playa-playa confidence and deemed him trouble with a capital *T.*

Sure, she appreciated the guy giving up the parking space for the day and she supposed she could've been nicer, but nice seemed to always wedge her butt in a crack when it came to devastatingly handsome men like him.

A young woman with two gnawed-up pencils tucked inside her brunette bun sat at the sleek wooden receptionist desk positioned near the newsroom entrance. She greeted Michelle with a warm expression on her round face. "Welcome to the *Detroit Herald.* May I help you?"

"Good morning. My name is Michelle Michaels," she said. "I was told to ask for Barbara Duncan."

"Yes. Nice to meet you, Ms. Michaels. I'm Carmen." She offered her hand and Michelle shook it. "I've been on the lookout for you. Let me check to see if Barbara is ready."

When Carmen picked up her phone to dial, Michelle scanned the newsroom where she would work for the next three months. It was just as large as the *Manhattan Business Journal* newsroom, only brighter. Early-morning sunshine dominated, slanting through opened blinds. Ceiling-to-floor windows stood where the *Business Journal* had solid plaster walls and pretentious art prints. Because the *Herald* was a daily morning newspaper, reporters already occupied most of the desks arranged in a neat gridlike pattern with low partitions.

Carmen placed the receiver back in its cradle. "Barbara is ready for you, Ms. Michaels."

"Please call me Michelle." Nervous energy fluttered inside her stomach as she followed Carmen across the thin carpet to a row of offices lined along the perimeter of the newsroom.

"I'll show you to Barb's office back in Features."

Uh-oh.

"Features? There must be some mistake." Michelle stopped in her tracks, trying to mask the displeasure and shock that must have shown on her face. She was a business reporter, not a dang features reporter. She covered *real* news—banking, big business, the stock market, CEOs, and corporate trends—not the frivolous lifestyle stories that often bored her senseless.

"Yeah, the 'Accent' section. Features," Carmen explained, giving Michelle a curious look. "Barbara Duncan is the *Herald* features editor."

Barbara, Michelle's new supervisor, could make her sentence at the *Herald* a breeze or make it feel like life in lockdown without parole. Getting off on the wrong foot with her . . . bad idea.

"Right, right, features." Michelle bobbed her head, managing a smile and a quick recovery.

Michelle took a deep breath. Heads snapped up as they passed. She drew her briefcase and purse closer to her body like shields against their blatant gawking. Was her slip hanging? Her blouse unbuttoned? Or worse, was her skirt tucked up in her panty hose in some embarrassingly revealing way? Moving her purse to the same hand that held her briefcase, she used the other hand to do a quick tactile check of her suit jacket and skirt.

"Here we are," Carmen announced when the pair reached the office. A dozen black-and-white postcards depicting scenes from *I Love Lucy* episodes covered the door.

"Thanks," Michelle said, starting to relax. Anybody who was a fan of Lucy had to have a sense of humor, therefore could not be all that bad, she reasoned.

"If you need anything or have questions, you know where to find me." Carmen gave Michelle a quick reassuring pat on the back before turning to leave.

"Come on inside," a friendly voice called out from the office.

Michelle stepped inside to find a wisp of a woman with short curly blond hair and big green eyes. "Hello, I'm Barbara Duncan."

"And I'm Michelle Michaels."

Barbara slipped her small hand in Michelle's for a warm shake.

Barbara barely cleared five feet, and with that high-pitched voice she'd probably had more than one telemarketer ask if her mother was home.

"Have a seat." Barbara gestured toward the chair in front of her neat desk. Though her too-cutesy short skirt and matching jacket screamed teen junior department, upon closer inspection the wrinkles fanning around her eyes and the slack skin around her neck revealed that this woman was probably in her late forties. "Welcome aboard."

"Thank you." Michelle set her briefcase and purse on the floor next to her feet. Barbara's immaculate office boasted a great view of the Detroit River. Kitschy pop culture bric-a-brac infused the space with loads of personality. Michelle felt at ease. A pair of *I Love Lucy* dolls, a Slinky, a glass bowl of colorful Koosh balls, a miniature model of the *Starship Enterprise* adorned bookshelves. On the walls, a couple of posters from sixties romantic comedies starring Doris Day and Rock Hudson.

"So you settled in okay?" Barbara asked. "I hear you're from these parts."

"Yes."

"Good. That means you have relatives here you can stay with, right?"

"Yeah, I'm in popular demand." Michelle chuckled lightly. "I'll shuttle back and forth between my mother's and my cousin's places."

"How nice. We've had loaners from other papers before, but most of them had to move into one of those extended-stay inns. Being with family is much nicer."

"Have you had many loaners from other papers in the chain?" Michelle asked, wondering just how much Barbara knew about her situation. Did Larry or the powers that be who arranged for this transfer fill in Barbara on Michelle's business with Stanford Chapelle?

"We had about three last year, but they were assigned to other departments—business, metro, and sports. You're the first one we've had at the paper this year and the very first one we get in the features department." Barbara tapped a pencil with a ladybug eraser against what looked like a Looney Tunes desktop planner.

"How exciting," Michelle chirped with enthusiasm she didn't feel.

"We're happy to have you. We can use the help now that Katie is out on maternity leave. As you know, you sit at her cubicle and take over her beat."

"So what kind of feature stories did Katie cover exactly?" Michelle realized that some features beats yielded serious, meaty stories. Features even had their own category for Pulitzer Prize honors. One winner had penned a heartrending and thoroughly reported story about a Honduran boy's perilous search for his mother, who had immigrated to the

United States. Another winner in that category had written a profile of a man who had been tried for negligence in the death of his son, and the judge who presided over the case. Then, the year before that, one winner had written a touching feature on a fourteen-year-old boy who chose to have potentially life-threatening surgery in an effort to improve his disfigured appearance. Michelle brightened with the knowledge that a stint in the features department could indeed have potential. Shoot, maybe she'd luck up on covering something she could really sink her teeth into while she was in the "Accent" department after all. Something that would have the *Business Journal* hopping to get her back long before her three months were up!

"Katie covers a little bit of this and a little bit of that," Barbara replied.

"So there's lots of variety, then. Good," Michelle said, restraining the urge to rub her hands together in glee. *Yes! The possibilities are endless!*

"Yup, but her mainstay is the pop culture and trends beats. That's what we'll expect from you. Katie had a nice, breezy writing style that lent itself to those kinds of stories."

"Is that right?" Michelle replied, her hopes sinking under the weight of her own leaden smile. Pickings from the pop culture and trends beat did not bode well for her fantasies of harnessing potential Pulitzer glory.

"I realize you're a bit out of your element in this department and this beat, coming from a publication such as the *Manhattan Business Journal,* but under the circumstances, after that ugly little business with that CEO and his disgruntled wife and all . . . Well, I don't need to rehash all of that now." Barbara made a little tsk-tsk sound. "Certain higher-ups at the *Business Journal* and Roswell, Inc., thought the publication and beat change would be good for you. And I do hope you see it that way, too." Barbara fingered through a stack of primary-colored folders on her desk. "I already have an assignment lined up for you—a phone interview actually. In about . . ." She flipped her slim wrist and checked the striped Swatch encircling it. "An hour."

Michelle's eyes went wide. "An interview in an hour? With whom?"

"The Yellow Wiggle," Barbara said matter-of-factly as she worked her way through the stack of folders.

"Excuse me? What is that exactly?" Michelle feared Barbara's reply.

"The Yellow Wiggle is not a *what* but a *who,*" Barbara explained affably. "No worries. Everything you need to know is . . . Where is it? Ahha! Found it! As I was saying, everything you need to know about the Wiggles is right in here."

"Could you give me the quick CliffsNotes version, please?" Michelle accepted the slick press kit that Barbara passed to her.

Barbara chuckled. "You're only out of the loop if there are little kids at home."

Barbara spent the next ten minutes filling in Michelle on Wiggle-ology. The Wiggles, four men from Australia who made up the traveling singing group, were an offshoot of the popular *Playhouse Disney* TV show of the same name.

Next week the Wiggly Safari Tour would make a pit stop at Detroit's Fox Theater for four sold-out shows. Michelle's first *Herald* assignment: write up a big blowout feature on what had become the hottest thing since Barney the dinosaur with the preschool set.

"I think you can have fun with Greg Page. He's the lead singer of the group," Barbara added.

"And this Mr. Page . . . He would be this Yellow Wiggly thing?"

"Yes. There's also one who dresses in blue, another in red, and a purple one. And assorted costumed characters, who are staples in the show. There's Captain Feathersword, Wags the Dog, Dorothy the Dinosaur, and Henry the Octopus."

Michelle peered down at the glossy color photo of the group pasted on the front of the press kit. Four white males, dressed in black jeans topped with either a blue, yellow, purple, or red turtleneck, smiled back at her in that exuberant but vacuous way that entranced those not so far removed from potty training. "And you know all this because you've read the press kit already?"

"I had the inside scoop. I have a three-year-old grandson who is just wild about 'em! Anyway, better hurry along now and study that press kit. In less than an hour the publicist coordinating the phoners will call you from Mobile, where the group has performed the last few days."

Michelle cradled the folder in one arm as she reached to gather her briefcase and purse. "Yeah, I'll get right on it." She tried ratcheting up her enthusiasm.

Just before Michelle turned to leave, Barbara leaned over her desk with a conspiratorial whisper. "Hey, between you and me, I think that the Blue Wiggle, Anthony, is pretty darn hot."

Was Barbara cracking an innocent joke or mocking Michelle's *Business Journal* troubles? Regardless, now was not the time to bristle with indignation. She vowed to do her time in Features without stirring up trouble, so she peered down again at the Blue Wiggle's toothy mug on the folder. He looked like Donnie Osmond before he got a lil' bit rock-'n'-rolled. She forced a smile. "Yeah, he's a real looker all right."

With Carmen's help, Michelle settled at Katie's workspace. Katie had left it nice and tidy. A Rolodex, ceramic mug of pencils and pens, and assorted reference manuals sat atop the desk, next to the phone equipped with one of those shoulder-prop thingies that made typing with a telephone receiver sandwiched between the ear and shoulder more comfortable. Michelle settled in the adjustable desk and chair with a heavy sigh, then noted that the keyboard was not ergonomically correct like the one at her desk at the *Business Journal*. Oh, how she missed that place!

"Would it be too much of a bother to get a replacement keyboard?" Michelle asked meekly.

"I have a little pull around here with the office supplies manager." Carmen plopped the big box on the desk, then reached for one of the pencils stuck in her bun and jotted a note on a tablet. "I'll see what I can do about getting you an office supply catalog to peruse." She waved a hand over the box. "Here are some things I thought you might need— spiral reporters' notebooks, additional pens, cassette tapes in case you like to tape interviews, your own Associated Press and *Detroit Herald* style manuals. Anything else before I head back to my post?"

"Looks as if I'll be all set when I get that catalog. Thank you." Michelle searched through the press kit Barbara had given her, then checked her watch. She didn't have much time to complete her Wiggles crash course, so she got busy.

Four

Wesley emerged from one of the *Herald*'s interview rooms. He often opted for seclusion to keep sensitive assignments under wraps and when he had to make personal phone calls using his cell phone. This time he'd used the room because he had a paranoid source at the mayor's office who feared exposure. The man would only talk from a pay phone and had insisted that Wes speak only when no one else was in earshot. Without those interview rooms, privacy was almost impossible during the peak morning hours in a newsroom the size of the *Herald*'s.

Wes reviewed his interview notes scribbled on a tablet as he strode back to his desk. He'd folded into his seat, booted up his computer, and reached for the phone on his desk when in his peripheral vision he caught sight of a body at Katie Carlton's cubicle just a few yards away. And oh, what a body! He did a drop-jawed double take; then a slow smile spread across his face as he recognized the good-looking honey who had usurped his parking space and blown him off near the bank of elevators. He'd been disappointed that he didn't at least get her name, but it looked as if he just might get a second chance. He tipped his head to one side and pursed his lips thoughtfully. Funny, she had made herself at home at Katie's desk as no typical newsroom visitor would. What was up with that?

With a telephone receiver sandwiched between her shoulder and an ear, her fingers tapped away on the keyboard as if . . . He stiffened, then shook his head. Naaah, couldn't be. No way would she be . . .

Working?

Here?

"Close your mouth, dude; you've got that look of a walleyed trout on ice," Craig Gordon quipped from Wes's right. Craig was Wesley's colleague, cubicle neighbor, and best friend. "Read the e-mail notice flashing on your monitor."

Wordlessly Wes glanced at Craig, then read the all-newsroom message in his e-mail basket from Barbara Duncan, the "Accent" editor:

> Herald staffers, please join me in welcoming Michelle Michaels, of the Manhattan Business Journal. Michelle has joined the "Accent" features staff as part of the Roswell Publications, Inc., interchain loaner program. She'll substitute for Katie, who as you all know is out on maternity leave for the next three months. We're fortunate to have Michelle, who is from these parts originally. Do drop by and introduce yourself to her.

Michelle Michaels, Wes thought with a grin, then turned in his seat to look in her direction again. He tilted the chair back, cradling the back of his head in his hands.

"Very attractive, isn't she?" Craig leaned toward the short partition separating their workspaces.

Wes kept his eyes trained on their newest co-worker and the look of deep concentration on her pretty face. "Just my type, too."

"Aren't they all?" Craig replied drily before his fingers did a rippling dance over his own keyboard.

Wes was just close enough to make out the crisp professionalism in Michelle's voice, but her words were indistinct. She was obviously in the midst of an interview, which could go on for an hour—maybe even longer. He tore his gaze away from her, realizing he had work to do. This Michelle would be at the *Herald* for three whole months. He had plenty of time to satisfy his curiosity.

An hour later Michelle knew more than enough about the Wiggles to pound out a feature that would work as an "Accent" "centerpiece" or lead story to go along with the color publicity glossies in the press kit. She craved coffee and planned to go in search of Carmen, who could provide directions to the closest supply. Michelle stretched and brought her hands to her neck to work out tight knots as she rose from her chair. The two flanking cubicles that had been vacant while Michelle conducted her interview now had occupants.

A thin woman with a rhinestone-pierced nostril and floppy brown hair stood at Michelle's right. "Hello, I'm Janie Howard. I'm the health reporter." Janie shook Michelle's hand with a too-firm grip and Janie's rhinestone thumb ring bit into Michelle's skin.

"Michelle Michaels," she said, quickly recoiling her hand.

"I know. I read Barb's e-mail," Janie said, her blue eyes shining.

"Barbara's e-mail?" Michelle's voice hitched, sounding a tad too paranoid.

"Yeah. She sent one to the newsroom staff about you."

"About me?" Michelle licked her lips and glanced around. Would she spend the next few weeks puzzling over how much everyone she encountered knew about her and the Chapelle debacle?

"Detroit is a big change from New York, but I hear you're from this area, so it shouldn't be too much of an adjustment," Janie assured her.

Michelle put a smile in place just as an older heavyset African-American woman who occupied the cubicle to her left stood and extended her hand. "Harriet Olsen, obit clerk. Glad to have you aboard." A thick black braid circled her head like a wreath, and raised black freckles sprinkled her plump brown cheeks.

Michelle didn't see any harm in fudging a bit. Everyone was nice so far. "Thanks. I'm very happy to be here."

"I couldn't help overhearing. Sounds as if Barbara has you plenty busy already," Janie said. "She couldn't wait to foist that Wiggles assignment on somebody."

"I survived the interview and I actually got a kick out of listening to the Yellow Wiggle's Russell Crowe accent." After what she'd already endured, it would take more than a kiddie-themed assignment to break her spirit. "Hey, I could use a caffeine hit. Was wondering where I might get a great cup of coffee."

"At the gourmet coffee shop about four blocks from here, but for emergencies there's a coffeemaker near the printers over there." Harriet pointed to a small alcove a few yards away. "But I wouldn't risk it if I were you. There's some in the Headliner, the newsroom cafeteria on the twelfth floor. It's not great, either, but it won't kill you."

"I appreciate the tip. Can I get you two anything?" Michelle reached for her bag.

"No, thanks for the offer. Would you like one of us to escort you?" Janie asked.

"I should be fine."

Michelle made a break for the bank of elevators without scanning the newsroom or the eyes she felt stared in her direction every time she made a move. These were journalists, but it was as if they hadn't seen an unfamiliar face in the newsroom before. Or maybe they knew about her troubles at the *Business Journal*! Michelle didn't like feeling so damn preoccupied with what other people thought of her. What happened to that confident, bulletproof young woman who had thumbed her nose at *Business Journal* newsroom gossip? She had ignored the rumors, because they were just that. Rumors. Her banishment from the *Business Journal* gave them the stench of truth. She pressed the DOWN button as she faced the elevators. A real trooper wouldn't allow herself to be distressed, always wondering and fretting about what these *Herald* staffers thought of her. True, she'd made a mistake—okay, more than one mistake—and getting too emotionally close to Stanford Chapelle while she was on the job was a real doozy, but she wasn't a gold digger or some skank who sexed old, married men to get ahead. She knew the truth and she still had her integrity, she decided, squaring her shoulders. From that moment on, no more! Cowering paranoia would not get the best of her. She was outta there in three months, maybe sooner, she hoped, as the elevator doors swooshed open.

Five

Inside the Headliner, Michelle had passed the checkout cashier two dollars for a cup of coffee with sugar and cream and two sticks of almond biscotti when a deep male voice piped up from behind, "I've got that."

She was too startled by his sudden appearance to protest. The hunk Michelle had encountered earlier that morning passed a ten-dollar bill to the cashier and disarmed Michelle and the cashier with a ten-thousand-watt sparkler of a smile.

It felt as if sawdust suddenly coated her tongue and throat, so Michelle swallowed with an audible gulp like a dork.

"Hello," purred the cashier, who had coasted through her job in a darn near comatose state just minutes before *he* appeared. She used one hand to fling her mop of lustrous microbraids over one shoulder like a supermodel preening before a clicking camera. All the better to give the well-dressed hottie a view of her comely mocha profile.

"Hello, Shawna. So how did it go with that big accounting exam?" he asked.

As far as tingle-inducing deep voices went, this man's bested them all because of its warmth. Michelle decided it had to be a practiced effect.

"Thanks for asking. I passed. Two more semesters and I'll finally have my degree," Shawna enthused. She took the ten-dollar bill, then passed him the change.

"That's wonderful news," he replied as if he meant it.

"Um, I can pay for my own coffee, Mr. . . . ," Michelle finally piped up, feeling like an interloper. Man! Was he ever built, and tall. Standing so close, she had to tip her head back to look up into killer brandy-brown eyes made at once soft and rugged by curly lashes and thick, jagged brows. She had always been good with names, but she played absentminded nonetheless as she moved away from the checkout. "Mr. . . . um . . ."

"Wesley Abbott." Hands in his trouser pockets, he strolled alongside her as she headed for a vacant table near one of the ceiling-to-floor windows. He pulled his hands out of his pockets and reached for her tray. "And you're Michelle Michaels. Let me carry that tray for you, Ms. Michaels."

Michelle swayed the tray in the opposite direction. "I'm doing just fine, thank you very much," she replied, noting his body language was that of a man with truckloads of confidence.

At the table, Michelle placed her tray on a faux wood surface, sat, then lifted a brow as he presumptuously claimed the chair across from hers at the same table. "And how do you know my name?"

"I could cop to possessing great psychic powers or chalk it up to my stellar investigative reporting skills, but you'd just find out it was all a ruse once you got back to your desk and signed on to your computer. I mean Katie's computer."

"And?"

"Barb Duncan sent an all-newsroom e-mail to announce your arrival."

"So you're on-staff at the *Herald*?" Michelle would've never guessed.

"That surprises you? Didn't I appear to know my way around earlier?"

"Yeah, but I assumed you were just visiting a friend who worked in the newsroom. Or that you might be an attorney at one of the chichi law firms I understand lease office space in this building."

"An attorney?" He blinked, feigning indignation. "And one who works at, what did you call it? A chichi law firm, too?" His lips turned up in an easy grin. "Is that a dig, Ms. Michaels?"

"Of course not. I happen to believe the law is an honorable profession." A reluctant smile found its way to her face; then she let her eyes skim over his impeccable white cotton shirt, deep burgundy silk necktie accented with a silver—most likely platinum-mercury–dime tie clip. "I don't see all that many working male newspaper journalists dressed as you are, tailored, custom-tailored perhaps . . . ?"

He gave her a slow nod.

"Masterfully *custom*-tailored suit trousers and dress shirt for the daily newsroom grind, that's all."

"Does my appearance make you uneasy?" he asked straight-faced, though his tone remained light. "I realize I'm not following the usual dress code for grunt male reporters. I understand the typical uniform is an ill-fitting sports jacket, golf shirt, khakis, or Dockers accented with ink scratches and coffee stains."

"And maybe a nicely pressed oxford shirt and a cheap clip-on tie when really trying to dress to impress. But that fancy car and those clothes of yours happen to say high-priced attorney or . . ." She paused. "At the very least, TV anchor. Very dapper."

"You think I look dapper?" he asked, that grin settling on his face again as he needlessly adjusted the knot of his necktie. "Why, thank you, Ms. Michaels."

As if he hadn't done his time before a movie screen–size mirror that morning to ensure that very effect. Michelle couldn't help rolling her eyes at his aw-shucks response to her inadvertent compliment.

"My desk is not too far from yours, ya know," he informed her.

"I hadn't noticed," Michelle couldn't wait to add, because she was enjoying the view, this exchange, and the clean sandalwood undertones of his cologne way too much.

He didn't miss a beat. "Barbara urged us all via e-mail to make the new staffer feel welcome."

"And that's why you're buying coffee and biscotti for me?" Michelle bit into her biscotti to offset the drool pooling around her tongue. This man was one big mouthwatering distraction! She could tell Wesley had a lean, athletic body underneath those tailored clothes of his. And those boudoir eyes coupled with his cologne stirred a yearning in Michelle's body from head to toe.

Wesley dazzled her with that smile, a blaze of pure white against flawless dark toffee. The dimple in his right cheek winked at her. *Lawd have mercy!*

"Well, actually, *you* paid for the coffee and biscotti," he said. "I used that ten you gave me to cover your 'squatter's rights,' if you'll recall. Speaking of which . . ." He reached inside his pocket and placed the change Shawna had given him—a five and a couple of singles—on the table in front of her. "The parking space is on me. I insist."

"Thanks." Michelle merely shrugged and took a dainty sip of her coffee.

"You don't have a problem with my joining you, do you?" Wesley finally asked. Michelle got the impression he was the type of guy who felt welcome anywhere he wanted to roam among womankind. Stunningly attractive people like him tended to glide through life with all-access passes.

"No, I don't mind," she replied, telling herself it was the least she could do to make up for the brusque way she'd treated him earlier. "So you're an investigative reporter, huh?"

"Yes." As he held her gaze, she felt the sensual heat radiating from him—like steam from an overheated race car.

After furtively noting that there was no wedding band or tan line on his left ring finger, she told herself there was no harm in continuing to admire his many obvious physical assets. First she took in more little details about him—the neatly zigzagging waves of his hair. Glossy onyx threaded with silver strands ever so faint they could be mistaken for reflections of overhead lighting.

"And you're on loan from the *Manhattan Business Journal.* Impressive," Wesley added in a way that let Michelle know he was not aware of her problems there—yet.

"Yup." Michelle allowed her eyes to feast on his smooth skin and full, soft lips that could do serious damage to a woman's self-control. A Bulgari watch peeked out from beneath one crisp cuff. His nails were neatly trimmed and had an attractive natural buff to them. The man was simply perfect.

Too perfect.

"I gather you're from here. Needed a break from the bustle of the Big Apple, eh?"

She looked down at her cup of coffee. "Yeah, something like that."

"Detroit's your hometown, right?"

Her gaze met his again. "Uh-huh."

"You're staying with relatives, then?"

"Yeah, at my mother's and cousin's places."

"So how did you get stuck in Features with Katie's beat? That's kinda odd. I mean with your hard business news credentials and all."

"I thought it might be nice to broaden my horizons a bit," she fibbed.

Wesley bobbed his head knowingly. "Oh, I get it. You're probably thinking of this stint as a vacation of sorts and Katie's beat is not exactly the most challenging one."

Michelle felt the same way, but hearing Wesley say it rankled her. "I hear her work is popular with readers, particularly those who get tired of reading all the doom and gloom that permeate most of the paper."

"True," he replied, then added quickly, "Please, don't quote me on that unchallenging part. I sounded pompous, didn't I? I wouldn't want that getting back to Katie. She'd hand me my head," he said with a wink and a quick chuckle. "I admire the fact that she not only is good at what she does but also enjoys it. So what hot story trail are you on, by the way?"

"The Wiggles," Michelle said, watching him closely. "They're coming to town; didn't you know?"

His expression went blank. "The who? Care to fill me in?"

"If you don't have pre-school-age kiddies at home, apparently it doesn't matter."

His steady gaze unnerved her, so Michelle took another bite of her biscotti and crunched with way too much gusto. She sounded like a squirrel pulverizing a jawful of acorns.

He gave her an arch look. "It's that delicious, huh?"

She stopped midchew. "Would you like a taste?" she asked, her voice suddenly dropping to a husky whisper.

A twinkle of anticipation lit his eyes as heat surged through Michelle's veins and settled as a tingling sensation between her thighs. What this man could do to her with a stare was scandalous! Her cheeks and the nape of her neck flamed with embarrassment. She squirmed as inconspicuously as possible, then cleared her throat, breaking his spell. "Would you like a taste *of biscotti*?" She shoved the napkin with the extra slice of biscotti in his direction.

All deep, dulcet tones and bedroom eyes, he simply replied, "No. I'm good."

No doubt he was *damn* good . . . and even better when he was bad. This man had to know his seductive power over women and probably played this game frequently—keeping them off-kilter for sport. A little flirting never hurt anyone, but Michelle wasn't allowed to indulge these days. She simply did not trust herself just yet. When the cell phone inside her bag chirped, she welcomed the interruption. Though impolite, she reached inside and removed the phone anyway, then flipped it open. "Please excuse me for a minute. I need to get this."

Chapelle. Again. Damn it. Why hadn't Michelle checked caller ID first? She glanced at Wesley, then down at the floor as she shifted left on her chair.

"It's not a good time," she said through clenched teeth into the phone while darting apologetic glances at Wesley.

Chapelle geared up for another speech about how genuine he'd been when he'd extended his "friendship." "I don't want to hear it," Michelle muttered. "Fool me once, shame on you. Fool me twice, shame on me. Don't call again, please. Good-bye." Michelle snapped the phone shut, then dropped it back inside her purse. She sucked her teeth and huffed, grasping for her composure as she prodded Wesley to continue, "You were saying?"

Curiosity lit his eyes. "Lovers' quarrel, Ms. Michaels?"

"No. I'm happily unattached," she replied breezily.

He leaned forward, clearly anxious for more info. "Is that right?"

"Yes, and that's *all* you're gonna get." She smiled. "I have a hunch you're very good when you're playing investigative journalist, but bamboo under my nails and Jimmy Choos three sizes too small wouldn't get me to spill it." Realizing she suddenly sounded too curt, she took a deep calming breath. She refused to take out her irritation at Chapelle on Wesley, so she softened her tone. "And pleeeease, no more 'Ms. Michaels.' 'Michelle' will do just fine. And I'll call you Wesley, if that's okay with you."

"How about Wes and Chelle?" His smile broadened, so that delightful dimple in his cheek made an appearance again.

The too-chummy Chelles were usually where the trouble began, but she didn't argue.

He took her silence as an agreement. "Chelle and Wes it is then. Great. And now that we're on a nickname basis . . ."

Michelle panicked, realizing he was about to bust his big move. "Don't mean to be rude, but I have to get back upstairs." She'd fumbled to gather her bag when he reached out to steady her hand with his large one. His felt firm but warm against her skin. A move that was way too familiar, but damn, it felt nice.

"This will only take a sec," he said smoothly.

Her gaze locked on his fingers encircling hers. She should pull hers away but didn't.

"Do you enjoy jazz, Chelle?"

Oh, how she loved what his deep voice did to her name.

He leaned in closer still, resting his elbows on the table. The movement drew his dress shirt taut, outlining his muscular chest, wide shoulders, and hard, rounded biceps.

"Yes. Why?" she replied tentatively.

"Ever hear of Ron Carter?"

"The legendary bassist? Of course I have." Her excitement was evident. "I have all of his recordings, starting with the stuff he did with Miles Davis back in the sixties. And oh, *The Complete Concert 1964*." Then she realized she was providing too much information. And while she couldn't pretend *not* to like Ron Carter, for crying out loud, she could pull her hand back from Wes's. She tried dismissing that she immediately missed the touch of warmth.

"I have *The Complete Concert 1964*, too," he said. "Along with everything else he ever recorded."

"Pure magic, isn't it? I mean, it was as if Carter, Herbie Hancock, and Tony Williams had some kind of otherworldly symbiotic thing going when they played together."

Wes settled back in his chair, studying her as if seeing her for the first time. "Wow."

"What?"

Wes smiled. "Just pleasantly surprised that you're a true fan, too, that's all. I'm going to see him and the quartet tomorrow night. I was going alone, but it would certainly be nice to have the pleasure of your company. Maybe we can even grab a bite before. We can talk about Carter and jazz in general. I'd also like to hear more about your work at the *Business Journal.*"

On the inside Michelle's rapidly shifting emotions flashed like a malfunctioning traffic light:

Say yes to the gorgeous man and great music!

Say no to canoodling with co-workers!

Michelle kept her expression calm and impassive. "You don't waste any time, do you? You're asking me out on a date?"

Wes studied her expression, obviously searching for the appropriate tone and words to yield a desirable response. "Not thinking *date,* actually. I mean, if you have a problem with that, let's think of it as two colleagues getting together after hours to enjoy one talented jazz bass player." His lips curled up in a smile. "And to get to know each other a little better at the same time."

"Now why would I need to get to know you better?" Michelle asked, trying not to smile back.

"Well, you *are* going to be here for three whole months. You're going to need some allies on-staff, don't you think? A friend who can share all the insider information on the politics and various players at the *Herald.* It could take you three whole months to learn what I could teach you in one night." His eyes sparkled with sensual mischief.

"Friends, huh?" Michelle took a sip of her coffee, which was now cool. She made a show of pausing thoughtfully as if she were actually entertaining the thought of accepting his invitation, though in reality, pigs would take flight first. She'd just made a promise to herself. *Never play where you work* traipsed through her mind. "Thanks for the offer, Wes, but I'm afraid I'll have to pass."

"I know it's short notice, but the show is here for a few days. We can go the night after next or the one after that," he suggested.

"I don't think going out together is a good idea with us working in the same newsroom and all."

Wes visibly deflated, which surprised Michelle. Could a date with her mean that much to him? She dismissed the thought. What she saw was more likely his reaction to the unfamiliar—rejection. "*But . . .* big but here," she added dramatically, "I can use a newsroom ally. I'd just feel more comfortable if we kept our interactions cordial but strictly professional." Michelle checked her watch, slung the strap of her bag over one shoulder, then came to her feet. "Just 'cause I nixed the concert and dinner doesn't mean we can't do lunch in here sometime, to talk *Herald* business."

"Lunch? Here? As in the Headliner, the company cafeteria?" he asked, sounding anything but thrilled.

"Yup. It's been nice chatting with you, Wes, but I'd better get back upstairs. I don't want to get a reputation for slacking off on my first day. Hey, before you go back upstairs, do have a cup of coffee and some biscotti." She shoved the money on the table back at him. "On me."

Michelle cleared her tray, placed it on a stack atop a trash can, then tossed Wes a smile before leaving the Headliner. She stepped inside the elevator, releasing a contented sigh and feeling proud of the way she'd handled him and herself.

When last week's memory of her date Ken Gerard blatantly flirting with Michelle's so-called friend Courtney resurfaced, Michelle shuddered. Ken's horn dog behavior was just the latest incident in a love life that had sucked for a long while now, but so far Michelle had resisted turning into the typical oft-scorned female. The type who either routinely huddled up in cold fear or brashly ball-busted *every* potential suitor she encountered, in the name of self-preservation, all because of a few rotten apples.

Michelle's romantic résumé included a morose poet named Felix, who turned out to be a little too enamored with her feet to make love to the rest of her; Emilio, the professional bodybuilder, who lifted everything—including one of Michelle's credit cards; James, the venture capitalist, who wouldn't stop boasting about his classic Lamborghini and vacation homes in the Hamptons and the Keys; and Bob Trumbell, the systems analyst, who had been mum about the *Mrs.* Trumbell, who wasn't his mother, tucked away in his Bronx brownstone.

Most women had their hearts battered and bruised at some point in their lives while searching for Mr. Right. Even Bliss Worthington, who had loved and lost every man in Dove Cove, including her bigamous stepbrother. But Bliss had soldiered on without giving up on her own happily-ever-after.

So would Michelle. She just had to be savvy and selective about who she let in, that's all. Newsroom romantic relationships were off-limits. And even if they weren't, what good would it do to meet Mr. Right in the Motor City when she planned to head back to the Big Apple in just a matter of weeks? Long-distance relationships were such a colossal pain in the ass. Why bother?

And Wesley Abbott had way too much going for him, which meant she had to keep him at arm's length. To her new way of thinking there was such a thing as oozing too much sex appeal. And Wesley Abbott practically hemorrhaged it—not only in the way he looked at a woman, making her feel as if she would spontaneously combust on the spot, but even in the way he moved and breathed. The bottom line: If a man looked *or* acted as if he were God's gift, way too many women had probably unwrapped his package. A man like that wasn't likely to settle for one anytime soon.

Six

After leaving the *Herald,* Wesley made several stops to gather the items for his parents' care package, which was positioned on the passenger seat of his car as he pulled into the circular stone driveway.

The 4,500-square-foot brick house, surrounded by acres of well-manicured lawn, was built on a gentle rise in the early 1900s in the upscale west side area of Detroit known as Palmer Woods. Wesley recalled the pride his mother took in decorating the historic dwelling, which featured marble floors, vaulted ceilings, a floating staircase, an Olympic in-ground backyard pool, a bluestone patio and fountain. To Wesley, who grew up there, it had been a massive enchanted playground filled with all sorts of cool places to romp, explore, and play hide-and-seek.

When he climbed out of his car, Margie, his parents' housekeeper of thirty-five years, stepped out of the house and greeted him before he could reach the door. Margie was a tall, slender woman with sharp dark eyes, a quick smile, and a slight limp, left by a bout with childhood polio.

Young Wes adored her because she'd always made up the best stories about dragons, wizards, gnomes, and kings. She'd had a tougher time winning over Patrick, who once slipped bug spray in her lemonade to avenge himself for one of the many times she'd banished him to his room for throwing a tantrum. Margie had lived and worked for the family full-time until Wes and Patrick moved away to attend college.

Wes's mother had always done most of the family cooking because she enjoyed it. And as his parents grew older their needs changed. Now Margie only came to the house twice a week to clean and take care of the laundry, though she was still paid the full-time salary with bonuses and cost-of-living increases for years of excellent, loyal service.

With the care package tucked securely underneath one arm, Wes mounted the steps. He placed a greeting kiss on Margie's soft brown face.

"You're here again?" Margie teased him. "Folks are going to start talking, saying you don't have much of a social life at all anymore, if you keep hanging around here with us old fogies."

"Old fogies? You? Never." Wes followed Margie as she led him deeper inside the spacious house. "I've got a few things I thought the 'rents might like."

"The 'rents? Speak English, son." Margie furrowed her brow as she reached for the box. "Need me to take that off your hands?"

"It's just some of their favorite magazines, newspapers, fruit, and some chicken soup."

"Like I can't whip up a decent bowl of something home-made." Margie pretended to take offense upon getting a peek at the Zoup! containers among Wes's stash.

"Hey, I thought it was your day off."

"I've been coming in all week because I know your parents haven't been feeling well."

"That's why I'm here, too, to check on them again. How are they?"

"Are you asking me if that bug still has a grip on them or if they're getting along?"

"Both."

"They're doing fine on both counts, I'm very pleased to report."

Wes set his box on a nearby chair and removed his suit jacket. "Maybe this forced time together has helped them come to terms with certain things. There's no rushing off here and there to tend to this and that to avoid really talking to each other."

"Could be." Margie took his jacket to hang in the coat closet. "Let me reheat that soup." She reached for the Styrofoam containers. "Go on up and say hello. I'm sure they'll be glad to see your hard head again. I did hear your mom specifically tell you not to come over for a few more days. They might still be contagious."

"What about you? You could get sick, too."

"The hired help always have an antibacterial force field around them. Comes with the territory. Besides, I get hazard pay," she joked.

"You know you've never been just the hired help, Margie," Wes replied, then did as she suggested. He took the stairs up to his parents' bedroom. Wes would have to steel himself for his mother. He was sure she would try to talk him into taking his five-year-old niece, Kelly, with him when he visited Patrick that weekend at Davenport. It had been too awkward for Lonette, Kelly's mother, to take Kelly to Davenport. After denying Kelly was his for quite some time and getting himself thrown into prison, Patrick was not one of Lonette's favorite people these days. And she'd already done her part by even agreeing to let Kelly see Patrick under the circumstances, Gloria had explained.

Meanwhile, Kelly had been so distressed about Patrick's absence she'd been acting out. Lonette had a devil of a time explaining why Patrick just disappeared four months ago and never came back to see his child. They all finally agreed that if Kelly saw Patrick soon—like that weekend—it could be good for her. Gloria and Winston were too ill to take Kelly to him.

When Gloria had first asked Wes about Kelly accompanying him to Davenport, Wes had flatly refused. He just didn't think a little girl should see her father in prison. Wes might have been overreacting, but he couldn't help believing that the experience might leave scars on the impressionable five-year-old. Kelly was a smart kid and she had to know that what was going on around her inside the Davenport Correctional Facility's visiting room was anything but normal.

Hell, Wes still had not gotten used to seeing Patrick in prison himself. His brother's incarceration shouldn't have caught him off-guard, not when Patrick had made a practice of letting them all down again and again. And he'd damn near single-handedly destroyed their parents' marriage over the years. The major source of the strain on their relationship had always been their philosophical differences on just how to handle their wayward firstborn.

Only two years separated the Abbotts' two children. As a boy, Wesley had always loved and looked up to his "cool" older brother, even after Patrick started to make trouble, beginning with a series of juvenile pranks, which included— and were not limited to—minor breaking and entering and destruction of property at his junior high school, resulting in a stint in a juvenile correctional center. Both boys had been blessed with money and loving parents, but a life of privilege and advantages had lacked the excitement and adrenaline rushes Patrick had obviously craved. He'd made his own thrills by breaking all the rules.

The allure of Patrick's rebellion wore off for Wes when they both entered high school. Patrick got bolder and progressed from taking their father's BMW for joyriding without permission to stealing stereo equipment from Alston Electronics, which was owned by a family friend, Prescott Alston. Fortunately, Alston hadn't pressed charges but allowed Winston to buy Patrick's way out of doing time by compensating him for the stolen goods.

Patrick had made trouble in college, too, getting kicked out for a year by a disciplinary committee after it was discovered he'd purchased term papers and passed them off to professors as his own work. At another college Patrick had managed to graduate with a bachelor's degree in computer science.

Patrick loved technology and knew computers in and out, but his grades had been unexceptional because he often missed tests and rarely showed up for class. It hadn't mattered that he barely eked by with a 2.2 grade point average. The Abbotts had been proud of him for graduating until he took his sweet time finding a job or other constructive way to fill his time because he still needed to travel to "find himself and more adventure first."

The Abbotts, their father's side of the family, and the Sinclairs, their mother's side, had inherited money from real estate and a string of hotels and car dealerships. While they were financially secure enough to live a full-time life of leisure, most family members—including Wes and his parents—believed in holding jobs they loved. Gloria had worked overseeing the family hotels until she had children. She resumed her career full-time once they were school age.

Wes and Patrick had inherited hefty trust funds on their twenty-fifth birthdays. While Wes indulged in great clothes, a tricked-out pad, and fancy wheels, he'd invested the bulk of his money and tripled its value. Ever the thrill seeker, Patrick had blown his in record time—jet-setting with a series of leeching females and sinking the rest in high-risk, often shady, business ventures, until he had to get a job out of necessity. He'd landed his first one at a marketing firm. Then the deadbeat-dad accusations and paternity suits weren't far behind. Patrick eventually botched up the marketing job when he was caught having sex with the barely legal temp in the office—during office hours. His second offense. The first had been downloading porn on the company computers. This pattern of irresponsibility and foolishness continued for years.

Then something miraculous happened. A year ago, all the Abbots had desperately wanted to believe Patrick had a desire to finally do right by everyone—especially Kelly, the child who was the product of a four-week fling he'd had with Lonette, a pretty cosmetologist he'd met at a Pistons game. He'd eventually accepted Kelly, but only after blood tests confirmed that she indeed shared his DNA.

Patrick had not only found himself, but he'd found Christ, he'd claimed. He described himself as "born-again." The family had been overjoyed by the positive changes in him. He went to church regularly. Sometimes twice a week. Had even joined the choir and spent lots of quality time with Kelly.

Winston, Gloria, and Wes had finally agreed as a family that simply forking over wads of cash to help Patrick take the easy way out again was only enabling him and sending the wrong message. The best thing for Patrick was to try to make it on his own. Patrick had agreed.

He sought another decent job, one that would enable him to use his computer skills so he could financially support himself and Kelly.

In a last-ditch attempt to help Patrick "do better," Wes had taken one last chance and called in a big favor from an old friend who'd helped Patrick land a sales job at Plexis, Inc., a local tech firm that specialized in bundling software for builders and resellers of nonbranded personal computers.

Soon after, Patrick managed to grow frustrated and bored with living paycheck to paycheck. He wanted more money. Fast. He'd lost his religion in record time by stealing and copying confidential documents, which included accounting records, profit-and-loss analyses of products, customer and prospect lists, and contracts with suppliers from restricted password-protected areas of Plexis's system, with the intent of selling the information to the highest bidder among the company's various competitors. At least that had been the plan before Patrick got busted.

Patrick had played them all for fools again.

Wes had been hiding behind a type of denial all this time. Would he ever realize there was no redeeming Patrick?

Outside his parents' bedroom door Wes knocked lightly until he heard his mother's voice beckoning him inside.

Gloria relaxed on a cream-colored chaise near a lilac silk–draped window with a best-selling hardcover thriller cracked open. Her usual glowing brown skin appeared dull from days of purging and bed rest.

Winston sat in a cushiony high-backed chair, engrossed in the pages of a glossy notebook. Both were dressed in comfortable loungewear.

Winston looked up from the notebook and removed his reading glasses when Wes entered.

"Wes, honey, it's good to see you." Gloria swung her legs off the chaise and stood. She took two steps in his direction, then stopped at a safe distance to scold him with her hands on her hips. "I thought I told you to stop coming around here until we're both sure we're not contagious."

"Thought I'd take my chances again," Wes said, unrepentant. "So how are you two doing? I come bearing gifts; hot chicken soup, new magazines and books."

"Come on in, Son, have a seat, but not too close," Winston said. "How was your day?"

Wes took a seat on the end of their king-size bed, then proceeded to make small talk about his latest assignments, but it wasn't long before his mother shifted the conversation to Patrick.

"Oh, honey, you're still going to see Pat this weekend, right? Did you change your mind about taking Kelly with you? Please tell me you did." Her eyes pleaded.

Wes waited for his father to pipe up in his defense as usual, saying something like "leave the man alone." But he didn't. Instead Winston said, "It'll give you a chance to spend some time with little Kelly, too. She's gonna need us all even more now that Pat's not readily accessible to her."

Though he missed his father's support on this issue, Wes definitely sensed a positive change in the dynamics of his parents' relationship. They were united again when it came to a decision involving Patrick. And Wes couldn't have been happier for them. This encouraged him to reconsider, and it must have shown on his face.

"So you'll do it, then?" His mother's voice broke through his reverie.

"Yeah, I'll do it."

"Good!" Gloria blew Wes a kiss. "Now where is that chicken soup?"

After spending a few hours at his folks' place Wes returned home. Clad only in loose cotton pajama bottoms, he punched PLAY on his stereo, sauntered to the leather sofa, and settled in with his headphones. He propped his long legs up on the glass coffee table, careful not to tip over the carved wooden Benin sculpture resting there. He positioned the stereo headphones over his ears, then snatched the headphones off and tossed them on the sofa cushion. He still had Patrick on his mind but didn't want to think about him anymore. He needed the vibrations of the music to wash all over his body as realizations that had shadowed him for months broke to the surface again. With them should come the kind of peace that resulted when one accepted that a big change was afoot.

He hummed along with Coltrane as he flipped through his mail. After tossing the bills on the coffee table, he opened the mini white envelope, which held a thank-you note from Julian and Maya Nelson for the wedding present he'd given them. He thought he'd never see the day. Someone had finally snared Julian, the last of Wesley's single running buddies. The rest of Wesley's friends not only were married but also had two or three rug rats.

The closest Wesley had come to parenthood was trying to be the best uncle he could to Kelly.

He also played godfather to Craig's twin boys. But all that required was doling out action figures, building sets, and toy trucks for birthdays and Christmases.

Would he ever have his own kids? Did he even want them? He hadn't given it much thought over the years.

It always seemed as if he had loads of time to savor everything else life had to offer. And Wes had been hardpressed to admit that time piled up on him. He knew he couldn't pluck away the few gray hairs streaking his waves forever. Like his father, full-fledged salt-and-pepper would probably strike in less than ten years. And with his stray gray came wisdom. He could only hope.

His feet moved in time with the music emanating from pricey state-of-the-art speakers. The plan had been to sip a bottle of fine wine and chill to the slammin' polyrhythms of Coltrane's *A Love Supreme* until sleep overtook him. A smile found its way to his lips when he thought about Michelle Michaels. He wanted to know her—even if it meant getting acquainted with her while choking down the Headliner's crappy coffee, bricklike doughnuts, and soggy tuna salad sandwiches.

Something about the twinkle in Michelle's catlike hazel eyes and that sweet little lopsided smile that found its way to her face—even as she struggled to maintain an air of indifference. Maybe it wasn't all that much of a struggle. After all, she had turned him down flat without giving his invitation much thought. He had a feeling once she set her mind to something, that was that. Would she ever take a chance on letting him in? Would he, if he were her?

When Wesley met women who weren't just in it for the

fun and games, he did not waste their time. For years he hadn't wanted any woman sacrificing or postponing her hopes for something meaningful while waiting for him to "come around." It would have been a sucker's bet.

He hadn't been interested in finding one woman to commit to. Like Patrick, Wes had been on his own new thrill-seeking path. But now he wasn't so sure how he felt anymore. He couldn't help wondering where Michelle's head was regarding relationships. The fact that he was still thinking about the damn woman both mystified and bothered him. He simply didn't do the daze and daydream thing after one meeting. Wasn't his style.

The CD player had slipped from "Kulu Su Mama" to "Ascension" when the doorbell buzzed, disrupting his groove.

"Damn," Wesley muttered, wondering who was visiting without phoning first. Only his parents had that privilege, but even they didn't abuse it with unexpected drop-ins.

He walked to the door and pressed the speaker. "Wes here."

"Hey, it's me. Brynn."

"Well, helloooo, Brynn," he said, managing to sound pleased that she was there, though he did not welcome the interruption. "What are you doing here?"

"I know you hate when people drop by unannounced, but—"

"Remember what we talked about before you left this morning? I thought we'd called it quits for a while."

"I know what we agreed, but—"

"I was just getting ready for bed, Brynn, baby," he said with a deep, playful lilt.

"Good." Her voice dropped to a seductive smokiness. "Sounds as if I showed up just in time, then."

Wes had initially found her aggressive damn near insatiability and lack of coy pretense a crazy-cool turn-on. The best kind of diversion when he needed it most—particularly during Patrick's arrest and trial. And she had been one of the few women who could almost hang with him stroke for stroke, creative position for creative position, "without stopping to lube up," Brynn had the crude audacity to boast.

Brynn was layered with thick curves that seemed to thrive and bloom with long, carnal rough riding. And she liked it that way.

When they started kickin' it, they had agreed that they weren't exclusive, so Wes did date other women, but Brynn was the only one he slept with, so to speak. Well, actually they'd done everything in his and her beds but sleep.

He didn't feel like doing the servicing stud thing that night. And nothing Brynn could pull out of her big bag of sexual tricks would change his mind.

Hadn't he just considered changing his swinging bachelor ways? He felt himself wavering already.

Maybe he'd grown bored with Brynn and their routine because he hadn't made a real effort to *know* her. Maybe he hadn't attempted to open up so she could know *him*. Maybe she'd held back, fearing that he would bolt if she tried to change the rules. Had he even given them a fair shot? Hell, no. Perhaps tonight would be an opportunity to test whether they had more in common than their routine bumping of private parts. Besides, he had too much on his mind. The usual thoughts of Patrick and the not-so-usual ones of Michelle were playing tag team, confusing him and making his head hurt. He needed the distraction of Brynn's company.

"So how 'bout it? You gonna leave a girl standing down here, wearing nothing but a trench coat, a red thong, and that strawberry/mango body lotion I know you like so much?" She laughed all low and husky.

"All right," Wes said. "Come on up."

Seven

Bowl-O-Rama was a dimly lit sixties throwback—part bowling alley, lounge, burger joint, and pool hall—tucked between Jake's old-fashioned ice-cream parlor and a shoe repair shop in Royal Oak. The kind of Saturday night dive frequented by men with greasy hair, pickup trucks, and beer bellies and women with cheap rings on every finger, tattoos, and dark roots. Mediocre static-laced pop tunes escaped from an archaic speaker system, background music for the roar of balls sliding down slick lanes and the clatter of toppling bowling pins. Tacky pine paneling clung to the walls. Red fluorescent running lights edged the time- and traffic-pummeled carpet. The Pin Stingers claimed lanes eleven and twelve. The Pin Stingers were a group of ten women on the Cherry Street Baptist usher board. For fun and fellowship they met at these lanes once every two weeks—all decked in pedal pushers, poodle skirts, and novelty bowling shirts with wacky embroidered patches. Liz, Michelle's mother, had been a member of the group for as long as Michelle could remember and had garnered a reputation as the best bowler among the fifty- and sixty-something bunch. Two days before, Liz had returned from a three-week trip to Atlanta, where she'd been visiting her nephew, Ahmad, his wife, and their new baby. Liz had not wanted to let the other Pin Stingers down by missing a third outing, nor did she want to abandon Michelle at her brick bungalow. Though Michelle needed to take some time to recover from a grueling day at the *Herald,* she tagged along that night because her mother had insisted.

Liz was way off her game and obviously preoccupied. Michelle couldn't help wondering if something besides a "sore shoulder" from the tetanus shot a doctor had administered to Liz the day before at her annual physical was the cause of the pitiful score.

Michelle sat on the plastic bench curving around the automated ball return. She wriggled her toes inside hard, stinky rental shoes and prayed that the antibacterial socks she'd purchased for the night did their job.

"C'mon, Liz, split those suckers. Blow a rack tonight! Lay it on out!" shouted Pin Stinger Ora Lee Welch, a short, gray-haired, and slightly overweight woman.

Liz now stood at their lane's approach area, her petite bird-boned frame devoured by an oversize bowling shirt stamped with hula girls who had colorful fringes for grass skirts. Black pedal pushers encased her thin legs. Her fingers gripped the glossy bubble gum–pink high-performance ball Michelle had purchased for her two Christmases ago. Liz hardly studied the pins, arranged in an equilateral triangle, before she took three steps forward, arms arced in a backswing. She released the ball, which flew up and out, then landed so harshly the rest of her team members winced. With very little power behind it, the ten-pound ball poked along a few feet, then sank inside the left gutter long before it got anywhere near the pins. On her second try she launched yet another creeper, which only clipped two pins. She'd turned to head back to the bench, tugging at the fingerless leather glove on her right hand, before the automated pinsetter descended.

Liz, who had been bowling since the age of sixteen, often boasted that her personal best score was 270 out of a possible 300. Her average was 180, but that night it looked as if she'd be lucky to hit 30. Instead of demonstrating her trademark clean hooks worthy of a champion on the PBA circuit, Michelle's mother had rolled gutter ball after gutter ball.

"That's all right, Liz." Edith Hightower, the Pin Stinger in rhinestone cat-eye glasses and too-tight leopard print clam diggers, slapped Liz on the back. "We all have an off-night. You're probably still suffering from a bit of jet lag."

"My doctor insisted that it was time for another tetanus shot, so I got one, and now my right arm is off," Liz explained. "I think I might've pulled something out of whack hauling my luggage off the baggage carousel at the airport the other day to boot." Liz rubbed her shoulder and looked at Michelle, who still sensed there was much more to her mother's inability to concentrate.

Ora Lee and Edith took their places before lanes eleven and twelve while the rest of the Pin Stingers watched and shouted encouragement.

"I tell you it looks as if Ahmad spit out that baby," Liz said, taking her place next to Michelle on the bench.

"How can you tell already?" Michelle inspected a row of bowling balls. "Don't all newborns look like worked-over prizefighters?"

"She's got Ahmad's eyes and that Matthews mouth." Liz stole one of Michelle's cold, greasy fries that were about as appetizing as wax candlesticks.

"I thought you were enjoying yourself in Atlanta. Why did you come back so soon?"

"I wanted to see *my* baby. You. And, if truth be told, I think I was getting on Wendy's nerves. I was only trying to help."

"Ma, I know how you can be when you're only to trying to help. Were you trying to run things?"

"No." Liz averted her gaze. "I merely had a few suggestions. It's not easy caring for a newborn who is not sleeping through the night, ya know."

Michelle could just imagine her mom "helping" until

Wendy was ready to pluck her own hair out—strand by strand.

When Michelle took her turn the ball glided along in the center of lane eleven smoothly, swiftly, its revolutions indistinct. It cracked into the front center pin and sent all but three pins toppling. Michelle finished the frame but didn't make a spare. She went back to the bench to join her mother, who suddenly threw her arms around her. "I'm so glad you're home, baby. You have no idea how much I've missed you," Liz said with a lazy smile, then rested her head on Michelle's shoulder.

"I've missed you, too, Ma. Promise I won't wait so long between visits next time." Michelle had not forgotten how good her mother's hugs felt.

"I'm just surprised you get to stay so long this time. I had no idea there was an exchange program among newspapers."

"Well, you can't get swapped out to *any* paper. Usually it's just a thing among affiliated newspapers, like those in the Roswell, Inc., chain. There was a time when the Gannett chain had a loaner program, which allowed reporters from its smaller papers to go to work for *USA Today* for short stints. But not every chain has done this."

"Oh, I see."

"I hope the *Herald* decides to keep you and never lets you go. I want my girl closer to home."

"Oh, Ma." Michelle patted Liz's leg. "Now don't go getting your hopes up. This is just a temporary thing."

Michelle had not shared the circumstances that led to her transfer to the *Herald* with her mother yet. But she would as soon as she got to the bottom of her mother's recent money problems. Michelle hadn't wanted to pepper her with questions so soon after her return from Atlanta, but after watching her performance that night she'd reconsidered. Something was most definitely up.

Michelle recalled that strange conversation that she'd had

with her mother last month. Liz had needed yet another loan. There was desperation in her voice that Michelle hadn't heard before. When she asked about the money shortages, her mother had become increasingly agitated, until Michelle dropped that line of questioning and agreed to send her the extra cash. When she phoned the following week all seemed back to normal again, so Michelle had not pressed. But upon Michelle's return to Detroit, her cousin Fatima mentioned that she'd given Liz money, too. And so had Liz's close friend Ed.

What the heck was Liz doing with all that extra cash? She had held the same job at the Winfrow Insurance Company for twenty-seven years and her standard of living hadn't changed that much. Her modest Ferndale bungalow and 1997 Honda Civic had been paid in full as far as Michelle knew.

As a seasoned journalist at a major national newspaper Michelle earned good money. A requisite to make it in Manhattan, even living a middle-class lifestyle. Michelle had believed in sharing the fruit of her labor. She regularly gave to her church and her favorite charities, such as Oprah's Angel Network and UNICEF. She'd also mailed monthly checks to her mother, Michelle's way of acknowledging and showing gratitude for the struggles the woman who had given birth to her had endured as a single mom. The last two months, however, those checks suddenly weren't enough.

Michelle decided the ride back to Ferndale was a good time to broach the subject of the money Liz had borrowed from Fatima, Ed, and her.

After climbing inside her mother's Civic, Michelle endured a rambling rundown about various Pin Stingers and the upcoming Women's Day celebration at Cherry Street Baptist.

As Michelle reached to turn down the volume on her

mother's favorite oldies radio station, she finally said, "Ma, I've been meaning to ask . . . is everything all right?"

"What do you mean?" Liz didn't take her eyes off the night road ahead.

"I mean, how's everything at work?"

"Same ol' same ol'. Chile, I know you don't want to hear about the boring ol' car insurance business." She faked some snores, then broke into a hearty, wheezy laugh.

Was Liz really happy? Michelle had never seen anyone with such sharply arcing mood swings as her mother. So full of bubbly cheer one month, then so droopy and melancholy the next. Over the years Michelle had pretty much learned to quickly identify Liz's various dispositions, then act accordingly. As a child Michelle knew which days would be good ones to hit her mother up for a pizza dinner or a new doll and which days to make herself scarce and focus on her coloring books.

Since Michelle's return Liz's signals weren't so clear, but Michelle thought she detected a hollowness in her abundant laughter and a sadness behind the smiling eyes. She couldn't put her finger on it. Things seemed the same as always on the surface, but her instincts told her something really wasn't right. Something was off. But what?

"How is everything with Ed?"

Ed was the fifty-something long-haul truck driver who had been her mother's "special friend" for the past year and a half. Liz would only concede that the relationship was based solely on their mutual interest in bowling and love for blues music. She claimed to have no use for romance. But since her day time with Ed had obviously merged into overnight visits, Michelle knew her mother had to be doing more with ol' Ed besides toppling pins and listening to Bobby "Blue" Bland recordings.

"Ed's fine, baby. He's in Albuquerque tonight, one of his many stops on the way to California."

"So he probably won't be back for a while, huh?"

"We're talking weeks. He'll take a short break in Los Angeles; then he's got another long run right after."

"And you're still okay with this?"

"Of course. I'm not the needy type who has to huddle up under some man all the time. I need my space."

"I am looking forward to seeing ol' Ed again, but I must admit I won't miss his wax-earplug-defying snoring," Michelle confessed. "It's like a fleet of Harleys at sunrise. This girl needs her beauty sleep."

The two women shared a quick laugh.

"He's a nice man, though," Michelle added. "I like him a lot, even his bent for bright-colored pimp wear and those jillion rings and things on his fingers. As long as he's still treating you well. And he is still treating you well, right?"

"Yes. We're fine, honey."

"Really?" Michelle was still not satisfied.

"You going Perry Mason on me or what?" Suddenly Liz clipped her words. "What's with all the questions?"

Michelle decided to just come out with it. "Ma, I've heard and noted some things that have me worried."

"Worried?" A flat chuckle. "About me?"

"Yes."

"What is it, baby?"

"It's about your borrowing . . . money."

"What I got from you a few weeks ago? Honey, I told you I would pay you back with interest. I always make good on my loans. Just give me a little time." Liz's voice strained; her eyes flickered with apprehension.

"Ma, it's not that. You know what's mine is yours and if you're ever in any trouble you can count on me."

"Everything is *fine*." A frown line settled between Liz's penciled-in brows. "Everything's under control, but I don't like the grilling you're giving me—not one bit. So back off, okay?"

"I'm just wondering why you had to borrow from me, Fatima, *and* Ed."

"That Fatima! She promised . . . !"

Michelle could tell from the flare of her mother's nostrils and the tight set of her thin lips she was thoroughly ticked off.

"She promised what?" Michelle pushed out a sigh. "Aren't you tired of all the secrets, Ma?"

"There's nothing to tell, all right?" Her posture went rigid, her voice cold. One hand flew off the steering wheel, flapping in frustration. "I got off my budget a little with a few bills. Must you take away the last little shred of my dignity by putting me on the spot?"

Dumbfounded, Michelle shook her head. "Last shred of dignity? And we call Fatima the drama queen of the family." She dropped the sarcasm to add gently, "Ma, you know I worry because I care."

"I didn't want to burden you by asking you for all of the money. Okay?" Liz stonewalled.

Michelle pressed on. "But I wired you a couple of grand. And if you had to get that and more from Fatima and Ed, that doesn't sound like you got a *little* off-budget."

"It's nothing, honey, please. Let's not spoil our time together bickering over nothing. Your ol' ma's fine." Her mother's manner shifted from irritable to ingratiating in a nanosecond. "You were always such a sweet, sensitive child." She patted Michelle's thigh. "Almost too sensitive. Your little radar picks up problems where there aren't any. Let's just drop this, okay? I'll get the money back to the three of you. Soon."

Michelle started, "Ma—"

"Would you reach inside the glove compartment and pull out the CD case for me, sweetheart?" Liz countered with a peremptory request. "Put a blues one in for me." The discussion about her loans had officially ended as far as she was concerned. "Your ma feels a monster headache coming on."

"Do you want me to drive?"

"No. Just put in B.B. That should do the trick."

Gritting her teeth, Michelle relented and pushed the B. B. King CD in the player. It was late and a headache pulsed at her own temples. She'd shelve this conversation for now, but they were far from done.

Once back at her mother's bungalow, Michelle went to her old bedroom, which had been redecorated with a more grown-up African safari theme a few years ago.

Michelle crawled between a thick comforter stamped with a lush palm leaf and zebra pattern. Settling in on matching plump pillows, she stared up at the bamboo hoop overhead. A mesh canopy reminiscent of mosquito netting flowed from it, making her feel cradled in an exotic sanctuary an ocean away. An hour later, however, sleep remained elusive. That conversation she'd had with her mother during the drive home from the bowling alley still played in her mind like a nonstop loop.

Then there was that other touchy subject that had always loomed over their relationship like a thick, unyielding fog: Michelle's father.

The man who had died before Michelle could know him the way her cousins Fatima and Ahmad had been blessed to know their own wonderful father.

The man whose memories Liz had hoarded from her.

That silence only fueled Michelle's curiosity and made her feel more incomplete inside. There were always the questions. So many questions plaguing her. If she could just get answers.

A disturbing childhood memory broke through as Michelle curled into a fetal position and hugged herself beneath the covers. She had been about ten years old at the time when she'd become attached to Pastor Herbert Wingate.

Pastor Wingate, a deep ebony–hued man, seemed as tall and as powerful as a comic book superhero. His teeth were big, white, and absolutely dazzling. He had no children of his own. And he smelled of soap and always had peppermint rounds in his pocket and jokes for Michelle and the other kids at Cherry Street Baptist. He'd been a widower for two months when Michelle had scrawled a four-page invitation to him on her yellow Josie and the Pussycats stationery, listing all the reasons that he should come to live with her and her mother now that his wife, Sister Edwina, had "gone on to glory," as the older folks put it:

> We can make up our on jokes after dinner every nite. We can take turns reeding Sharlote's Web to each other. Ma has a reely big bed that goes up on one end when you press a button. There's room for you to clime in with us for pillow fites. You wood never be lonely.

Her mother had been mortified when Pastor Wingate, touched by the "sweet" gesture, showed her the letter. Instead of providing a gentle explanation of why Pastor Wingate could not move in with them, her reaction had been cold and impatient. She'd scolded Michelle for embarrassing her and for "dippin' in grown folks' business with that silliness." Twice, in the heat of anger, Liz had pointed out that Michelle had not inherited that bent toward silliness from her. So Michelle assumed she must have gotten it from her father. She longed to know what other traits—good and bad—she might have inherited from him. Had the physical features that she didn't share with her mom, such as her hazel eyes, medium bones, auburn hair, and lighter skin come from his end of the gene pool, too? Michelle could only surmise. What about his immediate family and extended family? The questions went unanswered. As a child, she'd even tried pumping her aunt Carol, Fatima and Ahmad's mother, for information. But she'd claimed to know little about him.

There was no immediate family on Michelle's father's side, according to Liz. It was as if he had simply popped into existence one day in a cloud of smoke and drifted away mysteriously. Michelle had never even heard much detail about how he died. She had never seen a photo of the man, because they'd all been packed away in one box that was lost by movers, long before she was old enough to know that something that seemed as inconsequential as a few snapshots would create such a void in her life. But she'd thrived anyway and soon moved beyond it. Or had she? Michelle pondered that question before drifting off to sleep.

Eight

During the next four days, while yearning for a break on the edgier news side of the *Herald,* Michelle forced herself to settle into Katie's beat. She'd earned kudos from Barbara for the Wiggles feature and was jotting down notes for her next assignment, covering the Creative Coiffures National Competition. Hairdressers from all over the country would converge on Detroit at the Roostertail to flaunt avant-garde styles that were to locks what Milan haute couture was to frocks. She'd managed to avoid openly cringing when Barbara came by with the files containing clips and photos from previous hair shows.

Michelle sat at her desk, then glanced at Wesley's empty cubicle. Thoughts of him darted through her mind when she least expected it—too often. She could still smell his cologne and feel the flush induced by his provocative gaze. He hadn't spent a whole lot of time at his own desk that day, and the fact that she'd taken note of that troubled her. She'd found herself shifting to peek around Janie to steal furtive glances at Wes's cubicle often. Such an instant preoccupation did not bode well for Michelle's resolve. She must try to keep her interest in him platonic and professional. It was with great restraint that she'd managed to spare her cousin Fatima the gushing rundown on him so far.

Time to get to work, Michelle told herself as she flipped through the thick file of hair show photos. One model wore a style dubbed "Baby Hairy Copter," a molded mountain of neon orange curls with a bright yellow plastic propeller perched on top. According to the cutline on the back of the photo, the style actually had a switch to flip, which made the battery-operated rotary blade spin. The next style that caught Michelle's eye was something called Web Explosion. The jet-black hair had been twisted into a silky umbrella-sized spiderweb accessorized with a fat foil arachnid.

"Halloween in May. Treat or trick," Michelle muttered to herself. As she flipped through the stack, each photo was more ridiculous than the last.

"I don't think that look suits you," a rich male voice rumbled next to her right ear, startling her. The photos fell to her lap and to the floor.

Without turning, she identified the voice and the delicious cologne instantly. Wes.

"Please don't sneak up on me like that again." Michelle frowned.

Wes removed his hands from the front pockets of his dark navy trousers. "Sorry about that."

Both moved to retrieve the photos from the floor at the same time, then bumped heads.

"Ouch!" Michelle winced while he hardly flinched.

"Sorry again. Did I hurt you?" Looking concerned, Wes placed a large hand on her shoulder.

Michelle scowled, rubbing her forehead. "What you got up there? A metal plate?"

Wes gathered her photos, then placed them in a neat stack on her desk. "I do have a very hard head when it comes to going after something I want."

"I'm assuming you're talking about a story, right?" The dull ache above Michelle's eyes was quickly forgotten.

Wes paused as if measuring his words. "That . . . among other things."

The way he said "other things" caused Michelle's belly to

flutter, and though she recovered quickly she was awfully glad Janie and Harriet were not at their cubicles at the moment to see or overhear this exchange.

Wes lingered next to her, leaning against one of the gray partition walls of her cubicle, hands shoved back in his pockets, legs crossed casually at the ankles as if he had all the time in the world. "Looks as if you've settled right in and made this desk and beat your own. The fresh-cut flowers. Nice touch." He swept his fingertips across the bouquet of cheerful white daisies she'd picked up from a florist on the way to work.

"Thank you. Working on something hot?" she wanted to know. "I haven't seen you around the newsroom much for days."

"I had something, but turns out the source was all sizzle—"

"No steak," she completed his thought. "Boy, do I know how that feels. Were you shooting for A-One?"

"It involved alleged corruption in the mayor's office."

"The mayor? Whoa! Definitely page A-One."

"Not the mayor himself, mind you, but another high-ranking elected official."

"Next best thing. From what I hear, you're pretty good at what you do," Michelle revealed as she decided to give him her full attention now that the conversation was firmly planted on a professional level. "And you've made quite a name for yourself around here."

"So you've been asking around about me?" There was his cocksure grin again, complete with a flash of dimple.

"No, I wasn't exactly asking about you," Michelle said. "Your name just came up casually. Janie told me what a great job you did breaking the piece about the local pharmaceutical company that was secretly paying a dozen local doctors to test its drugs on patients."

Surprise, then earnestness played on his handsome features. "Janie actually said that? That I did a great job?"

"Yeah, she did," Michelle replied, her curiosity piqued by his odd reaction. She would've thought he'd have that built chest of his all puffed out right about then. "Is there some reason you think she shouldn't have said that?"

Silence fell between them as he appeared to stare at nothing in particular across the newsroom.

"Wes?" Michelle pressed.

He paused with a speculative look on his face. "You strike me as a real go-getter."

That took Michelle by surprise. "Somehow, though, I doubt you could glean all that from my Wiggles assignment," she said facetiously, assuming he was poking fun at her.

"I went and checked the online archived issues of the *Manhattan Business Journal* to browse some of your profiles on movers and shakers in big business. I also noted that you happened to get quite a few who have a reputation for not giving much to the media, but you managed to finesse gold out of them."

"Oh, thanks," Michelle said, still puzzled as to what that had to do with his strange reaction to Janie's praise. "I've checked out your work, too," she added with a smile as she watched him closely.

"The stories about the pharmaceutical company and the homes for the mentally ill were culled from Janie's health beat," he pointed out slowly.

It took a minute to register, but once Michelle got an idea what he was hinting at she nodded again. "Oh, I get it."

"You do?" he said, giving her a long, careful look.

"You're not supposed to roam on another reporter's territory, but in special investigative reporting that's where the story leads you all too often." She tipped her head to one side. "And I'll bet you get to do it with the senior editors' blessings because you're so damn good."

"I don't want to brag, but—"

"It's okay, Wes, really. You are good and I *get* you, but I also realize that the situation probably doesn't make you popular with some of your *Herald* colleagues."

He glanced around, checking once again to ensure that no one was listening in on their conversation. He proceeded, lowering his voice for good measure. "My tip, my source, my story, is the senior editors' reasoning. And then there's an opportunity to spur interstaff competition. I'm the spark management uses to light a fire under the butts of several beat reporters who are getting too lazy and complacent to really get out there and dig for the meat—"

"Choosing instead to feed this ever-voracious beast we call a daily newspaper with scraps of the mundane and mediocre," Michelle completed his thought. "Wiggles, anyone?"

"You *do* get it."

"So you've just told me how the senior editors feel about it. But how do *you* feel about your role?" Michelle asked, but before he could answer she took a stab at doing it for him. "Wait; let me guess. When it comes to your work you're passionately ambitious and aggressive, but because you're not truly ruthless about it, there's a prick of guilt here and there."

"Correction: I feel *like* a real prick."

Michelle chuckled at the bad pun. "Oh, but here's the rub. You feel bad, but obviously not enough to stop," she countered.

"Hell, no." His posture straightened. "I enjoy this beat with no boundaries, but I had hoped I could hang on to my integrity by at least dealing up front with the other reporters—"

"Other reporters whose beats you regularly poach and pirate from?" Michelle clarified.

He winced, then cleared his throat. "I don't like the words *poach* and *pirate*."

"I thought we were being real here. You're probably amazed that Janie can be so magnanimous about it all—to the point where she's actually praising your work on the pharmaceutical company story that probably should've been hers. Am I right?"

Wes didn't respond.

"Your feelings are natural and normal," she added, cutting him some slack. "You're doing your job. For what it's worth, I don't think that makes you a bad guy, Wesley Abbott. Relax."

He blinked, then tried to recover by changing the subject. "You'll send your bill in the mail?" He grinned. "So is workplace psychoanalysis just a hobby of yours or is it something you do on the side to help make ends meet, lady?"

"The latter would imply actually guiding people to solutions to their problems. I don't pretend to have all the answers—especially when I'm still trying to sort out my own damn workplace issues," she replied drily.

"Is that right? You just got here, so I'm assuming these 'issues' you're referring to are back at the *Business Journal.*"

"Yes, but let's just leave them there for now."

"Well, you're a good listener and perceptive, too, issues and all," he said, with an appreciation reflected in his eyes that made warmth skim up Michelle's spine. "How about we go down and grab some lunch together in the Headliner so I can return the favor? I can show you just what a good listener I can be, too. Hey, and you missed a really good concert the other night. Carter tore the roof off the joint. I mean, that guy and the quartet killed, *killed,* you hear me?" His smile broadened. "I could give you a detailed review. How about it?"

Michelle was at once pleased and anxious that Wes had extended another invitation. Although he'd ventured to open up, another part of her wasn't sure if it was a ploy or not. He could play vulnerable and guilt-riddled to suck her in.

He'd obviously sensed her hesitation. "I know you said no dating co-workers, but you said lunch at the Headliner was a definite possibility."

"I know. I'm sorry," Michelle said. "I'll have to pass." The gleam in his eyes muted, so she hurried to add, "On the way to work this morning I stopped by not only the florist but a deli, too. I picked up a pastrami, pickles, and rye sandwich."

"So? Bring your pastrami and pickles with you."

"I'm a little tight for time, so I'll have to eat lunch at my desk today while I work." She added with a quick note of disdain, "What with this thrilling hair show assignment at the Roostertail tonight. Rain check?"

Again there was that fleeting look of disappointment that he quickly covered with a cool veneer. "Another time, then," he replied, pushing away from the cubicle wall to balance his weight squarely on both feet. "Maybe I can recruit Craig to break bread with me today. Talk to you later," he tossed over his shoulder jauntily as he headed back to his own workspace.

Nine

Y ou sure it's the woman and not just the thrill of the chase?" Craig asked Wesley as they claimed a corner table in the Headliner, packed with workers from various *Herald* departments and companies leasing space in the building.

As usual Wes strolled ahead of Craig so he could claim the seat that provided a full view of the cafeteria.

Craig took the chair across from Wes, then immediately chomped into a thick submarine sandwich.

"This is no game, man. That Michelle, she's really something else." Wesley picked at the potato salad that was too heavy on the mustard. He preferred his mother's, which she made with sweet relish.

Davina and Cheryl, who worked at one of the law offices in the building, sashayed by, balancing Diet Pepsis, small cellophane-covered mixed green salads, and squares of bright red Jell-O on their plastic lunch trays.

"Hey, Wes." Davina smiled, stretching his name over her tongue like sweet taffy.

"Hello, Wes," Cheryl echoed in a similar fashion with a giggle, her female appreciation evident. Cheryl had slipped Wes her phone number five weeks ago, but he had yet to use it. He didn't *do* friends. Davina and Cheryl were the tightest. He'd dated Davina for a month when he first joined the *Herald* a few years ago. Things hadn't worked out, but they'd managed to remain on good terms because Wes had always been up-front about his intentions. He made no promises he couldn't keep. He'd found that most women were reasonable when plied with the truth *and* treated with respect.

"Hello, Davina, Cheryl." He smiled.

They were both nice ladies. If there had been room at the table Wes might have invited them to join him and Craig.

"Oh, hi, Craig," Cheryl and Davina said, almost as an afterthought. There was a time when Craig, an athletically built and glow-domed Michael Jordan ringer, had inspired a more awestruck greeting from the ladies, but that was before Bridget, the twins, and the wedding band on his finger.

Craig nodded in their direction. "Hello," he replied with equal indifference that indicated he didn't miss the fawning attention.

As the two women continued to an empty table on the opposite side, Wes discreetly checked out Cheryl's and Davina's appealing rear views. Then he turned his attention back to Craig.

Craig took a deep swallow of his Coke. "As I was saying, your motives are questionable where this new reporter is concerned. Face it. She's merely fresh meat and she's only in the newsroom for three months. But from what I can tell, Michelle Michaels appears to be immune to your Don Juan thing."

Wes's irritation smoked just beneath the surface; then Shawna, the cashier, sidled by, swinging her hips and grinning at Wes. She had a huge box of potato chips under one arm for restocking the nearby vending machines ringing the perimeter of the Headliner. She placed the box on the floor, then leaned over it to do a bag count.

"You don't know what you're talking about." Wes cleared his throat. He redirected his gaze away from Shawna's perfect cleavage, then back to Craig. "I've been stepping to Michelle correctly, meaning with the best of intentions. I've decided that I want to get to know the woman better. What's so wrong with that?" His appetite was suddenly gone, so he took a generous swallow of his drink and settled back in his chair. "I mean, check it out. I'm completely free. Broke it off with Brynn for good the other night."

Craig shrugged. "I'm not so sure about your definition of 'broke it off.' For most people that means the sex is over, too."

"Okay, so maybe I slipped up one last time." He'd tapped a long finger against the table to punctuate each word. He added, "But I'm done and she's done, too."

"And why is that, by the way? 'Done,' I mean? I'm wondering." Craig shook his head and pushed out a rueful sigh. "How can a beautiful, sexy, no-strings young tenderoni like Brynn—the emphasis is on no-strings, mind you—how can she become old hat to a man such as yourself?"

"A man such as myself?" Wes wasn't sure why he was egging Craig on.

"You know how you are. Do I have to spell it out?"

"Wooooo." Wes shuddered in a theatrical manner. "And I'm the big bad bogeyman—all sinister sexual menace. Quick! Everyone, lock up your wives, daughters, sisters," he added facetiously.

"And don't forget Granny, too," Craig added in his patented droll way.

"Ouch." Wes winced. "That's cold, man."

Craig shrugged as if to say, "Deal with it."

"Playing the simmering prig doesn't become you," Wes retaliated.

Craig's smug self-righteousness was really too much, but Wes kept his composure. Where did Craig get off? There was a time when he had the attention span of a gnat when it came to any particular woman—especially after he'd sexed her a few times. But now that he'd met and married Bridget and had the twins, he acted as if he'd always been in that settled, monogamous sort of mind. Nothing could be further from the truth, and Craig's superiority thing seriously chapped Wes's behind.

"Hey, if my interest was all about acquiring a new piece of ass I've got plenty of options, you know." Wes kept his tone even.

"But this woman is, ooooooh, right under your nose," Craig replied in taunting singsong. "And, hmmm, you see her just about every workday, too. But again, the beauty of that is . . . ," he lifted a finger as if emphasizing a significant point, "not for long, because she'll pack up and head back to New York in three short months, around the time a woman wears out her welcome with you. The time element kind of ratchets up the excitement and the stakes, don't you think? *Can* Wes nail her? *Will* he not nail her? Stay tuned, folks, for the heart-thumping conclusion."

"Look, man, I'm not going to argue with you about this." Wes kept his tone even. "I know what's in my heart."

"Heart?" The word rolled around Craig's mouth with a wad of bread, meat, and sarcasm. "New tactic. Smooth move. So you're dragging the ol' heart into it now, huh? Going for the jugular, the romance angle. Hmmmm, interesting."

Wes finally broke. "Fuck you, man."

Craig was goading him. All because Craig was still smarting over what he assumed happened between his sister, Lindsey, and Wes last Christmas.

Yes, Wes had ended up sharing dinner at the Rattlesnake Club with Lindsey one night. Before her trip from New York to Detroit for the holidays, she'd just been served divorce papers from that NBA baller she'd married. She'd tried to put on a strong front for her family. But that one night, after trying to drown her sorrows with a series of Asian pear martinis, she went off on a boozy confessional about just how devastated she was over the breakup of her marriage. Wes wasn't sure why she chose to confide in him instead when she and Craig had always been so close. But he'd willingly offered his shoulder and grappled to find the right words to comfort her as he would have done for any good friend. The next morning when Craig dropped by Wes's loft to draft him for an impromptu racquetball match at the gym, he'd found a disheveled and hungover Lindsey sprawled across Wes's platform bed. "Man, not my sister, too!" Craig had wailed before Wes could explain that things weren't as they seemed. Craig hit Wes with a withering look of betrayal, then nailed him with a quick left hook to the cheek that loosened a molar. It took an awful lot of restraint for Wes not to slug him back, but he knew how protective and crazed out of his head Craig could get when it came to his "baby" sister.

Wes and Lindsey had offered staunch denials that anything sexual, or romantic, for that matter, had transpired between them. And though Craig had later apologized for losing his temper, Wes wasn't sure Craig truly believed their version of the events that led up to Lindsey passing out in Wes's bed.

Wes and Craig had shared a friendship that dated back to grade school. Though Lindsey had briefly harbored a junior high crush on Wes, she'd apparently gotten beyond that once she entered high school and developed a taste for jocks. And though Wes would have to be blind not to notice that Lindsey had matured from a cute, curly-haired cheerleader to a real world-class beauty with a bangin' body, he knew where to draw the line. Fully realizing where his head had been with women and relationships at the time, he didn't dare try stepping to Lindsey any other way than as a "play" little sister, as he had from their elementary school days. The entire Gordon family's friendship and respect meant too much to him. He and Craig had had their ups and downs, but the bond had always endured. However, a part of Wes still hurt that Craig's first impulse that morning had not been to give him the benefit of the doubt—after everything they'd been through together over the years.

And that obvious distrust of Wes reared its head again.

"I like Michelle," Wes reiterated simply. "And yeah, I do think she's very attractive, of course, but that's not all. There's something different about her."

"I'll say." Craig snorted again. He bit into his sandwich, then added with a full mouth, "She hasn't melted into a warm puddle of quivering desire at the sight of you."

"Whatever," Wes replied wearily. He'd tired of pleading his case to a brick wall.

"I know I'm giving you a hard time." Craig eased up. "Forgive me if I'm skeptical. I mean, damn, just a few days ago you were still shakin' Brynn's chakras. I've gotta question where your sudden 'I'm vibin' with this Michelle babe on a whole different level' is really coming from. So I'm just being real with you, 'cause we never bullshit each other, right?"

"I hear ya. The thing is, yes, Brynn came over the other night and *spent* the night, if you catch my drift. But when I tried to see if there could possibly be more there than the routine bumping of private parts, I came up empty, okay?"

"In other words—"

"Great sex was all we had in common. I think I'm at the point in my life where I want and need more."

Craig still looked skeptical but said, "If your interest in Michelle is really about more than getting into her panties, then I'm happy for you."

"Can't I just be friends with a woman at first?" Wes said the words as if he wasn't so sure himself all of a sudden. Craig's lack of faith rubbing off on him?

"An attractive unattached one? Hmmm. Let me think about that." Craig set his half-eaten sandwich on a paper plate to rub his chin as if in deep thought. "The short answer?"

"Yes."

"No." Craig's reply emerged with such blunt and bullet-like certainty, Wes actually winced again.

"Man, you're just not even leaning toward giving me the benefit of the doubt, are you?"

"Look at your track record, dude." Without discretion Craig sucked his teeth, then used a fingernail to dislodge bits of his lettuce between them.

Wes passed him a toothpick. "Isn't it about time I at least started thinking about changing the MO? I am getting old. Hell, I'll be forty in three years. And there is nothing more pathetic than being the oldest cat up in the club trying to push up pretty young things."

"If you say so."

"The fact that you're acting as if I can't possibly step to a lady with something in mind beyond sexual seduction is getting real old, man. I'm only gonna take so much of your good-natured ribbing before I start whompin' ass," Wes added with a hollow chuckle. He shouldn't care what Craig thought at this point. Actions spoke louder than words, right?

"Just examine your true motivation is all I'm saying. Make sure this is what *you* really want before somebody, mainly Michelle, gets hurt."

"I have no intentions of hurting Michelle or anyone else," Wesley stated firmly, then tapped an index finger against a temple. "And as incredible as it sounds, it *is* possible for me to think with something besides the little head."

At that moment Shawna walked by, her cardboard box now emptied and the vending machines filled. "Take care, fellas."

"You, too, Shawna," Craig and Wes replied in unison.

Shawna tossed a special smile Wes's way. Wes knew Craig was studying him. As Shawna departed, Wes made a point not to let his eyes so much as drop to the curled ends of Shawna's mircobraids. The butt man in him usually dictated stealing a discreet peek at a woman's lower anatomy. He refused to yield to that habit this time.

"What?" Wes snapped as he leveled an annoyed gaze at Craig again.

"You know you want to inspect that bumper in those tight slacks. Don't let me stop you."

When Wes refused to check out Shawna's bottom, Craig lifted his brows and clapped his hands as if Wes's minor show of restraint had impressed him.

"The big head, huh?" Craig reached for a rippled chip from his plate; before he could bring it to his mouth, Wes plucked it out of his hand.

"Damn right," Wes said before shoving the chip inside his own mouth.

Ten

Saturday's drive toward Chippewa County in Michigan's Upper Eastern Peninsula took Wesley longer than usual due to extensive construction along Interstate 75. He'd also made an extra stop so Kelly could use the restroom and lunch on a McDonald's Happy Meal. Six hours cooped up in a sports car with only a couple of picture books for entertainment could prove torturous for even the most patient five-year-old.

Since Lonette turned over Kelly to Wes that morning, the child had been on her best behavior. She'd entertained Wes with her enthusiastic chatter about her Bratz doll collection; Mrs. Roundtree, her kindergarten teacher; and her gymnastics and dance classes. Kelly also shared her disdain for the midday naps Mrs. Roundtree ordered and a "stupid poo-poo butt" named Corey Johnson, a classmate who'd been teasing her relentlessly since she lost her two front teeth four weeks ago.

Before stirring up legal trouble at Plexis, Patrick had spent the past year getting to know his young daughter. And his efforts had obviously made a deep impression on the child, who had not forgotten him, though she had not seen him since his incarceration four months ago.

Just outside Kinross Township, near Sault Sainte Marie, Michigan, Wes slipped Ron Carter's jazz inside his CD player wedged in the car's console while Kelly napped with her small body belted against the reclined passenger seat. The car vibrated as it rolled over a patch of stripped asphalt that construction workers had prepped for paving. Kelly didn't stir. She was obviously a deep sleeper, just like Patrick.

Something compelling stirred inside of Wes as he reached over to caress her soft hair. He smiled at the bit of drool creeping from the right corner of her little mouth. She was such a beautiful child, with big brown deep-set eyes, golden skin, and brown corkscrew curls with natural sandy streaks.

Light rain fell from the gray sky, misting the car and fogging its windows. Wes activated the wipers and the defogger. Outside of the occasional cow herd or dilapidated barn, the fields flanking both sides of the highway provided little visual distraction.

The area boasted not one or two but five prisons—including Davenport, where Patrick was held. For the townspeople, life near thousands of felons and their jailers had proven that crime did indeed pay. The correctional facilities at the former Kincheloe Air Force Base, about fifteen miles south of the city limits, had also proven to provide a recession-proof economic boon for the little town that had been close to getting wiped from the map when the old air force base closed decades ago.

Davenport reminded Wes of a small military campus of silver barracks. Two thirty-foot-high fences with razor wire circled its perimeter. The lower-level security facilities housed mostly inmates like Patrick, in for nonviolent offenses. But there were also some inmates who had committed more serious crimes, such as rape and murder, and had started out at higher-security facilities but had been downgraded for good behavior and moved to lower-security institutions such as Davenport.

Wes parked, then got out, stuffing his driver's license and papers for Kelly in his pocket. He released Kelly's seat belt and helped tidy her pink skirt-and-matching-top ensemble emblazoned with a whimsical Hello Kitty motif.

Once inside Davenport, Kelly slipped her small hand inside Wes's. She looked around with wide wary eyes, taking in the cold, institutional surroundings as they stood in a long line of visitors waiting to submit to detailed searches. The guards used body patdowns and metal detectors.

Kelly tugged Wes's hand. "Why are we in line, Uncle Wes? Mrs. Roundtree makes our class line up to go to the playground and the cafeteria."

Davenport personnel instructed all visitors to remove their shoes and socks.

"But Mrs. Roundtree only makes us remove our shoes and socks at nap time," Kelly said, obviously confused. "We taking a nap? I don't want to take another nap! I thought we were going to see Daddy!" She stuck out her bottom lip and sniffled before her face started to crumble, only moments from a full-out bawl.

"We are seeing your daddy," Wes assured her. "We're only minutes away."

"Why I gotta take my shoes off, then?" she whined, her voice cracking with sobs. "I don't want to!"

"Aw, don't cry, honey." Wes knelt and attempted to draw her into a comforting hug, but she only tried wriggling away.

"Where's Daaaaaddy?" Her big eyes were bright with unshed tears.

"Sssssssssh. Please, honey." Wes couldn't remember the last time any female made him feel so flustered and clueless. His inexperience with the pint-size variety was painfully obvious. "We are going to see your daddy, but . . . but—"

She broke loose with a wail, drawing the surrounding crowd's attention.

Embarrassment flamed Wes's neck and cheeks as he grappled for a suitable explanation that didn't involve a hunt for weapons and contraband. "But they're only letting in folks with ten toes, sweetie," he blurted.

That did the trick. She went quiet, midsob, as if someone had snatched out her batteries.

It never failed to amaze Wes how abruptly kids could turn off the waterworks with the right bribe, diversion, or explanation. Kelly's small hands flew to her mouth. "What?" she gasped. "But everybody has ten toes, don't they?"

"I'm afraid not," Wes said, placing her on a bench so he could remove their shoes and socks before heading toward the line walking through the metal detectors. Once they'd passed inspection he lifted Kelly and gently set her on a wooden bench again to replace her socks and sneakers, and then replaced his own shoes and socks.

The gray-haired woman behind them set off a walk-through metal detector's alarm.

"Oops. Somebody's toes are missing!" Kelly shrieked, and squirmed off the bench. "I want to see her feet! Can I please go see the old lady's feet, Uncle Wes?"

More heat flushed Wes's cheeks as some of the visitors stared in their direction again. "Kelly, sit down," he said just firmly enough for her to hear. "She seems like a nice lady. We don't want to embarrass her. Remember how you said Corey Johnson teased you about your missing front teeth? That lady might feel the same way about her missing toes. We don't want to be stupid poo-poo butts like Corey Johnson, do we?"

Disappointed, Kelly poked out her lips. "No, I guess not," she grumbled.

Wes overheard the old woman explain that she'd had knee surgery. The metal replacement parts the doctors had used had triggered the alarm.

Soon Wes and Kelly joined a cluster of people who were ushered into the visiting area by another set of guards. The room had checkerboard-pattern tile floors and stark white cinder-block walls devoid of decorations. Decks of cards and worn Bibles dotted some of the mismatched wooden tables. The inmates, all in blue, sat awaiting their visitors, but there was no sign of Patrick.

"Where's Daddy?" Kelly scowled, rubbing her tired eyes.

The long drive had caught up with her. He'd never seen her so temperamental. He knew his bringing her had been a bad idea.

"Don't worry. He'll be here soon, I'm sure."

When Kelly wasn't checking out the other six children present, she was staring at that old woman who had triggered the alarm earlier. Actually, she gaped at the old woman's feet as if willing her orthopedic shoes to fall off.

Wes didn't make eye contact with anyone, but his hearing grew keener as he took in the conversations of other people who'd also come to see loved ones who'd lost their way.

"Daddy!" Kelly's outburst tore Wes from his reverie. She hopped off her chair, but Wes caught her by the wrist before she could bolt toward Patrick, who had suddenly appeared.

Wes softened his expression with a welcoming smile, but it still broke his heart to see his brother in a place like this. He and Patrick had always looked so similar that strangers guessed they were brothers. But at six-three, Wes had four inches and pounds of well-honed muscle on his older brother. These days Patrick looked as if he had even lost weight, Wes guessed about fifteen pounds, rendering him more wiry than usual. His rich toffee complexion had a grayish tinge. Deep crescents sank beneath his eyes. He'd grown out his dark wavy hair and gathered it in an elastic band. It stuck out like a blunt Doberman's tail at the nape of his neck.

"Daddy! Daddy!" Kelly jumped up and down.

When the nearby guard signaled to Wes with a nod, he released the eager child.

Patrick opened his arms and Kelly scrambled toward him,

then wrapped her thin arms around his long legs. "Daddy! Where have you been? Why haven't you come to see me?" she scolded, then hugged him hard, as if summoning all the strength her small body could muster. That crankiness spurred by travel fatigue obviously forgotten. With eyes closed, a rapturous expression brightened her baby face.

Patrick bent to pat her shoulders and kiss the top of her head.

Moisture welled up in Patrick's eyes. Tears of regret and joy, Wes suspected, as he swallowed the emotion that threatened to steal his own breath. His throat went dry and the backs of his eyeballs stung.

Kelly tipped her head of bouncy corkscrews back to look up at Patrick adoringly. Wes felt a twinge of envy. He'd just witnessed a pure, unconditional look of love, one usually exchanged between parent and child.

The guard discreetly signaled Wes to extract the child so they could sit.

Wes did so as gently and unobtrusively as possible.

"Got some sugar and a hug like that for a favorite uncle?" Wes forced a happy note into his voice as he spoke to Kelly. "I can sure use them right about now."

Obligingly Kelly turned. "Sure, Uncle Wes."

He squatted to her level so she could embrace him.

When Wes stood to his full height again he reached for Patrick and gave him a quick bear hug under a guard's watchful eye.

"How's it goin', Bro?" Wes managed cheerfully, despite the tightening in his chest.

Patrick, Wes, and Kelly then claimed a table and sat.

Kelly wanted to sit on Patrick's lap. That, however, was against Davenport rules on that particular day. There'd been some recent problems with "contact visits," and Davenport was still working out kinks in its policy.

"Buttercup, why don't you sit next to Wes on the other side of the table there so I can get a better view of your pretty face, okay?" Patrick said.

"'Kay, Daddy," she said, obviously befuddled and dismayed by the seating arrangement.

"How's Mom and Dad?" Patrick asked Wes.

"Fine."

"You look good, as usual," Patrick said with a hint of a smile. "Still a lady-killer, I'll bet."

"You killed some ladies, Uncle Wes?" Kelly tugged Wes's shirtsleeve. "Why?"

"Not the way you're thinking, Buttercup," Patrick explained with a light chuckle. "I meant in a way that makes all the ladies *love* Uncle Wes."

Kelly spent the next thirty minutes regaling Patrick with stories about her mother, school, dance/gym classes, Mrs. Roundtree, Corey Johnson, and her favorite TV shows. Then she moved on to her immense toy collection, courtesy of the Abbotts. But her favorite pastime was fiddling with the computer that Patrick had purchased for her.

"Like father, like daughter." Patrick beamed as she shared how proficient she had become with the computer and the *Clifford the Big Red Dog* game software he'd taught her to play before he went away.

She'd exhausted that topic to her satisfaction, then the two brothers engaged in forced chitchat. After Kelly reached for the deck of Old Maid cards that had obviously been placed on a bordering table for the youngest visitors she soon recruited one of the other children to play a game with her.

Once Kelly was distracted, the men could really talk.

"I know you still think I let you all down again." Patrick leaned forward, propping his elbows on the table. "I swear to you, man. I know it looks bad, but I'm innocent." He held Wes's gaze with an intensity Wes had not seen from him before. "You have my word, Wes. This time I had too much going for me. I'd gotten my life together. I had you, Mom, and Dad in my corner again, feeling proud of me. I had my Buttercup, there." Patrick winked at Kelly, who'd plopped down at an adjacent table with a blue-eyed brunette girl who reminded Wes of a ragamuffin from the musical *Annie*. The pair spread a blanket of cards across their tabletop.

"And I'd met a sweet lady at my church that I was dating. Why would I throw that all away?"

"I don't know, Patrick; why would you?" Wes replied, feeling uneasy. He didn't want to go over this again. They'd done this dozens of times already since Patrick's arrest. He had been working at Plexis for eight months and doing great. So great, in fact, they'd even offered him a promotion. But before the promotion could take place, word leaked to a company executive that confidential documents such as accounting records, profit-and-loss analyses of products, customer and prospect lists, and contracts with suppliers from restricted areas had been stolen and black-marketed to the highest bidder among Plexis's competitors.

"It just doesn't make any sense," Patrick said. "Why on earth would I sabotage Plexis like that? One of the few companies that gave me a chance at a fresh start?"

Wes had yet to comprehend that move himself, but then, Patrick had been an enigma to Wes most of their lives.

And Wes had also seen people greedily turncoat for less. There was a lot of money to be made off those documents. The evidence against Patrick was pretty damning, and obviously the court thought so, too. An examination of all the Plexis computers by the company's technical services director revealed that the document copying and an attempt to delete records related to copying were done on Patrick's laptop and office computer. Soon the High-Tech Crime Division of Michigan's Attorney General's Office got involved.

A search warrant was executed on Patrick's personal e-mail account and his apartment computer. A forensic evaluation revealed even more incriminating evidence.

"Not only do I *know* I was set up by somebody, but I didn't get a fair trial, either."

Wes had heard Patrick's conspiracy theories about Plexis before, but this was the first time he'd heard Patrick whine about judicial impropriety. "What about the trial?" he found himself asking.

"When I got here there was word going around that some foul stuff was going down in that particular courtroom."

"As in . . . ?" Wes prodded, telling himself that the investigative reporter in him was intrigued.

Patrick glanced at a nearby guard. Visitors at another table diverted his attention.

"It's about money changing hands for certain verdicts," Patrick whispered.

"As in bribes?" Wes asked, still unconvinced.

"What else? Man, I'm telling you, I knew something jacked up was going on, first at Plexis and then with that whole circus of a trial and that crooked-ass judge."

"But you're the one who requested a bench trial."

"I know. Sucker move. Only because I thought it would be easier to convince one person of my innocence rather than leave it up to a gang of folks who would bring all sorts of bias and personal baggage to the deliberations. In hindsight, I realize how stupid that decision was. And the clown I had as an attorney . . . he was pretty much sleep-walking through the whole thing."

"So you heard all this information about this judge from some inmate in here?"

"Not just one inmate. The upshot is, if you paid, you walked. Not-guilty verdicts don't come free or cheap—even when you're innocent."

When the guard returned to his post near their table, Wes

lowered his voice, using Patrick's earlier reference to his "clown" of an attorney as code. "And did Ronald McDonald mention anything about the setup?"

Patrick promptly got a clue. "Hell if I know, man. All I know is a co-worker highly recommended him. At the time, I was so pressed for legal representation I didn't get to do the thorough research I should have."

"And Mom and Dad refused to kick in more money by hiring a high-priced attorney to help you out." Wes briefly reflected on that *joint* decision and how significant it had been toward repairing their parents' frayed relationship.

"As bad as things looked, I was still convinced that my innocence was enough. Shoot, I was ready to defend my damn self at one point."

"I can't begin to tell you what a disaster that would've been."

"How much worse could've it have been, Wes? Tell me." Patrick leaned closer and whispered his rage to Wes. "Look where I ended up anyway, busting my ass for ninety-four cents a day working on the yard crew, bunking with seventy-nine other hard legs in a pole barn that smells like funky feet and sweaty armpits—"

"Nobody said this place was the Hilton. You know that ol' saying. 'Don't do the crime . . . ,'" Wes said flippantly, though hardening his heart was impossible.

Patrick continued as if Wes hadn't spoken, determined to break him down with a club of guilt. "Taking crap from the goon squad and other vindictive, power-drunk guards, and making sure I stay off the radar of warring cliques so I don't get my ass kicked on the regular."

"On the regular?" Wes's worst fears about his brother and this place surfaced full force. "You've had an altercation with somebody already?"

"Altercation?" Patrick repeated with a harsh chuckle. "Hell, man, we're not talking about two politicians debating

over Social Security reform and tax legislation. I'm talking a
serious beat down. Like the one I got four days ago over
something stupid, like unwittingly sitting on the free weight
bench that a six-four two-hundred-and-fifty-pound Davenport occupant nicknamed Bones had deemed off-limits to all
on the yard but members of his own gang. Pity I didn't know
anything about that rule until my chest was wrapped around
his freakin' wrecking ball of a fist."

"You all right?" Wes searched Patrick's face for injuries
to corroborate the story but didn't find any.

"Most of my bruises are concealed by the uniform,"
Patrick explained, as if he'd read Wes's mind.

Wes was ashamed of the doubt that flickered through his
mind, on and off like the light on a firefly, the push and pull
inside of him never ending when it came to Patrick. "So
what happened to this Bones character?"

"I wish I could say I got my licks in, but I didn't. His attack
came so quickly; then he got hauled off by guards. But he'll
be back, probably more pissed off than ever and out for more
blood, my blood. But hey," Patrick suddenly injected a false
upbeat note into his voice, "the highlight of my week is the
cheeseburgers served on Tuesday. Did you know that, Wes?
The rest of the week the food tastes like shit, but man oh man,
who'da thought a correctional facility could give Mickey D's
a run for the money, but then, how hard could that be, right?"

Wes felt nauseated. His thoughts scattered. Checking out
Patrick's allegations was the sort of thing the investigative
journalist in Wes usually thrived on. For the first time since
all hell broke loose at Plexis, Wes wondered if his brother
was actually innocent. Was he the victim of a conspiracy at
Plexis *and* corruption in the courts? What about this Bones
character? And most important, what about Kelly, who desperately missed and needed her father?

"The very best cheeseburgers—nice, thick, and juicy,"
Patrick said as if he were doing a television commercial.

Talk of tasty burgers in that setting eked up the jarring effect on Wes. Images of Patrick getting beaten to a pulp, Kelly crying, Old Maid cards, uniformed armed guards, the other prisoners in blue and their visitors conversing over small impromptu lunches—bags of chips, snack cakes, canned sodas purchased from prison vending machines—all blurred in Wes's head, the effect nightmarishly surreal.

Abruptly Patrick's cheery facade broke. "Wes, man, you gotta help get me get the hell outta here. You've just got to. I have to get back to my life, you guys, and my Buttercup."

"Look, Daddy, Uncle Wes!" Kelly flashed a snaggle-toothed smile. "I beat Missy at Old Maid three times!"

"That's my girl." Blinking back the tears that made his eyes glassy and overbright, Patrick smiled, gave a thumbs-up, and blew a kiss to his daughter, who blew a sweet kiss back. He looked at Wes again. "You're a big-time investigative reporter. You're brilliant, li'l bro. I know you've got sources and connections out the freakin' yin-yang. Just a little bit of digging in the right places for the goods on that dirty judge and you'll see. You won't have to take my word for it. Promise me you'll check it out and I'll do what I can in here."

Wes's gut churned. "You've lied to us more than once," he forced out through clenched teeth. "Too many times to count over the years, Patrick. And you're probably lying to me again—"

"But—" Patrick broke in.

"Wait. Let me finish." Wes paused to steady his voice. He looked at his niece and his heart squeezed. She and her little friend had moved on from the games of Old Maid. They'd built a house of cards with the deck. Wes wondered if he was doing the same by allowing Patrick to send him off on what was most likely a wild-goose chase for Patrick's version of the truth. "It's a chance I'm willing to take. But make no mistake. This time I'm doing it for Kelly."

Eleven

If anybody could defuse the bomb planted by evil Franco Cagnetti and save everyone at Dove Cove's annual Diamond & Pearl Gala without breaking a sweat in a beaded couture Christian Dior, Bliss Worthington could.

Michelle inched to the edge of the overstuffed sofa, eyes glued to the big-screen television. Her mouth fell open as her fingers plowed through a bowl of buttered microwave popcorn.

Ten, nine, eight, seven . . .

"The green wire!" Michelle squealed. "The green wire! Remember, with Dash's last breath, right after Franco knifed him in the neck with that shrimp fork. He told you, Bliss. Cut the green wire!"

Six, five . . .

Heart thumping in her chest, Michelle watched Bliss fiddle with a yellow, blue, and red wire before removing a tiny pair of manicure scissors from the matching beaded clutch bag.

Four, three, two . . .

"The green one! The green one!" Michelle shouted.

"But I think the green one makes me look fat," Fatima whined, snatching Michelle out of Dove Cove and Bliss Worthington's latest escapade.

Michelle had spent the last two nights at her cousin Fatima's condo, where watching her tapes of *If Tomorrow Never Comes* in peace had proven to be a challenge.

Fatima stood in the doorway leading to her bedroom, her petite form clad in a cream-colored satiny slip. She held up two short after-five party dresses, the sleek silk green one tasteful and sophisticated. The purplish one, appliquéd with ornate poofs all over it, would make Fatima look like the Fruit Of The Loom grapes.

Michelle tried dividing her attention between Fatima and the TV screen.

"I can't decide which one to wear. Didn't you hear me talking to you?" Fatima poked out her enhanced lips. She'd always been self-conscious about her smile and had finally gifted herself with collagen injections. With her shiny relaxer-commercial hair, creamy mocha complexion, and naturally tight body, Fatima was a beautiful woman by most people's standards. Michelle didn't think her cousin needed the artificially plumped-up lips but reminded herself she was in no position to judge. After all, she'd squashed her own square feet inside narrow isosceles-triangle designer shoes that kept her podiatrist in business.

Michelle cut more glances at the TV screen. "Whew, that was close!" She flumped against the sofa cushions and sighed with contentment now that Bliss had snipped the right wire. All was safe in Dove Cove—for one more day, or videotape, at least. She reached for the remote control and zapped off that day's recorded episode. "Sorry, Fatima. What was that you were saying?"

"You didn't hear a word I said!" Fatima sniffed. "Chelle, what's with you and your obsession with that damn soap opera? You claim to hate fluff and mindless news stories at work, yet you practically wallow in mindless crap during your leisure time."

"Oh no, you don't go there," Michelle said. The kooky

celebrity-phile wasn't criticizing her devotion to a daytime serial.

"It's just sort of—"

"Of what?"

"*Weird,* ya know, for a smart, single professional woman like yourself. I could see if you were some frumpy hausfrau with a rag on your head, the smell of Pine Sol on your skin. And no life beyond . . . beyond . . ." She shook one dress at Michelle in exasperation. "Tuna casseroles, screaming brats, and a neglectful husband with a shitty low-paying job."

Michelle's eyes went wide with shock. "Wait a dang minute here! What if I were some," she made quote marks with her fingers, " 'hausfrau' wearing eau de toilet cleaner? Would that be such a bad thing? Would that mean I had dust bunnies for brains?"

"I didn't mean that like it sounded, of course," Fatima said, backpedaling a bit. "My mom was a housewife, God rest her sweet soul."

"Look, I love the show, but I wouldn't say it's an obsession exactly," Michelle explained. "It's just one of the few guilty pleasures I have left I can indulge in that don't involve extra calories. And as for Bliss, well, she's the *Dove Cove Gazette*'s star investigative reporter. I just admire her smarts, her chutz-pah, her martial arts prowess, and her impeccable fashion sense. You should've seen the Dior gown she was wearing while she deactivated that bomb that was hidden under the pastry table. . . . Girl, it was da bomb!" Michelle chuckled at the absurdity of the story line and her own lousy pun.

Fatima didn't crack a dang smile. "Hel-loooo, Chelle. *Dove Cove* . . . and Bliss Worthington, for that matter, are not real."

"Do I criticize you for spending good money on those tabloid rags you read voraciously?" Michelle asked.

"So, you noticed those, huh?" Fatima's lips curved up in

a quick guilty grin as she clutched the two gowns and shifted her weight from one stocking foot to the other.

"Uuuh-huh." Michelle crossed her arms over her chest.

"So, what of it?" Fatima laced a challenge in her voice and stiffened her spine.

A long minute of silence passed during the stare-down that ensued, similar to the ones they'd had as teens living under the same roof, squabbling over whether to watch *Entertainment Tonight* or a *Dynasty* rerun.

The cousins suddenly burst out in peals of laughter, an official end to their spat.

At ages thirteen and fourteen, Fatima and her brother, Ahmad, after their own parents were killed in a car crash on the Santa Monica Freeway, had to leave their home in California to come live with Michelle and Liz. Though money had been tight when it was just the two of them, Liz Michaels hadn't hesitated to step in to assume guardianship of her younger sister's two teenage kids.

Michelle adored Fatima and Ahmad. They brought more warmth to the Michaelses' tiny home, but there was a part of her, a part that she loathed and resisted acknowledging, that had been unhappy when they first arrived. That part resented sharing the attention she had received from her one parent with two other people. As if Liz only had so much love to go around. Those unwanted thoughts had made fourteen-year-old Michelle feel deeply ashamed and selfish, knowing how devastating it had been for Fatima and Ahmad to adapt to the loss of their mom and dad at the same time. Nevertheless, the changes in Michelle's home dynamic had made her needier. She had yearned for her missing father even more.

Fatima placed the dresses on a nearby chair, then sat on the sofa next to Michelle. "I'm sorry. Will you forgive me for acting like such a witch?" Her eyes welled up and she fanned them dry to reduce mascara smears. "I think I'm letting my nerves about this date get the best of me. I need your help. I want to look perfect tonight."

"And you will." Michelle drew her into a quick hug. She'd never seen her cousin this flustered over anyone before. "Just relax."

Fatima took her advice, inhaling and exhaling deeply. Her makeup had been neatly applied to accentuate her deep brown eyes and her overly plumped-up lips, her jet hair fashioned in a shiny French twist. A nice loose one that didn't tug at the skin at her temples, making it look as if she'd had a bad face-lift.

"You really like this guy, don't you?"

Fatima nodded. "Oh, Chelle, he's sooo great."

Like Michelle, Fatima had experienced her share of clowns, but she believed she'd finally found a keeper in this one and was all atwitter about it.

"His name is Gabriel. And he's much older—"

"Older?" That made Michelle think of the gossip about her alleged affair with Chapelle. Even if he hadn't been married or an interview subject, Michelle doubted she would ever consider him dating material. *Gross!*

"So you're jonesin' for older men now?" Michelle teased.

"Make that Zeta-Jonesin'." Fatima winked.

"Excuse me?"

"Michael Douglas is twenty-something years Catherine's senior. Did you know Michael said it was love at first sight for him? He said he knew he wanted to be the father of Catherine's babies the moment he laid eyes on her in that *Zorro* movie. Isn't that romantic?" She sighed wistfully and fluttered her thick eyelashes.

There Fatima went, but this time Michelle honestly tried to keep up. "*Zorro* movie?"

"You know, *The Mask of Zorro,* released in 1998, starring Antonio Banderas, directed by Martin Campbell."

"Martin?" Michelle asked, always amazed by Fatima's nerdlike celebrity-cinemaphile encyclopedic recall.

"Of *GoldenEye,* hel-loooo? *GoldenEye* as in Bond-film fame." Fatima sucked her teeth with a definite "duh" in her tone.

"Ah yeah, right. *That* Martin Campbell," Michelle replied, nodding her head. They'd never get their conversation back on track if Michelle didn't at least pretend to have a clue.

"Anyway, Gabe is forty-eight. There's a sixteen-year-age difference between us, but he's a very well preserved forty-eight. For Gabe, think Billy Dee in that *Star Wars* sequel."

"And I know exactly which one, too!" Michelle piped up before Fatima went off on a *Star Wars* film credits tangent.

"That's how sexy Gabe is. He's my very own Lando Calrissian. Besides, what's sixteen measly years when we're clicking like castanets on all sorts of levels, honey!"

"As long as you're happy," Michelle replied honestly.

"I am! Hey, I'll bet Gabe's single younger brother is just as great as he is." Fatima's face lit up again. "I just got an idea!"

"I know where you're going with this and the answer is *n-o.* I'm just here to work. I start man-hunting again when I get back on my own turf."

"But it could be so great! We could even double-date! Sweet, dependable, do-right men like Gabe just don't come around all that often."

"That's no guarantee that his brother is a do-right man, too."

"Chauncey's a sweetie, a little on the short side, but a sweetie nonetheless. And besides, you're not as shallow as I am. I know you wouldn't let a few inches come between you and a possible dream guy. Look at Tom and Nicole—"

"Tom Cruise and Nicole Kidman are divorced."

"I just have this feeling Chauncey would be perfect," Fatima rattled on, oblivious to everything but her matchmaking plans.

"Even if he is, there's no use starting something with a great catch that I can't finish. I'm heading back to New York in a matter of weeks, I hope."

"So? It can't hurt to enjoy the company of a man while you're here. Who knows? If it turned into something special, there are planes, trains, automobiles. And between those, totally wicked phone and cybersex!"

"Cybersex? Are you nuts?" Michelle grabbed a fistful of popcorn and stuffed it inside her mouth. "Somehow I doubt Wesley Abbott would be content with merely letting his fingers do the walking over a keyboard, instant-messaging a woman into a passionate sweat."

Bemused, Michelle hadn't realized she'd verbalized her thoughts until Fatima slapped Michelle's thigh and hit her with a sidelong look, "Hey, who in the hell is Wesley Abbott?"

Michelle shot to her feet, almost knocking over the bowl of popcorn, just to avoid Fatima's curious gaze.

"C'mon, give it up. Who is he?" Fatima prodded. "Name sounds kinda familiar, though. Hmmm, is he on TV? Does he star on one of those new UPN sitcoms?"

"No, he's not on TV. And he's nobody you or I should be concerned about, okay?"

"We're talking men and dating, then his name suddenly tumbles out of your mouth. I say that sounds as if you're very concerned about him, Cuz. Now you come right back here and have a seat." She patted the cushion beside her. "Tell Fatima the story on him."

Michelle sat down again. "He's just a colleague at the *Herald*," she replied, realizing Fatima wouldn't ease up until she tossed her a bone or two. "I admire his body of work."

"And what about his body?" Fatima wiggled her neat

brows and rubbed her hands together gleefully. "Is he hot or what?"

"He's a very talented writer and a crack investigative journalist."

"Is that all?" Fatima screwed up her face.

"He's extremely charming, too."

Fatima brightened again, "And?"

"And he's very handsome, but in that polished, air-brushed, not-a-hair-out-of-place sorta way—"

"That would make most women who don't look like Halle Berry feel inadequate, right?"

"Right."

"Like that newscaster fella in New York you told me about?"

"Yes." Michelle waffled. "Wait! No!"

"Well, what is it? Yes or no?"

"Ken's good-looking and successful, too. But he's an ass. Big difference."

"I see."

"But Wesley, well . . ." Michelle's features wanted to soften into a dreamy expression, but she fought it. "Wesley is actually kinda nice . . . I think." A small smile found its way to her face anyway.

"You think?"

"We just met, Fatima."

"So there's a really good chance he's a good guy, then?"

"But I suspect only when you're dealing with him in that platonic, buddy-to-buddy sorta way. I don't think I'd ever feel comfortable actually dating someone that smooth."

"And sexy?"

"He does have this way about him." Michelle's smile dissolved and she suddenly snapped serious again. "The man's an outrageous flirt. Bottom-line, I doubt I'm the only woman who has felt as if she's connecting with him."

"So you're connecting with him?" Fatima said, barely containing her enthusiasm. "I'm lovin' this!"

"We *get* each other on journalistic and workplace issues."

"Workplace issues?"

"Yes, workplace issues."

Fatima scrunched up her nose to drone, "Stop. You're singeing my ears with the flaming passion."

"And we like the same type of jazz. He's into Ron Carter, too."

"I suppose that's a start." Fatima perked up again.

"Not for something of substance. He's not the one for me—plain and simple. End of story. Now what about getting ready for your hot date?"

Not willing to abandon Wes, Fatima pressed on. "So how do you know all this for sure? That he's not the one for you?"

Michelle shrugged. "I can just tell, that's all. And besides, word tends to get around, especially in a newsroom, where the stock-in-trade is poking noses into other people's business. One day when I was in a ladies' room I inadvertently heard some things. He's got quite the reputation as a ladies' man."

Boy, did he ever. And Michelle thought the whispering about her "CEO sugar daddies" at the *Manhattan Business Journal* was as bad as it got. According to the gossip she'd overheard, Wes clung to carefree bachelorhood with a firm, unyielding grip. He'd dated several women who worked for the various companies that leased office space in the twentyfive-story *Herald* building. With his charisma and good looks, Wes had dazzled many in the newsroom. But he had not dated anyone actually on the newsroom staff—yet. The three tongue waggers stopped dishing once they heard the flush of Michelle's toilet. They quickly scattered away from the liquid soap dispenser when she emerged from the restroom stall giving each of them a pointed reprimanding look. But that was not before she heard them say they suspected that a relationship with someone *inside* the newsroom was way too close for Wes's comfort, because the man obviously was only game for something short and sweet.

"You're the last one I'd expect to lap up newsroom gossip without proof. I mean, especially after what you went through at the *Business Journal* with people spreading crap about you and your so-called affairs with various CEOs—"

"And your point is?"

"Isn't it obvious?"

"Look, Fatima. I know you mean well, but between all of my screwups lately, my life resembles something straight out of *If Tomorrow Never Comes*. But I guess I'm good, under the circumstances. I'm already over Ken. Better I found out he was a jerk on the first date rather than later. But I'm just questioning my judgment these days. Work and personal life. I haven't been behaving like the savvy sistah I'm supposed to be, you know. I just need some time to get my bearings again."

"Aw, Chelle, you can't let all this shake your confidence, girly. I had a streak of bummers, too. But I hung in there and met Gabe."

Michelle reclined until her head rested along the back of the plush sofa. She studied the stucco-textured high ceiling and sighed. "But some serious soul-searching is on tap for me while I'm here."

"I hope you don't mean an extended bout of moping and navel gazing. That can't be good, either. Girl, don't worry." She gave Michelle a hug. "I'm gonna make sure you have some fun even if it means recruiting Chauncey for our group date! Trust me, you'll thank me later."

Michelle snapped upright again. "Fatima, no Chauncey! I mean it. I don't need you wrangling a man for me. I'm not that darn pathetic. Promise me you won't do anything."

Unfortunately, before Fatima could promise anything of the sort, the doorbell chimed.

"Omigosh!" Fatima popped up from the sofa. "That's gotta be Gabe and I'm not even dressed. Get that. And tell him I'll be right out."

Michelle went to the door, then waited for Fatima to vacate the living room.

Fatima shot to her bedroom, then U-turned to flit out and scoop up the two dresses she'd left behind on a living room chair. "Oops! Can't get dressed without these." She flitted away again.

Michelle was preparing to greet the visitor when Fatima poked her head out and called out with a stage whisper, "Pssssssst. Michelle, the purple or the green?"

"Green," Michelle advised just before greeting Fatima's handsome, well-dressed, and impeccably mannered suitor, who had arrived with an impressive bouquet of plump red roses.

In less than twenty minutes Michelle waved good-bye and watched the attractive couple climb into a blue BMW, Gabe in an elegant Italian suit and Fatima in Chanel No. 5 and that atrocious purple dress.

Michelle leaned against the doorjamb until Gabe started the engine and the night swallowed the taillights of his luxury vehicle. Before closing the door, she inhaled the crisp night air, thinking of the romantic evening ahead of Fatima. While happy for her, Michelle wondered if she'd ever get to experience a romantic evening of her own with a guy who was into her just as much as she was into him.

When Wesley Abbott's image came to mind again she muttered to herself dolefully, "Only in your dreams, girl, only in your dreams." She allowed herself to indulge for just a few minutes—fantasizing about curling her arms around his rock solid torso and kissing that cheek dimple of his as they slow danced to one of the more mellow Ron Carter tunes. The blood in her veins flowed slowly, like warm, thick nectar. She shook her head, erecting a mental roadblock to the more salacious thoughts that were sure to follow and linger. Like those of Wesley in her bed, wearing nothing but black satin sheets and a hungry-for-you grin. She plunked on the sofa, reached for the remote control and the half-eaten bowl of buttered popcorn on the coffee table. She took a big swig from her bottle of soda. The passion segued to melancholy. *Nothing a dose of recorded melodramatic mayhem couldn't cure,* she told herself with a heavy sigh.

When Michelle jabbed the ON button, the television and VCR clicked on where Franco, reeling from his foiled bomb attempt and wielding a chloroform-doused hankie, lunged at Bliss, who launched a kick and shish-kebabbed his groin with the heel of her designer pump.

Michelle cheered and stuffed more popcorn inside her mouth. "Go on, Bliss! Hit 'em where it matters most!"

When Michelle returned to the Ferndale house the following morning she found that her mother was out—*again.*

Since that talk during the ride home from the bowling alley, Michelle had found it increasingly difficult to pin down Liz for that serious heart-to-heart. Their weekday mornings were hectic, with them both gulping down cups of coffee and barely having enough time to exchange good-byes before rushing off to their jobs. Many early evenings Michelle would return home to find a nice dinner waiting and an apologetic note explaining why Liz wasn't there to share it with her. A Pin Stinger gathering at some unnamed location or overtime at the insurance agency, where Liz worked ate up more of her evenings.

Michelle wanted to give Liz the benefit of the doubt but couldn't help feeling that her mother was simply avoiding her and all of her questions. More determined than ever, Michelle decided to bide her time a little longer. Liz couldn't run or hide forever.

Twelve

If someone had told Wesley he'd spend a Saturday afternoon in the Fox Theater watching a group of grown men whip a bunch of preschoolers into a frenzy with such ditties as "Fruit Salad! Fruit Salad! Yummy! Yummy! Yummy!" he would have bet his Ferrari they were wrong. And he would've been footing it. Big-time. Because there Wesley sat. Coveted fourth row center seats listening to the Wiggles as they burrowed their way into his cerebral cortex with more inane musical stylings: "Shake Your Sillies Out" and "Willaby Wallaby Woo." A small price to pay to help out a friend in need.

Bridget, Craig's wife, was a systems analyst for a major automotive company. She had been called in to work after a hard-drive crash. That emergency meant she couldn't accompany Craig when they escorted their twins and a pair of neighborhood boys to this Wiggles concert as scheduled. Craig would've had to assume sole chauffeur and chaperone duties if he didn't get help. Fast! Not hesitating to call in one of many favors, he'd recruited Wesley to help—even offering to kick in an additional hard-to-come-by ticket for Kelly, who shimmied in her seat beside Wesley's.

"Aren't they great, Uncle Wes?" Kelly asked, flashing him a snaggletoothed grin that almost made him forget how bored he was.

She and the other kids came to their feet twisting their narrow butts and flailing their arms. They sang loudly and way off-key: "Fruit salad! Yummy! Yummy! Yummy!"

Wes felt a mild headache coming on, so he fished for one of those small foil convenience packs of Tylenol he'd had the forethought to tuck inside a pocket. He popped them inside his mouth, threw his head back to swallow them dry.

"You all right, dude?" Craig shouted over the noise and the five singing and swaying little kids who separated them.

The last thing Craig needed was another whiner in the bunch, so Wes forced a smile and shouted back, "I'm cool."

"Thanks for helping me out, man. Don't know if I could have wrangled these desperadoes without you. I don't know how Bridget does it when she takes them all out alone."

"No problem."

"Remember I promised the kids we'd get a bite to eat afterward. You still in, right?"

Kelly squealed, "Can we please, Uncle Wes?"

Earlier Craig had not mentioned that a meal was part of the deal, but Wes couldn't wimp out on his best friend now. "Sure, count us in," he replied wearily.

"Yay!" Kelly jumped up and down along with Craig's twins—Tim and Thaddeus—and his neighbors' kids, Josh and Scottie.

"Well, well, well," Craig said, suddenly looking over Wes's shoulder. "Would you look who's here?" He pointed midway up the aisle.

"Who? Where?" Wes turned to look; then a big smile found its way to his lips.

With pen and notebook in hand, Michelle had marched up and down the aisle looking for that open aisle seat that the PR rep for the Wiggles show had promised her. No luck. Little people packed the place. She had considered plopping down in the carpeted aisle to jot down her notes, but ushers enforcing the fire marshal's codes would not allow her to linger there for long.

She almost had enough material for yet another Wiggles piece. Seems Barbara simply could not have enough on them in the "Accent" section. She'd instructed Michelle to pen a combination review/"color" piece on the show and the kids attending. At that point her notes were all in her head, though. She had to find a suitable place inside the auditorium to jot them down.

Someone called her name. She looked in that direction and saw the last person she'd expect to find at a kiddie concert. Wesley Abbott!

She blinked. Twice.

He waved her over.

Robotically she closed the distance between them as if she still wasn't sure her eyes weren't playing tricks on her.

Michelle felt herself flush with pleasure the closer she got. "I never would've taken you for the Wiggles type," she said to him.

"I'm not. My being here was not strictly voluntary."

"Ditto here," Michelle replied, suddenly aware of the cute little girl of no more than five or six whose curious eyes were on her.

"Yours?" Michelle asked Wes, trying to keep the surprise out of her voice. It hadn't dawned on her that he might be a father.

Wes looked down at the child adoringly. "Nah, she's my brother's kid. This is Kelly."

"Well, hello there, Kelly." Michelle smiled.

Kelly just grinned and tried to hide behind one of Wes's long legs.

"Oh no, you don't," Wes teased. "Don't even pretend to be shy. She'll talk your ears off given half the chance," he revealed to Michelle, then looked back down at the girl. "Tell Ms. Michaels hello."

The child moved her lips to form the word, but the noise rendered her thin voice inaudible.

"What a cutie you are!" Michelle reached out to touch one of Kelly's springy corkscrew curls. It was then she also noted Wes cut an equally striking figure when dressed down. So far she'd only seen him in natty suits with pocket hankies, silk ties, and Italian calfskin leather shoes polished to a high gloss. Actually, she found this look more flattering to his sleek but muscular form. The short-sleeve black polo shirt—unbuttoned at the neck—hugged and flattered the hard biceps and pecs she'd only guessed were underneath those crisp dress shirts. His fashionably distressed jeans weren't skintight but a looser, casual fit that skimmed just enough to put an emphasis on the strong lines of his thighs and the really big curve near his . . . Michelle blushed and inwardly chided herself for having such racy thoughts while surrounded by children. She snatched her leer and her downward spiraling thoughts away from the man's doggone fly.

"These other two here," Wes pointed to the boys in the seats next to Kelly's, "are from Craig's neighborhood." He continued down the row. "The other two rug rats belong to Craig. And of course, you know Craig."

Michelle waved at Craig. It was the first time she'd seen him look light and free. In the newsroom he'd always had a serious, understated quality about him—the opposite of Wes, yet they were obviously extremely close.

After the intros, all but Wes resumed watching the show.

"I was just searching for a seat. All seem to be taken," Michelle said. "Well, technically not taken. Most of the kids are on their feet, but I think somebody's parent already claimed the one that was supposed to be mine."

Wes glanced around. "Sure looks that way. And you need to get somewhere so you can write a story. Am I right?"

"Yes. I'm just going to go back out in the lobby and find a spot on the stairs."

"You'll do no such thing."

"Excuse me."

"You'll miss the rest of the show. We can't have that. Take my seat."

"I can't do that."

"Yes, you can. No problem. As you can see, the kids will probably stand for the rest of the show. If Kelly gets tired, which I seriously doubt, and wants to sit, she can have the spot on my lap." Wes moved over to his niece's chair and patted the empty chair next to it. "Sit," he ordered Michelle.

"If you're sure," Michelle gratefully accepted his offer. She settled on the chair, neatly positioning her laptop computer case and purse near her feet. "I have my quotes already, got an official head count and descriptive detail to set the mood. This shouldn't take long at all."

"I gather you're writing on deadline to make tomorrow's paper?"

"Yeah, but it's just a small piece, more like a filler."

"What do you consider decent filler, Chelle?" His dark eyes gleamed and turned darker. A sly smile curled his lips.

"Huh?" Her throat went dry.

"Eight, nine, ten inches max?" Wes wore an arch look that made Michelle wonder if he was actually referring to story length or . . . *Nah, get your head out of the gutter, woman!* Why was she twisting the most innocent things into sexual innuendo? She flushed. Her brain turned to mush lately whenever Wes was around, that was why.

She cleared her throat. "Nine, ten inches is good."

"I'll close my trap then so you can get busy." Wes gestured toward her laptop before the show captured his attention again.

Michelle spent the next half hour composing her story. After quick proofreading, she excused herself to search for the nearest land phone line in the building to zap her story to the copy desk. She used her cell phone to call the copy desk chief to verify that the piece had made the cyberjourney intact. Fortunately, there would be no need for her to head back to the newsroom, and if there were questions about her copy, someone at the *Herald* would ring her cell. Technically she was all done with the Wiggles for the day—and forever. She could only hope. She could've left then, if she wanted. But it had not felt right leaving without saying goodbye to Wes, not after he'd been gallant about the seating thing and all.

When kids and adult chaperones spilled into the lobby she knew the show had ended. So many people, but it wasn't hard to find two tall, extremely handsome black men in this crowd. And sure enough, just a minute later she spotted Craig and Wes. She approached them, threading her way through a sea of kinetic humanity—all under five feet.

"Did you get your story to the newsroom?" Wes asked.

"Yes, all set. Thank you."

Kelly wandered away from Craig, who was lifting one of his little ones for a drink from a water fountain. She tugged at Wes's jeans. "C'mon, Uncle Wes. We're hungry."

"You're done with work, right? Join us," Wes said to Michelle.

"Um, I don't know if—"

"You've got other plans?" With tenderness, Wes's hands came to rest on Kelly's slim shoulders. Something about Wes with Kelly broke through the last of Michelle's resistance. What was it about big men with small children or dogs?

In Michelle's mind he wasn't the too-slick newsroom Lothario at the moment. He was a kind, doting uncle, who took his niece to concerts where the performers sang the praises of "fruit salad, hot potatoes, and crunchy, munchy honeycakes."

"No plans." Michelle adjusted the strap of her laptop case hanging from her shoulder.

"It wouldn't be like a date or anything. I mean, not with Craig and our gang of diminutive desperadoes."

"We're gonna have lots of fun!" Kelly piped up, catching Michelle off-guard.

"Now, I know you can't possibly turn that down. Whaddaya say?" Wes persisted.

"I say . . ." Michelle paused long and hard, knowing her answer but still hesitant.

"You have your car, right? So if we get to be too much for you, you can leave at your convenience."

"Pleeeeese?" Kelly pleaded.

Michelle wasn't sure why the child was so eager for her to tag along. Maybe she just liked the idea of at least one other female joining the gang of guys.

"Yes, pretty, pretty please with cream, sugar, and a big fat cherry on top?" Wes whined, trying to fake a bratty boy voice as he crossed his eyes. "I promise we'll behave."

When Wes poked out his tongue and made another silly face, Michelle laughed and her reticence evaporated. "Okay, now stop with the faces, will you? I'll go, but just for a little while. Where are we headed?"

A beaming Wes beckoned her with a sweep of one large hand. "Just hop in your car and follow my lead."

Thirteen

Only after driving at two hundred miles per hour up Pikes Peak in a turbocharged pickup truck and whizzing down the Alps on a snowboard did the post-Wiggles-concert crew finally settle down for its first taste of pizza.

Nothing like video game action to rouse the appetite, Michelle thought as she took her seat at their dining table. Chuck E. Cheese was not so much a restaurant as it was a giant playpen for kids.

Stepping inside had been a tremendous assault on Michelle's senses. Boisterous! Bright! Busy! Like getting sucked into a live-action version of a Looney Tunes cartoon. High-pitched squeals of delight punctuated with bells, chimes, and whistles from the arcade and mini–amusement park rides. Small bodies in perpetual motion crammed the place like ants in a maze.

It hadn't taken Michelle long, however, to doff the reservations she'd had about the wisdom of accepting Wes's invitation. She'd even gotten into the spirit of things. After she teamed up with Kelly, the pair had kicked Wes's butt at hockey, Skee-Ball, and Whack-a-Mole.

Ravenous, Michelle watched as Wes and Craig separated slices of one of three large pizzas they'd ordered for the group.

"I want cheese, please, Uncle Wes." Kelly rose up, planting her knees on her seat.

"Not until you sit down on your bottom first, young lady," Wes said with a gentle but reprimanding tone.

"Yes, sir." With her bottom lip poked out, Kelly slid down on her behind. The smile soon returned to her face when Wes placed a generous wedge of melted cheese pizza on her plate. "Thank you!" she said, then took a greedy bite from the pointed end.

Michelle had planned to order from the salad bar near the checkout counter, but the scent of oregano and fresh-baked crust had her salivating. She watched Craig and Wes serve the children. Tomatoes, lettuce, shredded carrots with a dollop of low-cal vinaigrette just wouldn't cut it when a hot pizza sat mere inches beneath her nose like a glistening pepperoni-laden welcome mat.

"Go ahead and dig in," Wes encouraged her.

"I'll have just a teeny sliver of the pepperoni," Michelle said, believing just a taste would take the edge off, then she could move on to more healthy, low-calorie fare.

"You should try the barbecue pizza." Craig tucked the edge of a paper napkin inside the front collar of his young son's shirt. "Now that's good eatin'."

Michelle usually preferred her barbecue cooked on a pit and not served in a pie. But what the hell? She'd sample anything once. "Maybe just a teeny sliver of the barbecue pizza."

An hour, six slices of pizza, three Italian breadsticks, two medium colas, and one jumbo chocolate chip cookie later, Michelle mentally tallied the caloric damage. Rather than berate herself for overindulging, she discreetly slipped her hand inside her blazer and under the edge of her knit top. She sighed contentedly once she released the top button of her slacks, which had suddenly grown too snug.

"Good, huh?" Wes took a big drink of his cola and crunched on the ice.

"Yes. I'm actually surprised." She reached inside her purse for a mint to pop inside her mouth, then offered one to Wes. "You know, in a place like this you don't expect the food to be good."

"Can we do the Sky Crawl now, Daddy?" Thaddeus had just finished his meal.

"Who else is ready to work off some of that pizza?" Craig boomed, and came to his feet.

In response the kids' hands shot up; then they broke into cheers and scrambled from their chairs.

"Need some help wrangling?" Wes asked, placing his cola back on the table and wadding a napkin.

"Nah. I've got this." Craig glanced at Michelle, and then Wes with a knowing grin.

"I have to use the little girls' room," Michelle announced.

"I'll go with you," Wes said.

When Michelle glared at him, he clarified, "Relax. The little boys' room is right next to it."

With the kids trailing behind him, Craig moved to the entrance of the Sky Crawl, a giant polyurethane tubelike play structure in which kids piled. It snaked around and was suspended over the restaurant's dining area. "You two take your time," Craig called out as Wes and Michelle made their way across the bright blue Berber toward the small alcove that led to the restrooms. That area was unexpectedly private.

"He's not very subtle." Michelle stood near the girls' restroom entrance. "What did you do? Pass him a note when you passed the salt and pepper shakers?"

"I did no such thing." Wesley wore a lazy smile. "But he probably feels as if he owes me. I mean, I don't make a practice of frequenting dining establishments with cups of crayons for centerpieces."

"But you must admit that a greeting by a big rodent sure beats the hell out of a stuffy ol' tuxedoed maître d' now, doesn't it? I think the two of you really bonded," Michelle teased, referring to the six-foot guy dressed as the restaurant's mascot and namesake, a rat named Chuck E. Cheese. The costumed character's job was to hang around the tables and pose for photos with excitable children.

Wes waved a warning finger at her. "If you tell anyone about that I'll—"

"You'll what?" Michelle laughed. "Remember, I've got the evidence to prove it." She reached inside her pocket and retrieved the Polaroid of Wes with Rat Man.

"Give me that!" Wes reached for it.

Michelle swatted his hands away. "Uh-uh." She taunted him, waving the snapshot under his nose until he caught her wrist.

The warmth of his hand on her skin caused a pleasant shiver to feather up her spine. They were no longer aware of the noise surrounding them as his brandy-brown gaze held hers. He placed his arms on each side of her shoulders, caging her in, then leaned toward her. Close enough for his chin to graze her forehead. He inhaled the scent of her hair. "You always smell nice. Like ambrosia."

"You smell nice, too." She enjoyed Wes's clean skin scent mingled with his now-familiar cologne. She dropped her chin. Muscles tensed as waves of yearning rolled through her body. Could she handle what would come next? Then initial awkwardness gave way to pleasure as he gently lifted her chin up, slid the back of his hand along her cheek, then dipped his head until the tips of their noses touched. She drew a shaky breath at the sparks of pleasure such minute contact created. The Eskimos were definitely onto something! Who knew the teasing tip of his nose and warm breath lightly skimming like sensual satin against her cheek, the shell of her ear, and that oh-so-sensitive spot behind her earlobe could cause her body to tremble with such a mighty yearning? She could not think too much. She would not think at all. She'd just enjoy. Her lashes fluttered closed as she opened to Wes, allowing him to brush her lips with a petal-soft kiss that was . . .

Simply perfect.

Wes didn't give a damn anymore. He wasn't feeling much like Michelle's buddy or *Herald* colleague. He liked this woman and he wasn't going to let Craig's suspicions about his intentions keep him from doing what had felt so natural and so right at that moment.

Tasting Michelle's lips, so lush and delicious, was worth any ribbing he'd have to endure from Craig. He suckled on her plump bottom lip, slowly, gently. It was with great restraint that he didn't go harder, deeper, for her tongue. As he remembered where they were and how hesitant she'd been to spend time with him, the last thing he wanted to do was overwhelm her. Or get them both thrown out of the joint.

He noted her sharp intake of breath and the flush across her cheeks when the kiss ended.

"Oh my." Her stunned whisper barely audible over the restaurant's merriment.

Wes bit his bottom lip, still relishing the cool, minty taste of her. He dropped his hands from the wall so he could entwine his fingers with hers. "Look, I'm going to be real with you. I like you. I mean *really* like you," he whispered with a sincere urgency in his voice that caught him by surprise. He couldn't remember ever feeling this way before, as if his next breaths depended on how she responded to this revelation. "I like talking to you, looking at you, being in the same room with you," he said. "But I'd like to get to know you better as a woman, not just as a colleague who I am restricted to coffee and doughnuts with in the Headliner. I want you to enjoy your stay in town. I want to show you a good time, take you to jazz concerts, movies, walks by the river, and share wonderful meals with you—"

"Like barbecue pizza?" Michelle joked, obviously trying to deflect the crackling intensity between them.

"Chuck E. Cheese it is, if that's your wish," Wes replied without hesitation. He could tell she was nervous. Her fingers trembled. He gently stroked them, hoping for a calming effect.

"I know you said you didn't want to date a colleague. I don't know about you, but I feel this powerful connection between us. Do you really want to spend the next three months fighting it? Denying it?"

"You're awfully sure of yourself, aren't you?" She slanted him a wary look.

"I'm not going to lie; usually I am, very sure, but with you," he hesitated, then sighed, "with you, not so sure."

"And I imagine that uncertainty must be exciting for a man like you."

There it was. That *man like you* thing again, but Wes wouldn't make an issue of it. After all, he'd made his bed— rather, he'd unmade his bed—too many times and with too many women over the years. Now he had to lie in it. "As I said before, I'm not going to play games with you. We're both adults. I'd love it if you'd give me an opportunity to spend more time with you while you're here. We could take things one day at a time, get to know each other better." He shrugged. "You know, see where things lead."

"And if that's *not* toward the bedroom?" She studied his reaction.

"I'm not going to pretend that I don't want you that way." Wes lifted her hand and let his lips skim over it. "But we go there only if *you* want to take it there. Deal? You have my word. No pushing. No pressure."

"No pressure, huh?" She lifted a skeptical brow. "And what do you call cornering me outside the little girls' room?"

"No pressure for sex. With the stipulation that I get to kiss and hold you." He grinned his rakish grin. "Deal?"

"Kissing and holding? And I'm supposed to be made of stone, am I? That's playing with fire." She chuckled, but he could tell she was giving his request some consideration. "I don't know, Wes—"

"If you're worried about people at work talking, it can be *our* secret. Nobody has to know."

"Somebody already knows." Michelle peered around Wes's broad shoulders and the corner at Craig, who was watching over the kids as they scooted through the Sky Crawl overhead toward a spiraling slide.

"Craig's cool and discreet. We've been friends since grade school. He's not a gossip." Wes prayed he'd eased the last of her fears. He didn't know what she'd heard about him exactly, but he could certainly guess. Newsroom gossip never fazed him in the past, but it did now. She was so guarded with him. That bothered him. A lot.

She looked down at her feet and stammered, "Y-you don't understand. I've . . . You see . . ."

"Is there someone back in New York?"

She shook her head. "It's not that."

"What, then?"

"In the past I've . . . ," she started, then thought better of revealing whatever it was that teetered on the tip of her tongue. When she inhaled and exhaled as if summoning a warrior's courage, once again Wes rued his freewheeling ways.

He gently lifted her chin until their gazes met again. He needed her to see the sincerity in his eyes. "I swear I won't try to play you, lie to you, or disrespect you. You have my word. Give it a chance. Just say yes."

Michelle's hands no longer trembled, steadied by his reassuring touch. Resistance fled from her body. Wes drew her closer, cupping her face in his hands. His thumbs stroked her cheeks.

She was about to make a big mistake. *Again.* But she'd

convinced herself that she was a big girl. She could handle it. Always trying to play it safe was no real life at all. And if she didn't at least try to get out and have fun, Fatima would have her shackled to Chauncey, aka the Unknown Entity. At least Michelle knew she liked and was attracted to Wesley Abbott. No use fighting it. She would enjoy his company, all the while proceeding with some caution, of course. The object: a good time, but a good time didn't have to include sex, did it? Sex could cause all sorts of complications. Somehow with her, deeper emotions always crept into the mix. As long as she knew where to draw the line from jump, there shouldn't be a problem, right? Once back in New York, she'd tuck away their time together as a harmless, pleasant distraction when she'd needed it most.

After all, she didn't believe in love at first, second, or tenth sight for that matter. Lust, what they obviously felt for each other, was instantaneous, but true love took time to take root, be nurtured, and grow. Why, before she knew it, she'd be packing it in to head back to her old job and life in the Big Apple, long before she could get into any *real* trouble with Wesley Abbott.

"Dinner tomorrow night," she said tentatively.

"Finally." Wes heaved a sigh, looking upward as if communicating with a higher power; then he looked back down into Michelle's eyes with obvious affection. "Sounds like we have a plan." He kissed her forehead. "Thank you for giving me, us, a chance."

Then, for the first time, she gave in to the soul-deep yearning to slip her arms around his beautiful solid body. Now close enough to enjoy the rhythmic beating of their hearts, she pressed her cheek against his sculpted chest and just squeezed with all she had for all those times she'd just wanted to touch him but didn't dare.

And it felt incredible.

• • •

That night when Michelle returned to her mother's place, she noted the Civic was not in the driveway or the garage. She stepped inside the living room and tossed her car keys and purse on the coffee table. This was getting ridiculous, she thought as hurt and anger stabbed her. Where the hell was Liz? This time Michelle searched for a note but didn't find one pinned to the bowl of golden fried chicken and the casserole dish of au gratin potatoes her mother had left on the stovetop.

Michelle checked her cell phone for messages, hoping Liz might have left her one, but only found a second good night from Wesley. She eagerly listened to it, smiling as the sultry vibrations of a deep baritone caressed her ear:

"Hello, lady, just wanted to call before I turned in to let you know I've been thinking about you. I'm looking forward to our date tomorrow night. And oh . . . I'm ecstatic that you said yes."

Michelle kicked off her shoes, then made her way to the living room sofa, determined to wait up for Liz. Hours passed. Still no sign of Liz, but fatigue had a grip on Michelle. The last thing she remembered before dozing off was a goofy infomercial about an exercise machine that resembled some medieval torture device.

Fourteen

After Wes left Chuck E. Cheese to take Kelly back home, he got the return phone call he'd been anxiously awaiting the last few days, from Antoinette "Toni" Frank, who worked as a courthouse clerk.

Conrad Sheldon, the *Herald*'s court reporter, had introduced the pair at his annual Fourth of July pool party a few years ago. Toni started off as Conrad's friend but soon became a close friend of Wesley, too.

Wes had the cell phone pressed against one ear as he navigated his car down Interstate 696. "Hey, Toni. I was starting to think you were putting me down," he said in a mock hurt tone. "Ignoring my phone messages and all."

"Been away on vacation with the hubby for a few days. The Bahamas, but I'm back now. What can I do you for?"

Wes glanced at his watch. "I know this is short notice, but can you meet me at Mitch's Tavern on Telegraph in about thirty minutes?"

"Dwayne just phoned to say he's running a few hours late. There's been a backup at the auto shop. Shouldn't be a problem."

"Cool."

"This isn't just about throwing down a few brewskies and catching up, is it?" Toni wanted to know.

"I'm checking out something. Need your help, but of course I'm willing to buy all the rounds, and I'll even throw in a platter of those hot as hell buffalo wings I know you like so much."

"An offer I can't refuse," Toni said. "See ya in a few."

Wes had slid inside a corner leather booth inside Mitch's Tavern and Sports Bar when he spotted flame-haired Toni as soon as she stepped through the front door. She waved in his direction, her compact but curvy build draped in her usual weekend attire—a large Pistons T-shirt and baggy frayed jeans. She moved with feminine ease as she maneuvered through the tables to get to Wes. Toni was a guy's girl, who despite her preference for comfy unisex clothing never forgot she was a woman. She preferred her nails superlong and highly ornamented with sparkly things. Toni loved to bake and was always sending friends and family the most decadent desserts. Wes and Conrad could always look forward to their favorite, a gut-busting multilayered cake, arriving at their *Herald* desk on or around their birthdays. Toni's signature tropical floral perfume was what Wes imagined the Garden of Eden must've smelled like. Toni could also spout off NBA player statistics with the best of them and outswear any basso profundo in the Palace of Auburn Hills, where the Pistons played their home games.

Wes slid out of his booth to greet her. She walked into his arms, planting a friendly kiss on his cheek.

"What you know good, dude?" Toni said, gray eyes sparkling. Her white skin had been baked to a deep pink that clashed angrily with her copper hair.

"You're the one living the good life." Wes took his seat in the booth again. "Running down to the Bahamas every chance you get. Some folks just have it like that, huh?"

Toni slid in on the opposite side. "What can I say? My honey-bunny gets all these frequent-flyer miles. Who am I to refuse or complain when he plans all these romantic getaways for us? But damn, it would be nice to go someplace where I don't have to worry about my fair, overly sensitive complexion."

"It's not that bad," Wes said, looking in her bright eyes instead of focusing on her nasty sunburn.

"Yeah, right?" Toni deadpanned. "I look like a boiled ham."

"You know you're still beautiful, though." Wes grinned. "The sun didn't fry all those curves in the right places."

"Awww, aren't you a sweetie." Her eyes went soft with gratitude. "Thanks for trying to make me feel better, but I've got eyes. It can be challenging enjoying a romp on the beach when you're Casper the Friendly Ghost. And that sunscreen I'm supposed to wear is in such high double digits that when I squeeze the bottle a full wool catsuit pops out!"

Wes choked back a chuckle as their waitress, a sun-streaked burnished blonde, appeared to take their orders.

Wes ordered a Heineken and Toni did the same but also requested a large platter of buffalo wings and onion rings on the side. "You're treating, right?" Toni smiled at Wes, who nodded. Toni looked at the waitress. "Add a jumbo order of potato skins to that with extra bacon bits and cheddar. I deserve it. I'm spoiling myself, at least until I've stopped peeling and flaking like a junkyard heap."

When the waitress turned to leave, Toni got right to business. "So what's up, player?"

"Was wondering what you can tell me about J. Ashton Pratt."

The waitress returned with their beers, so Toni waited until she departed to continue.

"He's an asshole." Toni twisted her shimmering pink-hued lips in distaste. "If you're not in his clique of 'acceptables'—other judges or attorneys—he acts as if you don't exist. It's as if the man never heard of common courtesy. He obviously decides a person's value based on their fancy degrees, zip codes, and bank accounts."

"So he's a snob? Anything else? Heard anything at all about the way he does business in the courtroom?"

Toni squared her slumped shoulders. "You got something on Pratt?" she asked, eyes shining with interest and satisfaction.

"Let's just say I've heard some things. Not even sure of the source," Wes said, his thoughts darting to Patrick. "Don't really have anything concrete, though. Just gossip."

"But your gut must be telling you there's something to it."

Wes shrugged, fiddling with the square metal napkin holder on the table. "Maybe, but you know me. I'll check out *anything,* 'cause you never know."

Toni looked at Wes and teased, "Man, to be you. The hotshot investigative reporter in pursuit of truth, justice, and the American way."

"More Clark Kent in a three-piece suit at the *Daily Planet* than Superman zipping through the air faster than a speeding bullet, right?"

"Bumbling Clark Kent? You?" Toni shook her head. "Never. Look up *smooth* in the dictionary and there's your photo there, player, along with photos of my personal fantasy crushes, Julio Iglesias and Pierce Brosnan, of course."

Wes made a face. "Thank you, I think."

"But listen up: none of you have anything on my Dwayne, of course," Toni added, as usual. She'd flirt and carry on with Wes and Conrad on occasion but never crossed that line where it could be interpreted as disrespect toward her marriage and beloved husband of ten years.

Their waitress returned with their orders.

"So you need *moi* to do some sniffing around to see what I can find out about Pratt's courtroom?"

"Just need you to ask a few questions, discreetly, to see what might turn up."

"You know, Conrad probably knows more about Pratt's

courtroom than I do." She sipped her beer but kept her gaze on Wes.

He knew Toni would bring up his colleague and potential competitor. "If Conrad suspected anything might be up with Pratt, he'd be all over this."

"For all we know he might be all over it already and just keeping it to himself," Toni speculated.

"That's a possibility, but I seriously doubt it," Wes replied with confidence. Conrad was a nice, pleasant guy and a great wordsmith, but he was a middling investigative reporter at best. He'd gotten the job done on the court beat, but he wasn't known for going that extra mile or wowing any of his editors with his ability to sniff out anything but the border-line obvious.

Wes was sure Conrad had only held on to the court beat because he was so well liked by the *Herald* powers-that-be and hadn't been scooped in any embarrassing way by court reporters at competing newspapers such as the *Detroit Free Press* and *Detroit News*. Yet. But Wes couldn't say what would happen if this thing with Pratt indeed turned into something and Wes was the one who broke it as a page A-1 exposé. As a result, Conrad could be forced to join Michelle in the "Accent" section, covering kiddie concerts and hair shows. The usual guilt nipped at Wes until he reminded himself that he was just doing his job as the *Herald*'s investigative journalist with no beat boundaries.

"If Conrad doesn't have a clue about Pratt, I'm certainly not going to be the one to give him one," Wes stated simply.

"Always the competitor, eh?" Toni lifted a brow.

Wes started, not liking the way Toni was looking at him. "This isn't just about hogging more journalistic glory—"

With her lips pursed, Toni looked dubious.

"I have to make sure this is done right—a lot is at stake." Wes trusted Toni and she'd never given him a reason to doubt their alliance. She'd become much closer to Wes than she ever was to Conrad over the last few years. Wes filled her in on Patrick's predicament and his motivation for pursuing the Pratt story. He kept the focus on Kelly.

"If it turns out there's something to the Pratt thing, I can't afford to have Conrad getting all ham-handed in his approach and possibly tipping off the wrong people," Wes explained.

"And you obviously trust me not to get ham-handed?"

"Absolutely," he stated so quickly and definitively he could tell she was flattered. If she wasn't so sunburned she'd probably be blushing. "I wouldn't have come to you if I didn't think you could handle it," Wes went on, smiling that charmer's smile. "You've got skills, woman. I think you missed your calling and could definitely give me some competition if you were in the same racket."

"I think I'll keep the day job for now," she said. "But I do enjoy playing spy games with you. I'll see what or who I come up with for you."

"Thanks, Toni. I owe you," Wes said, then finished his beer as the conversation circled back to Toni and Dwayne's trip to the Bahamas and the couple's parasailing adventure.

Later that evening when Wes returned to his loft he found himself leaving yet another good night message for Michelle. It was then he realized he'd lost his cool. He couldn't remember ever feeling like a schoolboy with a huge crush, even when he was a schoolboy.

But that was how he felt whenever he thought of Michelle. Damn, it was blowing his mind. And this sort of preoccupation with a woman had never happened to Wes. Though foreign, it felt good, he had to admit. He vowed not to try to fight or run from it. Overanalyzing the whys and hows might sully what was budding between them, he decided, climbing into bed with some papers. He still had work to do before he called it a night. Longer than usual days loomed now that he was clocking double duty. Not only was he working on a story for the *Herald* about the city's lax history of building code enforcement, but he would also spend a great deal of time checking into Patrick's case. He'd left Mitch's Tavern and Toni and made more calls during the drive home. Unfortunately, all the information he'd dug up on the Plexis case so far fell in line with what the prosecution had used against Patrick. Poring over a stack of records, nothing deviating from the state's findings, Wes did glean interesting tidbits that reeked of more unflattering gossip about the judge who'd heard the case. It was something. Now that he had Toni, someone inside the courthouse, helping him, Wes could only hope that where there was smoke . . .

Sunday morning, Michelle awoke with kinks stiffening her back and neck after falling asleep in an awkward position on the living room sofa the night before. She brushed her teeth, showered, then made her way to the country-style kitchen that felt bright and cheery even when gray skies loomed outside its windows. Its tones of lemon yellow and pale gold always evoked optimism, making it one of her favorite rooms in the house, second only to her own bedroom. A glass-front curio cabinet filled with thick pottery and stoneware sat opposite a white wood table. Quaint mismatched white chairs with perky tie-on cushions in a lemon yellow checkered pattern huddled around it.

Michelle secured the belt of a borrowed mauve terry bathrobe, then plucked a banana from a wire basket hanging near the fridge. Taking a bite, she peeked out the window overlooking the patio, an old birch, and a small but neat back lawn. She moved toward the coffeemaker and listened for sounds that her mother had also awakened, but there was only quiet save for her own puttering. The old clock/AM radio on the white tiled counter read 8:12 a.m.

Michelle was sure her mother would sleep in. Liz's car door closing and keys jingling at 4:00 a.m. had briefly awakened Michelle. What had the woman been doing out that time of morning?

Michelle had planned to ask her mother about it first thing. But three hours passed without so much as a peep from her room. Michelle and Fatima had made plans to go shopping as soon as the Somerset Collection opened at noon. Fatima needed to shop for a birthday gift for Gabe and had frantically begged Michelle for help. Fatima had no idea what to get the man who seemed to have everything. Michelle really wanted to cancel. She needed some alone time with Liz and now that she knew exactly where she was, Michelle didn't want to let her out of her sight again. Fatima had begged for a half hour, also pointing out that Michelle needed to comb the upmarket malls for a special outfit for her big evening out with Wesley. Michelle eventually caved.

Soon Fatima arrived, shod in peach mules and swathed in tight peach-colored Capri pants and a boat-neck top.

"I think you're being paranoid about Aunt Liz avoiding you," Fatima argued as her kitten heels clickety-clacked across the hardwood floor in the living room. "It's your imagination. All the bad timing is just a coincidence."

"There's got to be more to it." Michelle grabbed her shoulder bag, then stepped out the front door into a sparkling day that required slipping giant cognac-colored sunglasses over her eyes.

"Well, just the other day she was telling me how happy she was to have you home."

"She actually said that?" Michelle climbed inside Fatima's Crossfire. As the car rolled out of the driveway in reverse, she thought she saw the curtains on the front picture window flutter, as if someone was surreptitiously peeking out.

At the mall, Fatima marched inside the bookstore with a target in mind: the health/herbal medicine shelves. After scanning three rows of shelves, she'd apparently found what she was looking for: She tugged a book titled *Internal Cleansing: Rid Your Body of Toxins to Naturally and Effectively Fight Heart Disease, Chronic Pain, Fatigue, PMS and Menopause Symptoms, and More* off the shelf, then another: *Dr. Jensen's Guide to Better Bowel Care: A Complete Program for Tissue Cleansing through Bowel Management.*

"Fatima!" Michelle shrieked, crinkling her nose. "What in the world . . . ?"

"What?" Fatima took her books and sank into a cushy sofa to browse through the pages.

"Why are you suddenly so interested in such a gross subject?"

Fatima pursed her lips and studied the pages with great interest. "Didn't I tell you? The salon is adding high colonics, a type of internal hydrotherapy, to our services. They're all the rage with Hollywood A-listers, don't you know? Just thought I'd do my research first. We can get one together on your next day off."

"You're on your own with that one." Michelle shuddered at the thought. A leisure time enema ranked somewhere below a recreational root canal.

"Where's your sense of adventure?" Fatima teased, flipping the pages.

Michelle shrugged. *Different strokes,* she decided, settling on the couch next to her cousin with the latest glossy issue of *Soap Opera Times,* which she'd pulled off the magazine rack. She went straight to the scoop on her favorite show, of course. A blurb in one column teased that the show's producers were toying with the idea of bringing back the Elektra Vanderbrink character, Bliss's wicked nemesis, who had been presumed dead two years ago after her hot air balloon went down someplace over the Sierra Nevada Mountains. Translation: That actress who brought the character to life had demanded a hefty pay raise and had been canned as result. On the show the balloon and its passengers were never found, but everybody with half a brain knew in Soapland with or without a dead body characters could not only return as angelic or evil twins but also as their own perfect genetic clones these days. Michelle hoped the blurb was true. Bliss and Elektra's infamous martial arts clashes made *Dynasty*'s Krystle and Alexis's catfights look like playground games.

"So where is Wesley taking you tonight?"

"I don't know. It's a surprise. He strikes me as having excellent taste. I'll bet the restaurant will be spectacular." Michelle closed the magazine and fished her cell phone from her bag.

"Calling Wesley?"

"No, I'm checking to see if Ma is still home."

The phone rang several times; then the answering machine picked up.

"It's the machine," Michelle announced, clearly irritated.

"Relax. She's probably still snoozing," Fatima tried reassuring Michelle.

But when Michelle returned home three hours later, Liz was gone again. Keeping her irritation in check, Michelle emptied one of her many shopping bags crammed with several new outfits. Her stash included a silk chiffon off-the shoulder cocktail dress, a gold-plated cuff bracelet, brass tassel earrings, and a pair of matching designer shoes. The shoes, which passed a trek-around-the-mall test, were sprinkled with crystal dust. They were sexy and skinny heeled but not so elevated that Michelle would wobble on them like a toddler taking her first steps. She'd done okay on that date-clothes-hunting excursion though her mind kept wandering to her mother.

Soon after Michelle finished replacing the chipped polish on her nails, she grew even more worried and agitated about Liz's absence. She'd even considered phoning Wesley to cancel but ultimately took Fatima's advice. Michelle couldn't let her mother's mysterious behavior of late wreck her first official one-on-one date with Wes.

Michelle would go to dinner; then she and Liz were definitely going to have that serious talk before another sunrise, even if it meant waking Liz and dragging her out of her bed when Michelle returned home later that evening.

Wes spent the morning organizing the notes he'd gathered so far for his Pratt file, but by noon he'd met up with his parents and Lonette at a school auditorium, the location for Kelly's latest dance recital. Though he had too much on his agenda for that day, he managed to work the recital in by rescheduling several phone interviews. He really wanted to be at the recital, and though this was the first time Kelly had phoned to *personally* invite him to see her perform, Wes took in stride this new designation as Patrick's stand-in.

Lonette, a pretty, caramel-skinned woman with a trim figure, angular cheekbones, and neat, drinking straw–thin twists on her head, arrived earlier than the rest of the parents with kids performing had.

Lonette had saved seats on the first row for the Abbotts, beside her own parents, Howard and Nadine Warren. The Abbotts and the Warrens had all met before and managed to forge an easy camaraderie despite Patrick's deadbeat-dad history. The Warrens had vowed to give him a chance when it looked as if Patrick had finally gotten his act together and wanted to be a real father to Kelly.

"I'm so glad you all could make it." Lonette embraced Wes, Gloria, and Winston. "Kelly's going to be so happy to see you all here!"

They settled into their seats and watched a variety of dance numbers, which featured a range of skills, performed by young girls ages two to thirteen enrolled in Arabella's Tap, Toe, Tumble Dance Studio.

Wes, who had some trouble focusing on the performances, had settled in the seat between Lonette and an older, heavyset woman he didn't know. The woman wore a wide-brimmed flowered hat, short immaculate white gloves, and a jumbo gardenia corsage pinned near one throw-pillow-sized breast. Glasses with prescription lenses that made her peepers appear the size of black-eyed peas pinched the bridge of her nose. As if it were too hot in the air-conditioned auditorium, she kept fanning herself with a frilly-edged hankie, scattering a cloyingly sweet perfumed breeze in Wes's direction.

"That's my granddaughter, Emily-Raquel, up there." She nudged Wes and pointed toward the stage. "She's the third one to the left in the line."

"Is that right?" Wes smiled and showed polite interest when he spotted the little brown girl with a doll face and a round teddy bear body. She and her crew had squeezed into bright blue tights and ruffled red costumes reminiscent of a Carmen Miranda getup. The mini rumba line boogied to a fevered Latin beat, heavy on the horns.

"She's such a gifted child," the woman gushed, her eyes tearing up with pride. She sniffled and dabbed at them with the lace hankie. "Just look at the way she moves. She's so talented!"

Unfortunately, what Wes noticed was that Emily-Raquel had displayed all the agility and grace of a cactus, but he'd give the kid an A for effort. "Yes, talented. That she is," he replied without a hint of sarcasm.

The music stopped and the curtain came down, signaling the end of the Latin-themed performance. Obligatory applause rippled through the auditorium. To eke up the enthusiasm quotient, the prissily attired older woman next to him sank two fingers inside her mouth and let out a ballpark-style whistle, then cheered, "That's my Emily-Raquel! Yay, Emily-Raquel!"

Wes checked his program. Next up: Kelly Abbott performing a jazz and gymnastic number to a hip-hop version of the "Eeensy Weensy Spider."

The auditorium went dark as the curtain ascended. This time Kelly appeared, dressed in a cute purple and orange spider costume, black tights, and silver ballet slippers. Midstage, midspotlight, she struck a sassy pose, with her hands on her hips, as she awaited her cue. With the first few notes of music she wriggled to the up-tempo beat. The houselights lit up, illuminating the stage, then the entire auditorium.

Kelly perfectly executed a series of backflips and handstands that wowed the Abbotts and the rest of the audience as none of the other acts had. "Go, Kelly!" Wes cheered, pumping a fist.

"Yours?" the woman next to him asked, her brow pleated with displeasure.

"My niece, Kelly!" Wes boomed, feeling his chest expand with love and pride. He hadn't expected to experience such an intense emotional response.

"Do y'all feed the poor child? She's such a scrawny little thing." The woman chuckled good-naturedly in a futile attempt to mask a blatant dig.

Wes whistled his encouragement to Kelly, then shouted, "Yeah, get it, girl!"

"My goodness, who designed her costume?" the woman next to him asked with another chuckle. "I don't think I've ever seen a purple and orange spider before, have you?"

Watching Kelly as she smoothly segued into the jazz portion of her performance, Wes enjoyed himself too much to be distracted for long by the woman's annoying commentary.

"Emily-Raquel's the top scholar in her second-grade class," the woman suddenly blurted.

"That's nice," Wes replied with a prideful smile still on his face as Kelly performed a series of spins.

"Emily-Raquel was also crowned in the pre-Pro-Am division of the America's Little Darlings International beauty pageant just last weekend."

"Good for her." Wes reached out and squeezed Lonette's hand in a gesture of familial solidarity.

Kelly performed another impressive backhand spring that elicited even more enthusiastic clapping and shouts of encouragement.

"Look at her go!" a woman behind them cheered.

"Emily-Raquel speaks fluent Spanish and is working on French. Placed first for students in her age group at a city-wide spelling bee. She's also a whiz at math and will represent her class at an upcoming Math Bowl in a few weeks. What about Kiley?"

"Kelly," Wes corrected her.

"Kiley, Kelly, whatever," she said as she flapped a plump gloved hand and Kelly performed a comical little shuffle that showed the playful side of her personality. "What else does Kiley do, I mean, besides flip around like she's on something?"

In an uncharacteristically jingly voice Wes replied, "Well, if you must know. Our little Kelly speaks fluent pig Latin, maintains an age-appropriate messy bedroom, and whips up a mean peanut butter–banana sandwich. But that's not all. Give her a can of Pepsi and she'll burp any beer-guzzling frat boy under the table. Our little Kelly hates Brussels sprouts, rainy days, midday naps . . ." Then he turned and looked the woman in her black-eyed peas to make it clear to whom he was referring when he added, "And most of all, *overbearing grandmothers.*"

"Well, I never!" the woman gasped, her hand flying to her abundant chest.

Wes smirked, satisfied that he'd finally silenced the big-mouthed biddy so he could enjoy the rest of Kelly's performance.

Kelly had reached another jazz segment when she shimmied left, right, then suddenly went still as the hip-hop beat carried on. She did a little awkward shuffle, then froze again and stared out into the audience as if suddenly gripped by fear.

"Uh-oh," Lonette whispered to Wes. "It's that part we added to her routine at the last minute. She didn't have enough time to practice it as much. Was afraid she might forget it."

Wes's heart ached for his niece.

"C'mon, honey, you can do it. Sidestep, shuffle, shuffle, turn, turn," Lonette chanted to herself as if sending telepathic assistance to her daughter.

Kelly didn't budge but maintained that deer-caught-in-the-headlights stare, the confident tumbling dynamo she had been just a few seconds ago gone, replaced by a shamed five-year-old, who probably felt she'd let everyone down—with a slew of grown-up strangers gawking at her.

From where he sat he could see Kelly's bottom lip quiver, a tear slid down her cheek, then, her entire face broke, her chest heaving with sobs.

Lonette leaped to her feet and performed the steps Kelly had missed; the motion of the dancing woman on the front row caught Kelly's eye. But she just stood there sobbing. Wes heard Emily-Raquel's obnoxious granny snicker. It was then Wes knew he had to do something! So he found himself springing to his feet, too. Off the top of his head he unleashed some moves he remembered were akin to an awkward mix of the bunny hop, hokey pokey, electric slide, and Macarena. He knew he looked like a damn idiot, but that was the point. He'd captured Kelly's attention and then something wonderful happened: she laughed. She laughed so hard she clutched her midsection by the end of the song; then she took a graceful bow and accepted the audience's generous applause. She pranced toward the end of the stage and pointed to Wes, whom the crowd cheered for as well.

He turned and took a bow with a flourish. Instead of disappearing backstage when the curtain dropped, Kelly exited the stage at a set of side steps and ran out into the audience. She launched herself into Wes's arms and stamped kisses on his face.

"Uncle Wes, you were awful, just awful!" she said, with a smile so bright it rivaled the auditorium fluorescents.

"I know, sweetie, I know," he said, holding her tight and savoring the feel of her light weight and clinging embrace. "Think we'll take our act on the road?"

"No way!" Kelly giggled.

Lonette thanked Wes for his quick thinking. The rest of the family gathered around them and teased Wes for debunking the myth that all black folks had rhythm.

After the recital Wes had to part with the rest of the family, who had planned to gather for a barbecue in Kelly's honor at the Warrens' house. He had more work to do on the Pratt story before he prepared for his big date with Michelle that evening.

When Wesley arrived promptly at seven, Michelle stalled as long as she could without screwing up their reservations at the fabulous Keegen Harbor restaurant that she'd been dying to try. *How had he known?* Michelle wondered as a hostess escorted them to their table. The intimate dining room was tasteful, warm, and richly hued, with lush fabrics and shining oak floors. A black granite bar hugged one side. Diamondlike chandeliers dangled from rafters.

Wesley looked downright scrumptious in his dark Italian suit and crisp white shirt. As he eased a chair out for Michelle, she enjoyed his light but masculine cologne. "I thought you might like this place."

"Like it? It's wonderful," Michelle gushed, taking in her surroundings and not caring that she sounded like a bumpkin who'd only dined in restaurants with photos of food on giant laminated menus. "So, do you come here often?"

"I come here," Wes replied rather cagily.

Michelle refrained from trying to guess just how many of his dates he'd brought here. She was with him that night, and that was all that really mattered for now.

Their server appeared, a striking tanned, snow-haired man. Wes ordered a strip steak with sides of white cheddar mashed potatoes and green beans while Michelle chose the red snapper in yellow curry with somen noodles, bok choy, and shiitakes. The sommelier took their wine requests.

The conversation picked up where they'd left off during the drive there. Wes, who'd obviously sensed a bit of nervousness on Michelle's part, had broken the ice by discussing *Herald* goings-on first.

"So have you tried to get Jack to throw an assignment your way?" he asked, referring to the *Herald* business section editor.

"Yes, I even invited him to lunch to discuss that possibility, but before I could get the words out he told me he'd be thrilled to work with me—"

"Great!"

"*But,* big *but* here, he'd been warned by Barbara to keep hands off, that she had plenty of work for me and didn't want my attention divided," Michelle added glumly.

"I can certainly understand where she's coming from, what with Katie out and all, but I'm sure that was disappointing to you. Bummer." He took a sip from his water glass.

"Tell me about it," she grumbled. "But I should've known better. I don't think the object was to actually *enjoy* working here. I mean, it was supposed to be a punishment or reprimand."

Wes's brows shot up. "Punishment? What the hell? You're kiddin' me, right?"

"No."

"This is the first I'm hearing of this. Punishment for what?"

With eyes lowered Michelle pondered how much she really wanted to share about her troubles at the *Business Journal,* but if anyone would understand, it would be Wesley, who had shown that he was equally driven and ambitious. When their eyes met again she told him about the imbroglio involving Chapelle, Maxwell Coleman, the gossip, and the attacks on her journalistic ethics.

"Whoa," was all he said, with an unblinking gaze, when she was done.

Fortunately, their food and wine soon arrived to fill the uncomfortable contemplative silence that hovered.

So much for exuding a baggage-free vibe, Michelle thought ruefully. She knew there was a chance that he might think less of her after the big purge, but she had to admit it felt good to finally get it all out with someone in the business. She'd confided in Fatima, but it just wasn't the same.

As their server announced each silver-dome-covered dish Michelle found herself studying Wes, but his expression gave away none of what he might be thinking.

When the server departed, Wesley spoke. "So, you got too emotionally involved with *the* Stanford Chapelle?" he asked.

"Yeah, Chapelle, and there was Maxwell Coleman, and oh yeah, Bloomingthal, if I'm completely honest. But not in a lovey-dovey sense. I swear to you."

"I got that part. Besides being CEOs of multimillion-dollar corporations what did the three have in common?"

Michelle shrugged, then tucked into her entrée. "I don't know. . . . Well, they were very nice to me."

"So you get that emotionally involved with every subject who is nice to you? You don't strike me as the type." Wes ate a bite of his steak.

Michelle met his gaze. "You mean the foolish, flighty, and naive type?"

Wes's expression was frank. "Look, I wouldn't go that

far. We all make mistakes. Lord knows I have. Those three men being nice to you and all . . . Something just doesn't add up. There must be much more to it."

Michelle knew exactly what was up with those attachments but wasn't ready to go there with him just yet. "Let's not analyze it to death, please. Not right now, not on our first date." She took a sip of her white wine.

"As you wish," Wes said with a deferential smile. "Have I told you how lovely you look tonight?" His eyes skimmed over her dress, causing her to flush with delight.

"Yes, I believe this is the tenth time since we left my mother's house," she teased. "But don't stop."

"Sorry I didn't get to meet your mother by the way. Maybe another time."

"Yeah, another time." Dwelling on Liz would spoil her appetite, but Michelle couldn't help wondering where the woman could have been. She wasn't at church. Michelle knew that for a fact. Before Wes arrived, two Pin Stingers phoned to find out if Liz was feeling well. It had been her Sunday for ushering duties, yet she hadn't shown up at the 8:00 a.m or 11:00 a.m. services.

"Earth to Chelle," Wes's voice broke through her reverie.

Michelle blinked. "I'm sorry."

"Is everything all right?" Wes's concern was evident. "The *Journal* still on your mind? Look, after the way you patiently listened to me that time, I'm happy to return the favor if you still need to talk about it. You don't have to hold back. I'm in no position to judge you."

"It's not that," she began, then thought better of going into her mama drama. The man would discover she was just a bundle of problems and deep-rooted issues.

"What?" he prompted.

"This restaurant really is great," she said instead. "Rivals the very best in the Big Apple, I think. The food and wine are tops. I needed this. Thank you for inviting me."

"And thank you for coming."

They ate the rest of their entrées and engaged in a good-natured disagreement over whether jazz trumpeter Nicholas Payton had sold out. On the musician's latest album, *Sonic Trance,* he'd abandoned the traditional acoustic straight-ahead classic sound that had garnered him hordes of die-hard fans for a more modern, plugged-in, groove-oriented sound.

"When his horn was in classic jazz style it's like the second coming of Louis Armstrong," Wes said as he and Michelle worked their way through dessert: chocolate terrine with frozen coffee-almond ice cream. "Why would he turn his back on that?"

"I still say change can be good," Michelle countered. "Don't blame the guy for wanting to shake things up a bit. His new album is a masterpiece."

Wes couldn't remember the last time he'd enjoyed himself so much. He mentally took back that thought. The afternoon at Chuck E. Cheese had been pretty spectacular as well. It was then he realized that it wasn't about the setting or the food but the company.

Though Wes was stunned and bewildered by what she'd revealed about her departure from the *Manhattan Business Journal,* the fact that she'd confided in him felt good. He saw it as a sign that she was beginning to trust him.

Michelle finished off the last bite of chocolate on her plate. "I do need to come up for air here."

"Just enjoy until it's all gone; then order another if you like," he encouraged, thinking how Michelle's jazz acumen, quick wit, charm, unpretentiousness, hearty appetite, and sexy radiance clearly enchanted him. He'd thought she was a stunner the moment he met her, but her beauty tonight knocked him off his feet. She was simply a vision in gold that complemented the tawny smoothness of her skin, silky auburn hair, and hazel eyes. Her tall, curvy figure was shown to sensational advantage in that Viagra-punch of a dress.

Though he enjoyed nice butts, overall he'd never been all that exacting when it came to physical types. Slim. Fuller figured. Tall. Short. Fair. Dark. He could appreciate those most would consider classic beauties as well as their plainer or quirkier sisters. He just loved women. Period. Everything about them—their feminine auras, scents, softer bodies that were the cradles of life, and, most important, wonderfully different minds. He didn't think he could ever be truly happy with just one. But now . . . Now that he'd met Michelle, he wasn't so sure. She appeared to be everything he didn't know he was looking for. It was with great difficulty that he managed not to stare at her—bug-eyed and drop-jawed— during their meal.

She'd bewitched him so, not once had his gaze or attention been tempted to stray. Why would they? No need to do inventory to verify it. He knew he was with the most gorgeous, fascinating woman in the room.

"I have to go to the ladies' room." Michelle set her fork on her dessert dish to reach for the small golden clutch bag on her lap.

One incidental glimpse over Michelle's shoulder as she prepared to rise forced Wes to do a double, no, triple take.

He maintained his cool despite the sudden churning in his belly. If he didn't keep it together the expression on his face would read as mild terror.

Brynn Devereaux, dressed in full sexpot regalia, headed their way with a sphinxlike expression on her glossy red lips. Once towering over their cozy table she grinned down at both of them. "Well, well, well . . . if isn't Wesley Abbott."

Fifteen

Hello, Brynn, good to see you." Wes chased that blatant lie with a big gulp from his wineglass. "Dining here tonight, are you?"

"Yeah. This isn't usually my scene, though." Brynn spoke to Wes, but her curious gaze wandered to Michelle. "The food is good, but the atmosphere is a little too stuffy for me. My sister, Brooke, chose this place for my parents' anniversary dinner tonight."

"How many years?" he asked, still stuck on banal small talk.

"Thirty-five years of wedded bliss," she replied without a hint of sarcasm.

"So where is the rest of the family?" Wes cleared his throat, thinking how odd it was that he'd learned more about Brynn in the last minute than he had in three whole months.

"In one of the private dining rooms," she said, still eyeing Michelle.

"Sorry, where are my manners?" Wes finally said. "Michelle, this is Brynn Devereaux. Brynn, Michelle Michaels."

"Nice to meet you, Brynn." With a polite smile, Michelle extended her hand.

"Very nice to meet you, too." Brynn wrapped her long acrylic-tipped fingers around it.

"Excuse me, but I was just headed to the ladies' room." Michelle rose with her clutch bag in hand.

Minding his manners, Wes rose, too.

"I'll only be a minute," she said to Wes before looking to Brynn with a no-worries expression again. A few women might have opted to stay and sniff around for answers. Who the hell was this Brynn Devereaux in the shrink-wrapped dress? And what was she to Wes? They'd sit tight, even if it meant holding their water until their bladders burst. But not Michelle, who was a lot more calm and self-assured than he was at that moment.

In silence, Brynn and Wes watched Michelle depart. Once she was out of sight Wes took his seat again and Brynn commandeered Michelle's.

"Ooooh. She's *very* pretty, Wes. And those eyes and that hair. Kinda reminds you of Vanessa L. Williams, doesn't she?" Brynn whispered, then lifted Wes's wineglass for a big drink before setting it down again. "Got some back on her, too. Hmmp!"

Wes started again in a cautioning voice, "Look, Brynn—"

In a possessive gesture Brynn reached across the table to brush her fingertips along one of Wes's lapels. "Ermenegildo Zegna, correct? I don't think I've ever seen you in this one." She batted her eyelashes. "I usually just get the birthday suit."

Wes rolled his eyes but kept his impatience in check. He liked Brynn and didn't want to be rude.

"Have I ever seen you in a suit this nice?" Brynn pursed her lips and tipped her head for a moment. "Wait; that night we met at that nightclub, but I got you out of it pretty quickly, didn't I?" Her laughter floated across the quiet dining room. "In the backseat of my Lexus? Or was it the last stall inside the men's bathroom at the Voodoo Lounge? Silly me, maybe it was both. We had a lot of fun that night, remember?"

"Brynn," Wes bit out between clenched teeth; he darted anxious glances in the direction of the ladies' room. Michelle had been reluctant to give Wes a chance, and now it looked as if Brynn was going to screw it up for him.

"Relax, Romeo," Brynn murmured, sans the teasing lilt. "I don't think I've ever seen you looking so stiff and up-tight. I was just having a little fun messing with you. I didn't come over here to bust you out in front of your friend, all right?"

"Really?" Wes said, unconvinced.

"Get over yourself, dude." Brynn laughed again, throwing her curtain of inky black tresses behind her shoulders. "I understand that our little, um, arrangement is history. Fun while it lasted, though, wasn't it?"

"Is that right?" Wes still wasn't sure he was buying it.

Then she added drily, "So if truth be told, I ain't thinking 'bout you, okay? Old news."

Old news? Never in his life had Wes been so pleased to get dissed like that. He released the breath that he hadn't realized he was holding since Brynn appeared. She could be so damn unpredictable. Wes's concern and uncertainty about where he stood with Michelle had caused him to assume the worst. But he should've known that Brynn Devereaux hadn't ever cared enough to be jealous or possessive. He thanked heaven for that.

"That's not what you were saying not so long ago, though," he added.

"Oh, about that little popcorn visit to your loft that night . . ." She waved a dismissive hand at Wes, then crossed her long legs. "Puh-lease, Wes, I thought you of all people knew what *that* was about. Just one for the road, bro, just one for the road. When I spotted you and your friend, I thought I'd come over, be hospitable, and say hi, not give you a heart attack. But don't think I didn't catch that fleeting look of unveiled horror on your face when you first saw me."

Wes cocked a brow. "Glad there's at least one other way I can entertain you."

Brynn sat upright, then leaned toward Wes again, nearly resting her voluminous bosom on the table like a main course, but for once Wes wasn't the least bit hungry.

"You've got it bad for this one, huh?" Brynn asked, withdrawing to sit up straight again. "I could tell by the way you were looking at her googly-eyed and all."

"Is that right?"

"Right." Brynn stood, coaxing the clingy black jersey dress that rode up the curves of her thighs back to its proper place. "Well, I'd better get back to the rest of the Devereauxes. See ya around, player." She winked. "But remember, you're not the only one with game." She turned to walk away, hips swaying and trailing that distinctive musk fragrance she always wore.

"Hey, Brynn, tell your folks congratulations for me," Wes called out affably as his body went slack with more relief. Though he was sure Brynn had never spoken of him and the Devereauxes didn't know him from Adam, it felt like the right thing to say.

Michelle had more than a hunch that bodacious Brynn and Wes had seen each other naked.

Was Michelle supposed to care? She did. And how! But when you entered into a dating situation involving a man with an eye for the ladies, you took what thrills he had to offer, guarded your heart, maintained your dignity, and avoided situations that could wreak havoc on your self-esteem. Besides, she was headed to the restroom to use her cell phone to check on her mother *before* the microminied bombshell appeared. He knew that. Leaving Wes with Brynn had sent him the right message, she hoped. It wasn't a scaredy cat move but a cool one, she decided.

Three other women milled about the opulent powder

room. She slipped inside a stall for privacy, removed her cell phone from her clutch, then dialed. The phone rang four times before the answering machine clicked on. Darn it! Where could her mother be?

Michelle snapped the phone shut, then jammed it back inside her bag. She stepped out of her stall to an empty powder room. Soft classical music suffused the space. She moved across the lush carpeting to stand in front of an ornate mirror over the sinks to check her makeup.

Her index finger smoothed one neatly arched brow; then she checked her teeth for bits of spinach from her appetizer salad. Her lipstick needed a retouch, so she reached inside her bag for the tube of Spiced Raisin.

She looked up again to see Brynn's reflection behind hers. She gasped, "I thought I was alone."

The woman just stood there, staring, with a peculiar glimmer in her eyes. "Sorry. Didn't mean to startle you."

Ten minutes after Brynn left, Michelle still hadn't returned from the restroom. Women's "freshening up" tended to take a while, so Wes reached for his wineglass and relished his dodging of a bullet. A raw fear had rumbled inside his belly at the thought of Brynn blowing what he hoped to have with Michelle. He hadn't sweated past or present lady friends encountering one another, or he would not have dated more than one woman in the *Herald* building. The parting of ways had always been amiable.

"Would you like more wine, sir?" The server had returned, breaking into Wes's thoughts.

"I'm fine, thank you."

A few seconds later Michelle returned to the table, looking downright flummoxed. She reached for her half-full wineglass and took a big gulp.

"Chelle, are you all right?"

"Your friend Brynn—"

"Yeah, what about her?"

"Well, she came to the ladies' room while I was still in there . . ."

"And she said something to you?" Wesley braced for a bomb.

Michelle nodded.

Wesley might as well come forth with his version of their relationship. He just hoped it was enough to clean up whatever mess Brynn might have made. "Look, Chelle, about Brynn and me—"

"You two used to be an item, right?"

"You could say that. She's a fun girl, but let me make something clear: we're not an item anymore."

Michelle still looked shellshocked. "I gathered that part."

"Oh? So she told you that?"

"She told me you two were history. Done. Finished. But I believe her exact words were that you two were about 'as over as Gloria Vanderbilt jeans.'" Michelle took another big gulp of her wine.

"Hmmp." Wes didn't hide his pleasant surprise. "What else did she say to you about me?"

Michelle shrugged. "Not much actually . . . about you, I mean. But if I'm not mistaken, your friend Brynn . . ."

"What?"

"She just hit on *me*," she announced with utter wonderment.

"Say what?" Wes asked, forgetting to blink.

Michelle laughed heartily. "Took me several minutes to get a clue. After spending so many years in New York, I really should've been quicker on the uptake. It hasn't happened to me that often; I mean, a woman showing *that* kind of interest and all. But Brynn *definitely* made a pass at me."

Not only was Brynn full of surprises, but that chick was full-on *buck wild*—no holds barred. It shouldn't have thrown Wes off-guard to learn that she was all about equal opportunity when it came to getting her freak on. Wes shook his head and chuckled. "Sorry about that. I hope she didn't offend you."

"No offense taken. She was very nice actually." Michelle grinned, then placed a textured white card embellished with embossed letters and Brynn's loopy scrawl on the table between them. "In case I ever want to hang out she gave me her business card. See? Scribbled her home and cell phone numbers on it and everything."

When the server returned to refill Michelle's wineglass Wes used the distraction to discreetly pocket Brynn's card, with the intention of tearing it into a hundred bits at first chance. Hey, the male ego could only take so much.

"I know it's late, but I'd like to propose a toast," he said, at that moment feeling more contented than he thought possible.

"I'd like that."

They lifted their wineglasses.

He began, "To taking chances . . ."

"With no regrets," Michelle added, with a soft smile.

Sixteen

Michelle's first official date with Wesley came to an end with the most delicious, pulse-racing make-out session near the side entrance of her mother's brick bungalow.

Under the canopy of a velvety star-sprinkled sky, he was just supposed to walk her to the door and say good night. She was just supposed to thank him for a lovely evening with a sweet peck on the lips. Well, maybe not that sweet. She'd considered slipping him just a bit of tongue.

The lights in the house were still off and the Civic gone, which led Michelle to believe that her mother had yet to return. She'd planned to send Wesley on his way quickly so she could finally get to the bottom of the mystery that had been nipping at her attention all evening.

The streetlights provided enough illumination to appreciate his handsome face with its strong jaw, soft, full beckoning lips, and smoldering dark eyes tucked under a sharp ridge of brow. When he drew her into his protective arms and pressed her against his rock hard chest, Plan A was all but forgotten. She loved the way he always reached for her—his hand at the small of her back, curled around hers, or sweeping an errant lock away from her cheek. He made her feel as if not touching her was tantamount to not drawing another breath. And it felt so natural, as if his skin craved her skin. She hadn't wanted to consider that this was part of practiced protocol for him. He had to know what women wanted and responded to. And who wouldn't enjoy feeling like the most irresistible creature he'd ever met?

Wes started with pecks and gentle suckling of her bottom lip that soon gave way to a deep, tongue-tangling mating of mouths that turned the inside of her panties into sweltering jungle. Her sex thickened and throbbed for relief that only deep penetration could bring. She ground her hips against his hardness. One of his hands moved up to firmly cup one breast, inflaming her more. Moans floated out in the warm air and surrounded them. Before she surrendered to the urge to grab him by the collar and yank him toward the backyard to finish what they'd started on the vinyl cushions of her mother's Kmart patio furniture, Michelle tore her lips away from his. "Um . . . Wes . . ."

He latched on to them again, swallowing her protest, weakening her resolve.

But forcing her mind to scurry away from the pleasure she felt in Wes's arms to her mother's absence was like the splash of cold water Michelle needed.

Her hands crept to his chest to force space between them. But the heat of hard, sculpted pecs beneath her fingertips was enough to keep her libido whirling like jet turbines.

The bright glare of headlights pulling into the driveway provided the distraction she needed to disengage. For one hopeful moment Michelle thought her mother was home, but the late-model sedan was larger than her mother's car. The vehicle rolled forward, then retreated, merely using the driveway to change directions. Wes moved to pick up where they left off before the interruption, but Michelle withdrew. "I'm sorry. I'd better get inside before . . ."

"Before what?" With a rascal's grin, he skimmed his palms up and down her arms, leaving a trail of goose bumps that had nothing to do with the drop in the temperature. She maneuvered her lightweight wrap up over her bare shoulders and arms to foil the stimulating effects of his skilled touch,

but that only spurred Wes to be . . . well, more Wes. She'd
never been with a man so perceptive and attentive to her
every wish. During the drive to and from the restaurant he'd
let her choose the CD slipped inside the player. More than
once he'd inquired if the passenger seat and the car's interior
temperature were adjusted to her satisfaction. He'd even
noted the slight tensing of her muscles when the speedome-
ter's needle leaned more than ten miles over the speed limit.
Wordlessly he'd lightened his foot on the gas and switched
off that blasted fuzz buster that screeched radar frequencies
"X Band!" and "K Band!" every five miles or so.

"You cold?" he asked in a husky whisper, moving to draw
her back into his arms. "Come here; let me warm you up."

If he "warmed her up" any more her tooth fillings would
melt.

"I'm fine. Really." Michelle took a step back to maintain a
safe distance from his addictive embrace. "I really do have to
go." She smiled. "It has been a lovely evening. Thank you."

She opened her purse and removed her keys while he
teased with a mock-mournful expression.

"The sad puppy dog face is not going to work. We both
have work tomorrow, remember?" she reminded him with a
chuckle.

"I know. It's just that . . ." He took a step closer and
looked down at her with eyes so luminous with sincerity, she
found it disarming. "I've enjoyed you tonight. I don't want it
to end."

"Oh, Wes," she whispered. That inner schism widened after one date. How she wanted to believe that the look and
those kind words weren't just part of his repertoire, but she
knew better. *Keep your head and your heart in check and nobody gets hurt,* she reminded herself. She angled her head
and inched up on her toes to kiss that spot on his face that
dimpled when he smiled.

"Good night." Wes brushed a finger along her cheek as if

needing one last touch to tide him over until their next private meeting.

Michelle had made it clear that there would be no fooling around at work or anywhere near the *Herald* newsroom.

"Good night, Wesley." Not trusting what he or she might do next, she quickly turned away to insert her key inside the lock. She opened the door and stepped inside without looking back.

Michelle went to the living room and peeked out along the edge of a curtain to watch him climb inside his Ferrari, then pull away from the curb. A bundle of nervous energy, she reached for the cordless phone on the teak coffee table and phoned Fatima to find out if she'd seen or heard from Liz.

With the receiver tucked between her ear and a shoulder, Michelle went to the kitchen to pour herself a cold soft drink.

Fatima answered on the third ring. "So how did it go?"

"It was wonderful. The meal, the company. I kept wanting to pinch myself," Michelle admitted, feeling a dreamy smile tug at her lips.

"And?"

"And what?" Michelle removed a huge plastic cup with Greektown Casino stamped on it. It would hold a lot more cola and crushed ice than the glassware and crystal lined along the cabinet shelves.

"Details. Don't hold anything back on me now."

"I will fill you in. Promise. Just not right now. I'm still worried about Ma." Michelle removed a two-liter plastic container from the fridge, then filled her cup up with ice and cold, fizzing cola.

"She's still not home yet?"

"Doesn't look as if she's been back at all since I left for my date."

"That doesn't sound good."

"Tell me about it." Michelle took a big gulp from her cup. "Maybe I should have canceled my date with Wesley."

"Don't start beating yourself up for having a life. She's a grown woman and it's not as if she's been missing all that long. You heard her come in earlier this morning, right? And you peeked in her bedroom and saw her sleeping before we took off for the mall, right?"

"Yeah."

"Ed's not in town, is he?"

"Nope."

"So, she's probably not at his place. Hmm. Maybe we should phone some of her other friends. Maybe they've seen her."

Michelle sipped her cola. "I've already heard from three Pin Stingers. Nothing there. But there's still Fern, Dianne, and Charlene."

"I'll phone Fern and Dianne. You check on Charlene and any of her other friends you can think of. I'll buzz you right back in about ten minutes."

Michelle ended that connection. The last she'd heard, Charlene had moved, and Michelle no longer knew the woman's phone number. Directory assistance informed her that the listing was now private. She would have to search for the sunflower-print address book Liz always kept tucked in the nightstand drawer near her bed.

Michelle didn't usually rummage through other people's personal things, but this was an emergency. In her mother's bedroom, she sat on the queen-size four-poster bed encased in a luxurious green Calvin Klein comforter. Under the light of a Tiffany-style lamp she rifled through the nightstand drawer. Inside she found a stack of greeting cards for a variety of occasions, Unity Church Daily Word booklets, two spicy historical romance novels she made a mental note to borrow later, an old soap opera magazine, and reading glasses on a chain. The large mound of matchbooks and tokens, all stamped with that colorful five-torch logo for Greektown Casino, gave her pause.

Before she could locate the address book the phone rang. She picked up the old-fashioned rotary-style phone on the stand.

"I couldn't reach Fern, but Dianne is pretty sure where we can find Liz," Fatima said.

"I think I know where I might find her, too." Michelle lifted one of the matchbooks for closer inspection.

The rush of falling coins, slot machine bells, and whistles surrounded Michelle when she stepped inside Greektown Casino.

After security checked her pockets and her bag, they allowed her entry. To her immediate left sat a small alcove with pay phones and ATM machines.

Michelle was pretty sure she'd never wash out the thick stench of cigarette smoke that would cling to the pink sweatshirt and jeans she'd changed into for this trip.

Just ahead and to the right, the vast gaming area spread out over jewel-toned carpeting with a dizzying swirling design. In keeping with the Greek theme, a "Win This Chariot" sign loomed over a gleaming late-model burgundy Cadillac perched on a platform.

People packed the place. All so sure luck was more than a luxury. Some stood frozen, zombielike, hypnotized by the rolling dice or the bright blinking lights of video poker. Nearby a small sign from the Michigan Gaming Control Board that might as well have been printed in invisible ink read: YOU CAN REQUEST THAT THEY PERMANENTLY BAR YOU FROM ALL LICENSED-CONTROL DETROIT CASINOS.

It went on to provide instructions on how to request an application.

Slowly she walked by a bank of craps and poker tables, scanning the faces, just in case. But based on the pile of coins in her mother's nightstand, Michelle suspected the slot machines would be where she would find Liz. The building had two levels, both crammed with rows and rows of slots, according to the security guard she'd asked about the casino's layout.

After searching the first level, she took the stairway to the second, where she finally found her mother perched on a stool before a slot on the end of a one-dollar-machine row.

Michelle wasn't sure how long she'd stood there and watched her mother, who had that same scary glazed look in her eyes Michelle had seen on dozens of faces since she entered the place. She knew gambling was a form of entertainment, much like going to a movie, concert, or amusement park, but there was still something dark and desperate that lingered in the air there. Michelle didn't have moral opposition to gambling per se, but she did believe it could easily become destructive when bills went unpaid or basic needs got neglected because of it.

A poodle-haired brunette woman, wearing sheer black hosiery and a jewel-toned satin ensemble that coordinated with the casino's decor, approached Michelle. "Can I get you something to drink?"

"No thank you," Michelle replied before moving toward her mother.

Michelle settled on the stool next to Liz. Liz, however, didn't take her eyes off the face of the flashing Double Lucky Sevens slot machine until Michelle placed a hand on her shoulder. "Ma."

Jolted from her trancelike state, Liz shrieked Michelle's name. "Wh-what are you doing here?" The potent stench of alcohol heated Liz's breath.

Michelle recognized the denim crumpled up near Liz's feet. She slipped off the stool, crouched to scoop it up, then draped it around her mother's shoulders. "Let's go, Ma."

Liz stammered, "B-but—"

"I *said* let's go, Ma." Michelle's tone even but firm.

"But I was . . . was . . . just about to . . ." Her words slurred. "Things were turning around. I'm hot. This machine is hot. I can't leave now. See?" Liz moved to squeeze in another pull of the machine, then excitedly lifted the plastic cup filled to the brim with shiny coins. A whistle sounded and more coins gushed into the tray faster than Liz could scoop them up. "See?"

"I don't care. It's time to go." Michelle's voice went cold as her patience slipped away. "We're leaving. Now."

"Chelle!" Liz tugged her arm out of Michelle's grip and wobbled.

When Michelle latched on to her arm again, Liz set her jaw stubbornly and snatched her arm away again with a force that caused Michelle to momentarily lose her own balance.

Though startled by Liz's hostility, Chelle remained steadfast and took hold of her again. "Ma!" Michelle shouted, and shook Liz's shoulders, hoping to jar her from whatever alcohol-enhanced madness had possessed her.

A tall African-American female in a security uniform approached them. "Is there a problem here?"

"Ma, please," Michelle pleaded in a wan voice. "Please, Ma. Don't do this."

Liz paused, looking from the broad, stern face of the security guard to Michelle's anguished one—as if an inner battle between her common sense and a compulsion for Double Lucky Sevens tore her in opposite directions.

"Everything's fine." Liz stopped resisting, then slowly shrugged into her denim jacket.

Satisfied, the security guard kept moving.

"Will you at least help me gather my winnings?" Liz asked, obviously still rattled by Michelle's sudden appearance. She scooped coins inside a second large cup.

"Sure, Ma," Michelle relented, relieved that her mother had agreed to leave without causing a bigger scene.

• • •

After much debate Michelle convinced her mother, who'd obviously had more than a couple cocktails, to leave her Civic behind to ride with Michelle in the Taurus. They would return to retrieve Liz's car later in the day.

"How did you find me?" Liz wanted to know once inside Michelle's rented Taurus.

"It wasn't that hard." Michelle had been so distracted she only strapped on her seat belt after they'd pulled out of the casino parking garage and rolled onto the traffic-clogged streets bordering Greektown and Motor City casinos. A little past midnight, early on a Monday morning, and business still boomed.

"Who told you where I was? I want to know," Liz demanded, eyes flashing.

"*You* did, all right? You left plenty of clues that pointed to this particular casino. And then there's the issue of your recent money problems. Doesn't exactly take Columbo to figure it all out."

Just as expected, both women stank of stale cigarette smoke. Michelle opened the vents in the dash to let more cool night air circulate through the car.

Liz's shoulders slumped.

"Ma, you have a problem, don't you?"

Liz raked her fingers through her brown hair, pushed her head back against the rest, and sucked in a deep breath. Her slim body went slack, as if all anger had fled. She pushed out a thick sigh.

"These marathon sessions at the casino are the reason you've been coming up short on cash. C'mon, Ma. Out with it."

"I thought I could handle it. I was fine with a little recreational gaming here and there; then I started coming up short on a few bills."

Michelle maneuvered the car onto a ramp leading to the highway.

"Something snapped inside of me tonight. When you grabbed my arm and tried to pull me away from that hot machine . . . I swear I—"

"What?"

"I wanted to slap the damn snot out of you and I would have, too, had that security guard not intervened when she did."

"Oh, Ma!" Michelle wailed, reaching for her mother's hand for a squeeze.

"I'm sorry I let you down, again, Michelle." Tears welled up in Liz's eyes.

Again rang in Michelle's ears. She wondered what Liz meant by that, but interrupting her now was not a smart move. Liz had been more forthcoming during the past few minutes than she'd been the last two months.

"For months now I've suffered through long periods of insomnia, honey."

"Why didn't you go see a doctor?"

Liz shrugged. "I thought it would pass. But the sleep deprivation got to be too much after a while. It started affecting just about everything in my life. But then I discovered that when I was in front of that slot machine I became totally absorbed by playing and nothing else in the world. I felt this . . . this . . . intoxicating buzz . . . this overwhelming high." Tears slipped down her cheeks in earnest. Too much alcohol always made Liz weepy. Between the drinks and the drama that had just gone down in the casino, Michelle had anticipated this reaction.

"I have tissue in my bag." Michelle gestured toward her pocketbook on the floor near the passenger seat. "Ma, you know I'll always love you—no matter what. You can tell me anything. There should be no secrets between us, so if there's something else you need to get off your chest . . ."

A long, uncomfortable silence stretched between them before Liz spoke again.

"I started chasing the losses about four months ago. Feeling as if I'd hit it big eventually. And when that one big hit arrived . . . everything would be set right again. I'd come out of the hole and I could pay you, Ed, and Fatima back."

With the tissue she took from Michelle's purse Liz dabbed at her eyes, then blew her nose. "You were always such a good, sweet child. You've always made me so proud." Her lips turned up in a watery smile. "I hope you know that."

Michelle glanced away from the highway in front of her and gave her mother a small smile. "And you've made me proud. I'm sure it wasn't easy raising a child all alone. Not only did you provide for me, but you took in Fatima and Ahmad, too. I don't know how you did it, but we're forever indebted to you."

"There just wasn't any other alternative. I couldn't let my sister's children end up in foster care."

Michelle needed to circle back and get clarification on what her mother meant about *letting her down again*. "There's more you want to say, isn't there? Something beyond the gambling, right?"

"I'm tired, honey." Liz's eyelids drifted closed, a side effect of her long day and the alcohol. "So very tired." She reached for the adjuster, and the back of the passenger seat reclined. "I need to close my eyes for a bit. Just a minute. Give Ma a minute, okay?"

Before they reached the next highway mileage sign, sleep had claimed Liz. It was all Michelle could do not to reach over and shake her awake. But Liz was obviously in no shape to bear the full brunt of Michelle's interrogation.

Michelle relaxed, taking solace in the fact that the lines of communication were finally open and the reason behind the cash shortage exposed. Now she just hoped she could convince her mother to seek the professional help she obviously needed. However, something told Michelle the gambling, which seemed to have surfaced out of the blue, wasn't the real issue but just a symptom of something bigger and deeper.

Seventeen

Later that same morning Michelle sat at a table inside the Headliner sucking down cup after cup of the strongest black coffee, hoping that the caffeine overload would make up for the fact that she'd gotten very little shut-eye. Calling in sick wasn't an option. She didn't like the idea of slacking off so soon after joining the *Herald*.

She curled her hands around her Styrofoam cup, relishing the heat emanating from it and the morning sun pouring through the windows lining the right side of the cafeteria.

She settled back in the molded vinyl seat and gave the coffee time to work its way through her system. Before she left the house that morning she'd had an opportunity to go online to research counseling options and had compiled a short list of programs for Liz, who had agreed that it was time she sought help. Much to Michelle's surprise, her mother had already selected her own treatment program, Willow Grove, in West Bloomfield.

The twenty-day program had inpatient/outpatient components and a highly trained staff. In addition to one-on-one intensive counseling, the first ten days boasted a full schedule of educational group discussions as well as activities such as exercise and stress management classes. The second half, the outpatient program, put an emphasis on independence, getting the person assimilated back into the usual daily life while the group meetings continued. Michelle looked forward to participating in some of Liz's counseling sessions. Perhaps it was foolish and paranoid, but she couldn't help wondering if somehow she might have contributed to her mother's crisis.

She took another sip and bit into a stick of stale biscotti that tasted like cork.

Liz would request a leave from her job at the insurance company to enroll in the program. But Michelle advised her to avoid going into detail about her reason for needing time off. Employers sometimes didn't react well when they learned an employee had to seek inpatient psychological help. Michelle agreed to provide the money Liz needed to cover the cost of the counseling program and any other household expenses that had to be paid.

Two pretty women in business suits with supershort skirts walked by and smiled a polite greeting to Michelle, who smiled back.

Michelle looked out the window through which she could see the lazy Detroit River, a bright blue sky, and slices of Canada. She said a quick silent prayer of thanks. The unfortunate circumstances at the *Manhattan Business Journal* had more than one silver lining. They had forced her home just in the nick of time to check on her mother. Things had fallen into place too neatly, so Michelle couldn't shrug off all uneasiness. Maybe after Liz had completed some counseling sessions Michelle would feel more assured that her mother was indeed back on track.

Chairs at the table behind Michelle scraped against the tile. She quickly peered over her shoulder, then noted it was the friendly women who'd just walked by. They'd purchased cups of coffee and were also taking early-morning breaks.

With the intention of bringing her own break to an end, Michelle was digging inside her bag in search of a mint when she overheard the two women discussing Wes's page 1 feature on the Vatican's reinstatement of a local priest who was removed last year for alleged abuse of a minor. The controversial content of the story soon gave way to a gushing account of Wes's many physical assets.

"That's one fine brotha, I'll tell you," one said in a voice thick with desire.

"Like you have to tell me. I've got eyes," the other seconded.

"You're so lucky, Davina. I mean, what was it like?"

"Dating him, you mean?" The one named Davina chuckled like a woman with a juicy secret she obviously was not going to keep.

Michelle's ears hitched.

"Let's just say he *really* knows how to treat a lady, Cheryl."

"I'll bet," Cheryl replied. "Is he as good as he looks?"

"Better," Davina replied with a sultry little laugh. "In fact, I wouldn't mind getting another piece of *that*."

Michelle's mouth formed a big speechless O.

The heat of embarrassment for blatantly eavesdropping, feeling envious and something else she couldn't name spread to Michelle's cheeks and neck. She'd heard enough, she decided, quickly shoving the mint inside her mouth and surging to her feet. She slung the strap of her bag over her shoulder, gathered her briefcase, coffee, and biscotti. She stomped toward the exit, where she lobbed the biscotti inside an open trash chute.

Wes thought his frantic morning would take a turn for the better the minute he laid eyes on Michelle. But she'd just marched by his cubicle without so much as throwing him a polite glance.

After the magnificent evening they'd shared he had been counting the minutes until he'd see her again. And when she'd finally appeared she'd pretty much blown by like a swift, chilly wind.

He watched as she plunked down at her desk and pulled papers out of her briefcase. Sure, they'd agreed to be discreet in the newsroom, but did that mean they couldn't exchange professional smiles and a "good morning" here and there?

When it was obvious that Michelle did not plan to meet his gaze, he swiveled his chair toward his monitor with a frown, then started to type.

Michelle wasn't sure what to do with her feelings. She knew what she was getting into when she agreed to date a guy like Wesley Abbott. But jealousy was getting the best of her already. She'd handled that encounter with Brynn Devereaux with finesse because she only had to deal with the *concept* that Wes had gotten naked with her. That Davina woman was oohing and ahhing over feasting on Wesley's body and drooling at the thought of going back for seconds! Michelle had only gone out on an official date with the man once and had already encountered not one but two of his bed buddies in less than twenty-four hours. Who knew how many more would pop out of the woodwork! And if she felt as if she wanted to hurl her cookies every time, was it even worth it?

She signed on her computer and immediately noted the message-pending signal. An e-mail from Wesley. She wanted to ignore it and get to work but didn't. She clicked the pointer to open Wes's message.

It simply read: ☺ *Hi.*

A reluctant smile tugged at Michelle's lips upon seeing the singular perky symbol. She found herself typing this response: *Hi yourself.*

Wes: *Lunch at the Headliner?*

Michelle: *Too busy.*

Wes: ☹

Michelle: *Will ring later.*

Wes: ☺

She ventured to peek over at his cubicle. He'd swiveled his chair in her direction, and only when he was absolutely sure no one else was looking he winked at her, causing her pulse to race and insides to flip. And just that quickly her momentary meltdown was history and she put Wes's other dalliances and the conversation she'd overheard back in perspective again.

Four hours later, Wes had completed all he could that day on the building code piece he was working on for the *Herald*; he used the last two hours to follow up a tip he'd received on the judge who had heard Patrick's case. So far he'd learned that J. Ashton Pratt was a devoted family man with passions for fly-fishing, expensive properties, and exotic travel. These hobbies obviously weren't financed on his jurist's salary alone.

Wesley was not one to linger around the newsroom much when he wasn't actually pounding out a story, and his penchant for spending most workdays roving always paid off. He'd never underestimated the value of getting out there and talking to people—even when he wasn't on the trail of something specific. If he talked and stayed out long enough, he'd usually stumble upon something. It was time to check in with Toni. They'd planned to meet at the bleachers in Memorial Park, near Toni's house, in an hour.

Wesley found Toni where she said she would be. She wore business casual attire—cotton slacks and a long-sleeved tunic-style blouse. Her sunburn had healed to a lighter shade of pink.

It was a picture perfect day with a bright blue, nearly cloudless sky. He took the seat next to hers at the top row of the metal bleachers and passed her one of two bottles of lemonade he'd picked up from the gas station en route to the park.

They exchanged hugs and pleasantries, then immediately

got down to business, because Toni had plans to meet her husband for a movie in less than an hour.

"Ever heard of Nathan Busby?" Toni asked, screwing off the bottle cap.

Wesley watched a tall, athletically built young mother whiz around the track pushing a baby jogger stroller in front of her. "How could I forget the superslick bailiff who played those FBI agents for knuckleheads about three years ago?"

"The one and only."

Wes shook his head at the memory of how Busby had scammed the agents intent on setting up a sting to reveal two judges—Samuel P. Wood and Jerline Haliburton—who were under investigation for suspicion of fixing cases. For eight months Busby had strung the two stooges along, even setting up a meeting between the alleged crooked judges and the agents. As the bagman Busby acted as the go-between, collecting from the agents as much as seventy-five thousand dollars in payoffs earmarked for the judges—minus Busby's cut. That was how it went until the day one of the agents eventually got a clue. He'd stumbled upon a large photo of Judge Jerline Haliburton on the society pages of the *Detroit Free Press* and realized it wasn't the Jerline Haliburton he'd been doing business with. It didn't take much of a stretch to conclude that the Samuel P. Wood they'd been introduced to by Busby wasn't the real deal, either. The agents had been hoodwinked by Busby, who had recruited impostors to act as the judges during those meetings with them while Busby sat back and raked in the cash.

"Luck had been on Busby's side for months," Toni noted. "Can you believe it?"

"It ran out eventually, though. He lived large there for a while, but when the feds found out he'd been playing them and made them look like morons, it all caught up with him."

Toni took a sip of her drink and experienced a pensive moment. "What were the chances that things in those two courtrooms would go exactly the way Busby needed to keep his scam going for months? I mean, several cases the agents believed had ended in a favorable verdict just ended up that way because the defendants had a strong case or strong lawyer—not because of any fix."

"God forbid you or I get caught up with a character like Busby."

"No way!" Toni shook her head, causing her thick red curls to bounce about her shoulders. "I've got a whole brain while those two federal agents were obviously sharing one." She chuckled. "Anyway, I only brought up Busby because I happen to know the idea to go into that offshoot side business of his was inspired by a couple of bailiffs and clerks who are in on a different hustle, according to a certain courtroom janitor with the ears of a canine, the eyes of an eagle, and the hots for *moi*."

"So you trotted out the feminine wiles for my cause?"

With a mock self-important gesture, Toni blew on her long acrylic nails, then buffed them against her chest. "Well, you know, what can I say? Anything for a friend."

A wide grin spread across Wesley's face. "Damn, woman, you don't waste any time, do you? What you got for me?"

"If you hang around and do your thing around McLemore's Bar and Grill in Redford you're more than likely to get on track to find out everything you need to know. Buddy up with Titus Montesi if you can." Toni checked her watch and came to her feet. "I don't want to keep Dwayne waiting. I'm meeting him at the Star Southfield to catch the latest Pierce Brosnan flick."

Wesley pecked a quick kiss on Toni's cheek. "Thanks, Toni. You have no idea how much I appreciate this." He stood and took Toni's arm as they maneuvered down the bleachers.

When they reached her blue Toyota, Toni turned to face him. "You know, getting what you need from Titus is not going to be as easy as buying him a few brewskies and hoping the alcohol loosens his tongue. He's sharper than that, but being the horn dog that he is, I know he has been known to let down his guard with the right female distraction."

"Is that right?' Wesley's brain was already spinning, sorting through ideas and scenarios.

"Not me, of course. Titus and I don't get along and if I tried kissing up to him now he'd know I was up to something."

"You've already done enough," Wesley said, taking the keys she'd removed from her shoulder bag and opening the car door for her. "I'll take it from here and I'm sure I'll come up with something. There must be something else Titus is into."

"Besides babes and hustling fixes?" Toni's mirthless chuckle bubbled up from her throat as she climbed inside her car, then positioned her bottle of lemonade in the cup holder under the dash. "Good luck."

"You take care. Tell Dwayne I said hi." Wesley leaned into the window on the driver's side as Toni started the engine. "And remember, if you or Dwayne ever need anything . . ."

"I know. Just holler." Toni waved.

Wes backed away from the car and watched her drive off. He strolled to his vehicle with the information Toni had provided on his mind. He hoped this Titus character would turn out to be the needed connection to Pratt. It could mean a swifter new trial, a second chance for Patrick. And for Kelly the gift of having her father back. He'd keep exploring all leads on Pratt first, most on his own time; then when he'd gathered all the necessary facts and honed the writing to the best of his abilities, he'd let his immediate supervisor, editor Malone Hughes, in on what he'd been up to.

Wes had returned to his *Herald* desk a little after 4:00 p.m. when his mother rang to invite him to dinner that night.

"So you and Dad are obviously fully recovered," Wes said.

"I wouldn't invite you over, dear, if there was a chance we were still contagious." Gloria Abbott's laughter galloped through the phone line. "We both saw the doctor the day before and he gave us a clean bill of health. So can we expect you after work?"

It was then he got an idea. Excited about Michelle and their budding relationship, Wes couldn't wait to share her with his family. He turned his chair in the direction of Michelle's desk, but she wasn't there. She usually left the newsroom no earlier than five o'clock, so he assumed she had merely taken a break. He added, "May I bring a dinner guest?"

"You know Craig is always welcome over here. You don't have to ask. He's like family," his mother said.

"I'm not talking about Craig, Mom, but a lady friend I'm sure you're going to like." Wes couldn't suppress the big grin spreading across his face.

"A lady friend? Oh my, and you want us to meet her? This must be serious. Praise the Lord!"

Wes chuckled at his mother's overenthusiasm. "Now hold up; don't go jumping the gun on anything. I don't want you scaring her away."

"Scare *her* away? Did I hear you correctly? I could've sworn *you* were the one with jackrabbit in your butt, mister, so quick to turn tail and run at the first whiff of anything that reeked of long-term."

"Ah, Mom, not you, too," Wes groaned. "Is anybody willing to cut me some slack?"

"What's her name?"

Too many people in the vicinity to say. "If I can convince her to come with me, you'll find out this evening," he replied cryptically.

"Great. Dinner starts at six-thirty p.m. and not a minute later. If you're late you get to do dish duty for punishment."

"But you have a state-of-the-art washer."

"Nothing is as efficient as a good old hand scrubbing with plenty of soap and hot water. And if you're late—"

"I know. I know. My punishment, busting suds." Wes chuckled before ending the call.

He looked at Michelle's vacant desk again.

Craig leaned against the low partition dividing their cubicles. "Hey, man, I'm pretty sure she's gone," he whispered. "Saw her pack up her things about an hour ago."

Disappointed that he'd missed her, Wes checked the wall clock, which read 4:21 p.m. Done for the day, he packed his briefcase. He'd ring Michelle on her cell phone when he made it to his car.

Eighteen

Michelle's stomach rumbled as soon as she entered her mother's kitchen. "Yum! Something smells good!"

Liz stood over a big pot on a front stove burner. "Chicken and dumplings. I haven't made them in ages, but I remember how much you loved them when you were a little girl."

Michelle dropped her briefcase, then went to wrap her mother in a hug. "For me? Thank you." She pecked Liz's cheek, damp with steam from the bubbling pot.

Michelle released her to lean against the kitchen counter. She stifled a big yawn.

"It's the least I can do after keeping you up last night. You look exhausted. How was your day?"

"I managed with a massive caffeine transfusion. Had to compile a roundup of the hottest water toys for summer." Michelle plucked an apple from the fruit bowl on the counter and took a bite. "Here's an insider tip for you: the Wham-O Big Splash Slip N' Slide."

"Summer water toys? That doesn't sound like the kind of thing you usually write about." Liz set the wooden spoon she used to stir on the stove's surface to search for the celery salt and rosemary on the revolving spice rack. She added dashes of both to the pot.

"They have me on a different beat at the *Herald.*" Michelle was too tired to go into the particulars about her banishment from the *Manhattan Business Journal* but vowed to do so eventually. After all, she'd chided Liz more than once for keeping secrets. Michelle had already shared the circumstances with Fatima and Wesley. Her mother deserved the truth as well. "How much longer before dinner is ready?" Michelle asked to determine whether she had time to phone Wesley as promised. When she'd left the newsroom that day, he'd been out on assignment, according to Craig.

"We can eat now. The salad is already prepared. It's in the fridge." Liz went to the cabinets and removed two ceramic plates and soup bowls.

"It'll just take a minute for me to freshen up; then I can help you set the table." Michelle left the apple on the table, shed her blue blazer and sensible black pumps on the way to the bathroom. As she washed her hands she noted the puffed crescents beneath her eyes, then yawned again. Her soft bed called, but skipping that bowl of her mother's mouthwatering chicken and dumplings was not an option.

When Michelle returned to the dining room table there was little for her to do but take her seat and dig in.

"I made lemonade, too." Liz placed an ice-cold pitcher of it between them, right beside a vase of spritelike sunflowers.

After grace, they savored the plump dumplings and tender chunks of chicken seasoned to perfection.

Michelle had intended to keep the dinner conversation light, but when Liz broached the counseling program Michelle was more than willing to listen. It heartened Michelle to know Liz was serious about getting to the root of her problems.

"My boss approved my request for a short leave of absence and so I reserved some time at Willow Grove." Liz took a sip of lemonade. "I start tomorrow."

"So soon? That's great. What time do you have to be there? I can drive you over if you like."

"Because you don't trust that I'll get there on my own?"

"For emotional support," Michelle stated simply.

"Really?"

"Playing guard dog is useless. A program like that can't work unless *you're* ready for it. No one can do it for you, nor can they force you. If you say you're ready, then I'm willing to give you the benefit of the doubt and take your word for it . . . until you give me a reason not to."

"Thank you," Liz said softly.

"I noticed your car in the driveway. Am I to assume you went back to the casino to retrieve it?"

"Yes. Ora Lee gave me a ride. I explained everything to her."

"I'm so proud of you, Ma." Michelle's voice caught as she reached across the table to hold her mother's hand. "I do believe you're going to be all right."

"Hey! I have an idea." Liz popped up, suddenly crackling with good-natured energy. "Let's watch today's episode of *If Tomorrow Never Comes* together, like old times."

A full belly sapped away the last of Michelle's determination to stay awake. And even the lure of discovering that latest cliffhanger involving Bliss Worthington and a certain handsome international spy was not enough to keep Michelle from crashing.

"Sorry, Ma," Michelle begged off, rising on wobbly legs. "If you can hold off until I get a nap, maybe a little later."

Michelle dragged herself to her room and plopped on the thick, heavenly pillows of her bed. She'd watch her soap and phone Wesley after a nap, she thought just before drifting off.

Wes rang Michelle's cell phone a third time before he settled in the Abbott great room.

Gloria sat on the sofa next to her son. "So sorry your friend couldn't make it."

Though disappointed he hadn't reached Michelle in time, Wes realized he had no right to be pissed off. He hadn't given her any notice and she likely had other plans. She'd already made it clear that her world hardly revolved around him. And he must admit that was one of the dozens of things he'd noticed and decided he liked about her. In the newsroom she'd always carried herself like a journalist about to break the biggest story, which required quite an adjustment, considering what she'd been reduced to covering. When he'd peeked inside a planning meeting that morning he'd heard Barb mention something about Michelle's next "Accent" lead piece on popular water and pool toys. *Snore!* Wes was pretty sure he wouldn't have handled such a drastic beat change with as much grace and class. Michelle's roll-with-the-punches attitude was downright inspiring.

"Maybe another time," Wes said. "It was presumptuous of me to tell you she was coming when I hadn't even asked her yet. But I hope you'll get to meet her soon."

Winston helped his wife off the sofa. "Son, we were just excited to hear you've met someone. She must mean a lot to you."

"Tell me about it." Gloria linked arms with her husband and looked into his eyes.

Wes loved it when his parents smiled like that and touched each other like newlyweds these days. Quite a change from all those times they'd argued and frozen each other out because of clashing opinions on how to handle Patrick. How had they finally gotten over the hump and put it all in the proper perspective? Maybe Wes could learn a thing or two from them. They obviously didn't need Wes playing mediator for them anymore, a role he'd assumed in high school when their spats over Patrick began escalating on a regular basis.

For a minute Wes couldn't help wondering if his sudden interest in having Michelle meet his folks so soon had been spurred by his habit of distracting his parents. Nah, he decided, he cared deeply for Michelle. Since he'd met her, he was experiencing feelings he'd never had before for any woman. And those feelings had absolutely nothing to do with Patrick.

His mother continued, "I can't remember the last time you brought someone here to meet us. What was her name again?"

"Michelle Michaels."

"This Michelle must be someone special."

"She is." Wes felt a goofy grin tug at his lips.

When his mother and father exchanged gleeful glances, Wes thought maybe he needed to provide some clarification before their assumptions spun out of control.

"It's not that those other ladies weren't . . . um . . . s-s-pecial, too . . . ," Wes stammered, suddenly overly preoccupied with his platinum tie clip. "In . . . um . . . different ways."

"Different, you say?" his mother echoed, slanting Wes's father a knowing look.

"Yes. Every lady I've dealt with was unique and brought something different to the table. And those differences were just what I needed at that time. And what I could provide them was what they needed at the time."

"I find it hard to believe that none of those ladies ever once *needed* a good meal," Gloria quipped dubiously, then drew her berry-painted lips tight.

"I've taken plenty of them to nice five-star restaurants, Mother," Wes countered. He only went formal and called her Mother when she tried his patience.

Gloria clarified, "I'm talking a nice *home*-cooked meal—"

"At *Mother's* place," his father added with a chuckle. "You know she's giving you a hard time, don't you? What she's razzing you about is your failure to give her adequate opportunity to take a magnifying glass to your dates and crawl all up in your business."

"Winston!" Gloria swatted at Wes's father but didn't bother to smother the guilty smile breaking across her face.

"I have no doubt that Michelle would earn your seal of approval with flying colors," Wes assured her.

They went to the formal dining room and enjoyed their meal as Winston, who'd recently made a killing on a real estate investment, moved on to discuss recent changes in the market.

Gloria had just served after-dinner drinks and desserts in the great room when the phone rang. Judging by the shadowed look on her face upon returning to the room ten minutes later, Wes suspected the caller was none other than Patrick.

Gloria took her seat again. "Pat wants to speak to you, Wes."

For privacy Wes left the great room and picked up the extension in the kitchen. He was certain Patrick wanted an update on the investigation, which he'd planned to provide once he got back to his own place. He settled on a ladderback chair in the kitchen. In a tone just above a whisper, he told Patrick that he had indeed made progress on "their project"; then he advised his brother to keep it all to himself for the time being.

Patrick, excited about the news, sounded eager to agree to just about anything. "Thanks, Bro! I knew you'd come through for me. It's just a matter of time."

"The wrong word, leaked to the wrong person, especially to a fellow inmate, could potentially blow everything. And remember, I think it's best to keep Mom and Dad out of this, too."

"I don't get it. Mom always sounds so sad when we speak. This could be just the thing to—"

"Leave Mom and Dad out of this," Wes reiterated, rubbing his temples where pressure started to mount. "That's part of the deal."

"All right . . . all right. If that's how it's gotta be."

"That's how it's gotta be." Wes thought it best to keep his parents out of the loop on this for now. He hadn't wanted to get their hopes up prematurely in case things didn't work as he and Patrick hoped. "Gotta go. I don't like talking about this here. Check ya later."

"Later, Bro. And, Wes?"

"Yeah?"

"I love you, man."

Something slammed inside Wes's chest, but he quickly and casually replied, "Love you, too," as if he were ordering takeout.

His mother returned to the kitchen with a half-eaten platter of after-dinner petit fours and Godiva chocolates.

"You're done talking to Pat?" She placed the platter on the large granite kitchen island.

"Yes."

"That was quick."

"You know those conversations are timed, and apparently there were plenty of other inmates waiting their turn."

Gloria reached for a chocolate and stuffed it inside her mouth. "It would've been so nice if Pat were here with us tonight, like old times." She sighed. "I do miss him."

"Mom?" Wes rose from the chair and went to her.

"Yes, honey?"

"You and Dad . . . I've noticed that you two seem to be in a really good place these days . . . with each other I mean, despite everything."

"You mean despite all that mess with Pat?"

Wes nodded.

"As you're well aware, it wasn't always this way. Honey, when Pat got arrested your father and I were on the verge of divorce. Papers had been filed and everything."

"What? Oh, Mom." Wes dragged a hand down his face. He knew things had been bad, but not that bad that they'd taken steps to end it all.

"But neither of us could go through with it. We still love each other desperately, and the root of our problems isn't each other really. Never was. It was always a difference of opinion involving Pat. We'd practically never argue if it weren't for Pat. That realization hit us both like a freight train. We love both of our sons and always tried to do right by you two, but we both realized that you're grown men, responsible for yourselves. You have to live your own lives. Our own happiness has to come first now."

"I'm so glad you and Dad got it together." Wes drew his mother into his arms. "And you're absolutely right to put your marriage first."

It felt as if she squeezed Wes with all she had. "Oh, honey, it's not that we don't care. My heart will always ache and break for Pat and I'll always pray that he finally comes around to do right not only by us but by himself to have the kind of life he can be proud of, that Kelly can be proud of, but until then . . . Well, we simply cannot let him drag us down and destroy us, too."

"I hear ya, Mom, I hear ya . . . b-but . . . what if Patrick really got a bad break this time?"

Gloria loosened her embrace to look him in the eye, then shook her head. She kept her arms linked around his waist. "Honey, that would be a very nice pipe dream to buy into, but fortunately for us, your father and I just aren't in the market anymore. And I hope to God you aren't, either."

"But, Mom—"

"Don't do it, Wes. Don't," the warning note firm and clear. "It'll only cause you more pain and disappointment."

His mother's uncompromising admonishment startled him, but he was in too deep to consider her words of advice. Something was about to break; he could feel it in his gut. Once Patrick was vindicated, his parents would be pleased and she'd remember this conversation; then she'd thank Wes for not giving up.

When he left the Palmer Woods house and drove back to his own place, he found it difficult to settle down for the night. He had too much energy. The clock on the wall read 9:46 p.m. The perfect time to head down to McLemore's Bar and Grill again. He'd already been there twice since Toni mentioned the place, but his visits had been unfruitful. No sign of Titus Montesi or any of the others in his little clique of hustlers. But Wes knew Toni hadn't steered him wrong. A pretty young waitress who worked there told him that Titus did indeed frequent the place and always ordered the same thing—a Mega Burger with everything, a side order of fries, and in lieu of ketchup, a small bowl of sour cream for dipping. Titus and his friends would spend hours at the place talking trash between dart games. Titus was proud of his dart-throwing skills. The waitress pointed out a chalkboard with a list of the bar's dart game champs. Titus's name was scribbled at the top of the list of twenty in red block letters.

As Wesley changed out of his suit and into a pair of jeans, a short-sleeve pullover, sneakers, and a baseball hat, he got an idea.

Inside McLemore's the jukebox played old Motown classics and thick cigarette smoke crept from the designated smoking section to fill the entire space.

"I'll have a Heineken," Wes told the bartender after claiming a stool on the far end of the bar.

While Wes waited for his drink he surveyed the place, which had four pool tables on one end and an area where a boisterous crowd had gathered to watch two men engrossed in a dart-throwing match. Based on Toni's description Wes knew the shorter of the two was Titus Montesi, a spongy-haired African-American man of medium build with close-set dark eyes and a honker of a nose.

The bartender delivered Wes's cold bottle of beer. "Would you like to start a tab for the night?"

"Nah, one is my limit tonight." Wes paid for the beer;

then before the bartender could leave to tend to his other customers Wes removed additional bills. "I'd like you to do me a little favor."

Placing extra bills on the counter ensured that he maintained the man's attention.

"What's that?" the bartender asked.

"See that listing of dart player rankings over there?" Wes gestured to the large chalkboard perched on the wall bordering the bar mirror. The names of the bar's best pool players and dart throwers were listed in all their glory in bright blue chalk, but Titus's was still in red.

"Yeah, what about it?"

"I'd like you to put my name at the top of the darts champs list in red."

"Mister, I haven't seen you throw one dart. Why would I do that?"

"'Cause doing me a favor could fatten your wallet." Wes added extra bills to the ones on the counter and pointedly arranged them in a nice neat stack. "It's a temporary thing, just for tonight. Before you close you can restore the integrity of the list by erasing my name. Deal?"

The bartender eyed Wesley as if he had a screw loose, then simply shrugged and surrendered to the lure of the cash. "Sure, whatever you say. It's your money."

Wes slid the bills toward him. The bartender quickly pocketed them and kept his end of the bargain. He reached for the chalk tied to a string from the the board before he realized he didn't have enough information. "I didn't catch your name."

Because he wasn't sure how well read this Titus Montesi was, Wes couldn't take the chance on the dude recognizing his byline from the *Herald*. He'd need to use a fake name, just in case. "Joe Brown," Wes replied, thinking that was about as close as one could get to the only slightly more generic Joe Blow.

The bartender had written the first few letters when Wes interrupted to provide instructions. "Bigger, bolder block letters," he said, hoping to tweak Titus's ego. He'd heard the guy took the game and his top ranking at this bar and grill very seriously.

The bartender erased what he'd written and started again.

"Bigger," Wes said.

Clearly impatient, the bartender started again until the letters were the size of the largest line on an eye doctor's chart. *That should get ol' Titus's attention*, Wes thought with a smug smile as he gave the bartender a thumbs-up. Then Wes just settled in, finished his beer, and simply waited. Eventually, Titus ventured toward the bar for a refill as Wes assumed he would.

"Hey, Malloy, I need another Bud," Titus called out to the bartender in a voice that was surprisingly low and raspy, as if he was recovering from a bad cold or laryngitis.

While he waited for Malloy to deliver his drink, Titus removed a cigarette and disposable lighter from his pocket and lit up. He had tucked the cigarette between his thick lips when Malloy passed him a frosty mug of the draft with a thick white head.

Before Titus could turn to join his friends again he caught a glimpse of the chalkboard, then did a double take, sending his cigarette to the floor. "Hey, Malloy, when the hell did that happen?" Titus glared at the bartender fiercely.

"What you talking about?" Malloy appeared not to have a clue about what had rankled Titus.

"The freakin' board up there. Who the hell is Joe Brown and when did he become the bar's darts champ?"

Malloy tossed an uneasy glance toward Wes, then looked back at Titus. "Oh, that. He . . . um . . . beat your best game . . . last night . . . or the night before, I think it was. I'd been meaning to put it up there. Just got around to updating the board a minute ago."

"And he beat *my* game?" Titus's eyes went squinty in disbelief.

The bartender looked so anxious Wes thought he'd better speak up.

"Yeah, he did," Wes butted in quickly.

Still incredulous, Titus snapped his attention to Wes. "And you saw him? Beat my game, I mean?"

"Yes, he beat your score. I can vouch for that." Wes smiled, then extended his hand for a shake. "I'm Joe Brown."

Titus just stared at the hand for a long moment, then reluctantly wrapped his stubby fingers around it. He managed a diplomatic smile, then stooped to retrieve his cigarette from the floor. "Well, you know, I was the longtime reigning champ around here."

"So I'm told."

Titus took a deep drag on the cigarette, which seemed to have a calming effect on him. "No need for me to go ape-shit over a little competition, but I do think you owe me the opportunity to get my title—"

"And bragging rights back," Wes completed his thought. "Absolutely. You're on. When?"

"What about now?" Titus replied with a feral gleam in his close-set eyes and a challenge in his sandpaper voice.

Wes stepped down from the stool, thinking Titus would surely whip his ass at darts six ways to Sunday by night's end, but he had to believe he had just enough skill, albeit rusty skill, left over from his college days to give ol' Titus a run for his money. After all, Wes had been the dart-throwing champ for three years running at Alpha Omega Psi House. This was just the icebreaker he needed to get chatty with Titus.

"Three-O-One, Easy-In, Easy-Out?" Wes asked, thinking he could at least choose the game. In 301 all players start with 301 points. Where each dart lands on the board determines the number subtracted from the dart thrower's score at the beginning of each round. The player who reaches exactly zero first wins.

"What's your rush, my man? Here we do a version we call Nine-O-One, Easy-In, *Double*-Out," Titus countered, slapping him on the back and leading him to the tournament-quality Classic Bristle Dart board on the wall at the rear of McLemore's.

Wes agreed to 901, thinking it was going to be one long night.

Nineteen

The next morning before making his way to the news-room, Wes sat in his car in the *Herald* parking garage. He reached for his cell and dialed the phone at Michelle's desk.

"Where are you?" Michelle asked. The lilting cadence told him she was just as happy to hear his voice as he was to hear hers. But when she immediately blunted it to her business tone, he knew Janie and Harriet were in her vicinity.

"Sitting in the *Herald* garage. I know how paranoid you are about my e-mailing, speaking, looking, breathing in your direction in the newsroom." Wes took a sip from the cup of coffee he'd purchased at a convenience store on his way to work.

"Okay, okay, so I'm a tad jumpy. Shoot me." She laughed, then smothered it.

"A *tad* jumpy?" he scoffed. "Woman, you're as nervous as a tax cheat at an auditors convention."

"We had an agreement, remember?"

"I know. I know. No fooling around at work. But I'm also still trying to recover from the way you blew up my pager and cell phone yesterday," he added, heavy on the sarcasm.

"Sorry about that. I meant to keep my promise to call you. It's just that I went to lie down for a bit right after dinner with my mother. Had every intention of waking up after an hour or so. Well, I pigged out, then pretty much blacked out. The next thing I knew, the light of a brand-new day bombarded its way through my blinds. Ma didn't even bother to wake me so I could change out of my street clothes."

He lifted his briefcase from the passenger seat. "That tired, huh?"

"It's a wonder I was able to make it through dinner without falling face-first in the dumpling dish."

"You sound all rested and refreshed now."

"I feel like a new person."

Wes heard the smile in her voice. "Rested and refreshed enough to have dinner with me tonight?" He climbed out of the car with the cell phone pressed against his ear.

"Sure."

Her prompt response buoyed him. "At my place."

Silence.

"I just want to spend some time alone with you, baby, without a bunch of other people around. C'mon now," he prodded. "You can do the honors and cook for me at your mother's place."

"Ummm. I don't think that's a good idea."

"What? Your cooking?"

"I'm pretty good with Tuna Helper, but beyond that, things can get pretty dicey." Michelle spoke more openly, which led Wes to assume that her cubicle neighbors were too engrossed in their own business to pay her much attention.

"Tuna Helper it is then, as long as I get to spend some alone time with you."

"No. I can't subject you to that, not just yet." She laughed. "I'll get some takeout."

"That's cool." Wes paused. "I'll let you off the hook this time, but I'd really like you to see my place. My collections."

"Oh, brother!"

Wes pictured Michelle rolling her eyes. "What?"

"I know you don't have the nerve to try to lure women up to your lair using that ol' cheesy 'come-check-out-my-etchings' line."

Enjoying Michelle's tinkling laughter, he strode toward the garage elevators, Kenneth Cole wingtips tapping against gray concrete. "Not etchings." Wes wolfishly waggled his brows as if she could see him. "My jazz recordings and my art, Romare Bearden prints in particular. He's a visual artist, but his legendary collages have become synonymous with jazz music."

"You don't have to school me on Romare Bearden, dude."

"Meant no disrespect, of course."

Because Wes had skipped most of the early-morning building traffic, he stepped right on a waiting garage elevator and pressed the button for the twenty-fifth floor.

"Hmmmmm. I would like to see those Bearden prints of yours, though," Michelle said as if giving the invite to his loft serious thought.

Wes gave her a nudge. "So we're on tonight, then? My place?"

"You don't give up, do you?"

"Ain't no shame in my game. And I have a feeling that's what you like about me."

The elevator ascended smoothly, then dinged once it reached the newsroom floor.

"There you go again. So cocky. So smug."

"So right?"

She groaned with mock exasperation.

"Seven-thirty?"

"You promise to behave yourself?" Her voice was teasingly bouncy again.

He had her, he thought, stepping off the elevator onto the marbled hall floor just outside the newsroom.

"Do you promise to behave yourself?" she repeated.

"Only if you really want me to. Seven-thirty?"

"I can't stay late, ya know—"

"Of course, with it being a school night and all." He chuckled at their playful foolishness. "Seven-thirty?"

"Two hours tops—"

"And you're outta there, I know. Seven-thirty?"

"No cocktails, wine, beer—not even a Zima."

"Cola. Iced tea. Sunny D. Seven-thirty?"

"As long as I've made myself clear."

"Crystal. Seven-thirty?"

Long pause. Then her sigh of sweet surrender accompanied by a light chuckle. "Make it six-thirty and you've got yourself a dinner date."

"Six-thirty it is, then." Triumphant, he snapped his cell phone shut, tucked it inside a side pocket of his briefcase.

Wes strode inside the newsroom. "Good morning, Carmen. Beautiful day, isn't it?" he practically sang. "A new hairdo?"

"Yes. I thought it was time to give that dowdy ol' bun a rest." Carmen shook her head, flinging the trendier style that fell in soft layers around her round face.

When Wes gave her the thumbs-up, she primped, fluffing it with her fingers. "So you really like it?"

"Very becoming," Wes said sincerely. "Leonard is gonna have to beat the fellas off with a stick."

"A little incentive for him to finally propose, you think?"

"Hey, you know I'm rootin' for ya." Wes walked along the *Herald*'s sleek mahogany receptionist desk and lightly tapped its surface. He had to knock wood. He felt happier than he had in a long while. On top of the world, in fact. Between Michelle's entry into his life and his progress on the investigation into Judge Pratt, things couldn't be better.

Now whistling one of his favorite jazz melodies, he took a roundabout path through the newsroom's gridlike layout, chatting and spreading good cheer to everyone he encountered. He strolled by Michelle's cubicle before he reached his own.

As she would have wanted, he made a point of greeting her neighbors first. "Good morning, Harriet, Percy, Don,

Janie . . . And oh, hi, Michelle, almost didn't see you over there." The two exchanged quick knowing glances.

With the exception of Michelle, who tried to stifle a grin but failed, they all stared at Wes as if he'd lost his damn mind.

"Quick, somebody give me a gun so I can shoot Boy Wonder over there," Janie grumbled. "With the exception of Bill Gates, nobody should be so damn chipper about coming to work in the morning."

Twenty

That evening Michelle arrived at Wes's Royal Oak residence at 6:30 p.m. sharp.

Hidden speakers pumped soft jazz music through the cavernous loft, which was heavy on stainless steel, dark leathers, granite, and hard glass edges.

It echoed his urbane sense of style and looked like something out of those thick, glossy architectural magazines. She couldn't help wondering how he afforded such digs on a reporter's salary.

From their first real conversation she had suspected Wes came from money, but she wasn't so gauche as to come out and ask. Not that it mattered one way or the other. Michelle would always make sure she was in a position to take care of herself and those she loved. While a guy with bodacious moneybags would be a perk, landing such a man was never tops on her shopping list.

Gorgeous art hung from exposed brick walls and perched on decorative stands. A sparse king-size platform bed with a short, subtly bowed mahogany headboard held court on one end.

The punching bag, treadmill, three-tiered rack of dumbbells, exercise mats, and Bow Flex resistance training machine lent an edge to a neighboring corner.

The rest of the furniture was modern Italian, she guessed. A pendant lighting system gave the space a modern, minimalist feel. Ceiling-to-floor windows overlooking Royal Oak's Main Street lined one wall.

"This place is fantastic!" Michelle stepped on a silk Persian rug stretched across a portion of gleaming hardwood floor. Overhead, the high ceiling featured exposed trusses and ductwork with an overlay of the Eurostyle slick she'd first seen in the trendiest upscale living spaces. "Somebody's living awfully large. It's a damn football field."

"Not quite, but it's roughly three thousand square feet. You like?"

"So much room for one guy."

"Maybe someday I won't rattle around in here all by my lonesome." Wesley gave her what could've been interpreted as a meaningful look, but Michelle refused to read too much into it. Instead she watched as he checked out her cayenne-colored jacket ablaze with a textured jungle print. The jacket, matching skirt, and coordinating tank ensemble was just one of the more adventurous outfits she'd purchased during that recent shopping excursion with Fatima. All of those items had been selected specifically with Wes in mind.

Wes hung her jacket on a nearby coatrack. "You look . . ." He gave her a slow, appraising look—pausing where her breasts swelled at the low-scooped neck of her fitted tank top and where the skirt clung to the full curve of her bottom. "So hot." He let loose with a low growl.

"I felt kinda icky." Michelle chuckled, casually brushing by him to take in more of her surroundings. "Thought I'd go home first to freshen up a bit after a long day."

"Damn, baby, I'd say you did a lot more than freshen up." Wes reached for her hand, then curled his arms around her waist, tugging her close. "You were all buttoned up and the goodies locked down the last time I saw you."

Michelle savored the heat of his strong, sinewy physique underneath his waist-length off-white linen shirt. It was a casual, beach-style collarless number opened at the neck to reveal a generous swatch of brown skin, thick, silky chest hair, clavicles, and the hint of the muscular slabs just beneath them. Full, black, fashionably wrinkled linen bottoms and bare feet completed the look.

"I'll concede that this outfit is a little flirtier than what I'd wear to the newsroom," she said.

"A *little* flirtier?" Wes scoffed, appreciation gleaming in his dark eyes, making Michelle feel like the sexiest woman on earth. "Now why would you go to all that trouble if you wanted me to behave myself tonight?"

"You like?" Michelle asked, doing a little twirl.

"I love," he drawled.

Michelle let him hold her for a minute. When Wes went for her lips she pointedly and playfully offered him her left cheek instead.

With a lopsided grin, Wes kissed her there. "Oh, I get it. You intend to torture and tease me."

"You're a big boy; you can handle it," Michelle managed with a smile built on precarious bravado.

"Please make yourself at home." Wes gestured toward the living room area.

Michelle sat down on a sleek leather sofa, then crossed her legs at the knees. When the skirt slid up her thighs salaciously, she questioned the wisdom of her wardrobe choice—as she had at least a dozen times already during the drive over there. After she left the *Herald*, she'd been in such a hurry to shower, change, and fix her hair and makeup just so, she'd failed to take the time to see if the brief skirt passed the sofa test. Wes was most definitely checking out her long legs, along with everything else, but wasn't that the point? She decided she loved the attention.

When a series of pictures on the wall caught her eye she came to her feet again for a closer inspection.

"Ahhh, *Piano Lesson*." Michelle pointed to one of the

colorful framed pieces. "That's what this one is called, right?"

"Not only does she know her good jazz, but she knows her Romare Bearden, too. Damn." Wes placed one large hand on his chest. "Be still, my heart."

As she studied the print, Wes came up behind her, encircling her in the warmth of his arms.

"Such innovative use of color and texture," Michelle said, the awe evident in her voice.

"Just think, these are just reproductions." Wes nestled his chin in the hair she'd fashioned in a curly upsweep. "Imagine what the originals look like."

"Have you seen them?" As Michelle's wariness faded she found herself stroking his ropy forearms, coiling around her waist.

"Yeah," he said slipping into a soft voice and caressing the dip between her collarbones. "They had an exhibit at Washington, D.C.'s National Gallery of Art, which included not only his collages but paintings, drawings, and watercolors." His voice went low and his breath caressed her ear. "I lived in D.C. a few years before I moved back here."

"I would've loved to see all that." Michelle tilted her head to one side to allow him better access while he did the most delicious things to her earlobe and neck with his soft lips. Her nipples hardened, and liquid heat pulsed and pooled at all her pleasure zones. "You know," she said, her breathing suddenly quick and choppy, "I was just thinking, it's almost spooky how much we have in common."

"Spooky?" Wes's voice dropped lower. So sensitized to his touch, she felt the rumbling vibrations from his chest as he spoke. "*Spooky* has such negative connotations."

He gently suckled her earlobes, inflaming her to the core until she lost all train of thought.

"Huh?" Her lips slowly parted.

"It's going to be good between us, ya know." His thick, hot whisper was plush velvet against her ear. "The way our bodies feel together. The way we fit together. Connect. The chemistry. You feel it, don't you?" He nipped at the skin on her neck. "Tell me you feel it."

"I feel it." Michelle's skin goose-bumped. Her breasts rose and fell as her breathing grew more labored.

"When two people are meant to meet and click as we have, I'd like to think of it as . . . well . . . more like the right notes coming together to form the perfect riff."

"The perfect riff?" emerged on a breathy sigh; then she tried to laugh it off. "Like that ol' corny saying, huh? The one about making beautiful music together?"

"There's nothing corny about us, baby." When Wes drew her closer, her breath caught again.

"It's about harmony . . . the right rhythm," he continued with a deliberate and decadent grind against her rear. She swayed with him to the sultry sax solo, enjoying the feel of him, so hot and hard. That made her damp with yearning. "The time . . . and tempo . . ." He nuzzled her neck again. "The seamless duet."

She bit her lip to swallow the moan rising in her throat.

"Hmmmmmmm," he rasped languidly against her ear as tingles danced along her skin. "The right groove. The gradual, steady increase . . . mounting . . . mounting . . . just within reach, but still not close enough. Then . . ." He paused, leaving her teetering at a precipice.

Her heart hammered; her blood hummed in anticipation. "What?"

"The crescendo," he whispered thickly.

Michelle's sharp intake of breath broke through her pleasure haze. If she didn't move right then, the man was going to smooth-talk her right into an explosive orgasm—before the dinner! Gingerly she disentangled herself from him under the guise of checking out the rest of his artworks.

He appeared bereft when she skittered away, tugging at her skirt and adjusting her tank top.

"And all that . . ." Michelle felt breathlessly giddy. "All that starts with the perfect riff, huh?" She had gathered her composure again, but she felt her heart opening too much too soon to this risky man who probably trotted out lines about riffs and duets like a Social Security number. Still she couldn't deny that she was falling. Hard.

Beyond his obvious physical appeal, Wes had been nothing but kind, fun, and sexy. He was also intelligent and ambitious, but most important of all, he obviously cared about family. Just watching him with Kelly was proof of that.

Michelle walked over to the large-screen plasma television mounted on a wall. "This television is a work of art!"

"I thought monstrous televisions were strictly a man's domain—few things get better than watching the Super Bowl on a damn near life-size television screen."

"Change Super Bowl to *If Tomorrow Never Comes* and I'll agree with you."

"That's a soap opera, right?"

"Yeah. I live and breathe for that show." Michelle ran her fingertips over a black marble statue of two entwined nude bodies on the bar. It gave her naughty ideas, so she moved on to admire the Bantu mask next to it.

"I'm not a fan, but I'm pretty sure my mother is," Wes revealed. "Would you like a glass of wine?" He joined her at the bar. "Sorry. Almost forgot. No alcohol for you tonight, right? Iced tea, soda, juice?"

"I'll have just a splash of white wine to take the edge off," she said. On a lacquer pedestal, about waist high, she found a gorgeous handblown glass pitcher filled with water. "Oh, what have we here?"

"Careful, that's not for drinking," Wes warned from where he stood at a terra-cotta-colored counter.

As Michelle moved closer to the water pitcher she noticed the single blue and red fish swimming inside.

"That's Nemo. One guess who named him," Wes said wryly.

"Kelly."

"Yup."

"How precious." Michelle tapped the glass surface, then watched the fish flit to the opposite side.

"Pets just don't get more low-maintenance than that one." Wes went to Michelle carrying two wineglasses.

She accepted her drink and took a sip. "Do you see Kelly often?"

"As often as I can, what with her busy schedule and all. It's a wonder she doesn't have her own personal secretary."

"She's only five, isn't she?"

"Yeah, but when she's not at school Lonette has that child enrolled in gymnastics, jazz, tap, and ballet classes. She also meets with a regular play group and spends a lot of time at my parents' place."

"And her father is your brother, right? What's his name?"

Wes took a big drink of what looked like merlot. "Patrick." His tone and expression turned solemn.

"Who's older?"

"Patrick. Two years between us."

"You two close?"

"We used to be very close. Not so much these days." Wes paused as if unsure he wanted to wade too deep in those waters. "He's doing time in Davenport."

Michelle sensed his discomfort, then placed a comforting hand on his shoulder. "We don't have to go there if—"

"I don't want to keep anything from you." Wes went to the sofa and sat. "I want you to know me, and that includes knowing my family."

"Really? You're serious?" Michelle couldn't keep the skepticism out of her voice, but she went to him and sat, too.

He placed both of their wineglasses on the coffee table. Then resting one arm along the back of the couch, he angled his long body toward hers and used one hand to play with a lock of her hair. "Yes. In fact, I tried to hook up with you the night before so I could invite you to dinner at my parents' place. I told Mom and Dad all about you. They were disappointed that I couldn't reach you."

"They were?" Michelle asked, still stunned. Would a man poised for something short and sweet talk to his parents about her? Would he be eager for her to meet them?

"Yeah, they were." Wes's fingers dropped from her hair to stroke her cheek. "You have *the* most beautiful, catlike eyes. Startling hazel, or is it stunning amber, with a perfect hint of green and little flecks of gold that only show in certain light."

Awwwwwwwwwww. Michelle had never had a man take such detailed note of her irises before. She felt her resistance crumbling just a bit more as she inched to snuggle closer.

Then she gave herself a mental shake. *Not so fast!* The beautiful-eyes comment and his other effusive compliments were pretty standard for men trotting out their pickup lines. It also wasn't out of the realm of possibility that the "come-meet-my-folks" thing was merely a maneuver straight out of the ol' Wesley Abbott Player's Handbook. She imagined a leather tome, thick enough to rival the Oakland County telephone directory.

Because Michelle was still feeling Wes out, she couldn't be absolutely, positively sure he wasn't just working another Lothario angle. After all, she'd been in the newsroom the day before and spent most of the time at her desk. He'd had plenty of opportunity to mention dinner at his parents' place long before she left that day.

"Maybe another time," she said cheerily, satisfied that she managed to stay grounded in the reality of her situation.

"Absolutely. Next time I'll be sure to give you plenty of notice."

"Yeah, sure. Next time," she replied, still dubious.

"How does one day next week sound, then?"

"Huh?" *That* brought her up short.

"Whatever works for you. Just give me a couple of dates so I can coordinate with Mom."

So he was serious enough to try pinning her down for a day and time? Stumped for a reply, Michelle sputtered, "Um . . . well . . . sure." Maybe she had been too hard on him.

"Just let me know when. Now let's seal the deal." Wes leaned closer; his hand found its way to her nape; then he captured her lips and slipped his hot, sweet tongue inside to make magic. The indulgent kiss made her woozy with longing, but that wasn't where his talent ended. Just when she thought the kiss couldn't get any better, he angled her head just right so he could deepen the kiss and spend the next half hour tonguing her with bone-melting proficiency. She wrapped her arms around him, prepared to surrender and let him do whatever he wanted with her. Once reclined on the sofa with his beautiful strong body on top, she wriggled beneath him, enjoying the way his hardness pressed against her sweet spot. Her fingers roamed from the flare of wide defined shoulders and brawny back down to his tight, muscled bottom. There she grabbed a handful and squeezed him closer as they rocked together in that seamless duet he'd spoken of earlier.

And it was then that her blasted stomach decided it was the perfect time to roar like a belligerent beastie in a horror flick.

Michelle tried ignoring it, moving her lips over Wes's when the roar ripped again—only louder. The flush of embarrassment trumped the heat of passion.

Wes's lips went still, then he broke the connection, but he kept his face within kissing distance from hers. "Sorry." His eyes smiled as one hand reached up to caress her cheek. "I haven't been a very good host, have I? I invited you over for dinner and haven't fed you yet."

"I'm fine!" Michelle panted. On the verge of desperation, she clung to him like industrial-strength Velcro, but the double-crossing beastie persisted in rumbling its dissent. *Damn!* Her stomach wasn't going to quit until it was satiated.

Wes peeled himself off of her, then came to his feet, leaving her feeling more than a little frustrated. Her hunger for him overrode her hunger for food, but she kept that to herself. Instead, she chose to sit upright again, adjusting her disheveled clothing and hair.

"Come. Soup's on." Wes extended his hand to help Michelle to her feet.

At the dining table, Wes filled Michelle's plate with a Greek pasta dish. He served more wine along with hunks of crusty bread slathered with sweet, creamy butter.

"You cooked this?" Michelle twirled hot linguine around her fork.

"Yes, but it looks more impressive than it actually is. I can make two dishes. This and a mean eggplant casserole thingy. I don't pretend to be a gourmet cook."

"But this is delicious."

"Takes about fifteen minutes start to finish. Boil some pasta; sauté shrimp with a little butter, tomato, garlic, cilantro. Pour over the pasta. Sprinkle on the fresh feta, Parmigiano Reggiano. Voilà!"

Michelle kissed her fingertips. "My compliments to the chef."

"Why, thank you." Wes grinned.

"There's no way I can possibly repay you with Tuna Helper now. When I invite you to my place for dinner I'll definitely have to order out."

"Or let your mother do the honors. Most moms are great cooks."

A shadow fell over Michelle's features.

"Is everything all right?"

Michelle averted her gaze. "It will be."

"Meaning?"

She paused. "Things haven't been going so well for Ma lately."

"Her health?"

Michelle sipped her wine. "Let's just say she'd taken to stalking Lady Luck."

Wes was initially confused but quickly got a clue. "Ah, at the casinos downtown or horse races in Northville?"

"The casinos, but it's not really the gambling in itself. Something else is going on with her. I just know it. She's been suffering from insomnia for months, but she's enrolled in a counseling program right now, working on her second day."

"She enrolled herself." Wes took a pensive moment. "That's a great sign. At least she's trying to take responsibility."

"True, but if I hadn't stayed away for so long without visiting, maybe I could've gotten a clue that something was off much sooner." A frown line settled between Michelle's delicate brows.

"Maybe. Maybe not."

"I was always so wrapped up in my career and my profiles of America's most prominent movers and shakers," she added facetiously.

"Don't beat yourself up. There's really no guarantee that you would've discovered she had a problem any sooner had you been here. Lots of people are good at keeping things like that hidden from those closest to them, people living in the same house—spouses who share the same bed, even. But I know all about the worry that can take root when dealing with a loved one who just can't seem to get it together."

"Patrick?"

"Yes."

As they ate their meal Wes confided in her about Patrick—from his juvenile delinquency days to the circumstances with Plexis, which led to his recent incarceration.

Though Wes was skittish about word leaking to the wrong people, he knew he could trust Michelle, so he didn't leave out the part about his investigation of Judge J. Ashton Pratt.

"So you think Patrick's innocent?" Michelle placed her napkin on the table after finishing her last bite of the entrée. "And getting the goods on this judge is one way to get a speedier new trial."

"I didn't think he was innocent at first, but now, well, I'm not so sure." Wes walked across the floor to the stereo system to change CDs, then gestured for Michelle to take a seat on the sofa.

"I can't imagine how awful that must be, to go to prison for something you didn't do. What about an appeal, you know, the usual way?"

"Could take forever," Wes replied.

"So how's the investigation going?"

"Well, I can't give it my full attention because I have assignments for the *Herald*, but I'm making decent progress under the circumstances."

Michelle's hazel eyes sparkled with intense interest. "Care to share details? This is just the sort of thing that gets my journalistic juices flowing. With what I have to cover on my 'Accent' beat, I need to live vicariously through your stories."

Wes had never tipped his hand to another reporter on a big investigation before, but Michelle wasn't just any other reporter. He paused only for a minute to swear her to secrecy before he plunged ahead, giving her the complete rundown on what he'd learned so far and where he was stalled.

"So I gather this Titus person hasn't confirmed what you suspect about Pratt and how their littie hustle works—as in when and how the deals go down and how money is exchanged, et cetera?"

"Not yet, but I figured he wouldn't, not this soon," Wes said. "And I don't exactly have the type of assets that might help speed the loosening of his lips."

"As in . . . ?" Michelle prompted.

"I'm not exactly his type," Wes deadpanned.

Michelle nodded. "Ahhh, I get it. If you were a woman the ol' feminine touch might go a long, long way. I will be the first to admit that with certain male sources or moles a little flirting can get you gold." Michelle was lost in thought. She paused for a moment, with her full lips pursed, then suddenly snapped erect. "Okay, I'll do it!"

Confused, Wes furrowed his brow. "Do what?"

"I'll work Titus for you, of course," Michelle replied with a smile, practically rubbing her palms together with glee. "Should be exciting!"

Wes shook his head. "Ooooh, no, wait a minute, here. Not so fast. I wasn't trying to recruit you to do my work for me."

"I know you weren't. I want to help you, your brother, Kelly. Besides, this is the kind of thing that's right up my alley, getting tight-lipped males to spill the beans. Because everyone is always so eager to open up to nonthreatening lifestyle reporters who specialize in . . . and I'm quoting Barb here, 'feel-good, uplifting stories,' I feel as if I'm getting rusty on Katie's beat. I'd like to exercise my craftier interrogation muscles."

"No, Chelle." Wes set his jaw firmly, waving the CD in his hand.

"You used this one on me once and it worked: pretty, pretty please with cream, sugar, and a big fat cherry on top," Michelle pleaded, batting her long eyelashes and arranging herself on the sofa in such a way that her skirt slid an extra inch up her curvaceous thighs, just enough to make Wes's tongue stick to the roof of his mouth. He'd turned his back to her to sort through his CD collection when he heard her high heels clicking across the hardwood floor. She wrapped her arms around his waist and he felt the firm fullness of her breasts against his back. "I promise you won't be sorry. I'm good, damn good, with those press-shy CEO types. You even said so yourself. I have a feeling this Titus character will be a piece of cake. Let me have a bite of him. Please."

"No, Michelle." Wes pivoted within the loop for her embrace. "I just don't think it's a good idea for you to get involved."

She dropped her arms from his waist and crossed them over her breasts. "But why? You had no problem recruiting that Toni chick to help you out."

"That's different."

"How?" Michelle poked out her bottom lip.

"Well, um, Toni's always been a courthouse source and all I really needed her to do was keep her ears open and ask a few questions. This Titus character is still a big question mark. He's obviously involved with some shady dealings and I don't know what kind of unsavory characters he might be connected to. . . ." He shook his head. "It's just too risky."

"But not too risky for you? Look, Wes, I'm a big girl. I can handle this guy. I know it. Where did you say he hung out? At McLemore's, right? You can go with me to keep an eye on things. But of course, we'll pretend we don't know each other once we get inside."

"Chelle, no." Wes slammed his jaws shut and gritted his teeth.

Michelle's expression reflected a mix of determination and aggravation. It was a standoff.

Michelle then decided to use another angle. "Wait a minute." She softened her tone as if seeing Wes in a different light. "What's this *really* about?" Her hazel eyes narrowed in suspicion.

"I told you what it was about." He paced the floor. "It's about not putting you in harm's way. I'm still feeling out Titus myself. He seems fairly harmless, but I don't really know what this character is capable of."

"And this has nothing to do with my being a reporter, a

potential rival, competition for you?" Michelle studied his reaction intently.

"Of course not!" Wes snapped, clearly offended. "If I had any concerns about you trying to scoop me, why on earth would I have just spilled my guts to you about what I was doing and where I am with it? Does that make any sense?"

He stopped moving and watched Michelle bunch her lips in quiet speculation for a minute.

Michelle considered that logic. "Sorry. You're right. I am touched that you believe you could trust me with something so important, I really am, but—"

"But what?"

"There isn't just a touch of ego thing going on, huh?"

"Ego thing?"

"Let's not be coy. When it comes to our work we both have pretty much admitted we have humongous, man-eating egos. If you're thinking I'm going to expect double billing for any help I give you on this, relax. Don't worry. I wouldn't require a double byline or any public recognition for my time and input. Period. Promise."

Wes was losing his patience because Michelle still didn't get or believe his concern for her safety. He managed to keep an even tone. "Look, Michelle, sweetheart . . ." He ran his long fingers through his waves and drew in a deep breath. "Yeah, guilty as charged. We both have page-one-above-the-fold-*itus* in the worst kind of way, but I assure you my reluctance to bring you in is not about that."

"Will you at least think about reconsidering taking me up on my offer?" Michelle reached for his hand and stroked it.

"You never give up, do you?" Wes sighed, finally releasing a small smile, as he placed his palms on each side of her face and caressed her smooth cheeks with his thumbs.

She looked up at him through sexy half-mast eyes. "Neither do you, remember? That's why we're so good at what we do," she cooed.

"Okay, Michelle. I promise I'll *think* about your offer. If . . . it's a big *if* here . . . *if* I decide it's a go I'll have to make sure it's done in such a way that neither Titus nor any people connected to him can find out who you really are or track you down later. But I need to think on this some more. Deal?"

"Deal." Michelle eased up on her high heels and latched on to his lips for a kiss of gratitude that ended way too soon when she practically performed a little jig back toward the sofa, where she sat. "This is going to be so much fun! You and I working together!"

Wes regretted that he'd cracked under Michelle's seductive doggedness. The woman was like a swarm of ravenous locusts on corn when a story got her attention. But it was that very approach he'd admired in the exposés and profiles she'd written for the *Manhattan Business Journal.*

She was still blowing him kisses from the sofa and promising that he wouldn't regret recruiting her when the phone on the kitchen counter rang. The answering machine would pick it up, so he didn't budge from his spot in front of the stereo.

"You can get that if you like," Michelle said brightly. "It might be a source about the Pratt story."

"You have my complete undivided attention tonight, lady."

Then, much to Wes's dismay he heard his own voice, the prerecorded outgoing message, booming from the answering machine. It would look as if he had something to hide if he bolted for the damn thing now. He moved in that direction to lower the volume. He felt Michelle watching him, so he kept his gait cool and casual but hoped like hell it was his mother or father, Patrick, Kelly, or even a telemarketer calling. No such luck. A feathery female voice followed his:

"Weeees-leeeeey. It's Alana. United just changed my flight schedule and route again. You know what that means." Amorous chuckle. "I'll have a lot more layovers in Detroit for the time being. Was hoping we could hook up tonight. You haul that gorgeous ass of yours to the Airport Westin— Room Seven-twenty-three. I'll supply the Vanilla Crème Massage Oil and the—"

Wes jabbed at the VOLUME button, cutting the sound, then turned slowly to face Michelle. "An old friend," he explained with a sheepish grin.

"Sounds like a bedroom buddy." Michelle's expression and tone gave away none of what she might be feeling.

"*Former* bedroom buddy," he clarified.

Of all the nights for Alana to ring Wes for a reunion. Between this and that encounter with Brynn in the restaurant the other night, Wes could just imagine what Michelle was thinking. And it bothered him.

Michelle checked her watch and came to her feet. She stretched luxuriously, then said good-naturedly, "Well, I hate to eat and run, but I also don't want to wear out my welcome and—"

"That's been over for almost a year," Wes blurted, cutting her off.

"Excuse me?"

"That's over with Alana. I'm not interested in getting together with her tonight or any other night."

Michelle shrugged but wouldn't look at him. "Did I say you were?"

"Just thought I'd make myself clear. I'm interested in you and only you—"

"For now," Michelle added with an expression that was still unreadable. "Anyway, I really do have to go."

Frustration drop-kicked Wes in the gut. He didn't want her to leave, but he couldn't exactly duct tape her to his sofa. "I know." He sighed wearily. "You agreed to two hours and I promised not to give you a hard time about your terms." But he couldn't help pouting a bit.

Michelle gave him a consoling hug. "I've already stayed an hour and a half longer than I planned," she pointed out, as if to prove she wasn't completely inflexible. "We both have work tomorrow, remember?"

"Right." Wes went to retrieve her jacket from the coatrack and helped her put it on. He slipped a pair of soft leather huaraches on his bare feet to escort her to her car, parked near a meter out front.

Enveloped by the night's warm spring air, they kissed good night after he opened the driver's side door for her. Before things could get as steamy as they had earlier on his sofa, she gently tugged away. "I had a lovely evening, Wesley Abbott. I just want to say you're making good on your promise to show me a wonderful time while I'm in town. Thanks for inviting me over. We'll have to do it again soon."

Soon? Just the opening Wes needed. "Tomorrow?" He knew he was pushing it, but he couldn't help himself. He'd never been one to half-step when it came to going after what he wanted.

"Maybe." Her lips curled into a sincere smile that made him believe she wasn't holding that call from Alana against him after all.

"Your place? Tuna Helper?"

"My place. Takeout," Michelle countered, placing a sweet kiss on his cheek. She slipped inside the Taurus and started the engine.

Wes waited until she drove off to pump one fist in the air. *Yes!* Then he happily took the stairway back to his loft—two steps at a time.

Twenty-one

M ichelle awakened to the light and the ringing phone on the nightstand. Liz checking in from Willow Grove.

In sponge curlers, cotton pajama bottoms, and a tank top, Michelle sat upright, then dragged out of bed with the cordless phone to her ear. Her mother filled her in on program particulars and shared her daily schedule of activities.

In the sunny kitchen, Michelle removed a carton of Tropicana orange juice from the fridge, filled a tall glass, then took a seat at the homey white kitchen table.

"Ma, Ed called last night," Michelle said. "I didn't know how much you wanted him to know."

"Don't tell him about Willow Grove, honey, please!" Liz's voice strained with desperation.

"But, Ma, I thought you two were close. And I know he adores you. Don't you think he has the right to know? You have me, Fatima, and your girlfriends, of course, but don't you think he'd want to be here to support you, too?"

"I know he'd want to be here. But I don't want him messing up his runs and taking time off to hold my hand right now. Besides, visitation here is limited. What would he do with the rest of his time? I think it's best for me to get through these first two weeks without bothering Ed or making him feel as if he has to come in off the road. Promise me you won't say anything to him. Please, baby."

"Ma—"

"I think this way is best. I'll call Ed on his cell phone later. Promise me you won't say anything about my being in Willow Grove."

Reluctantly Michelle agreed, and Liz calmed again.

"I've met some people here in the various programs who are far worse off than I am," Liz said, her voice incredulous. "There are people who lost their jobs, their spouses, their homes. . . . One woman's addiction had such a grip on her she not only stayed in the casinos night and day, but she took to wearing Depends, can you believe that?" Before Michelle could respond, Liz continued, "Ya know, those adult diapers—"

"I know what they are. Please spare me the details," Michelle cut her off. She disapproved of the gossipy delight she thought she detected in her mother's voice. She decided or at least hoped she'd heard wrong.

"Anyway, so she'd taken to wearing those Depends things so she could hoard the same slot machine without bothering with the inconvenience of walking away from it to use the restroom. Hmmmp. Ain't that something?"

Michelle couldn't remember the last time she'd heard anything so shockingly pathetic. She didn't want to dwell on those kinds of stories. "Well, the upside is, this woman and *you* are getting the help you *both* so desperately need right now," she said with a mild rebuke in her voice. Liz might not have been pushed to the same brink of madness, but she was hardly in a position to judge anyone.

"Yes, you're right." Liz sounded contrite. "I didn't mean to . . . Well, you know."

Michelle opted to change the subject. "Have the coordinators told you when I can come visit?" She missed her mother already.

"Yes. The day after tomorrow. It's a workday for you, but do you think you can arrange it? I'd like us to have a long lunch and a talk together before we go see the counselor."

"Sure, Ma. No problem." Michelle tasted her juice. "I look forward to spending some time with you."

"And I look forward to seeing you, too. Well, gotta go. Breakfast in the cafeteria is over in fifteen minutes. Love you, sweetie."

"Love you, too, Ma," Michelle said before ending the call. She moved from the table to get her day started. She brushed her teeth, showered, and dressed for work. Before leaving the house she tidied up the living room and kitchen to prepare for her evening with Wesley.

Last night, she hadn't wanted to leave Wesley's place so soon and had seriously entertained picking up where they'd left off on the sofa when her growling stomach interrupted. But that phone call from Wesley's "friend" had made her reconsider.

Michelle hadn't relished listening to that *hussy*. Michelle sheathed her claws. Correction. It hadn't been easy listening to that *woman* purr about slicking up Wes's hot bod with sweet oils. In fact, it disturbed Michelle more than she'd let on. But she certainly was in no position to play the jealous girlfriend. It wasn't that kind of party. Last night she reminded herself what she was getting into with Wesley and managed to maintain her cool *again*. It was all about a good time. And wasn't she having a good time? Sure, sex could be a part of that good time, but she still feared what connecting with him in such an intimate way would do to her level head. She was still proceeding with caution. The many close calls with Wesley's former playmates had made it impossible for her to proceed in ignorant bliss.

As romantic, tender, and respectful as Wesley had been with her, Michelle was still starting to feel like a customer at a crowded deli counter, who'd taken a number and was waiting her turn to get served. Who knew when or where one of those other women would pop up next? Which was part of the reason Michelle had agreed to play hostess that night.

Her mother's house felt like a pretty safe location. There would be none of *those* kinds of intrusions that night.

But more disconcerting than feeling as if the competition was constantly breathing down her neck, her emotions regarding Wesley had deepened beyond her initial intention. She had real, honest-to-goodness feelings for this man, and it was all she could do to squash her foolish fantasies of fat babies, backyard barbecues, and happily-ever-afters with him. Despite the distractions, somehow the way he had looked at her, held her, and spoken her name made her think maybe, just maybe, those things *could* be possible with him. But once again, she shook off those foolish thoughts, banking on her ability to purge the man from her system once she returned to Manhattan.

Michelle arrived at the *Herald* just before noon and found four massive bouquets of the most gorgeous flowers she'd ever seen on her desk. Janie, Harriet, and two other female *Herald* staffers circled her desk like schoolgirls playing ring-around-the-rosy.

"Good morning," Michelle greeted them, then watched two of the women scatter.

"Oh, hi, Michelle! Well, I'd better get back to work!" The petite brunette copy clerk startled.

The mousy administrative assistant for the editorial board added, "Me, too!"

They bolted, leaving Janie and Harriet to explain.

"We were just admiring your beautiful flowers," Harriet announced, voice all jingly. "Somebody's been a good girl."

"Or bad one," Janie quipped, winking at a blushing Michelle.

Michelle wasn't comfortable with all this attention. "Excuse me, ladies." She maneuvered around them and took her seat. There was no room on her desk, so she set her briefcase by the wheels on her chair. Bouquets swelled from four glass vases. Brilliant red roses in one. Striking yellow tulips in another. Classic white orchids. And pretty pink peonies.

Harriet and Janie took their seats when Barbara, their supervisor, breezed by on her way to a senior editors planning meeting.

"Michelle, I'll need a sidebar and breakout box for your lead on summer camps," Barbara said. "Very niiiiiccce," she added, taking note of Michelle's flowers as she departed.

Michelle sniffed the velvety red roses. When she glanced at Wesley's cubicle, she caught his guilty grin before his face went impassive.

Too late, buddy! Busted. Michelle sucked her teeth. She couldn't stare at Wes for long or Harriet and Janie would get suspicious.

"So who are they from?" Janie blurted, blue eyes shining with curiosity. "A secret admirer? Or a boyfriend in New York you had to leave behind and didn't tell us about?"

Michelle just smiled and deflected Janie's questions politely. "Can't a girl have some secrets?"

This was just the sort of personal grilling Michelle had hoped to avoid during her stint here.

"Is it your birthday or something?" Harriet wanted to know.

"No," Michelle replied, just before she felt Wesley's sudden presence at her immediate right.

"Aren't you going to read the cards that came with the flowers?" Janie was relentless. "Aren't Michelle's flowers lovely, Wesley?"

"Quite lovely." Wes's brandy-brown eyes gleamed with devilment. "You could practically open a florist shop over here, Michelle."

"Somebody did something right," Harriet gushed, like the romantic she obviously was.

"You don't say," Wes replied.

"Make that *she* won't say." Janie nodded toward Michelle. "As in Michelle won't tell us anything about the sender. Her lips are sealed."

Wes chuckled. "Michelle, I was wondering if I could borrow Katie's *Farmer's Almanac*. I need to check something."

"What? *The Farmer's Almanac*? You got crops that need rotating or something?" Michelle slanted Wes a bothered look. She knew good and damn well he didn't need that almanac. He just came over to watch her squirm under Harriet and Janie's relentless interrogation.

"Katie keeps one over here." A sly smile settled on Wes's face. "Never mind; I've borrowed it before. I know exactly where Katie keeps it." Wes hitched the front of his pleated black suit trousers, then lowered himself to a squatting position near the bottom right desk drawer, practically out of Janie's and Harriet's sight due to the gray partition dividing the cubicles.

"So you're not going to tell us, then?" Janie tried again.

"Afraid not," Michelle replied with a coy smile for Harriet and Janie.

Wes had positioned himself in the perfect location to reach out and pinch Michelle's rear end undetected. And that's exactly what the prankster did.

Michelle whooped, then gasped but managed to play it off like a hiccup. She slapped his hand away inconspicuously.

"Here, I found it!" Wes announced as if he'd stumbled on gold. He stood to his full height with the almanac in his hand. "Well, better get back to work. Good day, ladies," he said smoothly before strolling back to his desk.

Janie and Harriet eventually realized Michelle would not reveal the sender's identity, so they got busy with their work.

When Michelle was sure no one was looking, she peeked over at Wesley's cubicle again until she caught his eye. He winked. She poked out her tongue at him.

Wes laughed heartily, pivoting his chair to face his computer monitor again. Michelle removed papers from her briefcase, then began typing story research notes on hers.

Despite that intense tag-team cross-examination from her co-workers, Michelle did adore the flowers Wes sent. A genuine smile found its way to her face as a fragrant floral scent enveloped her workspace. He'd pulled out all the stops. Still, he was gonna get it for having way too much fun teasing her. And she had all day to plan sweet revenge.

Michelle finished that day's assignment and left the newsroom an hour and a half earlier than usual. On the way back to the house, she picked up the steak fajitas with all the fixings that she'd ordered from a favorite Mexican restaurant for her dinner with Wesley that evening.

She pulled the Taurus beside her mother's Civic in the driveway, then climbed out.

Shirley Whitmeyer, from next door, was hauling trash to the curb for tomorrow morning's garbage pickup.

Michelle waved. "Hey, Shirley!"

Shirley, a big-boned woman with a wide, genial smile, had an extreme fondness for red sweat suits. She must've owned closets full of 'em, because Michelle couldn't recall ever seeing her wear anything else. "Hey, Chelle!" she shouted from the curb where she arranged the large mound of castoffs around the yellow and green paper recycling bin. "How long has it been since I've seen you last?"

"I came home for Christmas." Michelle moved near the small rock garden that separated the two properties. She carried her briefcase like a tray, balancing her hot bags of food on it. She'd have to make a second trip to the car to retrieve her flowers. She'd left two bouquets on her desk but brought two of them home to enjoy.

"You should come home more often, young lady," Shirley chided her. "We all miss you around here."

"I'm staying for several weeks this time, so you should get your fill of me."

"Where's Liz? I haven't seen her but once since she got back from Atlanta, and her car hasn't budged for days."

Just how Shirley knew the Civic hadn't moved for days was beyond Michelle. She chalked it up to that sixth sense that only the nosiest of neighbors had.

"She had to leave again to take care of business for a few days," Michelle replied vaguely, then quickly steered the conversation to the cart Shirley dragged. "Hey, what's all that you've got there?"

"Some of the junk I cleaned out of my basement." Shirley tapped a large oil painting of a silver unicorn with a sky blue horn and big pink eyes. The light colors didn't work on a black velvet background. And the gaudy gold frame didn't help. "My niece Rowena painted this when she was in high school and fancied herself an artist. Make that *artiste*." Shirley lifted her chin snootily, then broke out in laughter. "Thank God that was just a phase and that child went into real estate instead."

"You're throwing it out?"

"Why not? Look at it." Shirley crinkled her nose. "Besides, Rowena and Rowena's mother threw out their originals a long time ago. Ol' Shirley's been such a pack rat. Seems I'll never get around to having that garage sale I keep talking about. What do you think? Of the art, I mean?"

"Well, it's . . . it's . . . um, interesting," Michelle hedged instead of being crass and calling it what it was: butt freakin' ugly. She noted the disparity between it and what she'd just seen hanging in Wesley's personal collection last night. It was then that she got an idea. "Shirley, would you mind if I take it?" Michelle asked with a smile tilting her lips.

"Shoot, no, chile." Shirley flapped a hand at her. "One less thing for the trash collectors to haul away."

Twenty-two

O nce inside the house Michelle changed into floral cropped pants, a matching top, and comfy low-heeled sandals.

Wes had phoned from his car to let her know he was about five minutes from the house.

She set the dining room table with the peonies from Wes, candles, and enough food for several people.

Right after he stepped inside the house, Wes gathered her up for a dizzying kiss. "I've missed you."

"We practically see each other all day," she said, loving the way he always made her feel so irresistible.

He touched his nose to hers. "I think that makes things harder. Seeing you and not being able to hold you, touch you."

"Oh, today you touched all right." Michelle wriggled out of his embrace so she could playfully punch his arm for pinching her bottom at the office.

"Caught you off-guard, didn't I?" Wes laughed, loosening the knot of his red silk tie and shrugging out of the dark suit jacket he'd worn to work that day. He regarded her with sensual intensity, boldly allowing his gaze to roam over her body as he unbuttoned the French cuffs of his crisp white shirt and rolled its sleeves up past his forearms as if preparing to go to work.

He captured her in his well-built arms again. "I couldn't resist. I was down there and it was looking so good, so lush, so . . ." His words dropped off with a lustful hiss against her ear that lit erotic sparks inside of Michelle, causing her to shiver with bone-deep delight. Everything about the man was just so over-the-top sexy as far as she was concerned.

"So you just had to steal a grope? Remember, I told you no monkey business at work." Michelle tried to be serious but found his lighthearted yet sensual mood contagious. "Somebody could've seen you. If we're going to pull this off—keeping our after-hours relationship a secret—we must behave like professionals at work."

"I hear you." Then Wes slipped his warm, delicious tongue inside her mouth and skillfully stroked hers, making her question whether he was really paying attention to anything but pleasuring her. But she refused to be a spoilsport about it. Besides, she had her own trick up her sleeve.

When he finally released her again she was punch-drunk with desire and barely standing on wet noodle–like legs. She'd practically stumbled all the way to the entryway closet to hang up his suit jacket. "I hope you're hungry," she managed, grasping for her composure and balance again. "I have a ton of food."

"Tuna Helper?"

"No, fabulous Mexican takeout."

Michelle took his hand and led him to their dining room spread: generous portions of steak and chicken fajitas, grilled onions, peppers, salsa, guacamole, rice, beans, and nachos.

"Damn, baby! When is the rest of the party arriving?" Wes lifted a nacho chip, dipped it in the guacamole, and popped it inside his mouth.

"I also whipped up pitchers of sangria and margaritas. Your choice."

"Everything looks delicious. You went all out."

"No, you went all out with those flowers you sent me. I loved them. Thank you."

"I know I probably should've had them sent here or brought

them with me tonight, but I didn't want to wait. This morning I felt like a kid on Christmas Eve, waiting for you to get to work to see them. I saw Janie and the others checking them out. But I was careful. I instructed the florist not to put my name anywhere on the cards. The only way they'd learn I sent the flowers was if I told them. And I know you weren't going to."

"You probably think I'm militantly uptight about all of this, but if you only knew what I went through back at the *Business Journal*," she said with downcast eyes.

"Hey." Wes's voice was low and tender. He reached out to her, tipping her chin up so he could look into her eyes. "I'm cool. I was just teasing. I don't want to make this difficult for you."

"I know. I just don't want my hang-ups to—"

Wes placed a finger to her lips. "We're here to have a good time, right?" He maneuvered her into his arms again and kissed her forehead. "Now let's eat."

"You're right," Michelle agreed, thinking Wes always had a way of making her heart dance. "But wait, I have to show you the surprise I have for you first."

His eyes lit up. "A surprise for me?"

"Yes! I'll be right back!"

Michelle went to her bedroom and returned with the unicorn painting and presented it to him. "Ta-dah!"

Wes's eyes bugged out of their sockets just before he tried masking his astonishment—no, more like mortification. "*That's* my surprise?" His voice caught between skepticism and curiosity.

"Yup. Painted it myself." Michelle beamed with false pride. "This is the oil painting of my heart. I treasure this, but now I want you to have to it."

"Oh, Chelle, I'm touched . . . that . . . that . . . you . . . ," he sputtered. "That you'd part with it. I'm . . . um . . . not sure what to say. . . ."

"When I visited your loft last night I noticed how much

you really love art. I'm sure you'll find a good spot for it. I was thinking that space between one of the Romare Beardens and the Synthia Saint James." She lifted his hands and molded his long fingers along the frame to keep it from falling to the floor. "What do you think?"

"Uh . . ." For once Wes was at a loss for words, and Michelle was loving it.

She had to summon every bit of her resolve to keep a straight face. "So? Think you can find a good place for it?"

Long pause.

Wes's petrified expression was nearly Michelle's undoing.

"So what do you think? Got a good place for it?" she prodded again, straight-faced.

"I'm *sure* I do, sweetheart," he finally assured her, hugging her close.

"When I say a place for it, I mean a nice, *prominent* display," Michelle clarified.

"Of course, you can help me pick out the spot and I'll put it there. Because it's a handmade gift from you, I'll cherish it always."

Michelle studied him. "You really mean that, don't you?"

"Yes." Sincerity reflected in his eyes, and that touched her deeply.

She hadn't expected that.

What started off as a corny practical joke had a punch line that invoked an epiphany. *She loved this man.*

Michelle removed her hands from the painting and let it crash to the hardwood floor.

"Careful, you might damage it." He retrieved the canvas, but Michelle tugged it from his hands and propped it on the sofa.

Feeling sexy, predatory, and for once sure, she turned to face him. "Forget the painting for now," she said, letting her hot gaze sweep over him. Wes, obviously befuddled by her abrupt mood shift, just stood there.

She went to him.

With her palm against his cheek, Michelle gazed deep into his eyes and whispered, "I want you. Now."

"I want you, too. Have for a long time. Since *before* we met . . . if that makes any sense, I have wanted you."

"You have?"

"I've known something was missing for a while now. It was you," Wes revealed with stirring intensity before plunging his tongue inside her mouth again. With his fingers buried in her hair, he angled her head to deepen the kiss that left her disoriented once again from the pure pleasure of it. Michelle didn't know how long they'd stood there, entangled, feasting on each other's lips, before she paused long enough to point in the direction of her bedroom. She slipped her hand in his to lead him inside.

"Wow, I feel as if I'm taking a trip to the Motherland," Wes noted, admiring the bedroom's bold African safari theme. "It looks great."

"Ma's picking up decorating cues from the Home and Garden Channel. I'll be sure to pass along your compliment." Michelle smiled, then latched on to the mesh canopy dangling from the bamboo hoop overhead like mosquito netting, and dragged it to one side of the mattress.

Maintaining scorching eye contact with Michelle, Wes stripped off his necktie and undid the buttons on his dress shirt.

With a flourish and a frisky giggle Michelle kicked off her sandals, not caring where they landed. She pulled her top over her head, then parted the zipper on her cropped pants to shimmy her hips out of them, leaving two mounds of floral cotton fabric on the floor.

Wes's eyes darkened with furious desire, boosting Michelle's confidence and power as a woman. The way she felt about Wesley, how could this not be right? She tossed all doubts to the side and enjoyed watching him remove his shirt. Next, off came the T-shirt and trousers. Her pulse quickened with that first look at the product of exceptional genes and buckets of sweat. She'd been with good-looking naked men, even sneaked peeks in *Playgirl* here and there, but she'd never seen one as well put together as Wesley Abbott. He was simply her own personal erotic fantasy in the flesh—from the lean sweeps of his long legs and arms to the pleated abs tucked beneath his perfectly sculpted chest. He removed something, she guessed a condom, from his wallet. Eyes still on her, he held the packet between his teeth while he shoved his wallet back inside a pocket, then dropped the pants on the chair in a corner.

Just when she thought her pulse couldn't race any faster without rocketing her to the moon, he removed his black briefs, releasing his erection. Quite frankly, the man was blessed in more ways than one. . . . *Make that* extremely *blessed,* Michelle observed with a wicked grin and lift of one brow.

Giddy with anticipation, she crawled on the bed. She came up on her knees, then beckoned him with a crooked finger. "Come here, you."

"Yes, ma'am," he managed between clenched teeth.

Wes joined her in bed, also on his knees. He looked into her eyes, then leaned forward, passing the foil packet from his own mouth to hers. His lips gently brushed hers, setting off more sparks, during the exchange.

Eagerly she reached up to pluck the packet from between his clamped teeth. If she kept things quick, casual, and clinical, maybe she could stay grounded. And not get swept away by the sensual tsunami that was Wesley Abbott. She was about to rip that sucker open and roll it in place when he claimed it again.

He frowned. "What's the rush?" he whispered, tossing the condom to the side. "Just let me look at you," he crooned, his lips curved up in a lazy, crooked smile.

Wes admired the scraps of royal blue lace that barely covered her breasts and bottom. "You're so beautiful," he said with such quiet reverence she suddenly felt like a marauding boor. Make that a horny marauding boor.

Wes was obviously trying to set the tone for romance. He tenderly threaded his fingers through her hair, hypnotizing her with the sheer intensity of his heated stare. His fingertips massaged her scalp. Her nipples hardened and her breasts ached for the feel of those large hands, but he took the scenic route, lovingly and leisurely kneading her neck and shoulders along the way.

Michelle followed his lead, stroking steel shoulders before inching her way to the silky dark hair on his chest . . . and oh, what a chest! She played there until his flat male nipples beaded. She circled them with her tongue, then dallied at his rippled abs before seeking what she wanted most. She stroked his hardness, sliding its own moisture over the shaft and satin head as she tugged a husky groan out of him. Her hands slipped up and down. Up and down. He hissed and heat spiraled through her, coiled itself into a big knot of the fierce yearning that pulsated at her core.

"Oh, baby," Wes rasped with his head lolled back as she massaged him slowly and firmly, just the way he obviously loved it.

He looked into her eyes again, then eased the thin straps of the lacy bra off her shoulders. He'd wanted to take it slow, real slow, but Michelle made that a challenge. Why was he not surprised? he thought affectionately. She hadn't made things easy for him from day one. With the bra lowered he filled his hands with the weight of her ripe breasts, squeezed, then suckled the sepia tips, her skin like sweet butterscotch on his tongue. His hands slipped downward and cupped the lush bottom he'd only enjoyed in his dreams. He had to halt her eager fingers before she pushed him to the point of no return.

"Put your arms around me," he demanded in a husky whisper. "Tight."

She obliged, running fingers through the waves on his head at the same time.

"Ahhh, yeah, just like that," he praised in a low rumble. He pulled her close, wedging his erection against the soft curve of her belly. He heard the tandem beating of their hearts. He loved holding her like this and was determined to make it last.

He couldn't remember ever feeling so utterly turned on by someone—not just by the physical stimulation but also by the deep emotional connection he felt whenever he was with Michelle. Whether they were deconstructing a jazz CD, stuffing their faces with pizza, or dishing about *Herald* business, it was all good. Very good. For the first time his heart felt full . . . full of her.

When his lips found hers again she reclined against the pillows and let him cover her. He wanted to love on her lips forever, but he paused just long enough to slip the flimsy blue panties off her hips, drag them along her satiny limbs, then toss them aside. He drew a deep breath, admiring her voluptuous curves.

With the lightest touch, he teased, stroked, and strummed her wet center until short, quick bursts of breath tore from her throat and perspiration glowed on her skin. "Wesley, now," she panted.

"Soon," he crooned his promise. But even then he hesitated, because he so enjoyed the look of raw passion on her pretty face. He brushed an auburn lock from her wet brow and gazed into hazel eyes, half-mast with desire. He continued his ministration, reading her face and writhing body for cues on when to ebb and flow. He alternated from one beaded nipple to the next, suckling, nibbling, fanning the exquisite fire. She pleaded for more. But he watched and waited, relishing their deep breathing and passionate groans until they were both almost ready to explode with ecstasy heightened by delayed gratification. He quickly fished the packet out of the rumpled covers, covered himself, then wedged his hips between her thighs. By degrees he slipped inside. She thrust forward to fill her until his base grazed damp downy softness. A quiver raced through his muscled thighs. She felt too damn good to him, wrapping her smooth legs around him, fervently clutching his bottom.

As they moved to their own music, the sensual dance began, at first a slow and gentle grind together. Then he slid in and out of soft, sizzling walls that sheathed and stroked him into a wondrous delirium.

Her breathy moans and the scent of her skin surrounded him, spurring him on. A persistent pressure mounted in him and demanded release at once. A guttural curse slipped out of him from the sheer force of its call. It would've been so easy to get lost in his own satisfaction at that moment, but that had never been Wes's style. No one ever made him lose control before *he* was ready to lose it, but with Michelle he felt like a teenager enjoying his first sexual experience. As good as she made him feel, he wasn't going to succumb to the urge then—especially now that this wasn't just about pleasing the flesh. Michelle, of all people, deserved his very best. And contrary to popular male belief, the best wasn't always a stiff penis pounding in and out of a woman. He slowed down, lengthening his strokes, then tucked his bottom lip in determination and concentration. *Michelle first. Wesley second,* he reminded himself as he lifted one of her legs higher along his lean torso; then he precisely angled his hips so the base of him could tease the velvet wedge encircled by tight, moist auburn curls.

When she let out a long, soft moan, he knew . . . yes, he'd hit the perfect spot. So he kissed her lips and worshipped that spot, gladly, slowly, skillfully, for as long as it took, until she called out his name. Later, he wasn't sure how much later and didn't care, his baby came for him—hard and mightily if her hoarse cry and the way she wildly clutched his back were any indication. He rode out her rhythmic shocks and contractions, then thought, *My turn.* He grinned as he sank deep, then deeper into her, like a candle into a cake. Michelle must've known by then he was downright ravenous for her, so she grinned back, arching up, enticing him to give her all he had. Then and only then did he increase speed and force until every muscle in his body contracted and he surrendered to the sweet violence of his own climax.

A little before midnight Michelle, now dressed in an oversize University of Michigan T-shirt, sat on her bed lotus-style. Her body was tired, but her head and heart were light with a buzzy alive feeling.

With his back propped against the headboard, Wes sat across from her, looking sexy, mellow, and muscled in the black briefs.

They were supposed to be eating, but the shadowy wedge between Michelle's knees kept vying for his attention.

"Stop that!" She erupted in giggles.

"What?"

"Staring *down there.*"

"Woman, close your damn legs, then," Wes teased with a mischievous grin. "You're sitting there, all open and inviting, like a twenty-four-hour all-you-can-eat buffet. And have the nerve to tell me not to look or touch."

"Don't you ever get enough?"

"Of you? Never." Wes tugged at her T-shirt.

She slapped his hand away. "We must eat! Food! I can just see it now. My mother comes home a few days later and finds two corpses entwined in the missionary position."

Wes wriggled his brows. "But what a way to go!"

Michelle exploded with giggles again, then reached to

grab a flour tortilla from the tray of Mexican food positioned beside Wesley.

"I have a confession to make." Michelle stuffed the tortilla with charbroiled steak, peppers, onions, and salsa, which they'd had to reheat in the microwave.

"What?" he asked, building his own chicken fajita.

"About that unicorn painting—"

"Yeah?"

"The one you're going to put up on your wall between the Bearden and the Synthia Saint James as soon as you get a chance."

"I meant what I said," he reminded her.

"I know you did; oh, Wesley, that was sooooo very sweet of you to agree to do such a thing. So sweet that I now feel sorta bad for tricking you."

"Tricking me?" He stopped midchew. "How?"

"I lied. I didn't do that painting. I actually plucked it from the Whitmeyers' trash next door," she revealed impishly.

"You what?" Feigning indignation, Wesley wadded paper napkins, then pitched them at her.

She whooped and laughed loudly, blocking his shots with her hands. "It was just a joke to get back at you for putting me on the spot at work today."

"Oh yeah?" He released another knot of a napkin, clipping her on the forehead. Only then was he satisfied enough to cease fire.

"I know that thing is hideous, downright ghastly actually. Yet when you thought it was my work you were still willing to display it so you wouldn't hurt my feelings. It's not my crappy art, but you have no idea how much that meant to me."

"So your little trick backfired, huh?" Wes grinned, reaching over to slap her thigh.

Her expression went soft and dreamy as she leaned in his direction. She felt like a flower and he was the sun. "You're really a very nice guy, Wes," she said with conviction.

"And that obviously still comes as a surprise to you," he said wryly before taking another bite of his fajita.

Michelle flushed. "Yes, um. I mean, no." She set her fajita back on the tray uneaten. "I'm sorry if it seems as if I've been distant or dubious. It's just that I've been disappointed by one too many people lately. And I'm not just talking dating relationships. I'm talking friends, people I'd trusted and opened my heart to. It was quite a blow to discover they were either lying, using me, or angling to one-up or upstage me, whenever the opportunity presented itself. The last thing I want to turn into is a bitter or jaded ol' crone, but sometimes it's just so difficult to walk the fine lines. You want to be savvy but at the same time not overly suspicious. . . ." Her words trailed off. "But if you let your guard down too soon with the wrong people, you're suckered. People aren't always what they appear to be at first."

"True," Wesley stated simply as if weighing her words.

"Take Stanford Chapelle, for example. There I was thinking we'd bonded on a genuine level. Turns out he was just buttering me up so I would write a complimentary series about him."

Wes pushed out a sigh. "Do you want my honest opinion on that particular situation?"

"Yes."

"The complete and total truth without sugarcoating, right?"

"Nothing but." Michelle shifted, straightening her spine and tucking her legs beneath her.

"Michelle, what the hell did you expect from a man like Chapelle?"

Michelle shrugged. "I don't know. It's weird. It's as if he had some sort of spell over me for a while."

"The man is always manipulating people and things to get what he wants. That's how he got to be so powerful in the first place. You, of all people, should have known that. I still can't believe you crossed the line from journalist to . . . What? Friend? And let that man totally hoodwink you." Wes polished off his fajita. "And to take it further, I really don't understand where you get off being so judgmental about the way Chapelle handled you. Haven't you played the same or similar role to get what you need out of sources? You've even boasted about how well you can work people. I'm sure more than one interview subject or source probably felt he or she bonded with you on a personal level only to get dumped as soon as he or she was no longer useful."

"Well, I'm not sure *dump* is the right word, but I hear ya." Michelle considered Wes's words.

"Maybe you were more considerate and subtle, but admit it. There eventually came a time when maybe you didn't return his or her phone calls as quickly as you had before."

"True. Sounds pretty cold and self-serving now that I think about it."

"Yeah, but when it all boils down, we remind ourselves it's never really personal—just business. That's how journalists operate. It's all part of the game. Hell, when I was fresh out of college and working as a beat reporter I had the same thing happen to me—in reverse, though—with slick publicists and public relations reps, who acted if they were my best buddies in the entire world until my beat changed to something that didn't match anyone on their paying client lists. The free lunches, invites to A-list soirees, and perks suddenly dried up. I can't believe you lost sight of all this."

"I know. I can't believe it, either." Michelle sighed, bobbing her head. "I'm still asking myself how could I have been so stupid. There was just something about Chapelle, though. It's like, well, when I spent time with him he filled this void inside."

Wes gave her an odd look. "Keep it up and I'm liable to get very, very jealous."

"It wasn't a type of romantic or sexual attraction or connection, I assure you." She reached out to caress his cheek. "It was something else. But anyway, I'm trying desperately to move beyond it, but I think a big part of making sure it doesn't happen again is evaluating and analyzing where I jumped off-track. I can't afford to make any more career blunders like that. I'm sure it all circles back to this ever-growing hunger I have where my father is concerned."

"You never talk about him; where is he?"

"Dead," Michelle replied solemnly. "But the worst part is, I never knew him and I know very little about him. Ma has been staunchly closemouthed about him all these years."

"But why? It makes no sense."

"I've always been just as confused as you are about her attitude, but I was hoping that during this time at home I could get the information I needed out of her, perhaps if I had some of *her* old memories to cherish, even old photos, I could learn to be satisfied with that, but then the crisis with the gambling came up, and Willow Grove. I had to back off again."

"That stuff about your father is interesting," Wes said as if still weighing what she'd just revealed. "Try not to be too hard on yourself, baby. That misstep with Chapelle did have a silver lining. Don't you think?" Wes pulled her to his chest, then eased himself down the headboard to a reclined position.

"I got to come home and check on my mother and . . ."

"And?" He nuzzled her earlobes.

"I met you."

"Now *that's* what I want to hear." Wes smiled; then he rocked them until she was on her back. He covered her again. With one hand he pinned her arms above her head.

"Wes?"

"Huh?" He caressed her ear with the tip of his nose, then softly licked at her lobe.

"I was just wondering."

"What?"

"Have you made a decision about letting me help you with Titus Montesi?"

He ground his hips against hers so she could feel how much he wanted her, then groaned. "I don't want to talk about that right now. Later, okay? I'm still hungry; what about you?"

"Famished," she purred.

Wes used one hand to push her T-shirt up and over her breasts. He reached toward the tray to dip his fingers inside the salsa bowl.

He swiped spicy sauce on her pebbled nipples, then growled something in Spanish—something she suspected was very naughty—before he greedily licked the salsa off.

Michelle came up on her knees to pull the T-shirt over her head. She pitched it to the floor, then steadied her perfect naked body by latching on to the headboard. Over one shoulder she peered at Wes, then pushed her bottom toward him, unleashing a powerful sexual mojo that had him aching to bury himself deep inside of her.

"Wanna play a little game?" Michelle asked, raising one neat brow as if issuing a challenge. "A contest of sorts."

"A contest?"

"Yeah, we'll see who can make whom . . . um . . . *surrender* first. To borrow a line from an old *Seinfeld* episode, I'm queen of my castle, but are you master of your domain, Wesley Abbott?" Her hot gaze swept over his body, then lingered at his stiff manhood, straining against his silk briefs. Every pleasure-centered nerve-ending in his body jolted to life.

"Guess we'll see, won't we?" he said, instantly catching her drift and eager to take her on.

She licked her luscious lips. "Yes indeed. We shall see."

"Ahhhh, I love the way you think, lady." Wes grinned, memorizing the smoldering expression on her face. He'd see it in his most carnal fantasies again and again. He came up on his knees and positioned himself behind her.

"Well, what are you waiting for? Do me again. *Now*. But nice and *hard* this time around." Michelle reached back and tugged at his briefs until the elastic waistband slipped downward. She slapped her bottom against his naked hips. "Think you can handle that order? And just how long can you go? Or are rumors of your . . . um . . ." she cleared her throat, "legendary stamina greatly exaggerated?"

"Exaggerated? Oooh, woman, you're really asking for it now." Wes chuckled heartily, but was turned on nonetheless.

"I'm a bad girl. A really bad girl. Guess you'll have to teach me a lesson, then, huh?" Michelle wore a seductive smile as she separated her knees, then stabilized her position again.

She taunted him and he enjoyed it. He planted soft pecks to the delicate skin at the base of her neck and behind her earlobes before gingerly and reverently combing his fingers through her soft auburn hair. He skimmed his knuckles along her spine and breasts eliciting a needy moan from her, then a demanding, "Harder. More."

He cupped her full breasts firmly, then pinched and plucked her nipples to distended points. "Ahhh, yes, just like that," she hissed her praise. "But that's not all you've got, right?"

Whoa! Wes moved to stroke himself aggressively. He snatched the extra condom on the nightstand and quickly fitted it over his length. Once it was in place, he wrapped the other arm around her waist and yanked her flush against his chest. She gasped.

"Now what was that you were saying?" he issued his own challenge as he sank his teeth into her shoulder, then her earlobe. He threaded his fingers through her hair again, massaging her warm scalp just before he forcefully invaded her inner walls with one hell of a stroke and a husky grunt of need. Michelle turned her head to the side, then mewled as she accepted him.

"No smart words now? So cat's got your tongue now, huh?" He leaned and whispered hotly against her ear. He thrust again, filling his big hands with her hips until she gasped again.

On it went like that until his pulse escalated, his lungs expanded, and his blood pounded in his ears. Perspiration rolled from his neck, tickling the trench of his spine.

"And that's all you've got?" Michelle asked in a strangled voice, face still distorted in pleasure. The headboard played percussion against the wall. *Tap. Tap. Tap. Tap.* With his fingers tangled in her hair again, he jerked with just enough pressure to elicit another sound of pure delight from her.

Wes never got the hair-pulling thing, but it drove some women crazy and he aimed to please. He kept parting the silken cleft that seemed to tug him deeper inside with a suctioning sensation.

Tap. Tap. Tap. Tap.

A climax threatened to overtake him. But Wes, biting his bottom lip with unyielding concentration, shifted the angle, lengthened his stroke, and slowed his tempo.

Wes wanted to made her scream in surrender. He went deeply and steadily. "More?"

"More." Her moans grew louder and more frequent. Then his sweetie actually let loose with a string of dirty words that caught him by surprise, but propelled him to the next level of uninhibited ecstasy. "Ohhh, shame on you, such improper words for a proper lady."

She let loose again with more spicy words as he grunted something equally provocative and sizzling in her ear.

"Faster," she demanded.

"So you're really going to make a brotha work for it, huh?" Wes rasped against her ear, as he contracted his rippling abs, putting more of his back into it. The animalistic part of him reveled in this game. Despite the central air, sweat drenched them both. The tray of fajitas and fixings perched near the edge of the mattress crashed to the floor. But the bed would have to collapse *and* the house would have to crumble around them for Wes to stop now. He wanted to crawl inside of her and stay forever. Clearly dazed, Michelle threw her head back and arched her back as he tugged at her hair again. Her slow moans escalated to a piercing staccato string of "Ohs!"

Or just O, as an orgasm was imminent.

"I can't hear you. C'mon, speak up, now." His demand direct and throaty.

Michelle was too lost in her own pleasure to bother with a verbal taunt.

"Awww. Is that all *you've* got?" He playfully tsk-tsked her, feigning disapproval as his hips pumped.

Taptaptaptaptaptaptaptap.

Squeezing her eyes shut, Michelle's body convulsed as a climax rippled through her. She let it all out with a wail that he was sure the entire block could hear. Slick wetness pulsated, practically melting the latex enveloping his hardness. He released her hair.

"Yes," she panted, then went limp, collapsing on the bed.

"Damn right," Wes rumbled in haughty agreement with a smile.

He slapped her bottom before grabbing handfuls of her hips again. "You're not quitting on me now. We've still got work to do. Or are you giving in? Is somebody ready to cry uncle?"

"No way!" Michelle replied, obviously winded. But she rose to her knees again to signal that she was still game and had a lot more energy to spare. After all, *she* had started this, but Wes aimed to finish. They connected again. Then—just to prove a point—he took his sweet time giving in to his own release.

Over the next few hours, they made up for what had not happened after their first official dinner date and what had not happened on his sofa the previous night. As far as Wes was concerned, it had been worth the wait. Michelle had revealed her different facets to him. All sweet and tender in bed one minute. Brash, bawdy, skilled and sexy as hell the next. Their lovemaking would never grow mundane. They took compatibility between the sheets to a whole new level. From that day on he couldn't imagine ever needing or wanting to share this part of himself with anyone but her. Then there were the stirrings of something deeper and much more substantial going on inside of him whenever he thought about Michelle. These went beyond their mutual physical attraction or sex. If he wasn't sure of it before, he was damn sure of it now. She was made especially for him. A gift straight from heaven.

Twenty-three

The next day Wes had just enough time to drive to his place and change before a meeting with Titus, who wanted to share a quick lunch and another dart game at McLemore's.

As Wes suspected he would, Titus cleaned his clock at every match. Wes knew he was in trouble as soon as Titus whipped out a set of Black Widow Steel Tip Darts complete with movable black rough oxide-coated points and tungsten barrels. A set of high-performance darts like those cost a couple of hundred bucks. Wes, on the other hand, had to settle for the bar's way-too-light cheapo community set of Bud Light Steel Points that had been sent to the bar's owners as freebie promotional items. But the whole point of using the dart thing wasn't actually to win or impress anyone with his dart-throwing stroke or style; it was just a way to befriend Titus.

Titus had already mentioned that he worked as a courthouse bailiff. He'd also boasted about unleashing his entrepreneurial spirit by raking in extra cash on "a sideline gig." Wes knew it was the courthouse hustling, of course. However, Titus wasn't ready to reveal the details of his sideline thing, let alone any judges' names.

Titus had not become successful by spilling his guts to just any buddy-come-lately. Pumping Titus was going to take time, but for now Wes was still in. Every time Titus phoned Wes on his cell to extend an invite to hang with him and his clique at McLemore's, Wes believed he was getting a little closer to what he needed. Watching Titus act a plumb fool over just about anything warm-blooded with a uterus, Wes also believed what Toni had revealed about Titus's main weakness. Wes had discovered plenty, but he was still angling to figure out the best way to use that information, along with everything else he'd learned about Titus, to his advantage.

However, he didn't know Titus well enough to involve a third party in what could be a potentially dangerous situation. He couldn't just dangle anyone before Titus as bait. And as good as Michelle was at getting sources to open up to her, Wes still wasn't comfortable taking up her offer to help. She wasn't going to back down and he'd have to give her an answer soon.

His mind was sorting through the various possibilities when a bit of guilt pricked him. Where the hell did that come from? He thought about the conversation he'd had with Michelle the other night about the journalist modus operandi and the conflicting emotions it could sometimes evoke.

One minute he was considering Titus's possible underworld ties and how dangerous the man might be. Then the next Wes was questioning his own investigation tactics. He enjoyed the process, but he didn't always enjoy the deception necessary on his part to unearth what he needed. He did feel as if Titus was starting to consider him "one of his boys." It was then that Wes had to remind himself that he was investigating Titus for routinely breaking the law. Bottom line, Wes had started this whole investigation for Kelly . . . and Patrick, he admitted to himself reluctantly.

By the time he made it back in the newsroom he was ready to meet with his editor, Malone Hughes, about Titus and his possible criminal connection to Pratt.

When Wes emerged from the hour-long meeting Michelle had yet to return to the newsroom. He checked the clock:

3:12 p.m. Fearing his concern might rouse too much suspicion, he recruited Craig to ask questions for him.

Craig e-mailed Barbara, Michelle's editor, to inquire about Michelle's whereabouts. Craig relayed Barbara's reply.

"Michelle won't be in at all today, man," Craig told Wesley. "Seems she has some pressing family business."

It was then that he recalled Michelle had mentioned that a lunch and counseling session with her mother was on tap that day. He turned on his computer; while he waited for it to boot up, he wished the pair the best.

When the cell phone clipped to his hip rang, he answered it.

Patrick calling from Davenport. "Yo, Bro, what's shakin'?"

"I'm at work. I can't talk right now, but I do have an update for you."

"And I've got something big for you, too," Patrick said, obviously hyped up. "I know you advised that I keep things real chill in here, as in not discussing our project with anyone, but I got . . . What do you call it? A lead, a real hot lead, and a source for you that's guaranteed to blow this thing wide open."

Wes tightened his grip on the cell phone and listened intently.

"Of course, I can't go into the details, but call this number I'm about to give you. When the guy answers tell him the make and model of the car I totaled when you and I went to South Padre Island for spring break several years ago."

"What?"

"It's a code thing."

"We're not playing games here, Patrick. This sounds like crap from some cheesy spy flick," Wes said, his voice sharpened.

"I know it sounds crazy, but you know these lines aren't always the most secure. I did ring your cell. Anyway, that car's make and model is all the info you'll need to get clearance and the instructions."

"Instructions for what?"

"For where you'll hook up with my guy. I've arranged for you two to meet. He'll provide what you need and you'll know exactly what to do with it."

"What's the number?" Wes rubbed at the tension building near his temple and jotted down the phone number Patrick provided.

The brothers exchanged good-byes and Wes slipped out to his car and drove out of the parking garage to seek a pay phone away from the *Herald* premises just to play it safe. Pay phones, especially the booth variety, were getting harder to find these days, but outside a gas station a few blocks away he finally spotted one that didn't reek of urine. He stepped inside and dialed the number Patrick had given him.

When a male voice answered, Wes wasn't sure if he should introduce himself first or what. He just played it safe and went with the cryptic: "Porsche Carerra." The rented car Patrick had totaled that wild spring break weekend almost two decades ago that Wesley would rather forget.

"Meet me near the stage at Hart Plaza downtown. One hour," the voice instructed.

Willow Grove was housed in a brick office building softened by plush well-manicured grass and colorful annuals.

Michelle and Liz strolled outside to sit at a picnic table shaded by a hearty oak tree. The sun shone and the warm temperature hovered in the high seventies as residents received visitors outdoors.

So far their midwestern spring had felt more like summer, but Michelle wasn't complaining. Michigan wasn't exactly known for its mild weather.

Michelle had settled on one side of the table, while Liz sat across from her.

Liz looked at her only child with deep affection. "I'm so glad you could come."

"Ma, you know nothing is more important to me than you. Of course I was going to be here today, and any other day you need me. I love you and there's nothing I wouldn't do for you."

Liz's expression changed from pleasant to grave. "I hope you still feel that way after today, after hearing what I have to say to you."

"What is it, Ma?" Michelle's stomach quivered with dread. "You look so . . . I don't know. You're scaring me."

A soft wind blew, lifting Liz's thin brown locks off her shoulders. "What I have to tell you . . . I should have a long while ago. I just hope one day you'll understand why I made the choices I did, which seemed like the right thing at the time." Her hands trembled and she dropped the sunglasses in them on the table.

Michelle reached to steady the shaking. "Whatever it is, we'll work it out. We'll work through it together."

"I hope this doesn't seem cruel, but the only way I can finally do this is to just come out with it. Your father's not dead, honey." Liz dabbed at her eyes with the edge of her lightweight sea-foam green sweater.

Pole-axed, Michelle could barely move her lips. "What?" came out on a small puff of air.

"Your father didn't pass away all those years ago," Liz's voice akin to a weak but pained whimper.

Still dazed, Michelle just stared at the woman sitting across the table from her.

"Sweetie, I thought it was best. You see, it was all such a big mess. I was naive, single, and in love. We had an affair. He was married with two children at the time. He had a big career ahead of him that I soon discovered meant more to him than anything else in this world."

"So you slept with a married man. And had his baby?" Michelle managed in a thin voice. "Me?" In a stupor, she gazed out across the sweeping grass but focused on nothing in particular.

"I led you to believe he was dead all these years because I thought that was best for everyone involved," Liz explained, her voice shrill, pleading for understanding. "He didn't love me. Never did and had no intentions of leaving his wife and children for me, which I'd foolishly assumed."

Michelle looked into her mother's face. "So he knew that you were pregnant, then?"

"No, he didn't know about you. I didn't tell him."

"But why not? What possible reason could you have had for keeping something like that from him?" Michelle nailed Liz with an accusing look. "The truth, Ma! No more lies!"

Liz's chin quivered as she fumbled the sunglasses in her hands. "Okay. Yes. You're right. Yes. Yes. The truth. At long last the truth," she repeated like a mantra, then swiped at her tears. "He didn't want me. At the time I didn't think he deserved to know about you. I told myself I was shielding you, protecting you. And all these years I've not only lied to you, but I lied to myself to justify a decision that was purely selfish."

Michelle propped her elbows on the table and rubbed her throbbing temples. She couldn't believe what she was hearing. The jolt of what her mother had just confessed caused Michelle's stomach to roil violently. Suddenly she popped up from the bench and braced herself against the oak tree and heaved for several minutes. She felt like purging, but nothing would come up.

When Michelle felt her mother's arms on her shoulders,

she stiffened, then whirled around to glare at her fiercely. "Don't!"

Liz released her, giving Michelle the space she needed by remaining silent and taking her seat again.

Michelle stood for the longest time vibrating with righteous fury, unsure what to do or say next. Finally, she moved back to drop on the bench. She propped her elbows on the table and rested her head in her hands. "Why?" she finally asked in a feeble voice. "Why did you decide to drop this on me now?" But before Liz could answer, Michelle did it for her. "Wait. This is about you, isn't it? Of course it is. We're back to *you* and what *you* need again."

"Baby, just hear me out."

Michelle's rage flared up again. "All these years, I practically begged for scraps, any little bit of information you could give me about my *dead* father or his family, and you gave me nothing!" Michelle slammed a fist against the table and Liz startled. "Not a thing! Zip! Just kept me totally in the dark because it served your purpose best. And now, finally, after thirty-three years you're suddenly ready to purge all because that serves your purpose best." Michelle shook her head in disbelief. "And all the time I've been bitching and moaning about all the so-called friends who can't be trusted. And lo and behold, I find out my own mother's been lying to me all these years, too. Un-freakin'-believable." Michelle looked skyward with a mirthless chuckle. "God, I'm ready for the punch line when you're ready to deliver it."

"Honey, please, I understand how you feel. Just let me finish. I think you need to hear everything. Maybe it'll make a difference, help you understand a little better."

Though she wanted to bolt away from her mother and that place as soon as possible, curiosity kept Michelle grounded to that wooden bench.

"I've been struggling with bipolar disorder for the better

part of my life," Liz said, her eyes shadowed. "That's really what my stay here is about—not the gambling."

"Bipolar?　You　mean . . . You're . . . you're　manic-depressive?" Michelle's mouth fell open in alarm. Just when she thought she'd heard it all. At first she wasn't sure she could believe Liz. It could be a ploy, a fake-out to justify all her hurtful lies.

"You can speak to one of the doctors here about my diagnosis if you like," Liz added as if reading Michelle's mind. With eyes closed tightly Liz sighed and nodded. "They'll tell you. It's true."

"But I don't understand. . . . When did it start? How?"

Liz looked at Michelle again. "It first surfaced with unprovoked crying jags when I was sixteen. By seventeen I suffered from insomnia that I just assumed had been triggered by my own father's absence. He'd just left for work one day and never come back. But it was my mother's death a few years later that plunged me into a pitch-black emotional abyss." She paused as if to collect more memories, then struggled for a shaky breath. "The feeling of worthlessness that smothered me had gone beyond normal. I spent days at a time in bed, feeling so debilitated, just simply couldn't drag myself out. There were weeks and weeks of crushing, soul-wrenching sadness and despair; at times all I could think about was ending it all."

"You mean suicide?" Michelle needed Liz to clarify.

"Yes, but then there would be calm, relatively normal periods that could stretch for months at a time. I'd see the light at the end of the tunnel again. But that balance wouldn't last for too long. My mood kept escalating and escalating until I was sure I could conquer the world. I'd feel giddy, wonderfully alive, way over the moon! There was nothing Liz Michaels could not do!"

Michelle had read articles on various public figures who had come forward to reveal that they'd suffered from the disorder, but it had never occurred to her that her life would be touched by it in such a deeply personal way.

"Remember that time I blew off work at the last minute and swept you, Ahmad, and Fatima off to Disney World for an entire week?"

How could Michelle ever forget that crazy trip? Initially, she had sensed that something was peculiar about how Liz had impulsively requested that the three be released from their Wednesday classes before the lunch bell rang. From their school Liz had driven straight to the airport with the car stereo blasting Prince's "Raspberry Beret" as she merrily caterwauled along and coaxed her befuddled captives to do the same. The kids weren't even allowed to go back to the house to pack for the trip. Liz explained that they would buy whatever they needed in Orlando. And they did. Expenses included new wardrobes, the best suite at the Hilton, expensive meals in five-star restaurants, a rented red BMW convertible, and one night out on the town that ended with Liz getting a crucifix, along with her deceased sister's and brother-in-law's names, tattooed on her left ankle and right arm.

At the time, Michelle was too young to linger on how much damage her mother must have done to her Master-Card. Michelle had reasoned that the trip was her mother's way of helping them all—especially Ahmad and Fatima—work through their despair over the car crash that had taken their parents' lives.

"That trip wasn't just about my grief over losing my only sister," Liz explained, her dark brown eyes unblinking. "It was a perfect example of the manic side driving my impulses and my spinning completely out of control."

"If you knew all this at the time, why didn't you go for help, Ma? I don't understand. Please help me understand," Michelle pleaded.

"I did seek help on and off over the years," Liz said. "This is hardly my first stay at Willow Grove. But coming here was the smartest thing I ever did. Let me backtrack a bit. The first time I reached out to professionals the psychotherapy actually helped and I responded well to the prescribed medication. I thought I was cured. That was around the time I met your father at a concert on Belle Isle." A shadow of a smile found its way to her face. "Belle Isle used to pop with all kinds of fun activities back then. They used to have restaurants, refreshment stands, waterslides, and everything. The structures there weren't tattered and abandoned like they are now." She cast her eyes downward. "Anyway, I met your father there. He was so smart, funny, handsome, dashing."

"And he hid the fact that he was married?" Michelle asked with a heavy heart.

"At first. . . . Had I known earlier I would've never gotten involved with him. But then when I found out, I was too weak and too much in love with him to break it off." Liz sighed. "Lord help me. I knew it was wrong." Her eyes filled with fresh tears. "But, baby, I couldn't help myself. I really thought I was in love and he was the only man for me. I was twenty-two at the time and so foolish. And I was alone. No strong support system. No parents. And my only sister had moved to the West Coast after she got married. He had become my everything."

Though Michelle was still angry and confused, her heart squeezed for the lonely young woman her mother had been.

"So things got really heavy between us. It's the same ol' story you've probably heard from the other woman zillions of times. I gave him an ultimatum, told him it was time to choose—me or his wife." Her eyes went cold and glassy; then a scornful chuckle burst forth. "That joker didn't even hesitate. Pretty much said, 'See ya! Wouldn't want to be ya!' And then he just disappeared. Four weeks later I discovered I was pregnant with you. I'd made a big mistake getting involved with him, but how big of a mistake could it have been if it resulted in you? I had you. My beautiful cat-eyed baby, my Kitten. You have his coloring, you know."

Michelle swallowed the lump that swelled in her throat at the mention of the old nickname, Kitten. Her mother hadn't called her that in about two decades.

"I'm so sorry I kept all this from you, Chelle. As soon as you were old enough to understand the man and woman thing, I should've explained the situation to you. But with every passing year and lie piled on top of lie, it just seemed easier to keep quiet. Better to keep it all buried—especially when I was spending half the time struggling to keep the manic depression from consuming me again. I had to try to keep it together the best I could for you. And then I had my sister's kids to think about."

As she thought back on her mother's recurrent mood swings over the years, bipolar disorder more than rang true for Michelle. "So you said psychotherapy and medication helped."

"Yes, it did over the years, but I'd go through these periods when I felt fine, thought I could handle life like a normal person. How I wanted to be like a normal person, so I'd quit."

Michelle shook her head forlornly. "Oh, Ma."

"See, the therapy felt so overindulgent, like a luxury I really couldn't afford. I was paying out of pocket. Felt if I used company benefits my employer would find out, God forbid! Then I got tired of being a slave to all the little capsules and tablets. At one point I was taking up to nine medications, three times a day, always desperately trying to keep it a secret from you and anyone else in my close inner circle. It was like a reminder day in and out that my elevator didn't go all the way to the top. Do you know how that made me feel?"

"When was the last time you were on the medication?"

"A few months ago, just before Ed asked me to marry him."

"Ed asked you to marry him?" Michelle's eyes went wide with surprise.

"Yes, he did. But I never told him about the bipolar thing or the medication, either."

Michelle nodded her head disapprovingly. "Ma, see, the secrets and lying to those you love—"

"Don't you see? I had to try again to see if I could beat this thing, handle it on my own, before I could move forward with Ed. And oh, how I wanted to say yes to his proposal! I love him. He's such a good man. He deserves a wife that's whole, and I wanted to be that for him. I didn't want to think I would be dependent on psychotherapy and drugs for the rest of my life. And neither quite eased that other burden I'd been carrying around."

"Knowing you'd lied to me about my father all these years?" Michelle said, slowly putting pieces together.

Liz nodded. "That started festering again; then came insomnia again, and the obsessive tendencies, which led to the late-night trips to the casino, one of the few places in town open twenty-four hours. It became my refuge. You see, honey, your mother is just one big ol' sloppy, crazy mess."

"Stop it, Ma! You're not crazy; you just have . . . have . . ." Michelle searched for the right word. "Challenges."

"I tried to shield you from it, though, the best I could. I really did."

This time when Liz dissolved into tears again Michelle moved to her side and tried to comfort her, despite her own pain.

"It's going to be all right, Ma. You'll get through this, too. *We'll* get through this," Michelle promised, pressing a kiss on Liz's forehead.

"I realize now I'll be damned to deal with bipolar disorder for the rest of my life and just willing it away—without therapy and medication—and trying to hide it from those I care about is not the answer."

Michelle rocked her mother as sobs wracked her slim body.

"I'm so sorry, Chelle. So sorry I never told you, never told you about m-my . . . m-my," Liz stammered as if her lips could barely form the words, "*m-mental illness* or the truth about your father. But I can tell you everything I know about him now. You can seek him out yourself if you need more. I swear I won't try to stand in your way anymore. He's here in town. He was still in law school when we were involved. He's a very prominent judge these days. John Ashton Pratt."

Twenty-four

Wes took a seat in the first row near the stage at Hart Plaza. Minutes later a short, swarthy man with bulging bloodshot eyes and dark stringy hair seemed to materialize out of nowhere.

He approached Wes. "Porsche Carerra?" the man asked, tugging at one sleeve of his ill-fitting puke-beige suit.

"Yes." Wes stood.

Because it was just after lunchtime, most of the people milling about the park for their breaks were leaving to return to work.

The man removed a manila legal-size envelope from one jacket pocket and passed it to Wes, who quickly accepted it.

"What's this?" Wes asked.

"See with your own eyes, my friend," the man replied, casting glances in all directions to ensure no one was within earshot of their conversation.

Wes removed two sheets of paper that had photocopies of two checks on them. The checks had been made out to Titus Montesi and cashed at a party store on MacDougal called Big Bill's Beer Barrel. The checks had been written by a Wilma Urginovskiy for amounts totalling $15,000.

It didn't take much deduction for Wes to decide what to do with this new information. "I get to keep this copy?"

"Yes."

"And in return you expect . . . ?"

The man's purplish smoker's lips spread into an unctuous smile. "That's already been taken care of by—"

Lifting a hand to interrupt, Wes had second thoughts about pumping the guy for an answer. If cash was involved in the acquisition of these photocopies Wes didn't want or need to know the details.

From Hart Plaza he drove back to his place and removed his Pratt research files, which he kept in a safe in one of his walk-in closets. He removed records of the cases Pratt had heard in the past three years and skimmed the list. A Trevor Urginovskiy was on it. He'd beaten several theft/burglary raps and was now a free man. Wes picked up his cell phone and called a private investigator friend. He planned to meet him and have him run thorough checks on both Urginovskiys.

Michelle pulled out of the Willow Grove parking lot with too much on her mind. Since her mother's confession and the wrenching counseling session that followed, Michelle's jumbled emotions had whirled in a hundred different directions. One minute she felt blinded by hot smacks of anger, hurt, betrayal; the next, bright rays of hope and anticipation. Not only was her father not dead, but he was also right here, somewhere in town! And he had a legitimate full name. Over the years, the few times Liz ventured to mention him, she'd only referred to him as "your father." And Michelle could count the times she'd called him John, let alone used his full name. Liz had led Michelle to believe his last name had been Jones.

Only once in her life had a teenage Michelle questioned why Liz had not only kept her maiden name but also pinned it on Michelle. Liz's explanation at the time had sounded reasonable enough. Liz's parents never had boys—just two girls—Liz and Michelle's aunt Caroline, Fatima and Ahmad's mom. Retaining *Michaels* had been Liz's way of ensuring that the family name continued, she had said.

Michelle had never questioned whether her biological father and mother had been married. *John Ashton Pratt. John Ashton Pratt. John Ashton Pratt.* The name even danced in Michelle's consciousness during the counseling session when the focus shifted to her mother's bipolar disorder.

Michelle did not reveal that this was the man she'd been preparing to help Wesley investigate and take down for alleged courtroom crimes. She questioned whether even the scriptwriters for *If Tomorrow Never Comes* could come up with that one. What a hot mess!

She was pondering what to do with this new information when her cell phone rang. Wesley calling to check on her and to find out if they were still on for dinner that evening at his parents' house.

Michelle's first impulse: cancel. She just wasn't up to schmoozing that evening, but then she thought better of it. She didn't want to let Wesley down. Before her mother's heartrending revelation, Michelle had been looking forward to meeting Wesley's folks.

She had to try to eat dinner anyway. The distraction would be good for her, she decided. "Yes, we're still on," she said, merging onto the interstate. They made plans for Wesley to pick her up in Ferndale at 7:00 p.m.

"I can't wait to show you off," Wesley said.

She still had a few hours before then and she knew just where she had to go. McLemore's. The happy hour crowd would arrive soon. Maybe Titus Montesi would be among them.

McLemore's was alive with a boisterous crowd, eager to drink away any nine-to-five blues. Michelle stepped inside the smoky bar and took a seat in a booth near the pool tables and dartboards. It didn't take long before the string of break-the-ice free drinks arrived for a young woman alone in a dive like McLemore's.

Two grunge-band types wearing flannel shirts, T-shirts,

jeans, crocheted skullcaps, and dirt under their fingernails quickly swaggered over and claimed the seat across from Michelle's. They settled in to grin and flirt until she went on a too-much-info ramble about the icky ointment-resistant *mystery* rash that had suddenly cropped up in some of her more delicate feminine areas. A gross but highly effective whopper Michelle had used often whenever she attracted unwanted male attention at pickup watering holes. They both gaped at Michelle, then at each other, before scramming, leaving only the scent of sweat, mingled with clashing aftershaves, behind.

Soon Dart Thrower Extraordinaire, as her waitress had identified Titus Montesi, ambled over, with a slew of bird feather–adorned darts in his stubby little hands.

"You play?" he asked, letting his appreciative gaze drop to admire Michelle's bosom in her form-fitting knit top. Any other time, she would've shielded her assets from his beady eyes, but she had to use everything she had to pry what she could from this guy about Pratt.

Wes would hit the roof when he heard that, without his go-ahead, Michelle had started in on Titus but she could only hope he'd understand why she *needed* to get involved and get to the bottom of things for herself. Learning that J. Ashton Pratt was her father had changed everything.

"So Wesley tells us you're from this area originally. What part?" Winston Abbott poured chilled chardonnay in a glass, then passed it to Michelle.

"Ferndale." Michelle accepted the glass. She took a sip and took her place on a love seat next to Wesley. "You two have such a lovely home."

"Thank you." Gloria Abbott smiled.

Wesley's mother was a regal woman with a chic super-short haircut and gravity-defying curves that belied her age. Tasteful diamond jewelry winked on her neck, earlobes, and fingers. She moved with a languid sort of grace as she, too, took a seat, then perched Kelly on her lap.

Michelle noted that Wes had obviously inherited his dimple, brandy-brown eyes, and smooth dark toffee skin tone from his mother.

But Wes's tall, broad-shouldered, sleekly muscular build was clearly a gift from his father. Winton Abbott's grizzled waves gave him a distinguished and scholarly quality. Yet his warm eyes, quick smile, and easy manner rendered him open and accessible.

"Gloria is a whiz at decorating, as you can see," Lonette, Kelly's mom, added. "You can give any professional a run for his or her money."

"Now you all stop. My head's starting to swell," Gloria said with a burst of musical laughter.

The family had gathered in the magnificent great room for conversation before dinner.

The Tudor-style residence was nestled in one of the older upscale communities. Towering oak and beech trees leaned in close to elaborately landscaped lawns and posh, sprawling homes.

So far everyone had made Michelle feel so welcome. She and Lonette had even swapped phone numbers and promised to get together for lunch and shopping. Guilt nipped at Michelle because she found herself rudely casting furtive glances at her watch. Maybe she should've rescheduled. She was simply way too distracted, and it wasn't fair to Wesley or his family.

"When are we going to Chuck E. Cheese again?" Kelly asked, practically shouting.

"Sssh, honey, not so loud. Use your indoor voice," Lonette gently chided her child.

"I want to play the video games." Kelly lowered her voice. "I don't get to play them at home no more."

"*Any*more," Lonette corrected her.

"Why not? Don't you have a ton of games?" Wesley curled one arm around Michelle's shoulder.

"My 'puter's broke," Kelly told him.

"The computer is not broken," Lonette corrected her again. "We're just having some problems with the game software. You know Patrick set up all that stuff. I'm such a computer illiterate. I have no idea what's wrong exactly or how to fix it."

"I can look at it, but I'm not as skilled as Patrick at that sort of thing."

"Wesley, you've got to be light-years ahead of me," Lonette said. "Anything you can do is bound to work. If you can't figure it out I'll have to hire someone."

"So I can play my *Clifford the Big Red Dog* 'puter game again?" Kelly asked, relaxing against Gloria's bosom.

Wes crossed his fingers. "Uncle Wes is going to *try* to hook you up, sweetie. But I'm not making any promises. Better come here and give me some sugar for incentive."

Kelly slid off Gloria's lap and walked into Wes's arms.

"I hope everyone's hungry." Gloria got to her feet, ushering the group toward the dining room.

Dinner was delicious and conversation flowed smoothly, though Michelle's thoughts kept drifting off. She managed to put on a good front, or at least she thought she had until Wes whispered to her during dessert, "Are you all right, baby? You seem a little distracted."

"I'm fine." Michelle picked at her apple pie. "I just have a bit of a headache."

"Would anyone like a coffee, cappuccino, or liqueur?" Gloria played the attentive hostess.

"We can cut this short and I can take you home," Wes said to Michelle.

"Could you?" Michelle whispered with gratitude. "Here I am eating and running. I'm sorry."

Wes touched his napkin to his lips. "No problem. I'll take care of it."

"Let's all go back into the great room to relax and chat some more," Gloria chirped. "Michelle, Wesley tells me you're a big fan of *If Tomorrow Never Comes*. I don't miss an episode, either."

"Ditto for me!" Lonette's eyes lit up. "Do you think Bliss will get back with Shiloh Forrester now that Dash is dead?"

"I hope so," Michelle replied. "I always thought he was her one true love."

"I hate to cut in here, but I'm afraid we have to leave." Gallantly Wes assumed the blame for cutting their visit short. "It's been a long day at work and I've got an even longer one tomorrow."

The Abbotts graciously allowed the couple to depart without pelting them with questions.

At the door Gloria gave Michelle a Tupperware container full of the apple pie Michelle had been too full and preoccupied to enjoy. Michelle and Lonette promised to get together soon.

Kelly climbed Wes's long legs until he swooped her up for a kiss. She wagged a finger at him. "Now you promise to come over and fix my 'puter."

Wes eased her back to her feet and saluted her. "Yes, ma'am. I promise to come over one day soon, right after work."

"You promise you gonna take me to see Daddy again, too." Kelly peered at him with big, guileless eyes.

Wes looked uncomfortable.

There was strained silence among the adults until Gloria piped up, "Your grandpa and I are going to see Patrick this weekend. You get to go with us this time. Weather permitting, we'll make a quick stop at Mackinac Island either on the way to Davenport or on the way back. How does that sound?"

"We'll stop at McDonald's, too, right?" Kelly negotiated. "Uncle Wes took me there."

"McDonald's, too." Gloria, who obviously had something against fast food, shot Wes an irritated glance.

Wes merely shrugged. "Hey, she earned it. That long, boring drive wasn't easy with only a couple of picture books for entertainment."

They all said their good-byes. When Michelle absently rubbed her arms, Wes removed his suit jacket, then draped it around her shoulders.

Her mind was so far away from the Palmer Woods neighborhood, she hadn't consciously realized the night temperature had dropped drastically.

"You want to tell me what's going on now?" Wes opened the passenger side door of the Ferrari to help her inside.

Once she was settled in, he moved to the driver's side, then belted himself in. "How did that meeting with your mother go?"

Michelle collapsed against the headrest, massaging her brow. "You're not going to believe what I have to tell you."

By the time Wes pulled into the driveway of Liz's bungalow, Michelle had told him that her mother had just revealed that Michelle's father was not dead. But she wasn't sure if she was ready to tell Wesley her father's identity. The implications were just so heavy and overwhelming.

He cut the engine and sat there studying her. "Are you all right?" He entwined his fingers with hers.

"I think I am. It's just all so much to take in and absorb, ya know."

"I can't even begin to imagine."

"He's not dead. He's really not dead! Can you believe it? Not only is he not dead, but he's here! Right here in town. I can look him up if I want to."

"And you will, right?"

Michelle's hesitation to answer the question stunned her. "From what I understand he was married and had a family when he was involved with my mother. That probably hasn't changed. I feel weird, you know. Like I have no right."

"But if that's what you need. . ."

Then Michelle decided she had to come clean with Wes so he could completely understand her predicament. "There's more, Wesley. Much more. He's a prominent judge."

Wesley raised his eyebrows. "Who?"

"John Ashton Pratt."

Wesley's eyebrows shot up about another mile. "Oh no, hell, no! Tell me you're joking!"

"No, I'm afraid not. I wouldn't joke about something like this." Michelle felt so mentally and physically drained, it seemed as if she'd gone a month without sleep. She sat upright and raked a hand through her hair. "And there's something else I need to tell you."

"What?"

"Right after I found out, I drove to McLemore's," she said.

Wesley closed his eyes and sighed. "To see if you could find Titus?"

"Yes," she replied softly. "Please don't be angry. But . . . but . . . You see, after what I had learned I just had to try to find out what Titus knew, what Titus could confirm."

"Michelle," Wes uttered through a clenched jaw.

"I didn't blow it. I swear it. I handled myself well under the circumstances."

"And?"

"It was a long shot, but he started hitting on me and all."

"As we figured he would."

"And he was really trying to impress me, telling me about all about the money he made and all the big boys' toys he had, the nice car, the house in West Bloomfield, the whole nine yards. I fibbed, told him I had a real weakness for legal types and how Court TV was my favorite channel. And how I live to watch shows like *Law & Order* and *Celebrity Jus-*

tice. The next thing I knew, he was telling me about all these judges he was tight with and how he'd even gone into lucrative business with a few of them."

"Pratt being one of them?" Wes paused, as if trying to corral his thoughts. "You believe him?"

"He'd obviously had too much to drink, but the next thing I knew he was revealing details about exactly how the hustle worked and who was involved."

"All this because of the promise of a date with you?" Wes rolled his eyes "Unbelievable!"

"Well, if truth be told, I didn't hint at just *dating.* I had to lie and act as if I was willing to provide more—*much more.* You'd be surprised what some lunkhead men will do for the promise of getting in someone's panties."

"So you cheapened yourself and played on that?" He knew he had to be more understanding, but the idea of some horny operator even thinking about having his way with Michelle's body made Wes boil with rage.

"It was just business, remember? And I was desperate, Wes!"

Wes's nostrils flared. "You didn't let him touch you!"

"No!" Michelle frowned. "I know what I'm doing! I know where to draw the darn line!"

"You didn't tell him anything about yourself, did you?"

"Of course not! All he got is a fake profile I'd made up a long time ago for undercover assignments. I used the name Sharla Denver."

"Did he or anyone follow you when you left McLemore's?"

"No, I didn't see anyone. After I got what I needed I told him I had to go to the ladies' room to freshen up. I'd promised him we could go back to his place so we could—"

"Spare me the details," Wes clipped his words.

"Anyway, I climbed out of a window in the ladies' bathroom."

"You're lucky there was a window."

"Luck had nothing to do with it, Wes. I checked *before* I launched my plan. And I wouldn't have even tried that stunt with Titus if I couldn't map out a decent escape route."

"I still don't believe this! You're not some character in that stupid soap opera you like to watch, you know!" he exploded again, arms flailing. "What you did was not cool, Michelle, not cool at all. Why didn't you call me? You could've been in real danger! I could've been there with you, watched over you!"

"I know, Wes. You're right. I still can't believe all this is happening."

Wes managed to calm down after releasing his rant and took her hand. "I'm sorry I blew up at you, okay? It's just that . . . if anything had happened to you . . . Of course, you must feel pretty traumatized after all you've learned today. I didn't mean to shout."

Michelle drew her hand from his. "So we've got confirmation from Titus. Is that even enough?"

"I've got more. Copies of checks from a dear ol' granny who got a second mortgage on her little Redford house to pay Montesi to keep her grandson out of jail. That was an idiot move on Montesi's part, accepting those checks and all. Up until that point and from then on his hustle was a strictly cash-and-carry proposition. Who knows what kinda sob story Granny came up with to convince him to accept the checks? From what I understand the woman is in a wheelchair. I'm thinking she had problems arranging transportation and in a weak, greedy, and impatient moment his brain checked out and Montesi agreed to let her mail him the checks. Now, any wagers on how long you think it's gonna take before Montesi rats out Pratt under oath? I mean, he shot his mouth off to you when he didn't even know his ass was on the line."

"But how did you—?"

"I always work more than one angle. I've spoken to Malone already."

"Your editor?" Michelle didn't mask her surprise. "I thought you were going to wait awhile before going to him."

"I was, but I changed my mind. I've gotten the go-ahead to move ahead and write the story. Malone thinks it's going to be big."

"Of course, you wouldn't be bothered if it were anything but." Michelle's voice suddenly took on a harder edge.

"Excuse me, but was that some sort of snipe?"

"Let's not play games here. Remember, I know all about your relentless ambition." The words bolted out of her mouth before she had a chance to think.

"And I also know the pot ain't calling the kettle black, is it?" he bit out, then quickly softened his tone and reached to embrace her.

But she recoiled. "Didn't you hear what I just said, Wesley? John Ashton Pratt is my father!"

Wes paused for a long moment. "Look, Chelle, I can't even begin to imagine how confused you must feel right now—after everything that's been dumped on you today. But my interest in taking Pratt down is not just about scoring another Page A-One lead. I thought I explained that to you. He worked Patrick's case and if he's corrupt, it should be exposed."

"Your editor knows Pratt worked your brother's case, right?"

Wes's hesitation and the uneasy expression revealed that he knew exactly where she was headed with that question.

"Does Malone Hughes know that Pratt worked your brother's case? I'm going to go out on a limb here and say he doesn't, because he knows it reeks of a serious conflict of interest if you, someone with a big, *obvious* ax to grind, are breaking this particular story. Hardly makes you the best candidate for being fair and impartial."

"And we both know you're the paragon of professional and ethical virtue," Wes parried.

Drop-jawed, Michelle shrank and glared at him. Then in a huff she moved to scramble out of his car; when Wes latched on to her wrist, she snatched it out of his grip.

"Wait. Wait. Chelle, please. I'm sorry. I shouldn't have said that," he said, issuing a swift mea culpa. "I did not mean that. Look. . . ." He pushed out a heavy breath, balled his fist, and pounded the steering wheel. "We both need to chill out. We need to think about what we're saying and stop acting so ugly with each other, 'cause that's getting us nowhere."

Heeding his voice of reason, Michelle sagged against the passenger seat again. "I'm sorry, too. It's just that . . . Well, I'm not sure what to feel about Pratt right now. The man's literally a stranger to me. Yet, yet—"

"He's *still* your father," Wes said, sounding sympathetic.

"Yes. And Patrick's your brother. He needs your help. How could you choose?" Michelle went on to answer her own question. "You don't. You do what you have to do. I won't stand in your way or guilt you into backing off." She kissed his cheek. "Good night, Wesley."

Michelle wouldn't wait for him to help her out. She nudged his jacket off of her shoulders, opened the door, then stepped onto the concrete driveway.

Wes sprang out of the car and skirted the grille to stop her. "Chelle, wait! You shouldn't be alone tonight. Let me come in with you. We could talk this thing through some more."

"Thanks, but I'll be fine," she said, not meeting his eyes. "I just need some time alone. And I'm very tired. I wouldn't be good company."

"We don't have to talk. I could just hold you," he offered softly.

Michelle placed her hand on his chest, then palmed his cheek. "Thanks for the offer." She managed a weak smile. "I really do appreciate it, but the best thing for us both right now is space before both of us say something else we don't mean but can't take back."

Wesley escorted her to the front door, took the keys from her hand, then slipped the house key in the lock until it clicked. "You sure you want to be alone?"

She retrieved her keys. "Yes."

He looked down into her hazel eyes. "You do know this is all going to work itself out, right?"

"Right," Michelle replied, forcing an optimistic note into her voice.

She watched him reluctantly trudge back to his car and fold himself inside. The Ferrari disappeared into the night. With her gut still in knots, she went to the kitchen and by rote prepared a cup of herbal tea.

As she sipped, she tried sorting through the rush of conflicting feelings. The emotion that disturbed her most was the anger still simmering just below the surface of the calm and reason she tried so desperately to cling to. She wanted to will the anger away, but it ran deep, starting with the anger at her mother for lying to her all these years. And now she felt herself starting to resent Wesley's role in it all. If she was completely honest, she'd admit that what she really wanted was for Wes to back off on the Pratt piece until she could make sense of it all and decide if she wanted to pursue a relationship with Pratt or not. But how irrational was that? God, if Pratt indeed was a criminal, soliciting bribes for verdicts . . . She shuddered at the thought. Didn't he deserve to go to prison? Yes, her rational, sensible side knew that was the right thing. But that little girl inside of her who had scrawled that pathetic letter to Pastor Wingate, inviting him to move in with her and her mother, still wanted her father. Her eyes welled up with tears until they slipped down her cheeks. God help her. She loathed feeling so weak and needy for that connection. She was a thirty-three-year-old woman, for crying out loud! When would she get it together, grow up, and *stop yearning for Daddy*? It all crushed her down now, making it difficult to breathe. Her unwise attachments to older, successful men like Stanford Chapelle, Desmond Bloomingthal, Maxwell Coleman. Men who represented something she'd never had. Now hunched over the table she sobbed outright, her tears mingling with the taste of mint tea on her lips. She cried until she felt spent, but suddenly a tremendous urge to seek and know more overwhelmed her. She snatched her purse and car keys from the coffee table, then took off.

Twenty-five

At the loft Wes fell on his bed, staring up at the exposed ductwork and trusses on the ceiling. He wrestled with his wrenching dilemma. Sure, a huge part of what he did was about pacifying his restless ambition. But at the same time he derived huge satisfaction from digging for the truth and righting wrongs with his splashy exposés.

Even if Pratt hadn't had ties to Patrick's case, could Wes just turn a blind eye to his unlawful machinations? Wes wasn't so sure he could.

Wes recalled that desolate look in Michelle's eyes when they'd exchanged their good nights. He reached for the phone on his nightstand to dial her number but decided to leave her be—at least for tonight.

Everything would work itself out. She just needed some time to think it all through, he decided, coming to his feet again. He moved to the bar to fill a snifter with cognac.

Though Michelle's last words and kisses were obviously meant to be reassuring, Wes still sensed her pulling away emotionally. He couldn't let that happen. He wouldn't let that happen.

The guard stationed at the reception desk in the *Herald*'s main lobby pushed a clipboard at Michelle. She signed it and passed him her *Herald* photo ID for inspection.

"Squeezing in more overtime?" the brown-haired guard with a scraggly beard asked cheerily. Michelle caught a glimpse of David Letterman on the TV screen no bigger than a child's lunch box positioned to the guard's right.

"Yup," Michelle said with a curt nod as she dashed toward the bank of elevators. This time of night she had her pick; all eight were grounded at the lobby level, doors open and waiting.

She stepped inside and punched the button for a floor. When the doors wouldn't budge, she remembered that late-night security required punching in designated codes to activate the elevators. Michelle cursed under her breath as she rummaged through her bag for the numbers she had yet to use because she'd never tried to enter the newsroom that late before.

With a sigh of relief, Michelle removed the slip of blue paper tucked in a side pocket of her purse. It had the elevator security code numbers for all the floors occupied by *Herald* staff. Each floor in the building had a different series of eight numbers. Carmen had passed them along to Michelle the day she'd given her the official orientation tour of the building. Thank God for that woman!

Michelle punched in the series for Floor 24, where the newsroom library was located.

Inside the library two fluorescent panels overhead were lit, just enough to see the layout of the place and avoid tripping over things, but it wasn't nearly bright enough for Michelle's purposes. She flipped several switches, bathing the library in light.

She dropped her belongings at one of the desks that had a computer. She turned it on to search the *Herald* computerized clip files, but while it booted up she would scour the paper archives that had yet to be converted. She went straight for the shelves housing the P folders—for Pratt. She should've known the paper files and photos would be missing. Most likely Wesley had checked them out, but she still had the online archive to peruse.

Michelle was awakened by a gentle pat on her shoulder.

"I've heard of burning the midnight oil and all, but don't you think you pushed it a little too far?" Thelma Baldwin, the *Herald*'s head librarian, looked down through reading glasses perched low on her prominent nose.

Michelle blinked, then remembered that at 5:00 a.m. she'd put her head down to rest her eyes for a few minutes— after staring at the computer monitor for hours, reading all she could on her father. She must have fallen asleep.

"What?" Michelle cleared the sandpaper rasp from her voice. "What time is it?"

Thelma pointed to the wall clock. It read 8:32 a.m. Michelle's workday was supposed to start at 9:00 a.m. and she had an interview scheduled at 9:30 a.m, she realized in panic. Not only did she have no toothbrush, but she looked disheveled, in the same clothes she'd worn to work the day before. If no one else noticed that the fuchsia blouse was a repeat, hawkeyed Wesley surely would.

"Did you come to work early or did you spend the night?" Thelma asked.

Lying was pointless, Michelle decided. "I inadvertently spent the night."

"Must be some story you're working on to get all engrossed like that," Thelma said.

But Michelle didn't touch that one. "I have an interview shortly and I don't have time to dash home first."

Thelma nodded toward a closet near the library exit. "I have a clean sweater I keep in there when the central air gets too cool. You're welcome to borrow it if you like. You have on black slacks, but with a different top maybe it won't look so obvious that you're wearing yesterday's clothes."

"Thank you, Thelma. You have no idea how much that

means to me. I'll have it cleaned before I get it back to you."

"Don't worry about it." Thelma smiled at Michelle. "Glad I can help."

Michelle gathered her purse and went to the closet to remove the sweater. *Yikes!* It was one of those holiday-themed sweaters. Halloween at that! Stamped with multiple arched-back black cats and grinning jack-o'-lanterns, it clearly wasn't Michelle. But was it anyone's style?

Still grateful for Thelma's generosity, Michelle quickly shoved her arms inside its sleeves and secured its plastic black goblin buttons to cover the silk fuchsia blouse underneath.

Groggy-eyed, Michelle made her way to the Headliner's vending machines on the twelfth floor to load up on mints and gum until she could get her hands on a toothbrush and toothpaste. She also needed caffeine, so she grabbed a big cup of coffee, then stood in line behind a short man with a bad toupee and a chubby one wearing thick glasses whose magnifying lenses made his eyeballs look big as boiled eggs. Snapping her gum, Shawna hardly acknowledged them as she took their money. Fawning customer service was obviously only reserved for men who looked like Wesley.

When the two men in front departed, Michelle passed Shawna the coffee money.

"So how's accounting coming?" Michelle thought she'd at least take a stab at being friendly to Shawna, because Wes seemed to like her.

"Fine," the young woman managed in a flat-affect voice, between gum snaps, then went back to reading her *Bronze Thrills* confessions magazine.

Why was Michelle not surprised by Shawna's disinterest? Not only could Wes work his special kind of magic on an apathetic cashier, but he also could charm the dot off the letter *i*.

With twenty minutes until her interview subject arrived

Michelle decided she deserved a five-minute coffee break. She'd just sat down when Craig came over.

He pulled out the chair across from hers and settled in. "I hope you don't mind if I join you."

She did mind. She just needed the alone time to get her head together. But Craig was always so pleasant to her, she didn't want to be rude. "No, not at all." She smiled.

"So how's it going?" he asked.

"Okay."

"I hear you're settling into Katie's beat just fine. Barbara's been raving about you."

"So how are your wife and the twins? Those boys really put away some pizza that day at Chuck E. Cheese." Michelle made an effort to make small talk.

"They're fine. They're all excited about having a big birthday party coming up in a few weeks. We're inviting all their friends and family. My mom, Dad, and sister Lindsey is even flying in from New York. Of course, Wes will be there. I'm sure he'll want to bring you, so I hope you'll consider joining us."

Michelle replied with a mysterious smile instead of committing right then. She didn't know if she and Wes would still be an item in a few weeks. She changed the subject. "So you say you have a sister who lives in New York? What does she do there?"

"She's a television news producer."

"Another journalist in the family."

"Lindsey called last night to catch up. We usually speak at least a couple of times every week, but we've both been so busy lately we let more than a few weeks pass. Anyway, we finally had a chance to talk last night," Craig chattered on amiably. "Lindsey needed updates on family and friends and of course she got around to asking about Wesley as usual."

"Wesley, huh?" Michelle instinctively knew there was a story there and did her best not to react.

"Anyway, I know I promised to keep quiet about your relationship and I swear I have here at work. But Lindsey, well, Lindsey is family, so I didn't think Wes would mind my telling her. I hope you don't, either."

"So you told her Wes was seeing someone?"

"Yes. When she heard about you and Wes she was surprised." He grinned. "She didn't think Wes would ever really fall for anyone."

"You told her Wes had fallen for someone? These words came from Wes?"

"Not just from his mouth, but his behavior. He's a different guy since he met you, and Lindsey couldn't be more pleased . . . I must admit I'm surprised to note."

"So Lindsey and Wes are close?" Michelle found herself asking as curiosity practically choked her.

"She's really happy for you two," Craig announced pointedly, instead of answering Michelle's question. "That's good, because I wasn't sure how . . ." He seemed distracted, then stopped himself.

"You weren't sure about what?" Michelle prompted. Her heart thumped against her chest. Hard.

"Oh, nothing. I need to shut my damn trap. The brain is too foggy early in the morning without coffee. I'd better go grab a cup and get back to work before my editor puts out an APB on me." Craig clammed up, then surged to his feet. He flashed her a uneasy grin before departing.

As Craig paid for his coffee and sweet roll, he kept darting antsy glances in Michelle's direction, probably well aware that his reticence to elaborate on Wesley and Lindsey's closeness had revealed way too much.

Craig was hiding more. Michelle had a hunch what it was. And just thinking about it made her ill. Who *hadn't* Wesley hooked up with?

Twenty-six

One glimpse at Michelle and Wesley knew she hadn't spent the previous night in her own bed. That thought unnerved him. He knew he should not have left her alone, but she'd practically begged for space the evening before. What could he do but give it to her?

Not only did he recognize the black slacks and the sliver of fuchsia blouse peeking out from the edge of that ugly sweater as clothing she'd worn the day before, but he could even see the crest-shaped shadows beneath her eyes from where he sat at his desk.

He positioned his chair to face his monitor and typed her an e-mail: *U-O-K?*

Michelle looked over and nodded.

Still not satisfied, Wes sent a second e-mail: *Will buzz you.*

He walked to one of the private interview rooms with his cell phone. He was starting to feel silly going to such measures to speak to her when she was just a few yards away.

He punched in the number to her desk phone.

She answered using her official work voice: "The *Herald*, Michelle Michaels speaking."

"You sure you're all right? You don't look so good," Wes said, hoping she might want to explain her appearance.

"I'm fine."

"I'm not buying it. You look worn-out and you're still

dressed in yesterday's clothes. Meet me in the parking garage, at my car, in ten minutes. Level fifteen, slot fifty-eight."

"I have an interview in five minutes. I can't take off now."

"We meet after your interview, then." He paced the small room that only had a tiny table and two chairs.

"I'm on deadline. Barbara will want the piece before noon."

"After you turn it in, we'll go for lunch."

"But—"

"I know, I know, *away* from the *Herald* building. I'll hang close to my desk today."

Realizing Wesley wasn't going to take no for an answer, she relented. "Okay."

By 2:17 p.m. Wesley wheeled his car out of the *Herald*'s parking garage for his very late lunch with Michelle.

"So why are you dressed in that god-awful Halloween sweater and yesterday's clothes?" Worried, Wesley wasted little time getting to the questions that had plagued him for the past five hours. "Did you get any sleep last night?"

"I must really look like shit to you right about now," Michelle wryly said.

"After yesterday and all, I am concerned about you." Wes cast glances between the road ahead of him and Michelle. "Have you had anything to eat?"

"I don't feel up to dining in; can we just get carryout from somewhere?"

"What would you like?"

"Food. I don't much care. I could eat that if you'd slather a little butter on it," she grumbled, pointing at the empty Styrofoam cup that had held his morning coffee.

He pulled into the first fast-food restaurant they came upon, a burger joint. Then he eased behind a train of four cars in the drive-through service lane.

While they waited to place their order, he'd get answers. "So what did you do after I left last night?"

"I went to the *Herald*."

"That late? Why?"

"I wanted to read up on Pratt."

Wes immediately felt a wave of guilt. Of course she'd want to find out as much as she could about her biological father.

"I figured they'd have more in their archives than what I could surf up on the Internet for free."

"I see. And you spent all night there?" Wes inched the Ferrari forward as the line ahead shortened.

"I didn't mean to stay all night. You know how time can fly when you're engrossed in research."

Because Wes had done his own thorough research on Pratt he had a good idea what kind of personal information she'd come across. "And do you feel better now?"

"If truth be told, I think I got walloped by TMI." Her chuckle was humorless.

"Too much information?" he asked.

"By all accounts Pratt has been happily married to the same woman for almost four decades." Michelle forced an upbeat note in her voice, but Wes could tell she was hurting, very badly, as she tried rattling off Pratt's family ties like a grocery list. "Has three children. Two of whom, the sons, John Junior, thirty-seven, and Brock, thirty-five, graduated with top honors from Harvard Law and are now very successful practicing attorneys. One here in town and the other at a very prestigious firm in Chicago. Pratt has a daughter, Shelby, a doctor, specializes in orthopedic surgery. And get this: she's thirty-three."

Wesley knew the significance of that number and felt tremendous empathy for Michelle at that moment. "Oh, honey, I don't know what to say." He wanted to draw her into his arms, but the driver in the black Hummer behind them slapped his horn, urging Wesley to close the car-length-and-a-half space between his Ferrari and the Toyota ahead of him.

"Sounds as if his wife and my mother were carrying babies about the same time. So if I really let myself go wild, venturing down memory lane, when I was blowing out candles on birthday cakes wishing I had a dad, he was probably right there with Shelby, helping to light hers. Isn't that a trip?" Michelle's eyes brightened with tears. "I'm sorry, Wes, I'm acting like a blubbering fool. I should be way over these perceived slights by now. I mean, it's not as if he knew about me, then rejected me, right?"

As Wes eased the car to the menu, he removed a travel package of Kleenex he kept in the glove compartment for her.

Michelle took one. "I mean, Ma never told him about me. He doesn't even know I exist."

Wes seriously doubted knowing Michelle's mother was pregnant would have made a difference to a man like Pratt but kept that to himself. "Have you decided if you want to change that or not?"

Michelle shook her head, then blew her nose.

A voice blared from the speaker mounted beneath the menu, "Welcome. May I take your order?"

"I'll have two cheeseburgers and a Coke," Michelle said.

Wes had no appetite. "I'll just have a medium Coke."

"I just don't see how I'd fit into the pretty little picture that is his perfect life." Then she caught herself. "Wait; once your story on him is published his life won't be so perfect anymore, will it?"

"Look, Chelle, I've been doing a lot of thinking and I don't have to be the one breaking the story. In fact, I don't *want* to break it now that I know Pratt is your father."

"What difference does it make? I mean, you can't exactly cork the genie back inside its bottle now," Michelle said, snipping her words. "You've told a senior editor about it.

There's no way he would back down on the story. If you don't do it, he'll just put another reporter on it."

"Then so be it." Wes knew Michelle was right. Stopping the story now would be akin to stopping a runaway train.

"Somebody else will get the glory, the credit. Do you understand what you're giving up? Your editor might even demand that you turn over all of your hard work, your notes and sources."

"So be it," he repeated without the least bit of regret.

"I understand why you want to take Pratt down."

"But that doesn't mean you like it, either."

"It could mean a second, quicker shot at freedom for your brother."

"But *I* don't have to actually write the story. And I'm not going to. Besides, when Malone finds out I have a connection to Pratt through my brother he won't let me write the damn thing anyway."

"And you're going to tell him about Patrick?" Michelle looked dubious.

"I'm going to tell him about Patrick."

Wesley drove up to the drive-through window where he paid for the food, then reached for the aromatic bags containing the cheeseburgers. "I know I have to get you back to the newsroom, but I don't think you should be alone again tonight."

"I need to be alone tonight. I'm going to crash as soon as I get home. I'm bone tired and I have a stiff neck and shoulders from falling asleep hunched over a desk." Michelle wouldn't look at him.

Wesley steered out of the parking lot and pointed the car in the *Herald*'s direction. "Where does it hurt exactly?" He put one hand on her shoulder to massage away the pain.

As he kneaded with just the right amount of pressure Michelle couldn't help thinking about how skilled his touch always felt. And then how he got so experienced. She tried not to linger on the women before her, but that was becoming more difficult by the day. Then that conversation she'd had with Craig that morning rushed back to her.

"Wesley?" Michelle dug inside her bag for a burger. She unwrapped one and took a greedy bite.

"Yes, sweetheart?"

"Craig says Lindsey is coming down for the twins' big birthday bash," she tossed out casually, studying Wes's reaction.

"Yeah, so?"

"So what's the deal between you and Lindsey?"

Michelle just quietly waited for a reply to her question.

"She's my best friend's sister. We all practically grew up together. Great girl."

Michelle snorted and muttered something under her breath that she wouldn't repeat.

"Excuse me?" he said.

"And that's all she ever was to you?" She cocked an accusing brow. "Your best friend's sister?"

Wes glanced in her direction, then back at the road. "Yes. Why?"

"Okay, if you say so," Michelle replied a mite too quickly.

Wes knew there was a lot more behind that remark. He went on the defensive. "I swear nothing ever went down between us."

"Lack of opportunity lately, huh? I mean with her living in New York now and all." Michelle didn't like feeling like a jealous harpy, but she couldn't seem to help herself.

"Lack of interest *always*," Wes said coolly, not liking where this conversation was headed. "Is that so difficult for you to believe?"

"It's just that . . . well, I know you."

"Well, whatever you think you *know* about us, as in Lindsey and me having some sort of romantic tryst, you're dead wrong." Wes shifted the gear stick roughly and shook his head. "Man, I'm gonna bust Craig's head if he was the one telling you otherwise."

"Craig didn't say anything actually. It was what he didn't say that got me curious."

"Well, for the record, let me make myself clear. I haven't lied to you about anybody I've been involved with so far and I won't start lying now. There's never been a man-woman thing between Lindsey and me." Wes couldn't tell if she believed him or not, but he was glad he'd spelled it out. "So what do you say? May I come over tonight and rub you down?"

He pulled the car into the *Herald* parking garage.

"Thanks for the offer, but I really just need to be alone tonight," she repeated coolly.

Wes tried not to take it personally, but two nights in a row? On Wes, insecurity was not a good fit; it chafed like hell. He couldn't help feeling as if she was pushing him away.

He parked, then helped her out of the car. As they moved toward the bank of elevators, he tried reaching for her hand, but she drew away.

"We're back on *Herald* property." She walked ahead of him. "Remember, anybody could see us."

Wes, who was losing his patience with the routine, threw up his hands in exasperation. "Of course. How could I forget?"

"Would you like to go in first or do I go in first?"

"That's right," he said facetiously. "We couldn't possibly walk back in the newsroom at the *same* time. Someone might assume we've spent the past hour making out in the office supplies closet."

"Look, Wesley, you know the rules," she spat.

"How could I ever forget when you keep pounding me over the head with them?"

Michelle stopped, mouth drawn tight, arms crossed over

her chest. "Ya know, Wesley, I really don't need to deal with your whining about this right now."

"*My* whining?" His laughter sounded harsher than intended. "Isn't that rich when that's all you've been doing since we met!" He immediately wanted to snatch the words back, but it was too late.

Michelle's eyes ignited and then wordlessly she stalked toward the garage elevator. He reached and hooked her arm, but she snatched it out of his grasp.

"Michelle, I'm sorry. I didn't mean that. Let me make it up to you. Let me—"

"Look, Wesley, if truth be told, I think—"

"What?"

"This whole thing with us is getting to be more than I bargained for. We've had our fun and gotten some things out of our system—"

He felt his face heat with fury. "Gotten some things out of our system? You make it sound like food poisoning, diarrhea, or something."

Narrowing her eyes, Michelle tsked. "You know what I mean. You know what our hooking up was about. And I know what it was about. Scratching an itch. We've done it. Now we move on and maybe still salvage a working relationship."

"A working relationship?" Wesley felt as if he'd been kicked in the stomach. She sounded so cold and distant. Was this the woman he'd eagerly opened his heart up to?

Michelle continued in that all-business tone that was like icicles stabbing his eardrums. "You must have done this dozens of times, Wesley. You get around, remember? Why would this time be any different?"

Wes had to gulp for air. He swallowed but managed to will his lips to move. "Why is this time different, you ask?" His voice now a strained whisper. "Because, because I fell in love with you, Chelle. It's just that simple. I love you."

Michelle gasped; then her face crumbled. "Stop it, Wesley!" Her eyes filled with angry tears. "Just stop it!" Her heart had momentarily leaped for joy. She loved him, too! Oh, how she wanted to believe that her love would be reciprocated beyond a few wonderful weeks. But her head wouldn't let her—not for long—knowing such emotions were too risky with a man like Wesley. Yes, he was nice and sincere. He probably never set out to leave or lose interest in the women he became involved with, but the bottom line was, he had, time and time again. He couldn't help himself. He obviously thrived on not only the thrill of the chase but also variety. Had he only been interested in her because she hadn't been one of his more willing conquests at first? And now that she needed to end things he'd gone and upped the ante by tossing out the *l*-word. He might even *think* he loved her now, but would he grow bored and restless once she completely surrendered her heart and soul to him? What would happen when the tedium of a sure thing set in? How long would it take before his eye started to rove again? A month? Maybe six if she was lucky? Could Michelle handle the anxiety of always wondering when some hot chick would make him do more than sneak a peek at her butt in a micromini? The constant insecurity would eat her alive. Drive even the most self-assured woman plumb crazy. Even now her head wouldn't let her buy into his beautiful words without wondering if they were just a tactic from the Wesley Abbott Player's Handbook.

"It's all about the game for you." Tears slipped down her cheeks. "The chase, isn't it? And it's all about winning at all costs. You'll do or say anything to get your way."

Wesley went to her, then gripped her shoulders. "Look at me, Michelle."

She refused, knowing, as mentally and physically exhausted as she was, her resolve was way too weak.

Wes lifted her chin and forced her to look him in the face. "Look at me." His nostrils flared and fire danced in his eyes.

"I have *never* told any woman outside family that I loved her." He gave her a little shake. "Do you hear me?"

Before she could reply, they heard the *ding* of the elevator and voices. A group of people Michelle recognized as *Herald* employees stepped off, laughing and chatting. Wes tried to shift himself and Michelle into a shadowed corner out of sight, but she used the distraction to break out of his embrace and run.

"Michelle!" he called after her, but she wouldn't look back. "Michelle!"

She bolted for the elevators and jabbed at the buttons. The door closed before he could get in, Michelle slumped against the wall.

Once inside the ladies' restroom on the newsroom floor, Michelle splashed her face with cold water, smoothed her mussed hair, and adjusted the tacky borrowed Halloween sweater. She still looked like crap.

A toilet flushed and her editor, Barbara, emerged from one of the stalls. She caught a glimpse of Michelle's red, puffy eyes in the mirror. "You coming down with something?" she asked in a concerned voice as she pumped pink liquid from the soap dispenser.

"I don't know." Michelle's voice trembled as she touched the back of her hand to her own forehead. "I might be. I was hoping I could leave a little early today. I don't feel well at all."

Barb's brow pleated. "Of course, you can. I'm not a slave driver."

"Thank you. I'll work overtime tomorrow to make up for it."

"Don't worry about that. You just go on home and take good care of yourself." Barbara dried her hands with a paper towel, then touched Michelle's shoulder lightly. "Hey, I also want you to know what a great job you've done so far. I wasn't so sure you could handle it, coming from an edgier

news side and all, but you've done just fine. Great, in fact."
She smiled. "And I've told the managing and hiring editors
they should consider offering you a permanent position
here—in the business section, of course. Not that I wouldn't
mind keeping you on in Features, but I know that's not
where your heart is. So if you want a permanent job here, it's
yours."

"Oh, Barbara, thank you. You have no idea how nice it is
to have your approval." Michelle meant that. And in turn she
had acquired a newfound respect for everyone's contribu-
tions to such a solid newspaper. Everyone's role was
important—from the clerks who penned the obituaries to the
graphic artist who drew the weather maps.

When Barbara departed, Michelle splashed more water on
her face to prepare for the drive home. She had her purse and
she'd left her briefcase at home. There was no need to go back
to her desk. No need to face Wesley again so soon. It was over
between them and she needed time to let that sink in.

Michelle left the restroom, bypassed the bank of elevators for the stairwell used during fire drills.

Later, Wes pulled out of the *Herald* parking garage, still not
believing that day's turn of events. The very first time he'd
ever told a woman he loved her. Her response? She ran from
him! Not only ran but also left freakin' skid marks!

He considered tearing straight over to Michelle's house
to finish that conversation, but he thought better of it. After
all, if he hadn't pushed after she refused to hold his hand,
they might not have had that argument and she might not
have tried to break things off. She'd had to cope with too
much in the last few days. She obviously wasn't thinking
straight, but pushing Wesley away and sabotaging their good
thing was no way to deal.

He remembered that he'd told Lonette and Kelly he'd
drop by after work that day to check out Kelly's computer.

He might as well keep that promise, he decided, taking the interstate toward their Southfield neighborhood.

It blew Wesley's mind that Michelle was still so terrified of him. If he could kick his own ass, he would, for always playing it so fast and loose with women over the years.

Somehow he had hoped Michelle would see in his eyes and feel in his touch that she was indeed different and meant so much more to him. He merged with early-evening highway traffic, mulling over this setback.

He couldn't depend on time helping him get through to Michelle—because he didn't have a lot of it. How could he convince her that his heart was true before she left for Manhattan? That would be next to impossible if she refused to spend any more time with him outside the *Herald*. Words weren't enough. It was going to take a grander gesture. Something significant. Something serious. Something damn impossible for her to dismiss as just another player's ploy. And he knew exactly what he had to do.

Lonette led Wesley to Kelly's computer set up in the neat family room of her light and airy condo.

"Let me get you a regular chair." Lonette rolled the pink one meant for child-sized romps to the side.

Kelly claimed it so she could watch and chat with Wesley.

"Can I get you something to drink, Wesley?" Lonette asked.

After the day he'd had Wes could use a drink, make that good stiff drinks, but he still had to drive home. "No, I'm good. Thanks, Lonette."

"I need to check on my casserole in the oven," Lonette said. "Holler if you need anything."

Wes turned on the computer. "Come here, Kelly."

She popped up from one of her pink chairs.

"Show me what you do when you want to play a game,"

Wes said, positioning the child on his lap in front of the keyboard.

Kelly's small hand covered the mouse. She clicked, then tapped a few keys. It still amazed Wes how computer proficient the youngest kids were these days. When he was Kelly's age the most technologically advanced toys he'd owned were an electric train set and remote control car. And even then he recalled his father enjoying them a lot more than he had.

"See, the *Clifford* game won't act right." With a pout, Kelly peered over her shoulder.

Wesley looked at the screen and then determined that the problem was relatively minor. He called out to Lonette, who returned wearing bright red oven mitts.

"Where do you keep the game software?"

"Game software?" Lonette obviously didn't have a clue.

"Yeah, the CDs. They're what's used to install the games on the computer. I think I just need to reload the *Clifford* software."

"CDs?" Kelly piped up. "You talking about those shiny round things? I watched Daddy when he put shiny round things in to make my 'puter work."

"Yeah, exactly. Did you see where your daddy put those shiny round things?"

Kelly slipped off Wesley's lap and went to a towering bookshelf. She pointed to the top shelf. "He put them way up there."

Strange, Wesley thought; that shelf was out of not only Kelly's reach but also Lonette's, who Wes guessed was about five-seven. Even she would require a chair or step stool to reach them. Why would Patrick store them in such an inconvenient location?

Wes tipped his head back to check out the shelf. He didn't see anything but dusty potted plastic plants and decorative bric-a-brac.

"I saw him put it behind those leaves there," Kelly told Wes.

"You mean the plant here?" Wes touched the one in the middle.

"The one on the other side." Kelly pointed to Wes's right.

On his toes, Wes reached up, shoved the plant aside, and found a small cardboard box filled with computer CDs.

He sat back down before the computer and flipped through the game software until he came upon the case for the *Clifford the Big Red Dog* game. Inside he found an unmarked CD.

He slipped it inside the computer anyway, and what he found on it saddened, then enraged him.

Twenty-seven

The next morning Michelle asked Fatima to accompany her to Willow Grove. Liz, who had completed the inpatient portion of the program, had been released.

"Do you really think ten days is enough?" Fatima asked, her expression grave, as they climbed the steps to the center's entrance.

"Her treatment is far from over," Michelle explained. "She's still required to visit regularly for intensive group, family, and individual counseling."

"They ain't playing in those sessions, are they?" Fatima shook her head. "When I think about what she finally purged as a result, that stuff about your father in particular. I wonder if my mother even had a clue about him or Aunt Liz's bipolar disorder."

"Aunt Caroline probably suspected that something was wrong, but back when they were young, people didn't speak of mental illness the way we do now. And you know how black folks are about that sorta thing. Shrinks and counseling are strictly for bored, rich, overindulgent white folks. After all the hardships our ancestors endured with slavery and all . . . what we have to deal with now, comparatively, is a piece of cake. We're expected to keep on truckin'—no matter what." Michelle walked to the sign-in desk and introduced herself to the dark-haired young woman there.

"I'll let Liz know you're here. I'll just be a minute," the

woman said. She left and returned five minutes later with Liz, who was carrying a small suitcase and garment bag.

Tentatively Liz approached Michelle and Fatima.

Michelle, who was still reeling from her mother's revelations, decided she had to make an effort to move beyond her hurt feelings and frayed trust. Wallowing in self-pity was not going to do either of them any good.

"Ma." Michelle met her halfway with outstretched arms.

Liz dropped her luggage. Mother and daughter embraced. Fatima joined them.

Michelle realized she and her mother still had a long way to go to repair their damaged relationship, but both were willing to make the effort by committing to mother-daughter counseling sessions for the duration of Michelle's stay in Detroit and beyond. She'd made a promise to fly back there at least once every six weeks for the next year.

Because Michelle still had work, she dropped Fatima and Liz off at the Ferndale bungalow with a promise to return and join them for a quick lunch. She dreaded going back to the *Herald,* where she would surely see Wesley.

Fortunately, Wesley wasn't at his desk when she arrived and by the time she left for the day he had yet to return to the newsroom.

Twenty-eight

First thing the next morning, instead of heading directly to the *Herald* building, Michelle found herself steering her car in the direction of the courthouse.

Twenty minutes later, wearing a brimmed hat and sunglasses she'd picked up at a drugstore as a disguise in case Titus Montesi was around, she took a seat in the back of Pratt's busy courtroom and just watched the man.

Her mother had been right. Michelle had inherited many of his features—the auburn hair, butterscotch skin, and light-hued eyes. He had a commanding presence and deep voice that would've been wonderful reading the Prince Charming parts of her childhood fairy tales. All the woulda-coulda-shouldas seemed so lame right then.

She sat there for hours, taking in as many details as she could about the man—the firm set of his mouth, full brows, aquiline nose where small round-framed spectacles sat. She considered his list of transgressions—from cheating on his wife to abandoning Liz coldly, as well as the courtroom crimes he'd allegedly committed. Between the hours spent poring over his *Herald* online files and studying him in the flesh, all of the cracks, gapes, and holes slowly began to fill. A barren dryness had been drenched by a cloudburst. Everything was suddenly clear. It was then that Michelle finally knew exactly what she had to do.

• • •

A bundle of restless energy, Wes dropped on an exercise mat in the corner of his loft and performed so many ab crunches and push-ups he lost count. He couldn't stop even when his muscles quivered and screamed for mercy.

He'd informed his editor, Malone Hughes, that he planned to work from home that day, but so far he'd done very little real work.

Every time the phone rang he'd prayed it was Michelle or Patrick. But neither had called, much to Wes's dismay. Since he left Lonette's place the night before he had been willing the damn phone to ring. It was not as if he could just call Patrick anytime the mood struck him and get him on the line. There were prison rules and restrictions; however, that hadn't stopped Wes from leaving about a dozen messages for Patrick to phone him. All he could do now was wait.

He really wanted to see to Patrick, but because correctional center visiting days were on a rotating schedule, determined by inmate last names, Wes would have to wait four more days before he could drive up to Davenport for a face-to-face meeting with his brother.

Clad only in sweat-soaked sweatpants, Wes lifted himself off the floor, wrapped his hands with Ace bandage, then tugged on a pair of sparring gloves. He pummeled the hell out of his punching bag, grunting from the gut each time his fists made contact with the leather surface. *Thwack!* Perspiration rolled off his face and the pumped muscles of his arms and torso.

He'd already made up his mind that he was driving to Michelle's later that evening and he was going to *make* her talk to him—even if it meant camping outside her doorstep. Michelle was his. *Thwack!* She'd brought him nothing but satisfaction in every way. *Thwack! Thwack!* She'd opened his eyes to the possibilities and dreams he'd never seriously considered.

Their blowup would not keep him down. *Thwack! Thwack!* In his heart he knew it wasn't over. And it was just a matter of time before Michelle realized that, too. *Thwack!* He thought about the little velvet drawstring pouch he'd gotten from his mother earlier that morning.

He looked at the clock, estimated the time it would take for Michelle to get to her mother's Ferndale home, factoring in rush hour traffic.

When the phone rang he stopped midjab, then reached out to steady the swaying punching bag before tugging off his gloves and dashing to the phone.

He was winded as he tossed the gloves on the terra-cotta-colored counter. "Wes here."

An operator's voice informed him that an inmate from Davenport Correctional Facility was on the line, then asked if Wes wanted to accept the call. He did.

Finally, Patrick checking in.

"So is everything with our project still on schedule?" Patrick wanted to know.

"If you mean the exposé, yes, it is."

"I heard you got the envelope? We got 'im now."

"But I'm not writing the story, Patrick."

"What?" Patrick's voice was panicked and confused. "I . . . I . . . don't understand."

"It's a huge conflict of interest for me to break the story." Wes thought it wise that they not talk specifics on the phone. "It could mean trouble for the *Herald* if the connection between you, me, and the subject gets out."

"But somebody is writing it, right?"

"Yeah, another reporter is on it."

"Good." Patrick sighed.

"A lot of good it's going to do you, though," Wes announced casually. "Even if you get a new trial, the same ol' evidence is out there."

"But I'm innocent."

"Tell it to somebody else, Patrick. You can't fool me anymore."

"But I was right about that judge," Patrick insisted, now in a huff.

"And so wrong about everything else."

"What you talking about?" Patrick had the nerve to explode.

"Keep your voice down."

"You'd better tell me what you're talking about right this minute or—"

"Or what?" Wes challenged him. "What can you do where you are? And where you're obviously going to stay for the next three years."

Patrick shifted his tone from edgy to placatory. "I'm sorry, Bro. Didn't mean to lose my temper. It's just that it's so damn difficult being in here and all. It gets to me sometimes. I spout off when I don't mean to. Just come out with whatever it is you have to say. I can take it. But God, Wes, if you only knew how hard it is to have your freedom snatched away from you, to hear the clanging of locks closing around you and having people tell you what to do all the time and never getting a moment to yourself. It's driving me crazy."

"Sorry, that dog just don't hunt no more, *Bro*."

"What?"

"Your sad sack stories about life in prison. There was a time just a few weeks ago when that had the desired effect. I'd be wracked with guilt and willing to bust my hump to work harder to help prove your innocence. But no more."

"What are you saying?"

"I'm saying I finally have hard evidence what a lying, thieving bastard you are," Wes said matter-of-factly. "How stupid can you be, Patrick? Or a better question is, How stupid did you think I was? I guess I played the part, though.

King of all suckers, in the name of brotherly allegiance. Always trying to sniff out that loophole so I can give you a break or the benefit of the doubt."

"What have you been smoking, man? What are you talking about?"

"Kelly was having problems with her computer. Lonette asked me to come over and look at it. I had to reload the game software for that *Clifford* game."

"Oh, shit," Patrick hissed.

"Oh, shit, indeed."

"Wes, wait! I-I can explain," Patrick stammered. "Really, I can. But hey, listen up. I can't do it on the phone. But I will when you come see me again. This weekend."

"This weekend?" Wes gave a dry laugh. "That gives you plenty of time to come up with a real doozy, a real wollopolooza, doesn't it?"

"Wes, man, you're always supposed to have my back; you're my brother."

"And I'll always be your brother, but I'm not your savior. I still love you and will always love you, career con man that you are, but I can't do this rescue thing. Not anymore. And this time I mean it."

"But, Wes . . . Wes!"

"Mom says she'll be sure to make up a batch of those computer magazines you like so much and mail them to you." Wes kept his tone calm and even as he segued to small talk, which further infuriated Patrick. "And oh, Dad made a killing off that Phillips commercial real estate deal . . . and oh, as always, Kelly sends her love."

"Wes!"

"Anyway, I think that's everything. Gotta run. See ya, at your next visitation. Good-bye."

Wes heard Patrick shouting his name as he pushed the disconnect button. He placed the receiver back in its cradle, then braced his arms against the counter as his legs went weak. Over the next half hour the phone rang again and again. Each ring more excruciating to ignore than the last. He checked caller ID and knew they were operator-assisted phone calls from Davenport. Wes swallowed the emotion welling up in his throat and told himself that he'd done the right thing. Finding that CD containing copies of those stolen Plexis documents was just the jolt he needed to clear up all doubt and confusion regarding Patrick's so-called innocence—once and for all. The only way they could've gotten there was if Patrick put them there. There was no disputing that. As much as it pained Wesley, he now had to finally admit that Patrick was just where he needed to be, with the rest of the creeps and crooks. Maybe the next three years would force Patrick to reflect and make some authentic, lasting changes this time. Wes could only hope and pray. But in the meantime, he had his own life to live and enjoy.

One down, and one to go.

Michelle.

Twenty-nine

S o have you made a decision about whether you're going to contact John or not?" Liz opened the suitcase on her bed and removed items she'd packed for her stay at Willow Grove.

"I saw him . . . at the courthouse today," Michelle said.

She heard Liz's sharp intake of breath.

"I just watched him," Michelle added quickly. "I didn't approach him."

"But why?"

"I've been doing a lot of thinking, Ma." Michelle reached inside the suitcase side pocket for the toiletries and lined them up on her mother's dresser. "That fact that I still have the option to seek him out when I'm ready is a good thing, but . . ."

"What?" Liz stopped her perfunctory movement, sat on the bed, then coaxed Michelle to sit next to her.

Michelle sighed. "I've decided I'm in no hurry to do that."

"Oh?" Liz didn't hide her surprise.

"Maybe I'll never seek him out. Maybe I will. I just don't know. The point is, there's no rush, no desperation, anymore. I finally feel this freedom I've never had before. Like something heavy and dark lifted."

Michelle shared what she knew about that upcoming *Herald* exposé and the criminal allegations mounting against J. Ashton Pratt.

"I'm not sure how all that will turn out for him, but it doesn't look good at all. I'm sure the feds are going to jump all over it when the story is published. Maybe Pratt will learn something from it all. But most important, I have. What I've come to realize is that I have to feel complete and content within myself. And move beyond feeling somehow lesser, not whole, or slighted because I missed having a father around. I mean, there are a lot of people out there who had to deal with much worse and they're not wallowing, no, practically marinating, in self-pity like I was. Look at Fatima and Ahmad: they didn't lose just one parent, but they lost them both at a young age." When Michelle shifted to face her mother fully, Liz reached out to touch her cheek. "I had a mother—"

"An imperfect mother," Liz added.

"An imperfect mother, who still loved her imperfect daughter with all her heart, the best way she knew how." Michelle wore a melancholy smile. "But, Ma . . . ?"

"Yes, baby?"

"What are you going to do about Ed's marriage proposal?"

"There were others before Ed's, you know. Remember when I dated Frank? You, Fatima, and Ahmad were in high school."

Michelle recalled the soft-spoken general contractor who was a deacon at their church. "After we dated for a while he asked me to marry him, too, but I ran into the same road-block I've encountered with Ed. I just couldn't."

"Didn't you love him?"

"Your ma had too much fear, baby. After John I simply didn't trust men for a long time. Then when I started to loosen up enough to enjoy their company I didn't trust myself. I can't promise that I won't have to check in at Willow Grove again for another stay."

"You won't," Michelle tried to reassure her.

"I hope not, and thanks for having faith in me. But I still

can't be absolutely sure. I just have to take it one day at a time."

"You can do it."

"You don't understand. The medications that keep me from plunging back into emotional valleys also numb that feeling of overwhelming intoxicating pleasure. I still struggle to suppress impulses to ride that white lightning rod again. Anyone I married would have to know and accept that this is a part of me. And there's still such stigma attached to any mental illness."

"But if that person really and truly loves you—"

"I just didn't want to put anyone through that." She shook her head. "I didn't want to test anyone like that, especially after what happened with John." Liz got to her feet and went to look out the window. "John walked away and he didn't even know about it. I couldn't guarantee that another man wouldn't walk away once he found out."

"Oh, Ma." Michelle reached out for Liz and a hug. "So you've been so lonely all those years because of your fear?"

Liz nodded.

"You can't let fear rule your life. You love Ed. I've seen you two together. He's such a great guy, Ma. And he's perfect for you."

"He is a good one, isn't he?" When she released her daughter, a smile played on her lips.

"Yes, and you'd better rope him in before he gets away." Michelle brightened and found herself laughing from the heart for the first time in days. And it felt so good. She flopped face-first on her mother's bed and propped her face in her hands.

"You really like Ed, huh?" Liz asked.

"Yeah! Fatima and Ahmad do, too!"

"Hmmmmm." Liz tapped a finger to her chin. "Maybe I *will* finally accept his proposal when he gets back from California."

"But first you will tell him everything—"

"Yes, everything first . . . about John, my stays at Willow Grove, and my illness. And if . . . *big if* . . . he *still* wants me after hearing it all, we'll have . . . What do the kids say these days? The phattest, flashiest wedding of them all . . . in the backyard."

"I'm not sure how phat and flashy you can get in that postage-stamp-sized yard, but the planning is going to be fun. Of course, I'll help you." Michelle sprang from the bed and grabbed her mother. They embraced again, rocking together until the doorbell chimed.

"I'll get that." Michelle moved to answer it.

She found Wesley at her doorstep.

And she was so glad to see him. Her heart leaped as usual at the sight of him. As it always would—even if they both lived to be a hundred.

She'd been swept up in an emotional sleep-deprived tailspin the last few days, but now that things had slowed and settled, she was rested and could think clearly. She knew one thing for sure: she loved, needed, and wanted Wesley in every way that mattered. She'd just lectured to her mother about fear and moving beyond it to accept love when it was offered. Now she had an opportunity to practice what she'd just preached. And if Wesley said he loved her she should take him not only at his word but at his actions. Wes hadn't been anything but wonderful to her, she thought with hard-won clarity. Quite simply he'd swept her off her feet . . . the way she'd always dreamed a man would someday.

And no soap opera, epic theatrical saga, or romance novel hero could touch him.

Keeping his past where it belonged, in the past, she had to focus on the present if she was going to have that dazzling future with him.

When she opened the door Wes stepped inside and immediately got down on one knee.

Michelle's lips formed a giant O.

He took her hand. "Michelle Michaels, I love you with all my heart and soul. I want to spend the rest of my life with you. And only you. You hear that? *Only* you. And if it takes telling you a million times, I'll tell you a million and one times. It's us, baby, all the way, as in two's company, three's a crowd . . . As in you're not gettin' rid of me that easily."

"But—"

"I want a wife and kids. I want us to make a real home together with stain-resistant rugs, childproof furnishings, and a big backyard."

"But—"

"Wait. I'm not done yet. A bodacious backyard for a giant jungle gym, swing set, a lake-sized pool, putt-putt golf. And a huge family room. You and I can snuggle up together in front of a big ol' monstrosity of a television set. Of course, I'll watch *Monday Night Football* and the Pistons, but you can even get me up to speed on Brooke . . . Blaine . . . Blaire?" He furrowed his brow, then continued, "Oh, you know, that Worthington woman on *If Tomorrow Never Comes*. I hope you like the picture I'm painting, baby. Because it looks darn good to me." Wes removed a gorgeous sapphire and diamond ring from a small velvet pouch. "This ring has been in my family for generations, so this ain't nothing to play with."

Michelle's hand flew to her mouth at the sight of the headlight-sized rock.

"This is straight-up serious Abbott business, you hear? My mother has been champing at the bit for years to pass this ring along to me or Patrick when either of us wised up and snagged the right woman. It's been a long, slow haul but looks as if I'm the lucky one, who made it to the finish line first, by more than a nose, I should add. This ring, I'm not about to give it back to Mom now that I've gotten her hopes up 'cause I'd never hear the end of it, so you *must* accept it."

Wes smiled, then kissed the back of Michelle's hand tenderly. He looked up at her, eyes shining with anticipation of the glorious life they could have together. "Michelle Michaels, will you marry me?"

Michelle dropped to her knees. Happy tears slipped down her cheeks. As she let him slip the gorgeous ring on her finger, her heart expanded with so much love, hope, and joy it rendered her speechless—make that practically speechless.

Actually, there was one perfect word. Of course she told him . . .

"Yes."

Epilogue

One year later

Lazy Sundays were Michelle's favorites. She and Wes often stayed in bed until some decadent hour of the day, making love and reading a stack of voluminous newspapers. It was nearly noon, but they'd only left the comfort of their king-size bed long enough to get orange juice, bagels, and cream cheese from the kitchen. Then they'd crawled back between the soft sheets and into each others' arms. They'd been married for nine months, three weeks, and three days.

"You did a great job on this Ludwig Industries piece, babe." Wesley sat up in bed and folded the pages of the *Detroit Herald* as he read Michelle's column a second time. "You should include this one in your contest entries file. Between this and the other columns you've written the past six months I think you're well on your way to a solid Pulitzer Prize entry."

"You really think so?" Michelle, who had been resting her head against Wesley's bare chest, turned up her face to kiss his cheek. His praise and obvious pride always warmed her heart. She was thrilled about her new position as the lead columnist for the *Herald* business section. Of course, she hadn't missed that features beat at all, but surprisingly she hadn't missed the *Manhattan Business Journal* either. Detroit was where she needed and wanted to be.

Despite seeking ongoing professional help, Liz had experienced a relapse that required another brief stay at Willow

Grove and more tweaking of her prescription medications. With Michelle, Fatima, and Liz's new husband, Ed, by her side, Liz was more determined than ever to win the battle for her mental health.

"Speaking of the Pulitzers, are you sure there are no second thoughts about walking away from the story on Pratt?" Michelle asked softly.

Wes put the paper aside and drew Michelle into his arms. "No regrets whatsoever," he said quickly, planting kisses on her forehead to reassure her. "There will be other stories. I'm on something so hot now, it'll make the Pratt piece look like high school newspaper journalism."

Wes had passed over his Pratt notes and research to Conrad Sheldon, who covered the courts beat for the *Herald*. Conrad went on to win a slew of regional journalism awards for the series of front-page stories that resulted in the arrest and indictment of Judge John Ashton Pratt and his "bagman" Titus Montesi for racketeering. Justice had moved at a more glacial pace for the defendants who had received guilty verdicts in Pratt's courtroom. Most had yet to receive new trials, but it was unlikely Patrick was going anywhere, even with a second chance. Despite the shady goings, where Pratt was concerned, the state still had a strong case against Patrick, and Wes had accepted that prison was where his brother needed to stay for his crime. Patrick, who was still upset over the fact that he couldn't manipulate Wes anymore, hadn't made things easier. The brothers' relationship was strained, but Wes dutifully continued his visits to Davenport, often with Kelly in tow. Michelle, however, had yet to take a trip to the federal prison to see Pratt or inform him that he was her biological father. Initially, she had written a few letters to him that she had yet to mail. She had followed his trial closely and the more she'd learned about the selfish, greedy, and unscrupulous man, the more she didn't believe a sappy Hallmark-movie–style reunion was possible. And she could honestly say she was okay with that. She knew what was important. She knew who she was and that gave her true inner strength. Inviting Pratt into her life would only complicate things. She just wanted to count her many blessings. She had more than enough family to love, which now included a really cool stepfather, Ed Porter, and the Abbotts. What a difference a year made, she thought, sighing contentedly and snuggling deeper into her husband's warm embrace.

R. Laudat

REON LAUDAT is the author of twelve novels (traditionally and independently published). She has a bachelor's degree in journalism from the University of Missouri–Columbia. As a features and lifestyle reporter, Reon covered the fun stuff—pop culture, fitness, television, and fashion. She lives in the southeast with her family. Check in at www.reonlaudat.com.